ANOTHER KIND

CAIT MAY & TREVOR BREAM

HARPER
alley

An Imprint of HarperCollinsPublishers

CHAPTER ONE

WE KNOW WHAT YOU ARE

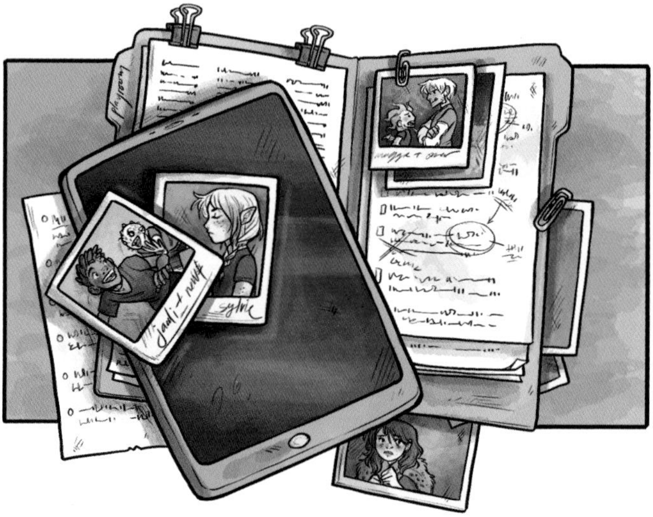
sylvie

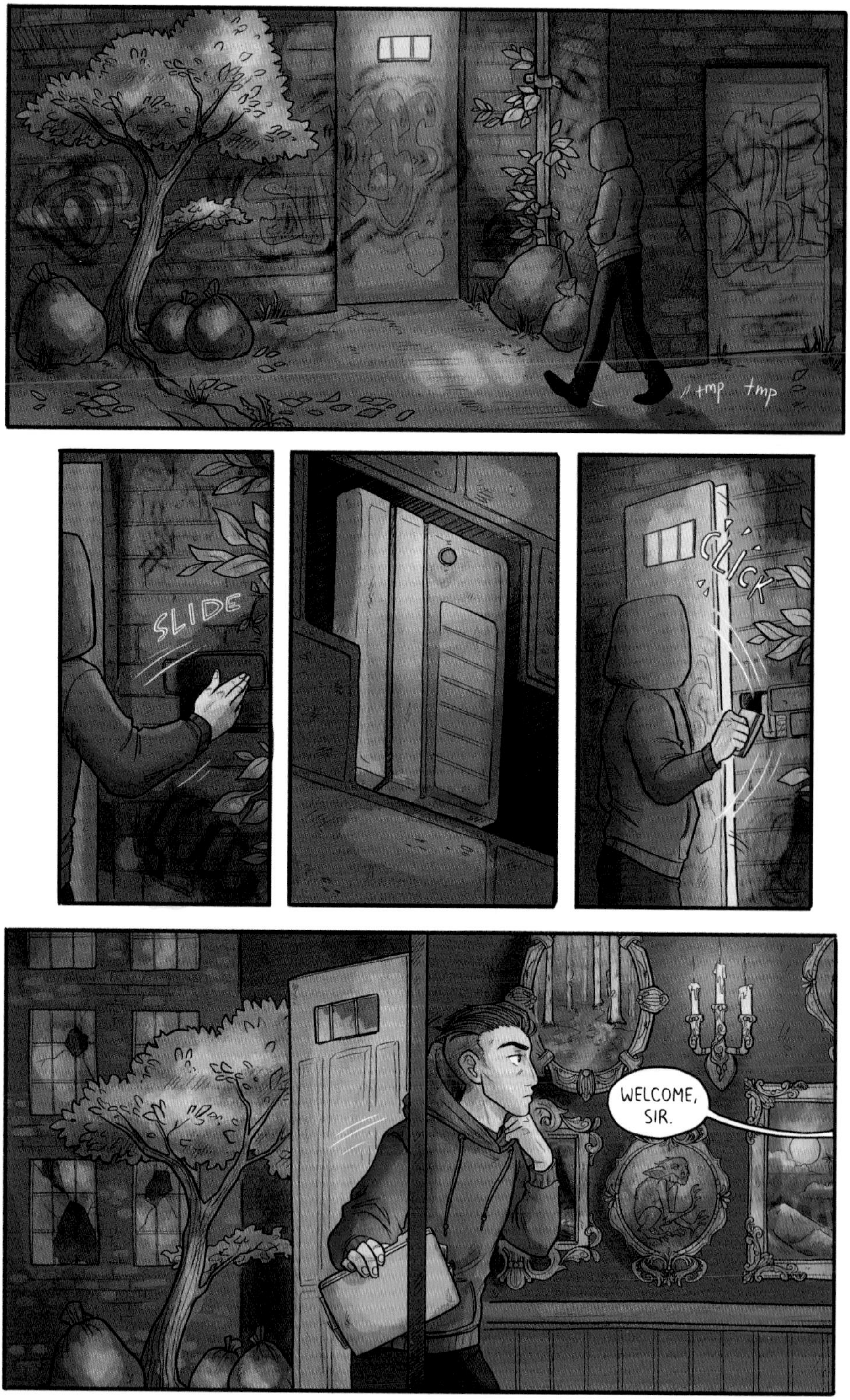
tmp tmp
SLIDE
CLICK
WELCOME, SIR.

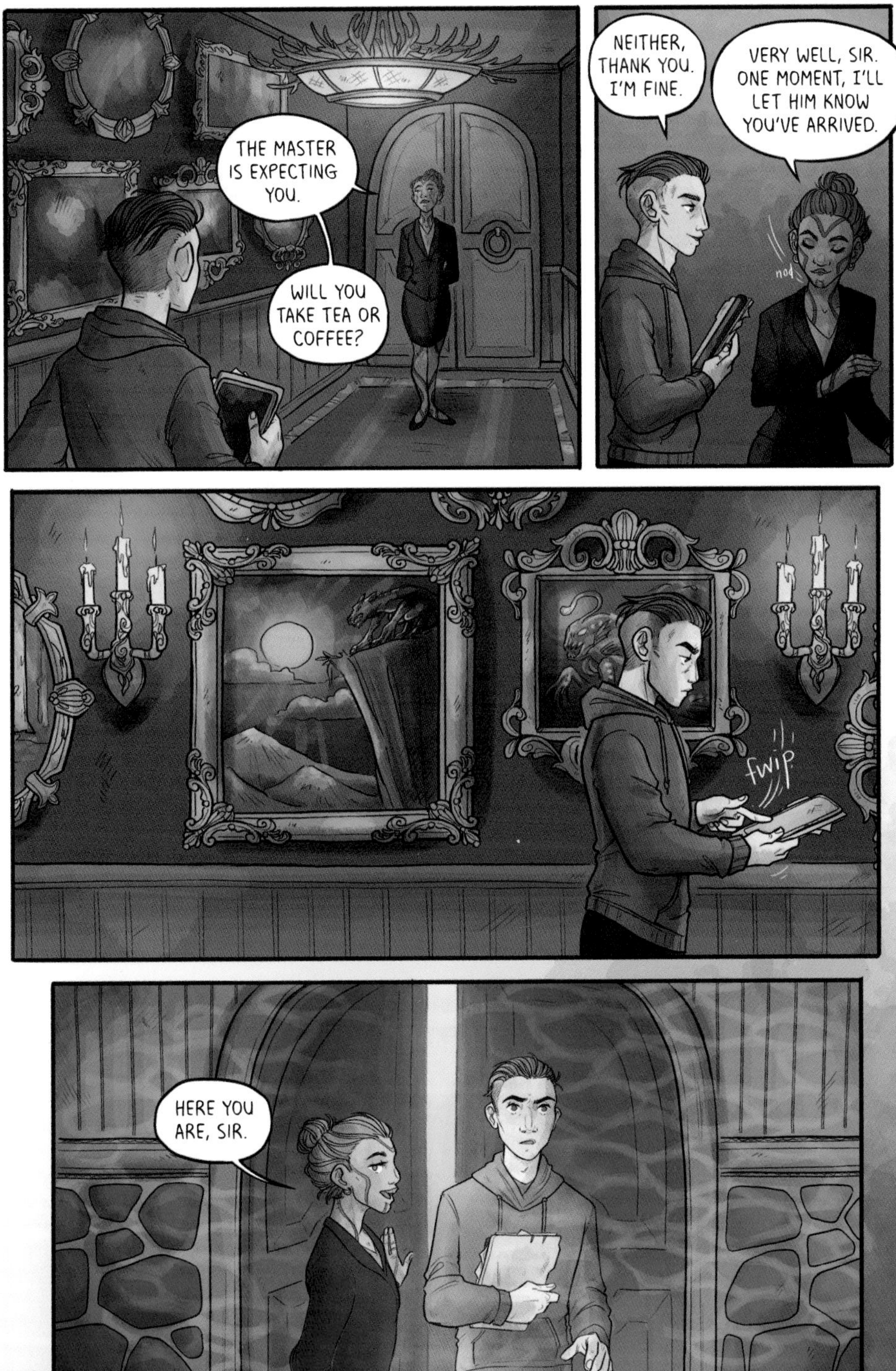
THE MASTER IS EXPECTING YOU.
WILL YOU TAKE TEA OR COFFEE?
NEITHER, THANK YOU. I'M FINE.
VERY WELL, SIR. ONE MOMENT, I'LL LET HIM KNOW YOU'VE ARRIVED.
nod
fwip
HERE YOU ARE, SIR.

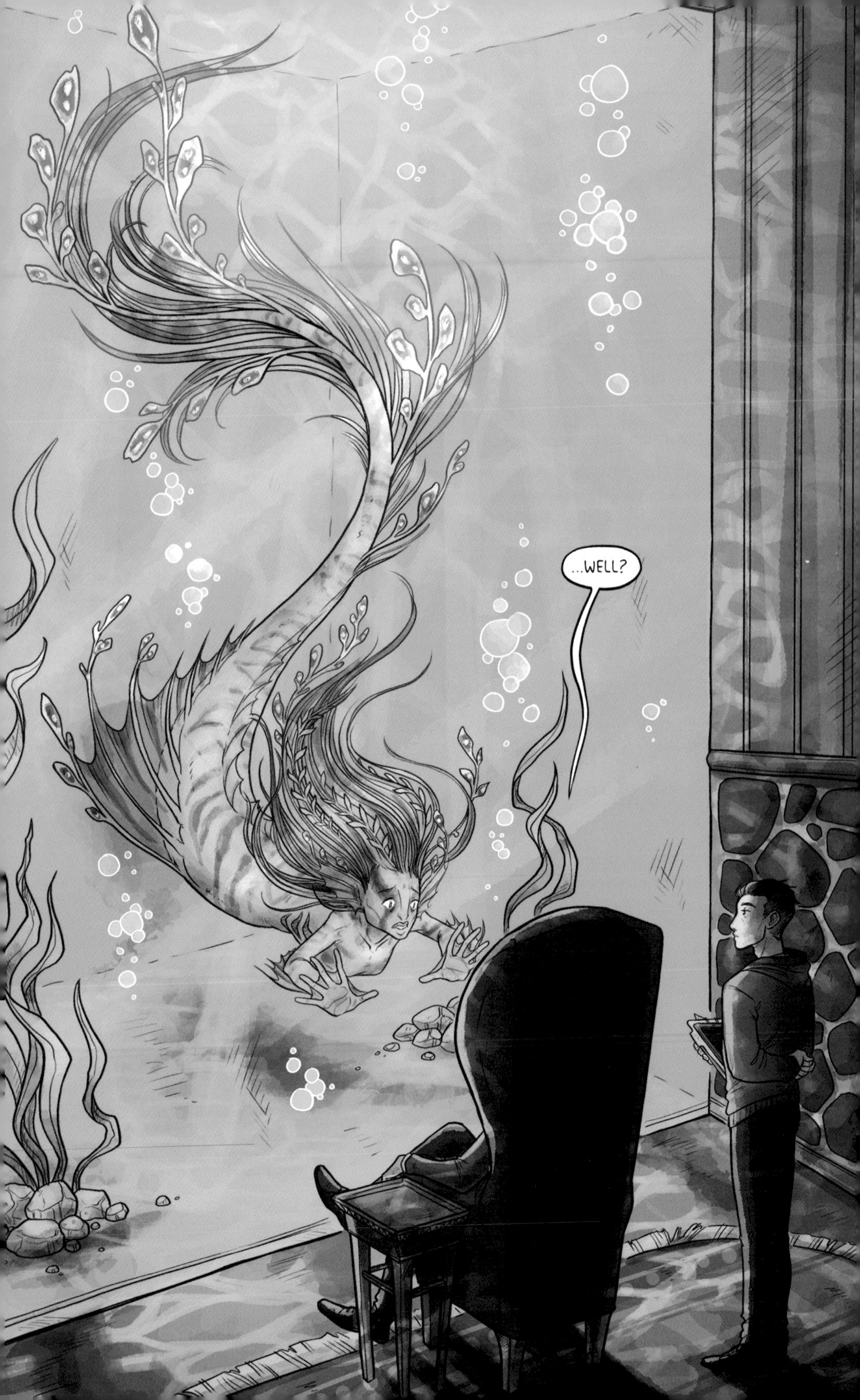
...WELL?

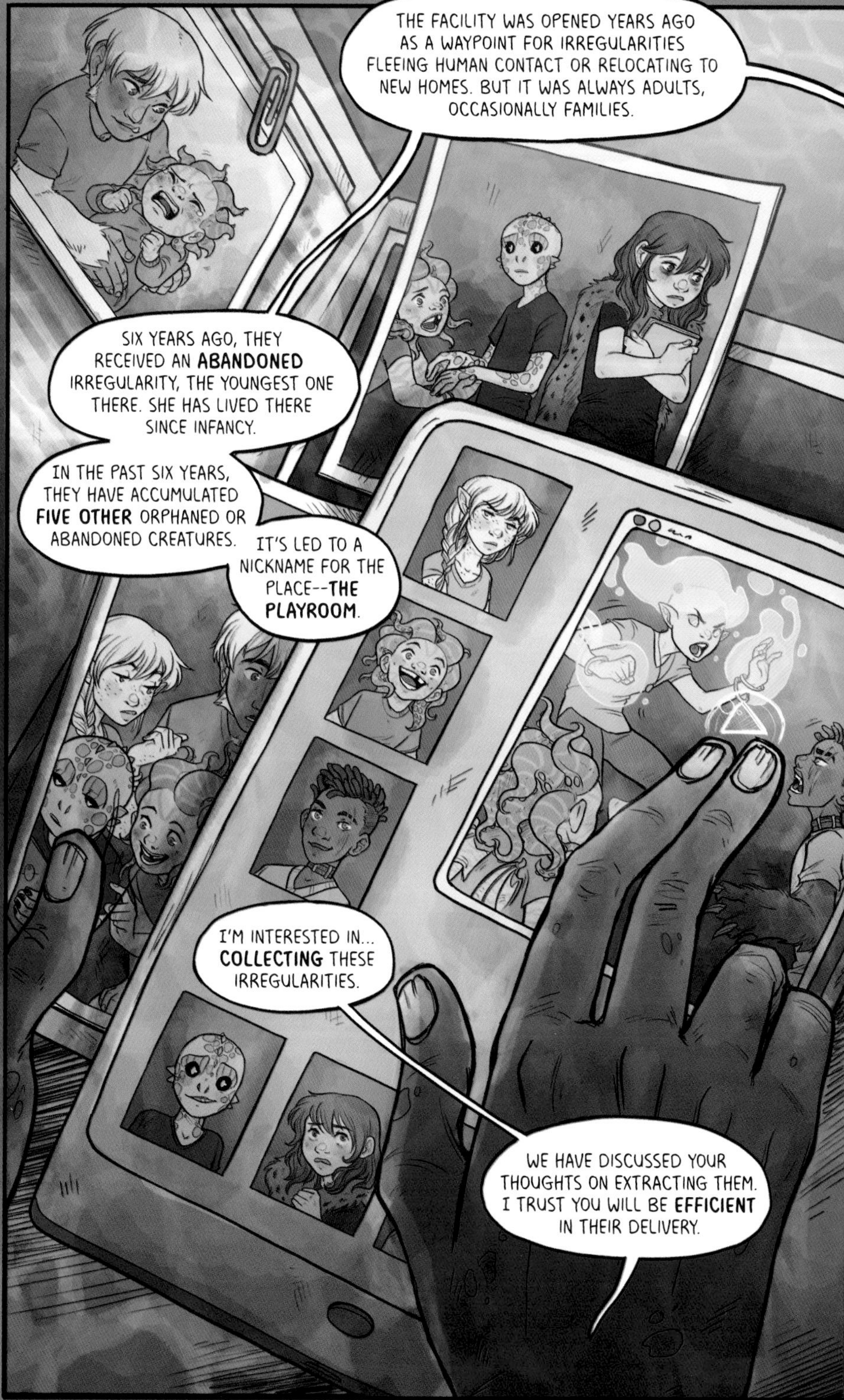
THE FACILITY WAS OPENED YEARS AGO AS A WAYPOINT FOR IRREGULARITIES FLEEING HUMAN CONTACT OR RELOCATING TO NEW HOMES. BUT IT WAS ALWAYS ADULTS, OCCASIONALLY FAMILIES.
SIX YEARS AGO, THEY RECEIVED AN **ABANDONED** IRREGULARITY, THE YOUNGEST ONE THERE. SHE HAS LIVED THERE SINCE INFANCY.
IN THE PAST SIX YEARS, THEY HAVE ACCUMULATED **FIVE OTHER** ORPHANED OR ABANDONED CREATURES.
IT'S LED TO A NICKNAME FOR THE PLACE--**THE PLAYROOM**.
I'M INTERESTED IN... **COLLECTING** THESE IRREGULARITIES.
WE HAVE DISCUSSED YOUR THOUGHTS ON EXTRACTING THEM. I TRUST YOU WILL BE **EFFICIENT** IN THEIR DELIVERY.

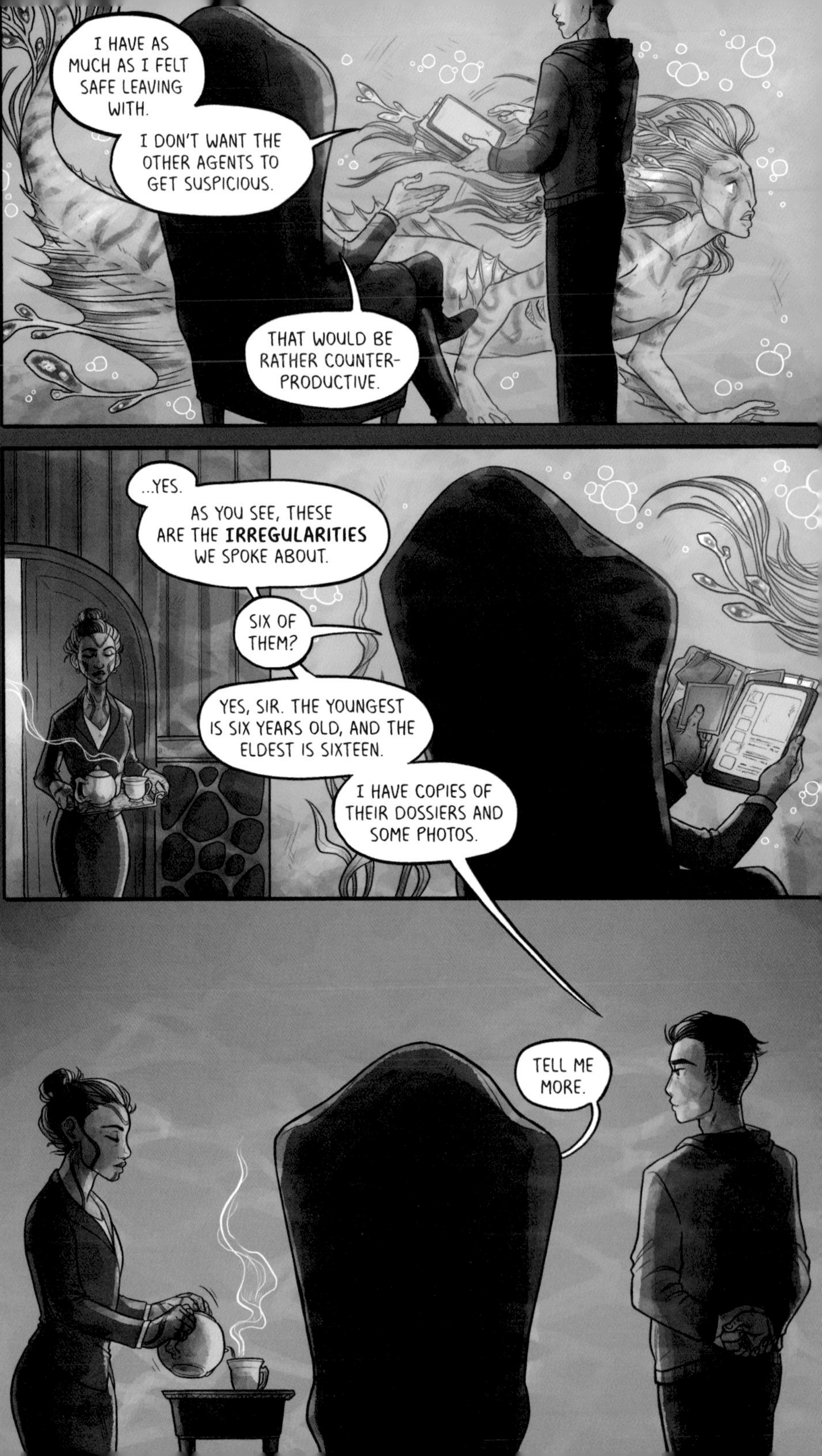
I HAVE AS MUCH AS I FELT SAFE LEAVING WITH.
I DON'T WANT THE OTHER AGENTS TO GET SUSPICIOUS.
THAT WOULD BE RATHER COUNTER-PRODUCTIVE.
...YES.
AS YOU SEE, THESE ARE THE **IRREGULARITIES** WE SPOKE ABOUT.
SIX OF THEM?
YES, SIR. THE YOUNGEST IS SIX YEARS OLD, AND THE ELDEST IS SIXTEEN.
I HAVE COPIES OF THEIR DOSSIERS AND SOME PHOTOS.
TELL ME MORE.

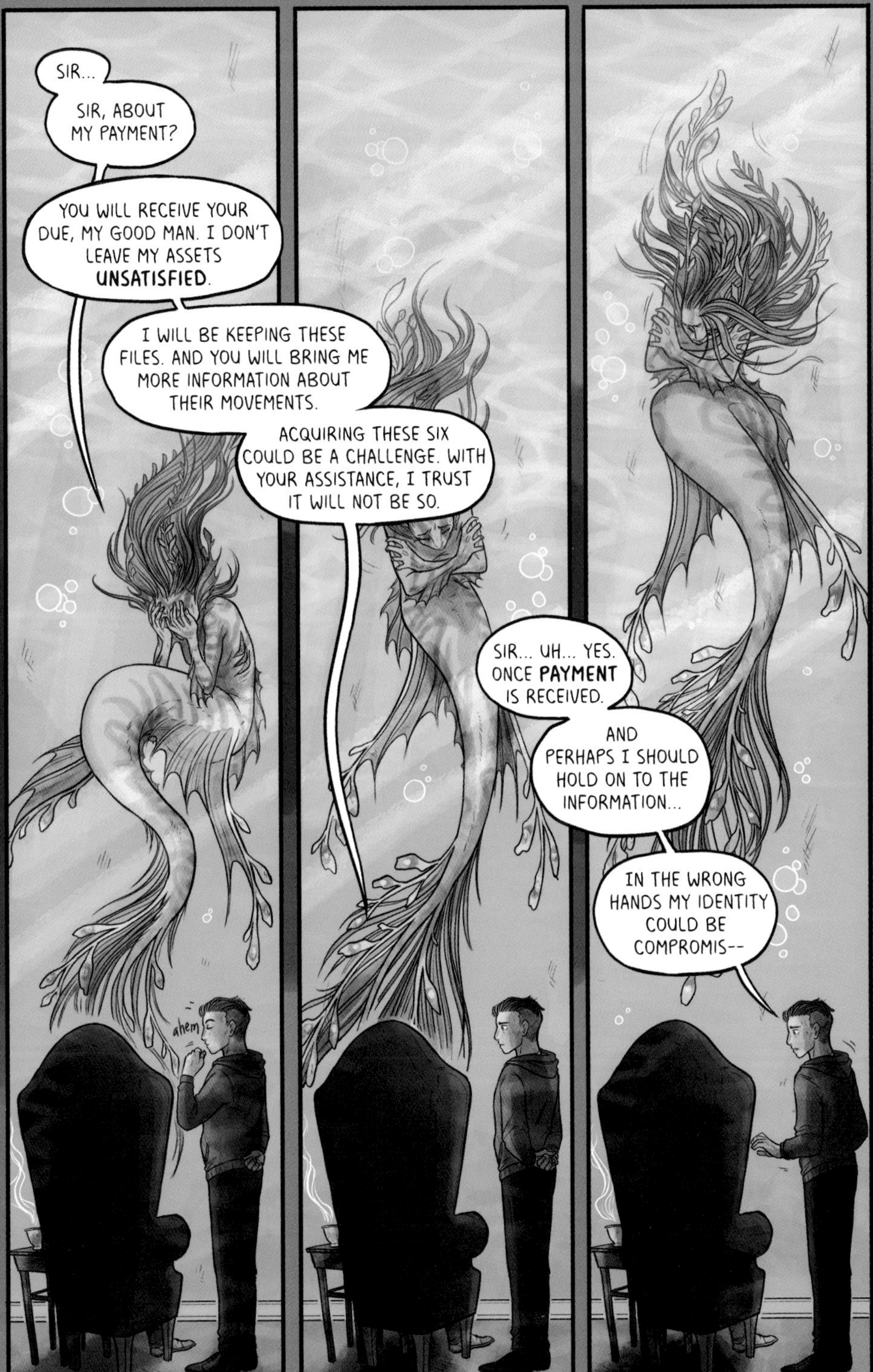
SIR...
SIR, ABOUT MY PAYMENT?
ahem
YOU WILL RECEIVE YOUR DUE, MY GOOD MAN. I DON'T LEAVE MY ASSETS **UNSATISFIED**.
I WILL BE KEEPING THESE FILES. AND YOU WILL BRING ME MORE INFORMATION ABOUT THEIR MOVEMENTS.
ACQUIRING THESE SIX COULD BE A CHALLENGE. WITH YOUR ASSISTANCE, I TRUST IT WILL NOT BE SO.
SIR... UH... YES. ONCE **PAYMENT** IS RECEIVED.
AND PERHAPS I SHOULD HOLD ON TO THE INFORMATION...
IN THE WRONG HANDS MY IDENTITY COULD BE COMPROMIS--

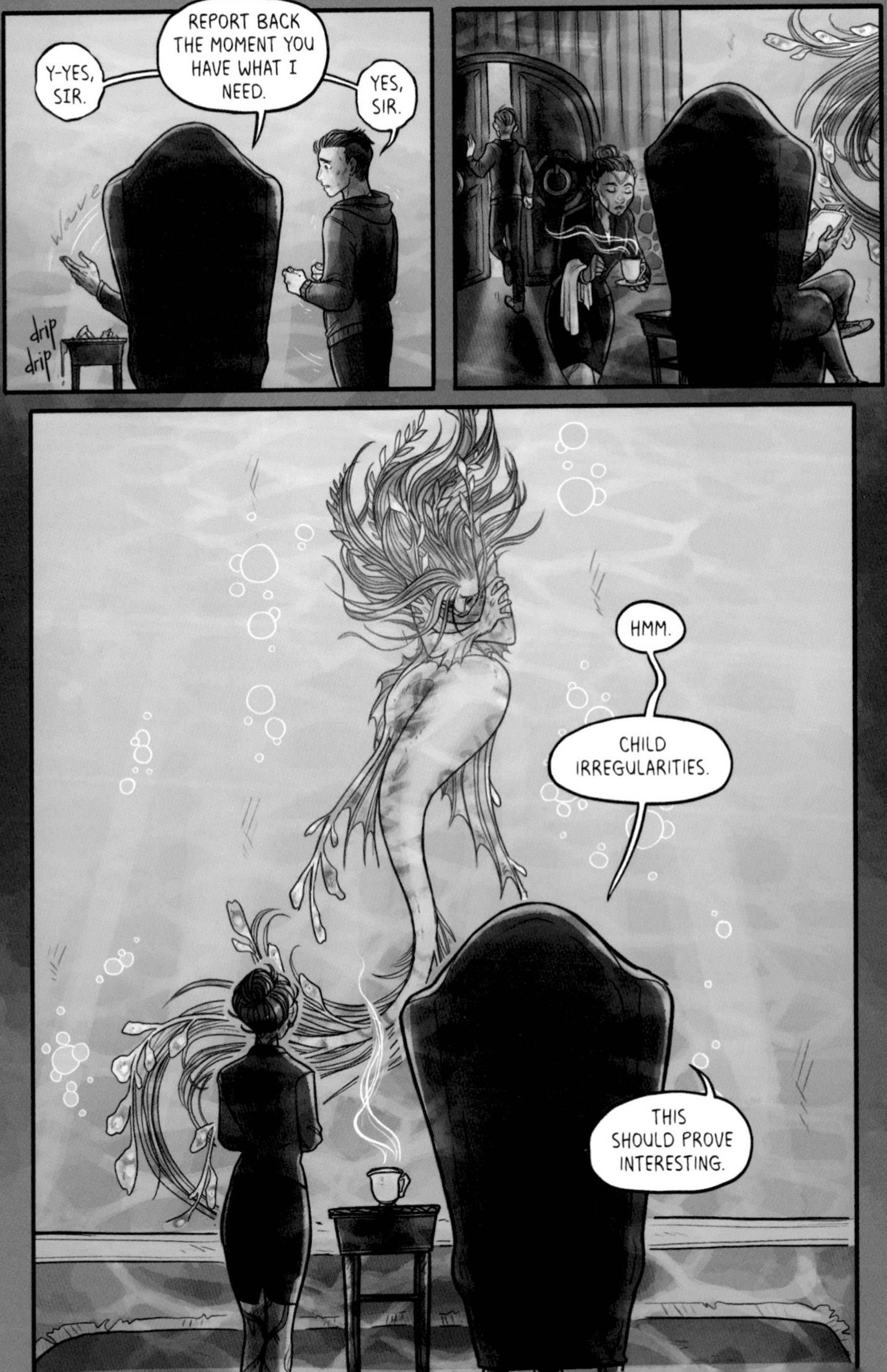
Y-YES, SIR.
REPORT BACK THE MOMENT YOU HAVE WHAT I NEED.
YES, SIR.
Wave
drip drip
HMM.
CHILD IRREGULARITIES.
THIS SHOULD PROVE INTERESTING.

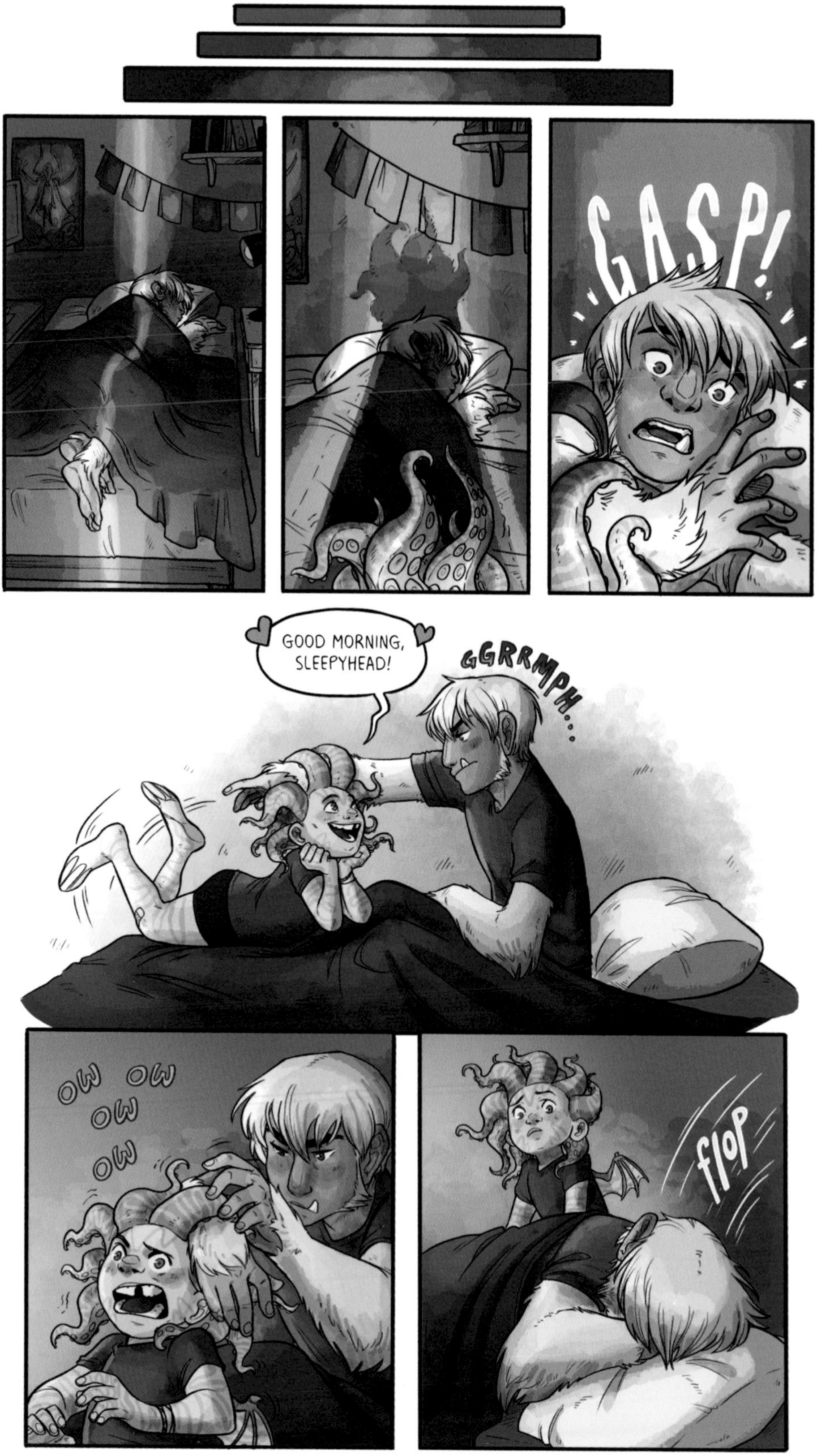
GASP!
GOOD MORNING, SLEEPYHEAD!
GGRRRMPH...
OW OW OW OW
flop

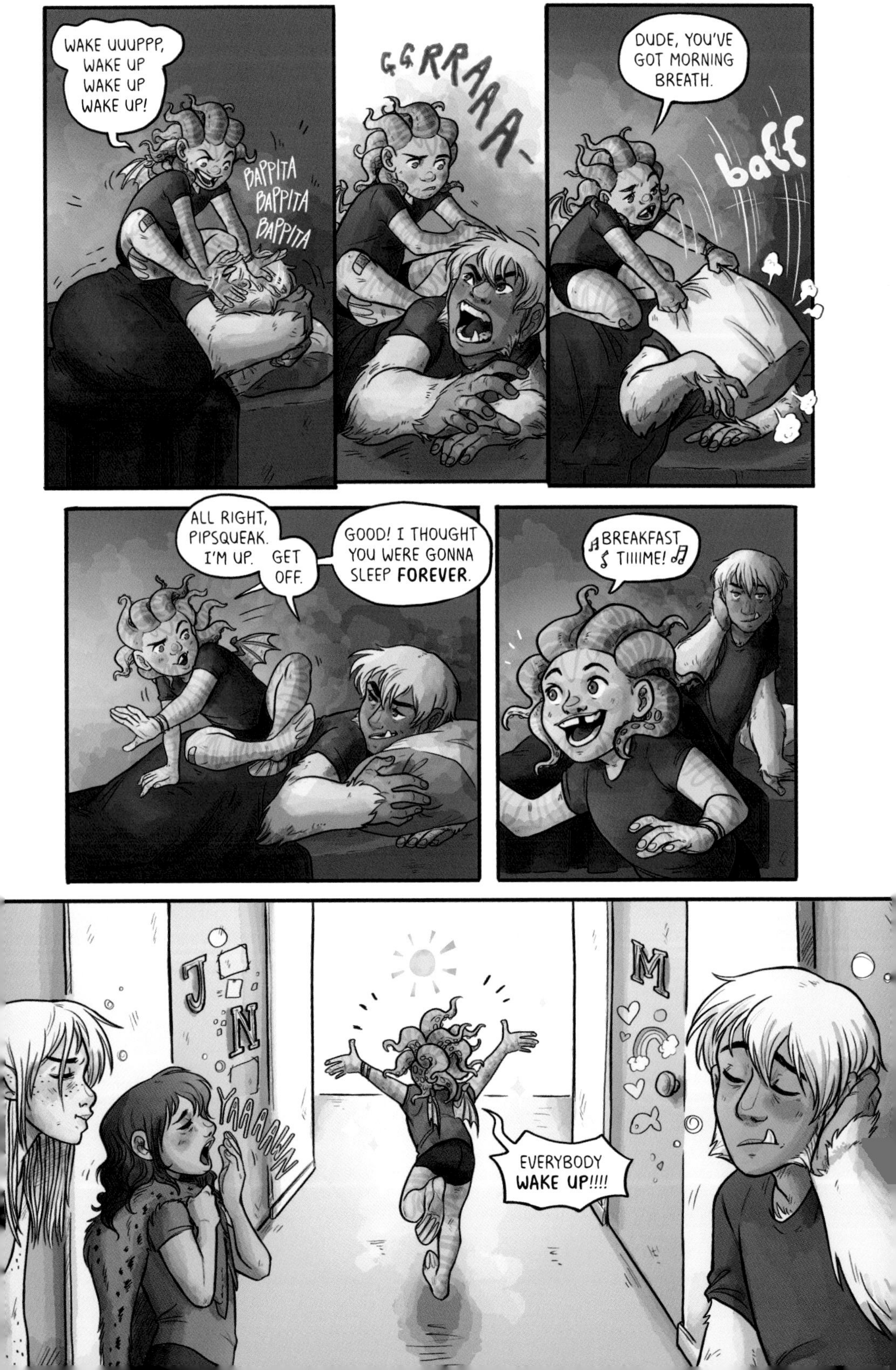
WAKE UUUPPP, WAKE UP WAKE UP WAKE UP!
BAPPITA BAPPITA BAPPITA
GGRRAAA-
DUDE, YOU'VE GOT MORNING BREATH.
baff
ALL RIGHT, PIPSQUEAK. I'M UP.
GET OFF.
GOOD! I THOUGHT YOU WERE GONNA SLEEP **FOREVER**.
BREAKFAST TIIIIME!
J
N
YAAAAWN
M
EVERYBODY **WAKE UP**!!!!

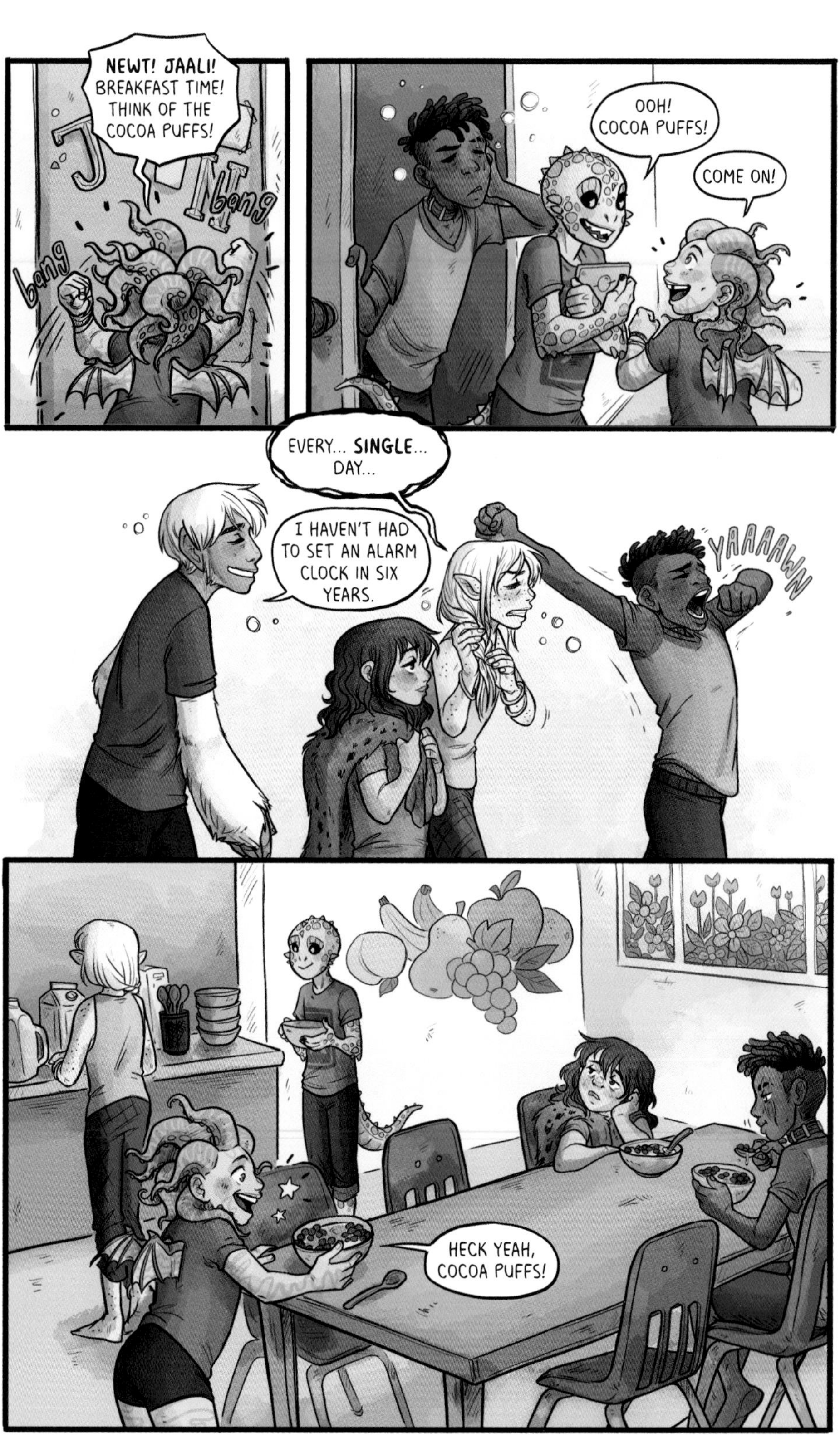
NEWT! JAALI! BREAKFAST TIME! THINK OF THE COCOA PUFFS!
bang
bang
OOH! COCOA PUFFS!
COME ON!
EVERY... SINGLE... DAY...
I HAVEN'T HAD TO SET AN ALARM CLOCK IN SIX YEARS.
YAAAAWN
HECK YEAH, COCOA PUFFS!

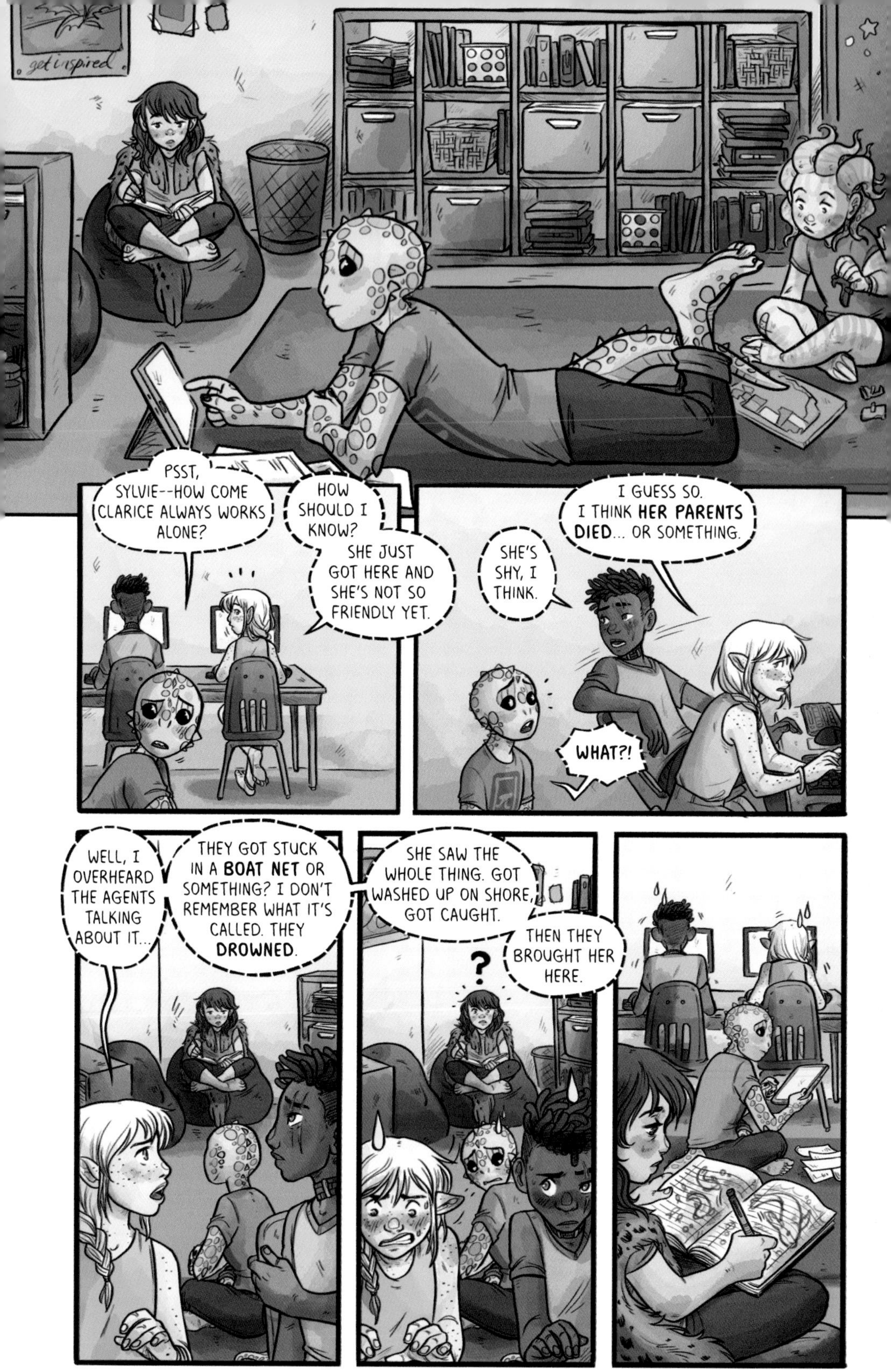
get inspired
PSST, SYLVIE--HOW COME CLARICE ALWAYS WORKS ALONE?
HOW SHOULD I KNOW?
SHE JUST GOT HERE AND SHE'S NOT SO FRIENDLY YET.
SHE'S SHY, I THINK.
I GUESS SO. I THINK **HER PARENTS DIED**... OR SOMETHING.
WHAT?!
WELL, I OVERHEARD THE AGENTS TALKING ABOUT IT...
THEY GOT STUCK IN A **BOAT NET** OR SOMETHING? I DON'T REMEMBER WHAT IT'S CALLED. THEY **DROWNED**.
SHE SAW THE WHOLE THING. GOT WASHED UP ON SHORE, GOT CAUGHT.
THEN THEY BROUGHT HER HERE.
?

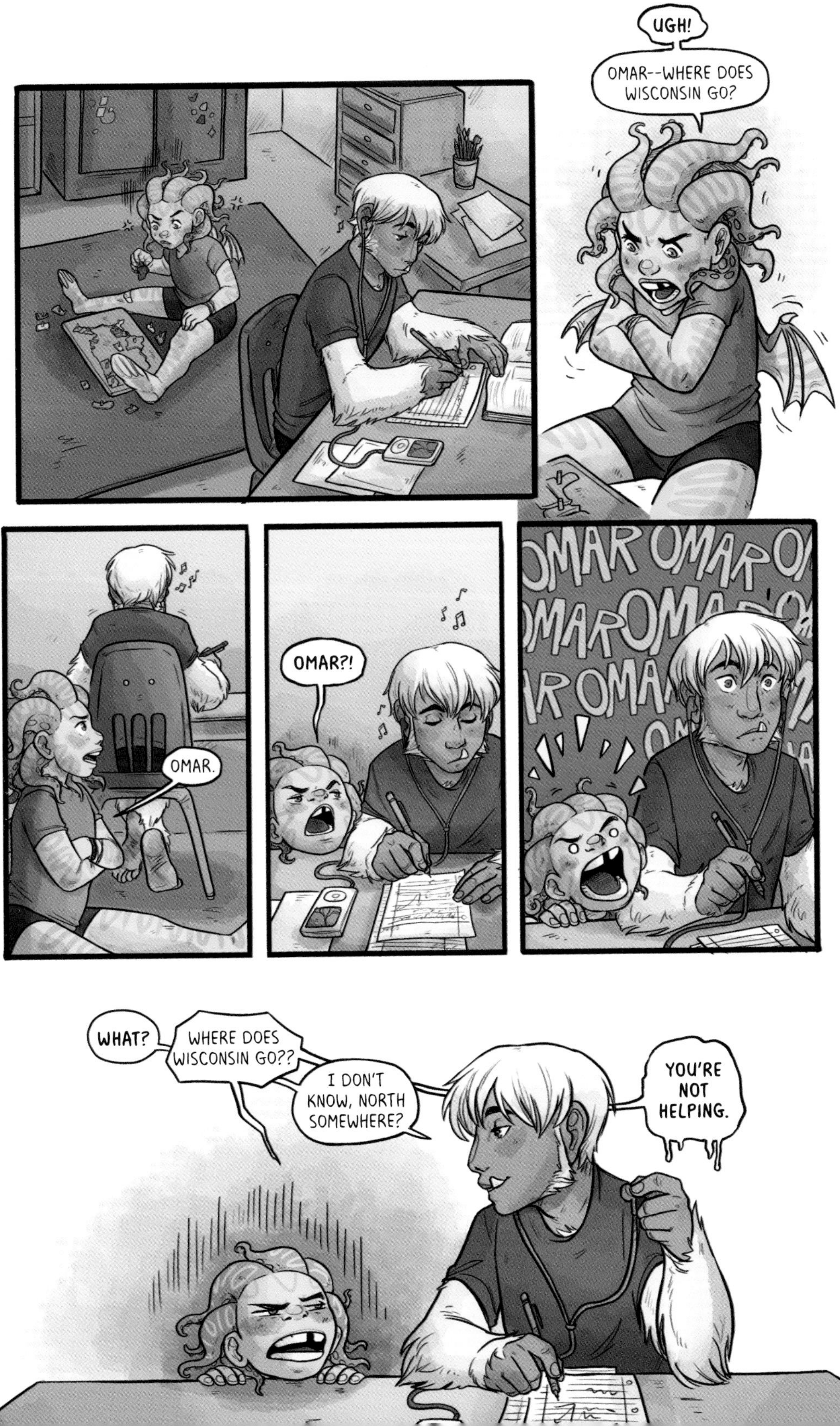
UGH!
OMAR--WHERE DOES WISCONSIN GO?
OMAR.
OMAR?!
OMAR OMAR OMAR
WHAT?
WHERE DOES WISCONSIN GO??
I DON'T KNOW, NORTH SOMEWHERE?
YOU'RE NOT HELPING.

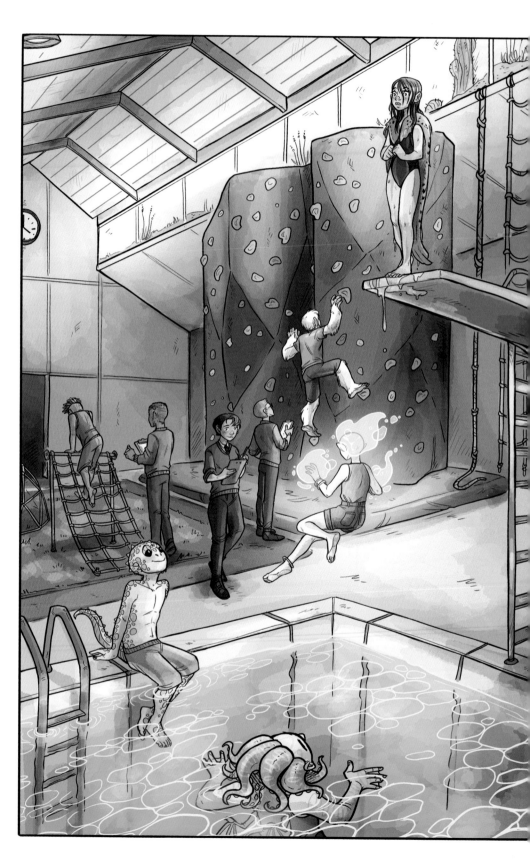

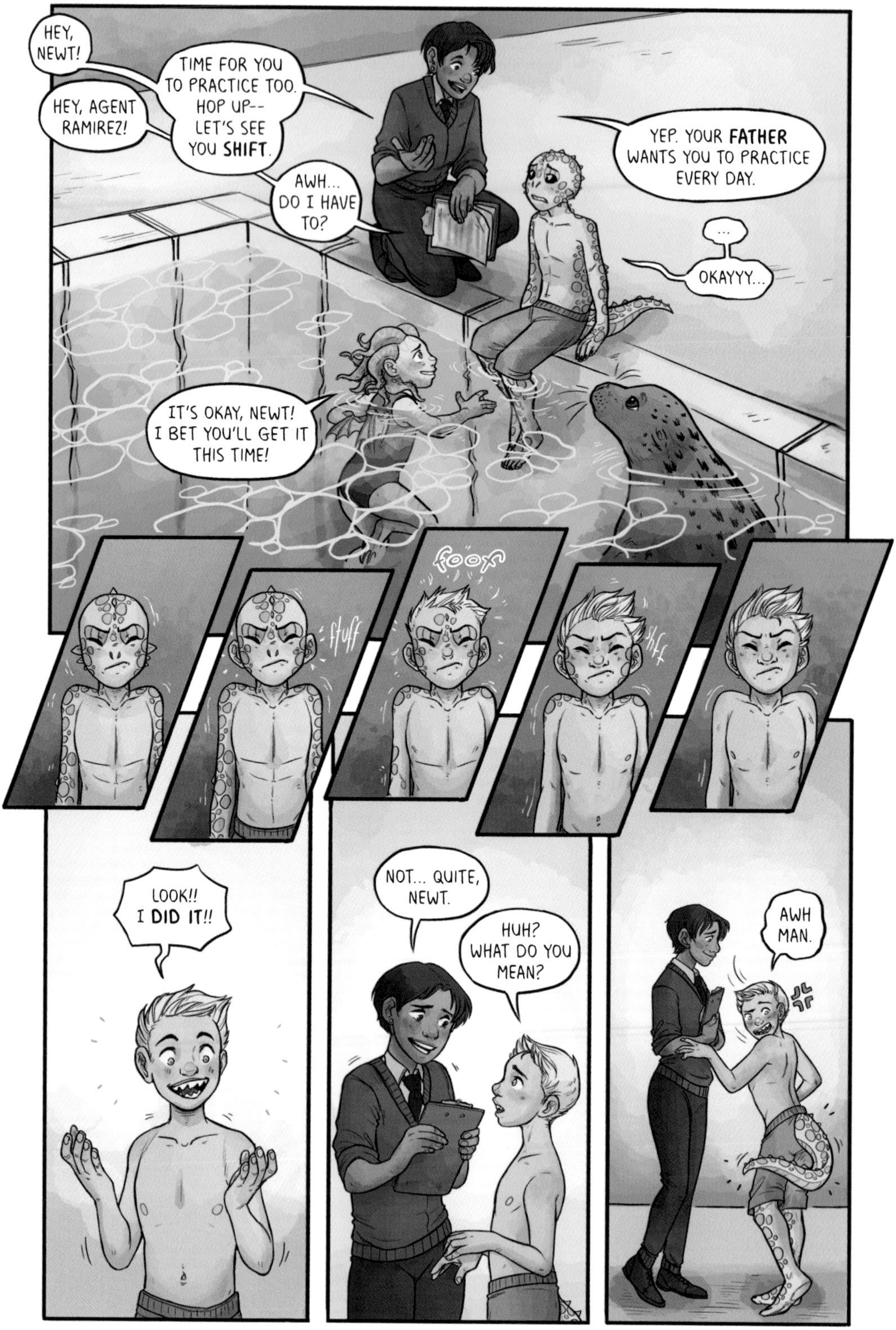
HEY, NEWT!
HEY, AGENT RAMIREZ!
TIME FOR YOU TO PRACTICE TOO. HOP UP-- LET'S SEE YOU **SHIFT**.
AWH... DO I HAVE TO?
YEP. YOUR **FATHER** WANTS YOU TO PRACTICE EVERY DAY.
...
OKAYYY...
IT'S OKAY, NEWT! I BET YOU'LL GET IT THIS TIME!
ffuff
foof
LOOK!! I **DID IT**!!
NOT... QUITE, NEWT.
HUH? WHAT DO YOU MEAN?
AWH MAN.

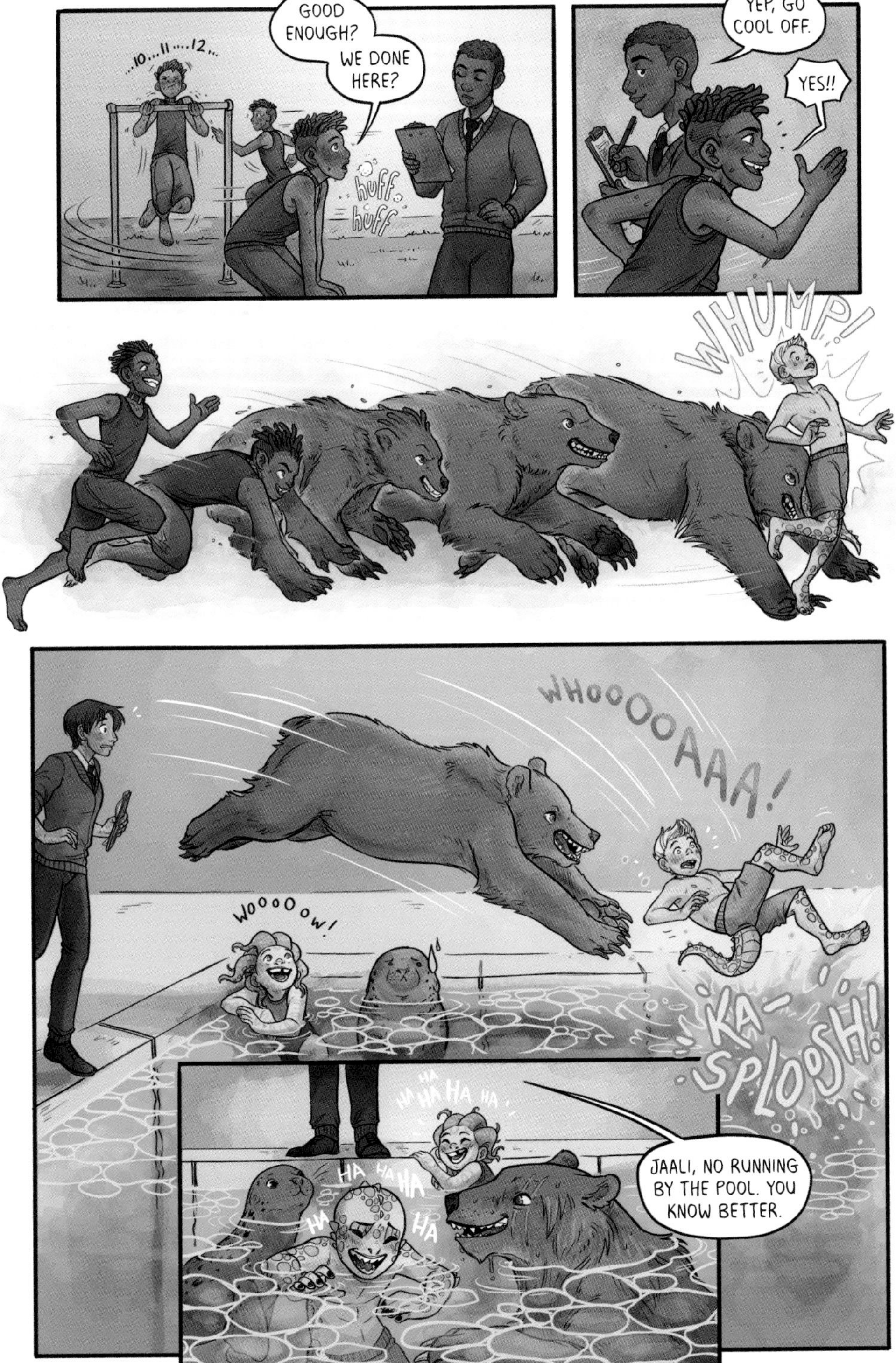
...10...11...12...
GOOD ENOUGH?
WE DONE HERE?
huff huff
YEP, GO COOL OFF.
YES!!
WHUMP!
WHOOOOAAA!
WOOOOow!
KA-SPLOOSH!
HA HA HA HA HA
HA HA HA HA HA
JAALI, NO RUNNING BY THE POOL. YOU KNOW BETTER.

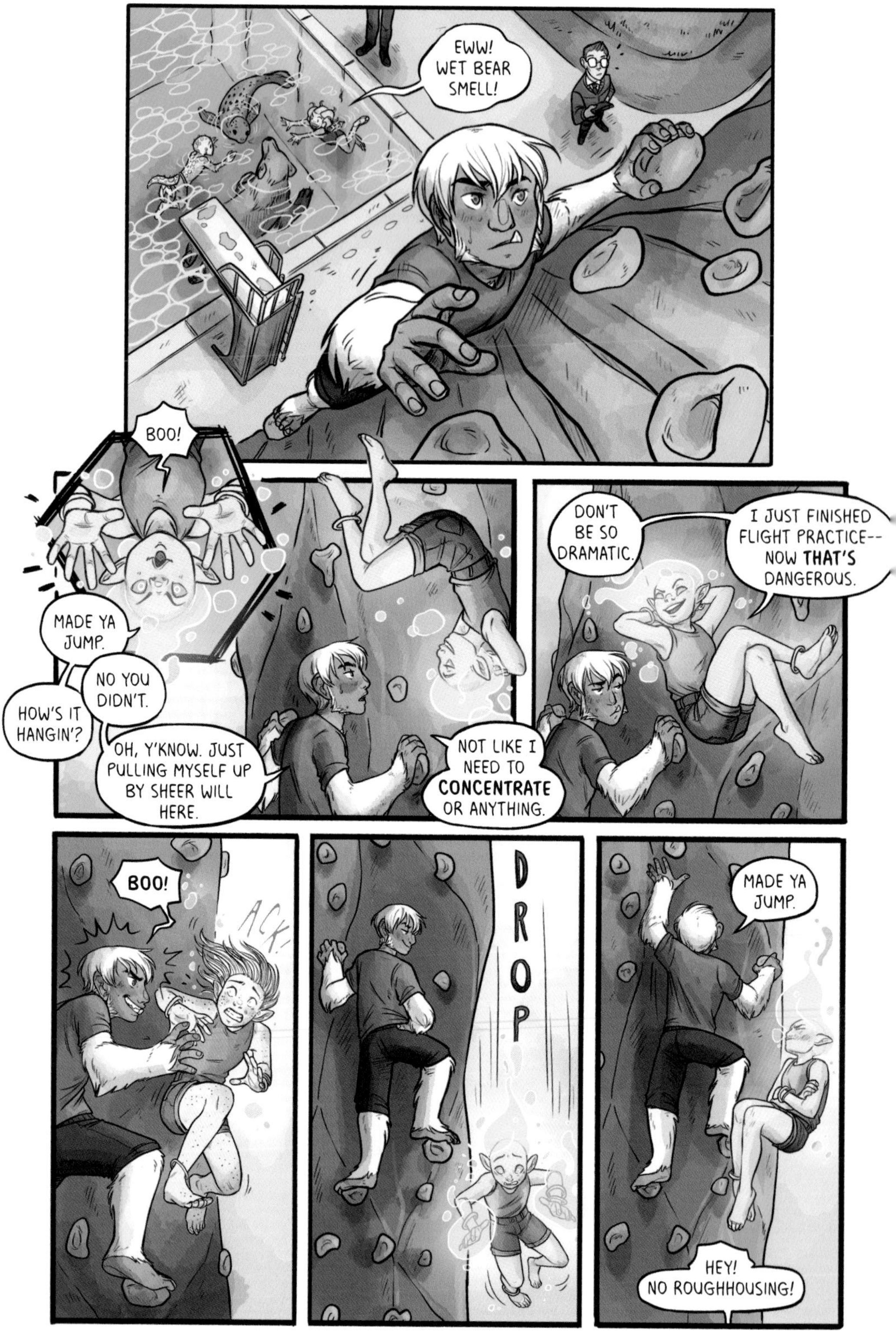
EWW! WET BEAR SMELL!
BOO!
MADE YA JUMP.
NO YOU DIDN'T.
HOW'S IT HANGIN'?
OH, Y'KNOW. JUST PULLING MYSELF UP BY SHEER WILL HERE.
NOT LIKE I NEED TO **CONCENTRATE** OR ANYTHING.
DON'T BE SO DRAMATIC.
I JUST FINISHED FLIGHT PRACTICE--NOW **THAT'S** DANGEROUS.
BOO!
ACK!
DROP
MADE YA JUMP.
HEY! NO ROUGHHOUSING!

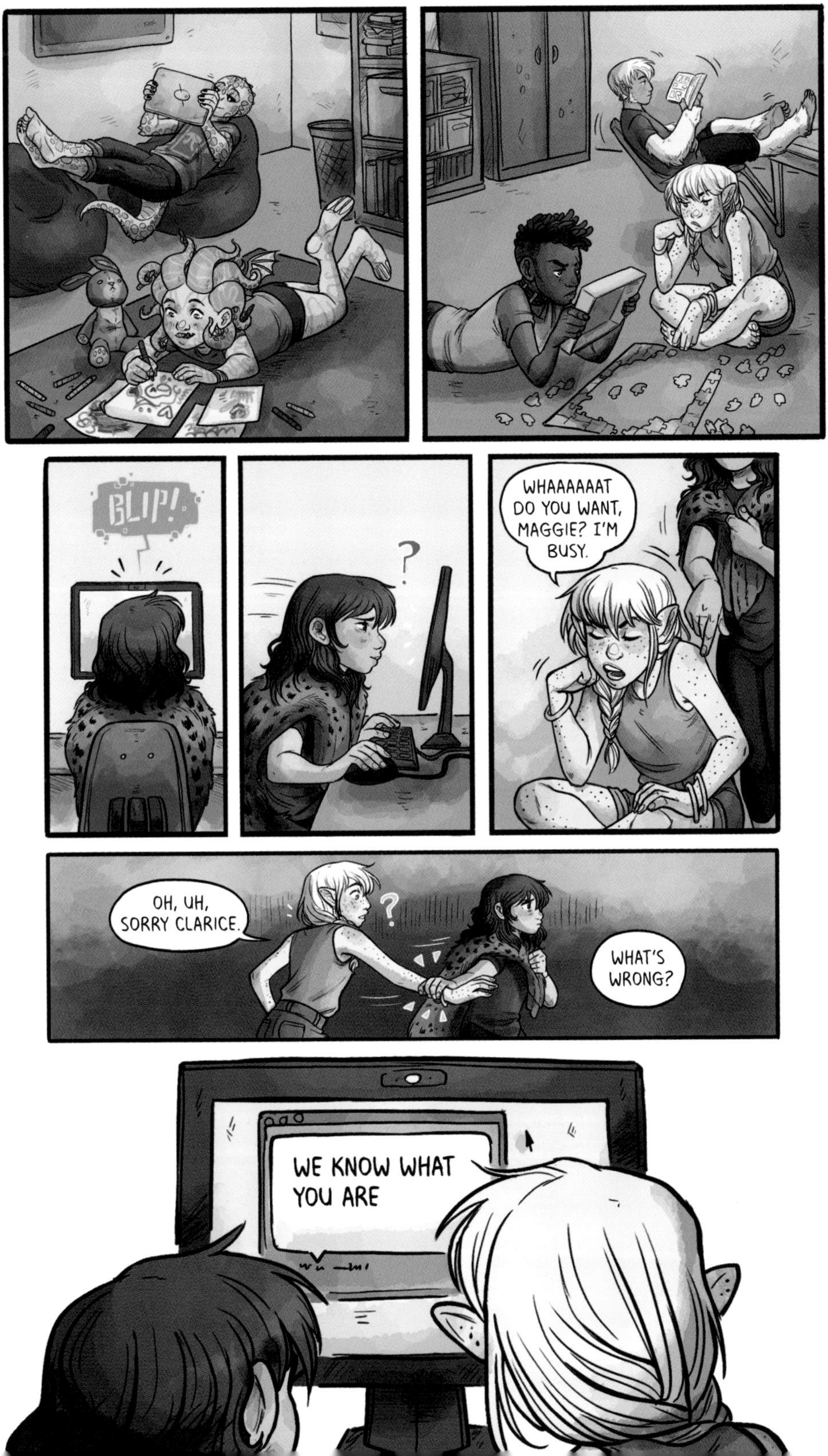
BLIP!
?
WHAAAAAAT DO YOU WANT, MAGGIE? I'M BUSY.
OH, UH, SORRY CLARICE.
?
WHAT'S WRONG?
WE KNOW WHAT YOU ARE

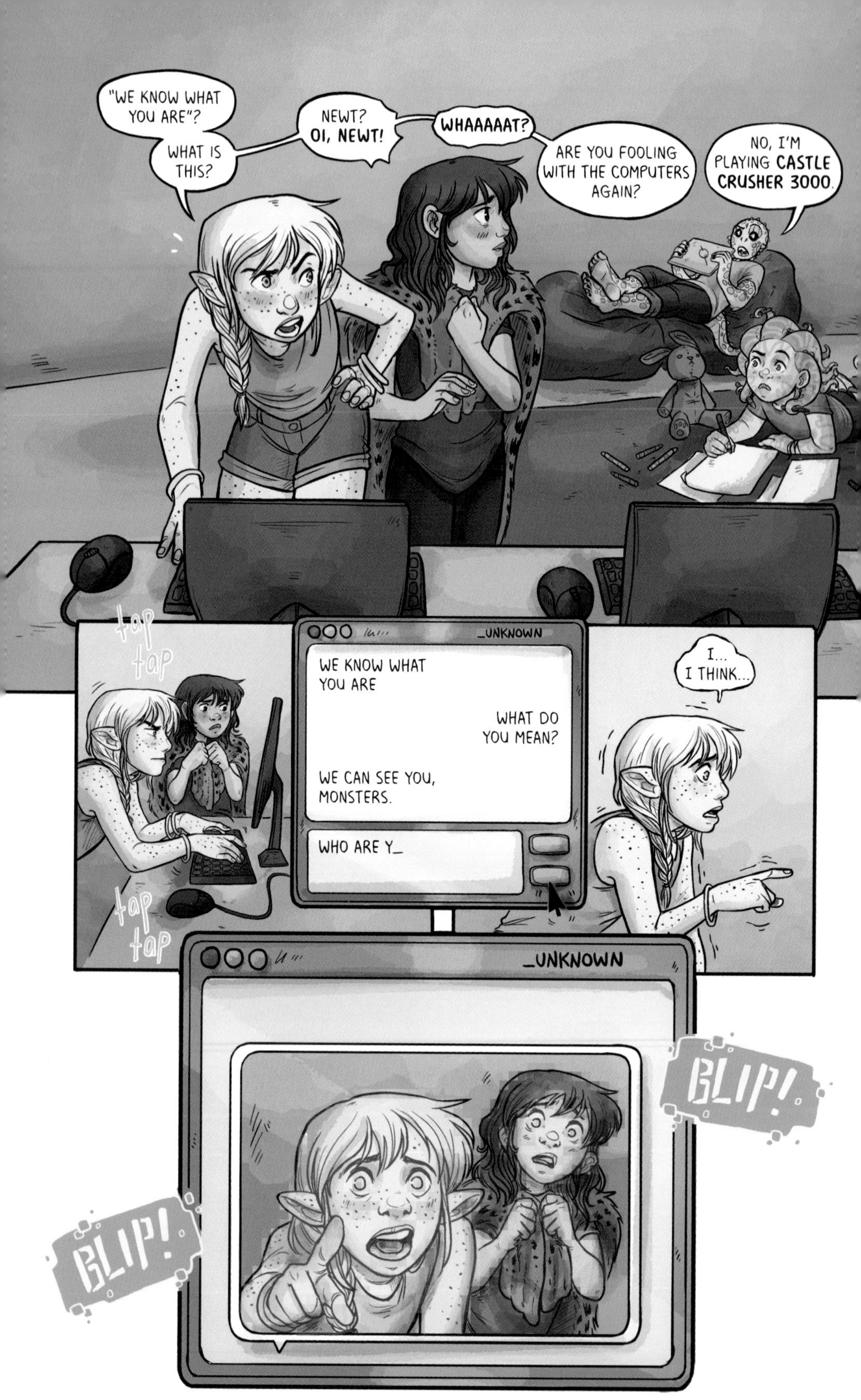
"WE KNOW WHAT YOU ARE"?
WHAT IS THIS?
NEWT? **OI, NEWT!**
WHAAAAAAT?
ARE YOU FOOLING WITH THE COMPUTERS AGAIN?
NO, I'M PLAYING **CASTLE CRUSHER 3000**.
tap tap
_UNKNOWN
WE KNOW WHAT YOU ARE
WHAT DO YOU MEAN?
WE CAN SEE YOU, MONSTERS.
WHO ARE Y_
I... I THINK...
tap tap
_UNKNOWN
BLIP!
BLIP!

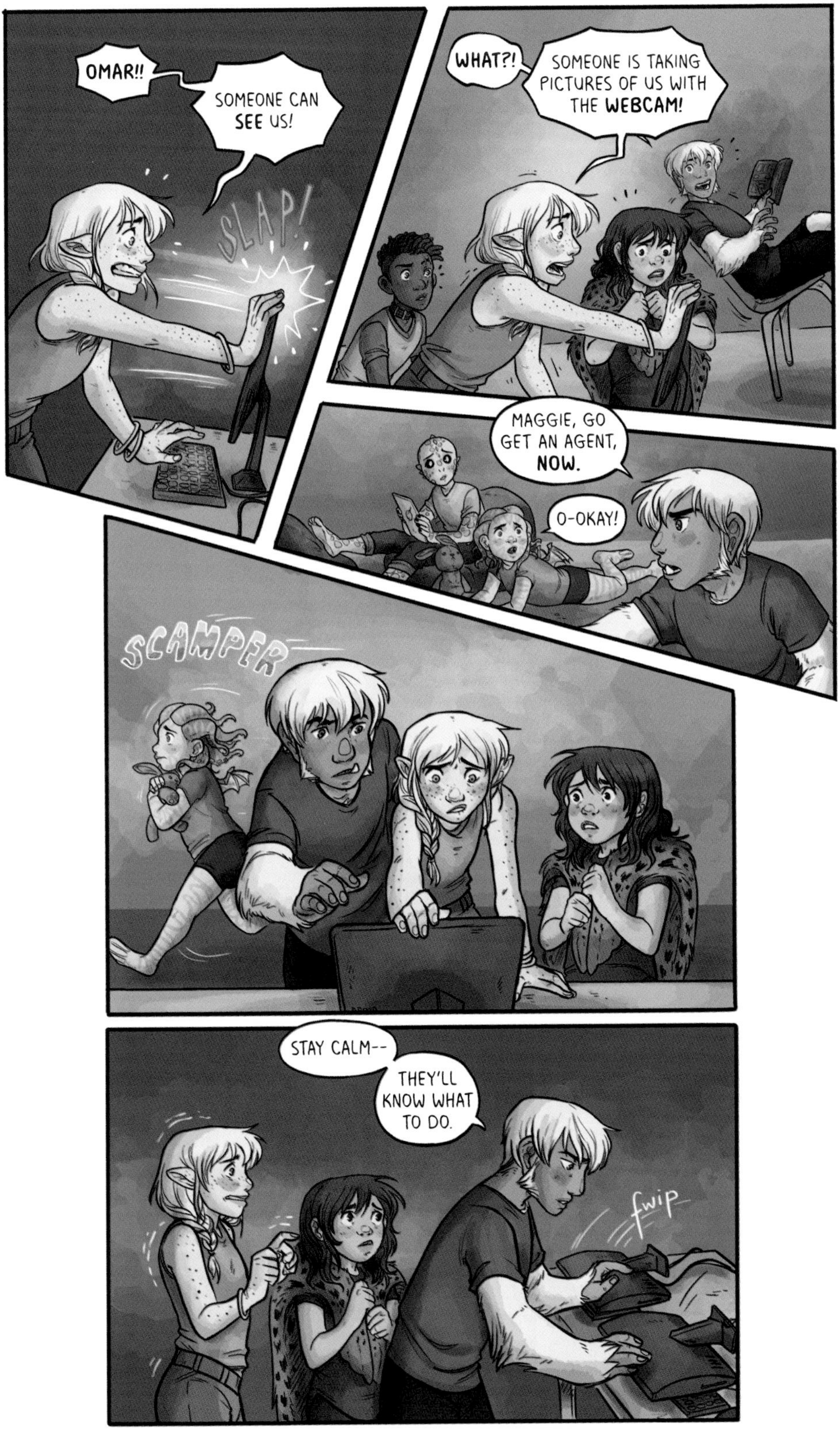
OMAR!!
SOMEONE CAN SEE US!
SLAP!
WHAT?!
SOMEONE IS TAKING PICTURES OF US WITH THE WEBCAM!
MAGGIE, GO GET AN AGENT, NOW.
O-OKAY!
SCAMPER
STAY CALM--
THEY'LL KNOW WHAT TO DO.
fwip

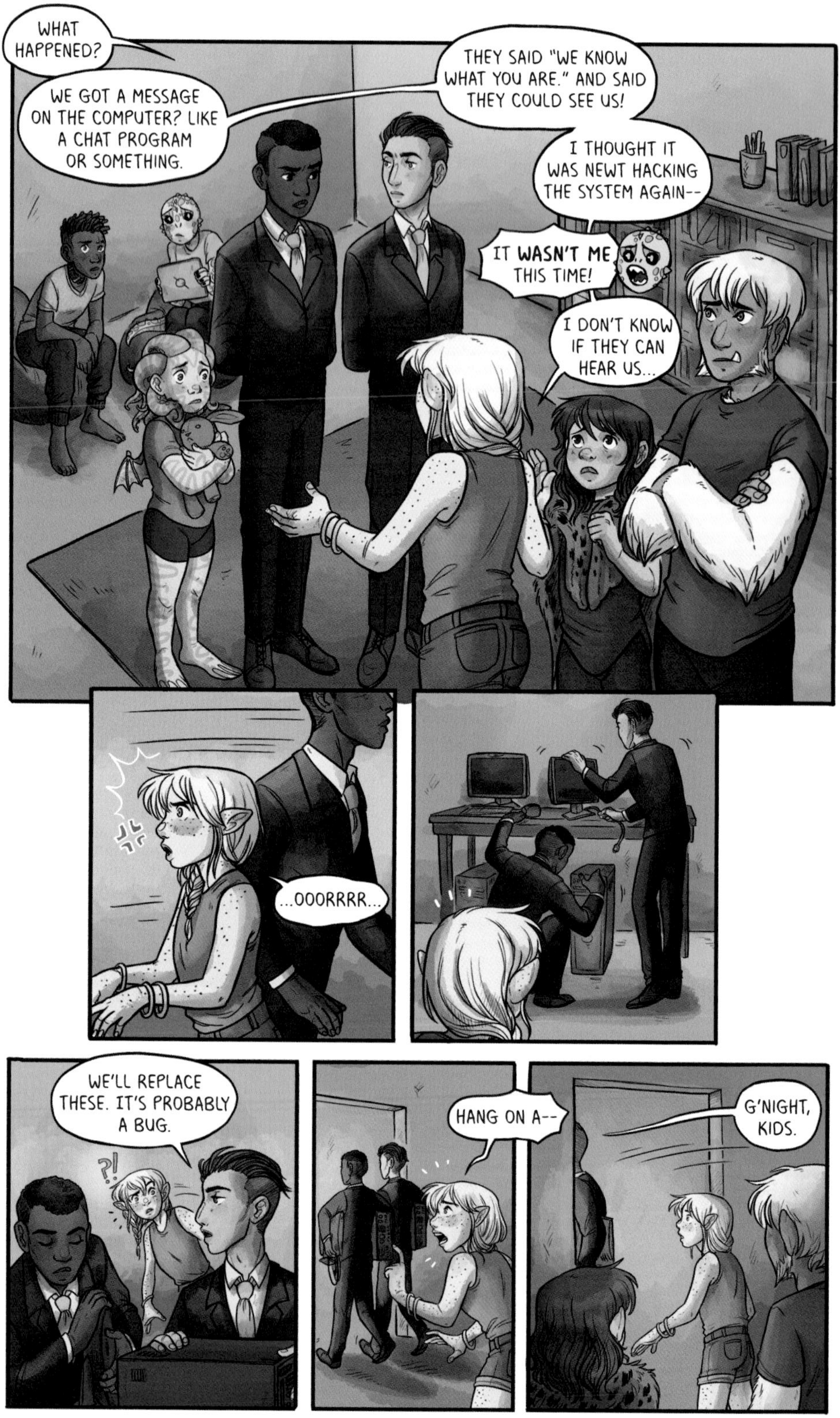
WHAT HAPPENED?
WE GOT A MESSAGE ON THE COMPUTER? LIKE A CHAT PROGRAM OR SOMETHING.
THEY SAID "WE KNOW WHAT YOU ARE." AND SAID THEY COULD SEE US!
I THOUGHT IT WAS NEWT HACKING THE SYSTEM AGAIN--
IT **WASN'T ME** THIS TIME!
I DON'T KNOW IF THEY CAN HEAR US...
...OOORRRR...
WE'LL REPLACE THESE. IT'S PROBABLY A BUG.
?!
HANG ON A--
G'NIGHT, KIDS.

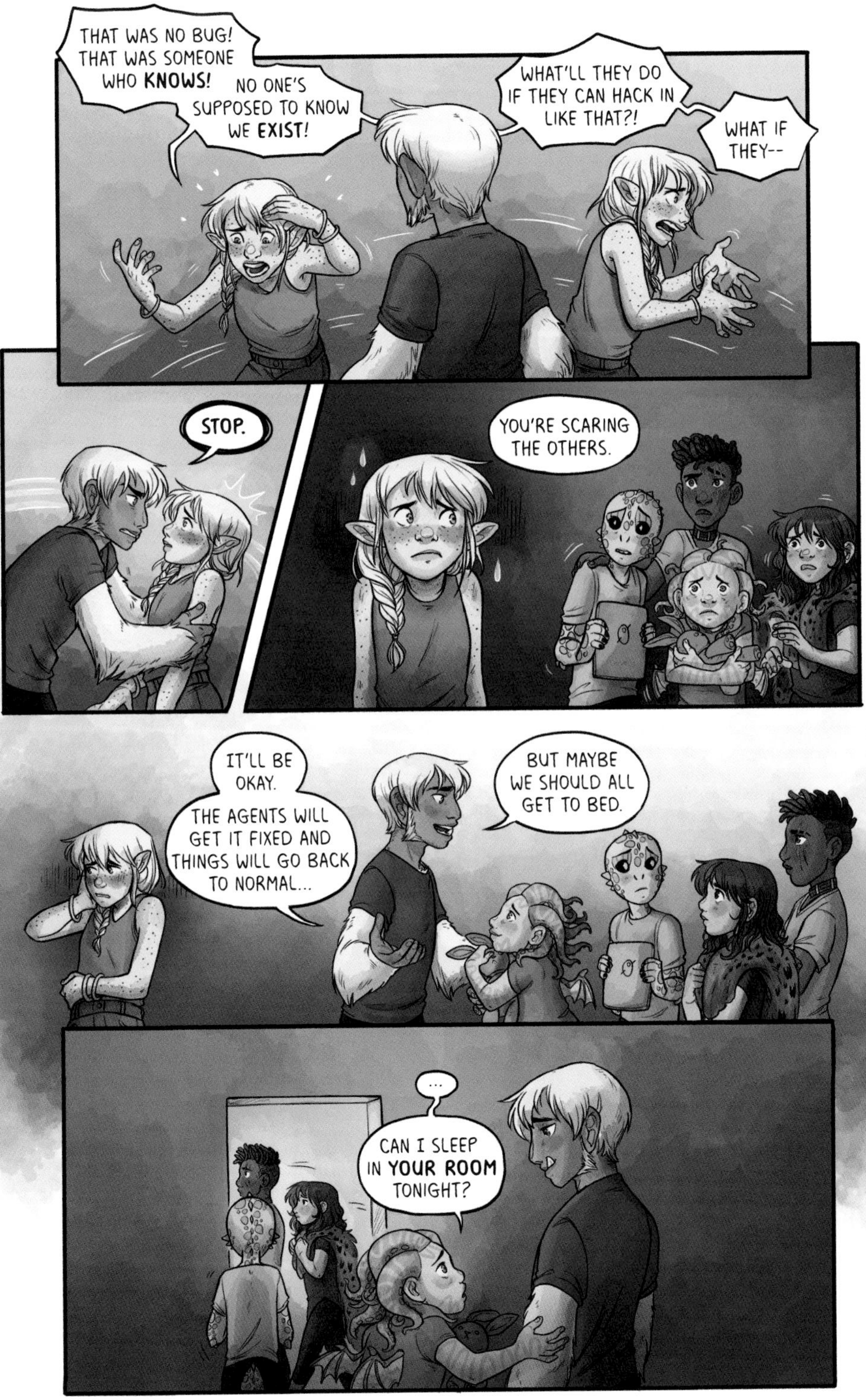
THAT WAS NO BUG! THAT WAS SOMEONE WHO **KNOWS**!
NO ONE'S SUPPOSED TO KNOW WE **EXIST**!
WHAT'LL THEY DO IF THEY CAN HACK IN LIKE THAT?!
WHAT IF THEY--
STOP.
YOU'RE SCARING THE OTHERS.
IT'LL BE OKAY.
THE AGENTS WILL GET IT FIXED AND THINGS WILL GO BACK TO NORMAL...
BUT MAYBE WE SHOULD ALL GET TO BED.
...
CAN I SLEEP IN **YOUR ROOM** TONIGHT?

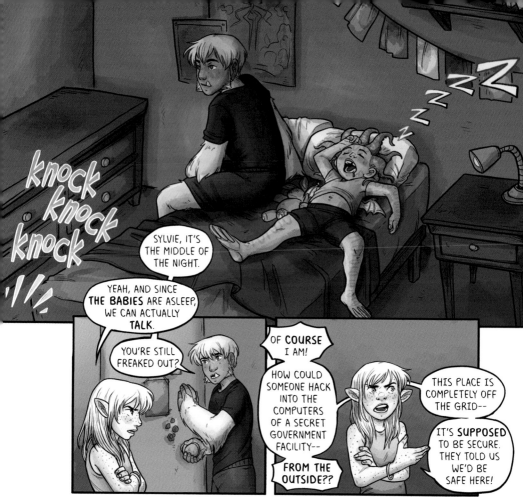

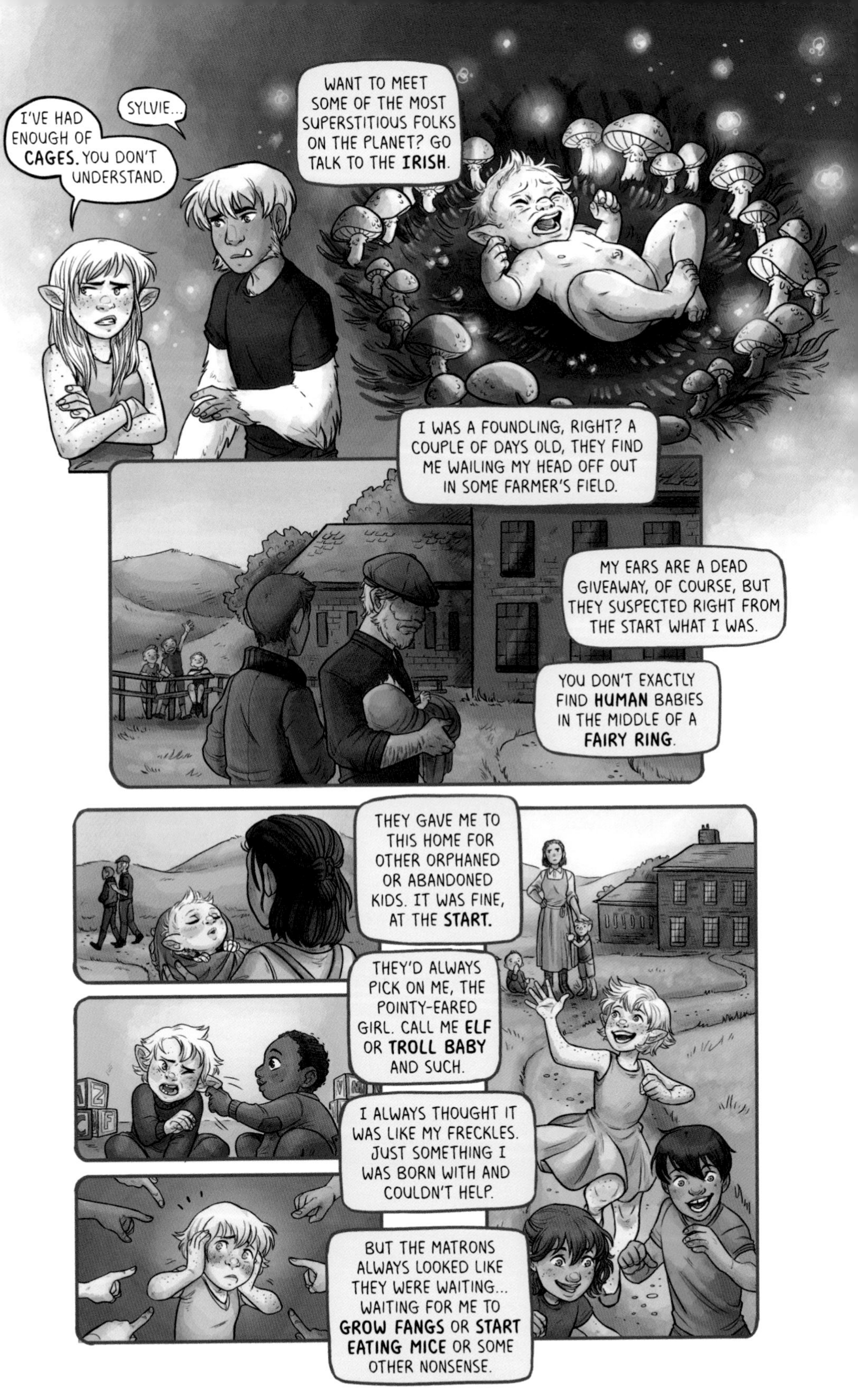

I'VE HAD ENOUGH OF **CAGES.** YOU DON'T UNDERSTAND.
SYLVIE...
WANT TO MEET SOME OF THE MOST SUPERSTITIOUS FOLKS ON THE PLANET? GO TALK TO THE **IRISH**.
I WAS A FOUNDLING, RIGHT? A COUPLE OF DAYS OLD, THEY FIND ME WAILING MY HEAD OFF OUT IN SOME FARMER'S FIELD.
MY EARS ARE A DEAD GIVEAWAY, OF COURSE, BUT THEY SUSPECTED RIGHT FROM THE START WHAT I WAS.
YOU DON'T EXACTLY FIND **HUMAN** BABIES IN THE MIDDLE OF A **FAIRY RING**.
THEY GAVE ME TO THIS HOME FOR OTHER ORPHANED OR ABANDONED KIDS. IT WAS FINE, AT THE **START.**
THEY'D ALWAYS PICK ON ME, THE POINTY-EARED GIRL. CALL ME **ELF** OR **TROLL BABY** AND SUCH.
I ALWAYS THOUGHT IT WAS LIKE MY FRECKLES. JUST SOMETHING I WAS BORN WITH AND COULDN'T HELP.
BUT THE MATRONS ALWAYS LOOKED LIKE THEY WERE WAITING... WAITING FOR ME TO **GROW FANGS** OR **START EATING MICE** OR SOME OTHER NONSENSE.

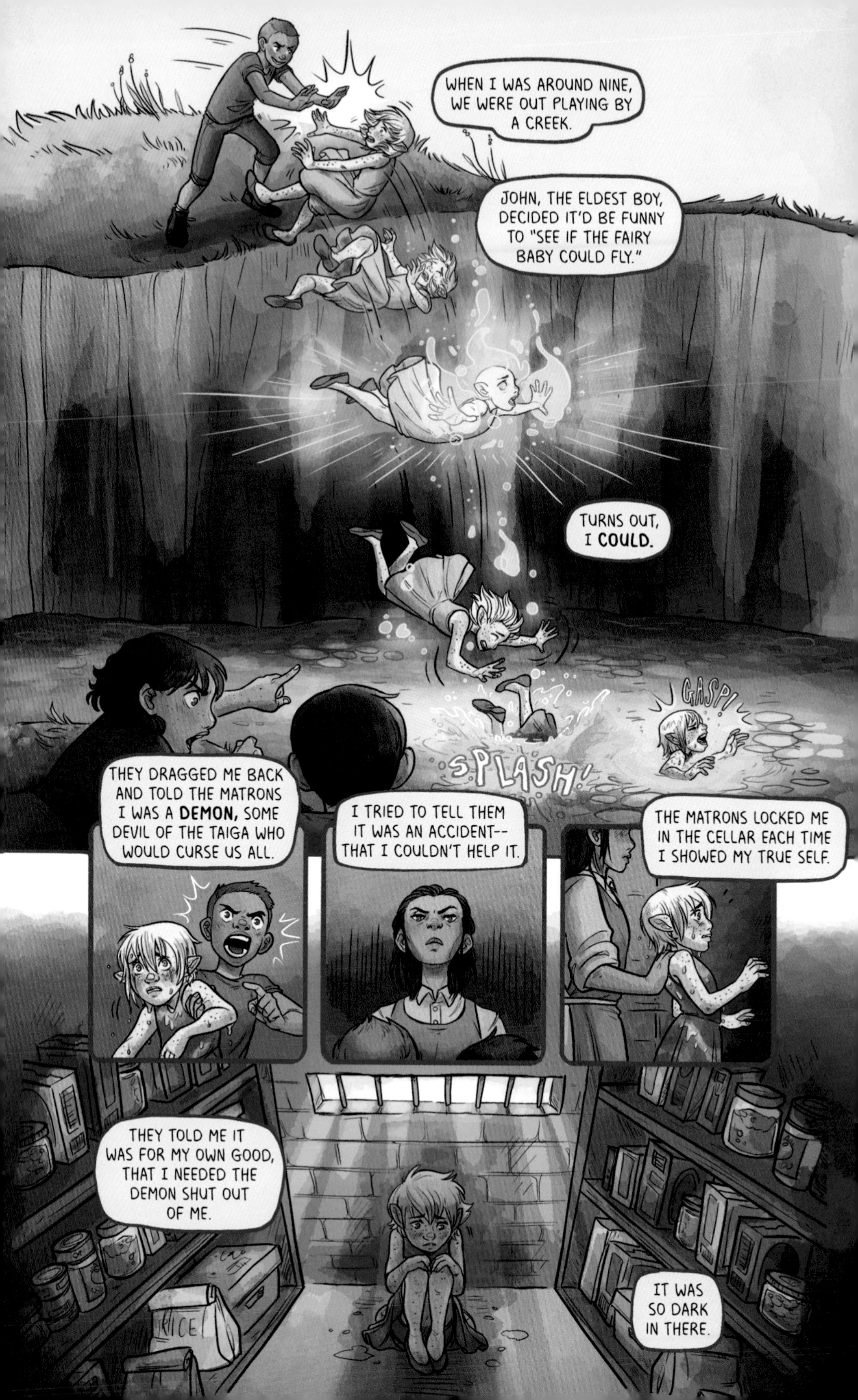
WHEN I WAS AROUND NINE, WE WERE OUT PLAYING BY A CREEK.
JOHN, THE ELDEST BOY, DECIDED IT'D BE FUNNY TO "SEE IF THE FAIRY BABY COULD FLY."
TURNS OUT, I **COULD.**
GASP!
SPLASH!
THEY DRAGGED ME BACK AND TOLD THE MATRONS I WAS A **DEMON,** SOME DEVIL OF THE TAIGA WHO WOULD CURSE US ALL.
I TRIED TO TELL THEM IT WAS AN ACCIDENT--THAT I COULDN'T HELP IT.
THE MATRONS LOCKED ME IN THE CELLAR EACH TIME I SHOWED MY TRUE SELF.
THEY TOLD ME IT WAS FOR MY OWN GOOD, THAT I NEEDED THE DEMON SHUT OUT OF ME.
RICE
IT WAS SO DARK IN THERE.

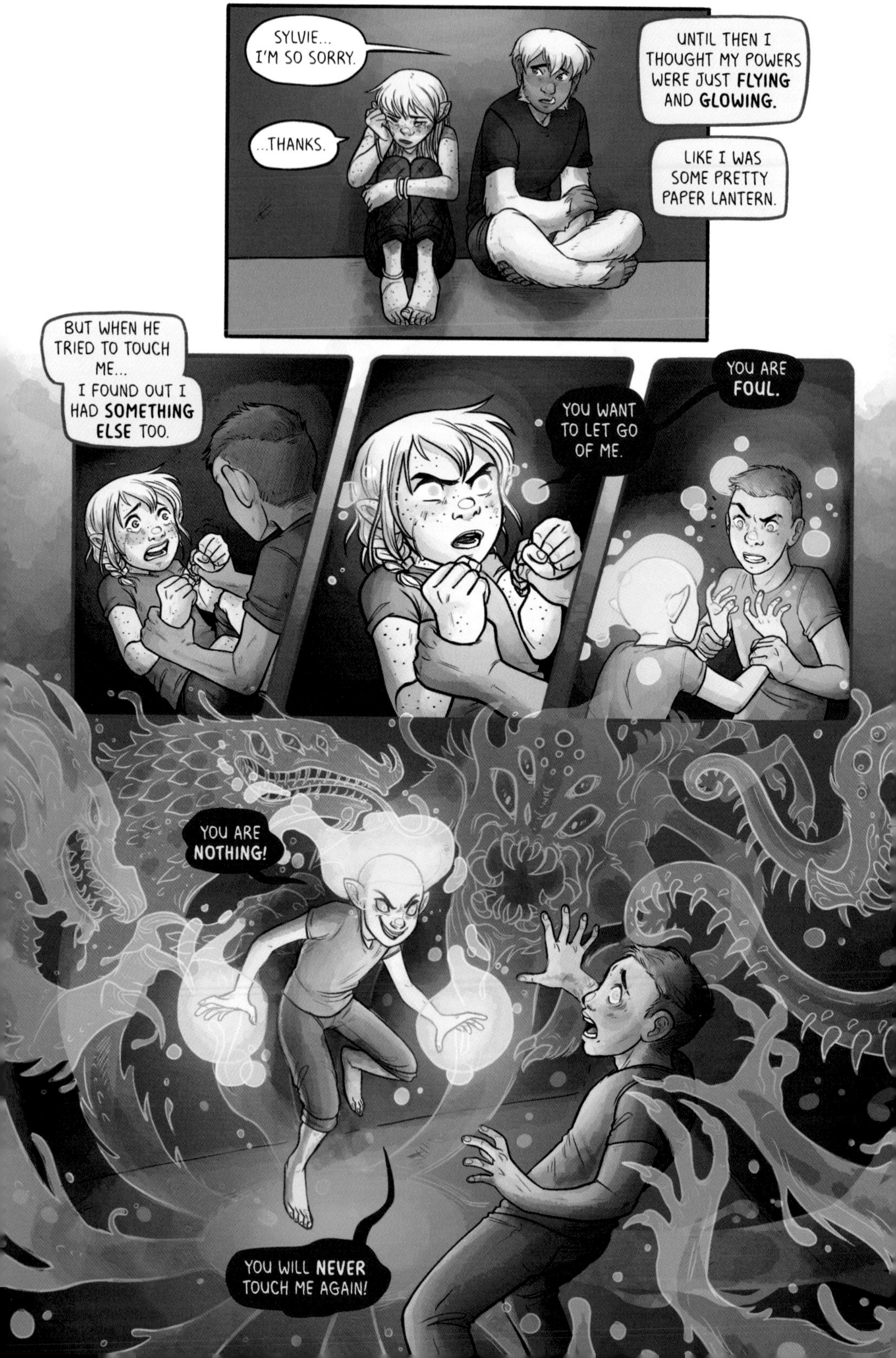
SYLVIE...
I'M SO SORRY.
...THANKS.
UNTIL THEN I THOUGHT MY POWERS WERE JUST **FLYING** AND **GLOWING.**
LIKE I WAS SOME PRETTY PAPER LANTERN.
BUT WHEN HE TRIED TO TOUCH ME...
I FOUND OUT I HAD **SOMETHING ELSE** TOO.
YOU WANT TO LET GO OF ME.
YOU ARE **FOUL.**
YOU ARE **NOTHING!**
YOU WILL **NEVER** TOUCH ME AGAIN!

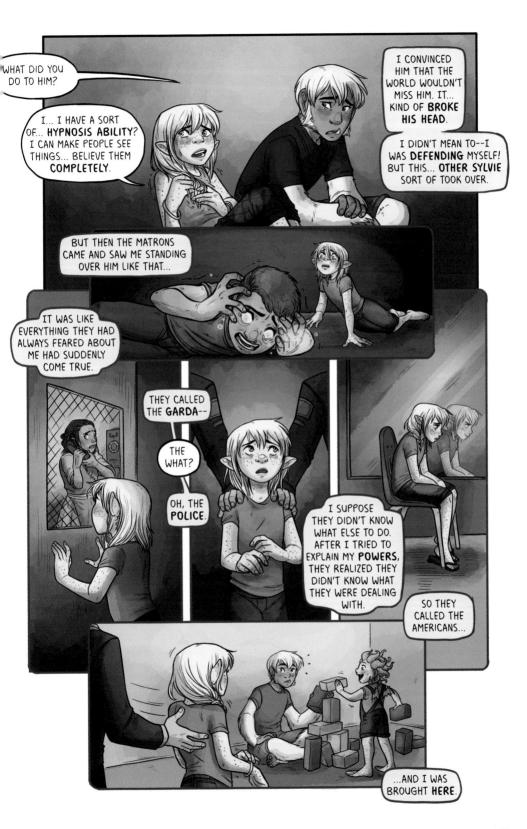

WHAT DID YOU DO TO HIM?

I CONVINCED HIM THAT THE WORLD WOULDN'T MISS HIM. IT... KIND OF **BROKE HIS HEAD.**

I... I HAVE A SORT OF... **HYPNOSIS ABILITY?** I CAN MAKE PEOPLE SEE THINGS... BELIEVE THEM **COMPLETELY.**

I DIDN'T MEAN TO--I WAS **DEFENDING** MYSELF! BUT THIS... **OTHER SYLVIE** SORT OF TOOK OVER.

BUT THEN THE MATRONS CAME AND SAW ME STANDING OVER HIM LIKE THAT...

IT WAS LIKE EVERYTHING THEY HAD ALWAYS FEARED ABOUT ME HAD SUDDENLY COME TRUE.

THEY CALLED THE **GARDA**--

THE WHAT?

OH, THE **POLICE.**

I SUPPOSE THEY DIDN'T KNOW WHAT ELSE TO DO. AFTER I TRIED TO EXPLAIN MY **POWERS,** THEY REALIZED THEY DIDN'T KNOW WHAT THEY WERE DEALING WITH.

SO THEY CALLED THE AMERICANS...

...AND I WAS BROUGHT **HERE.**

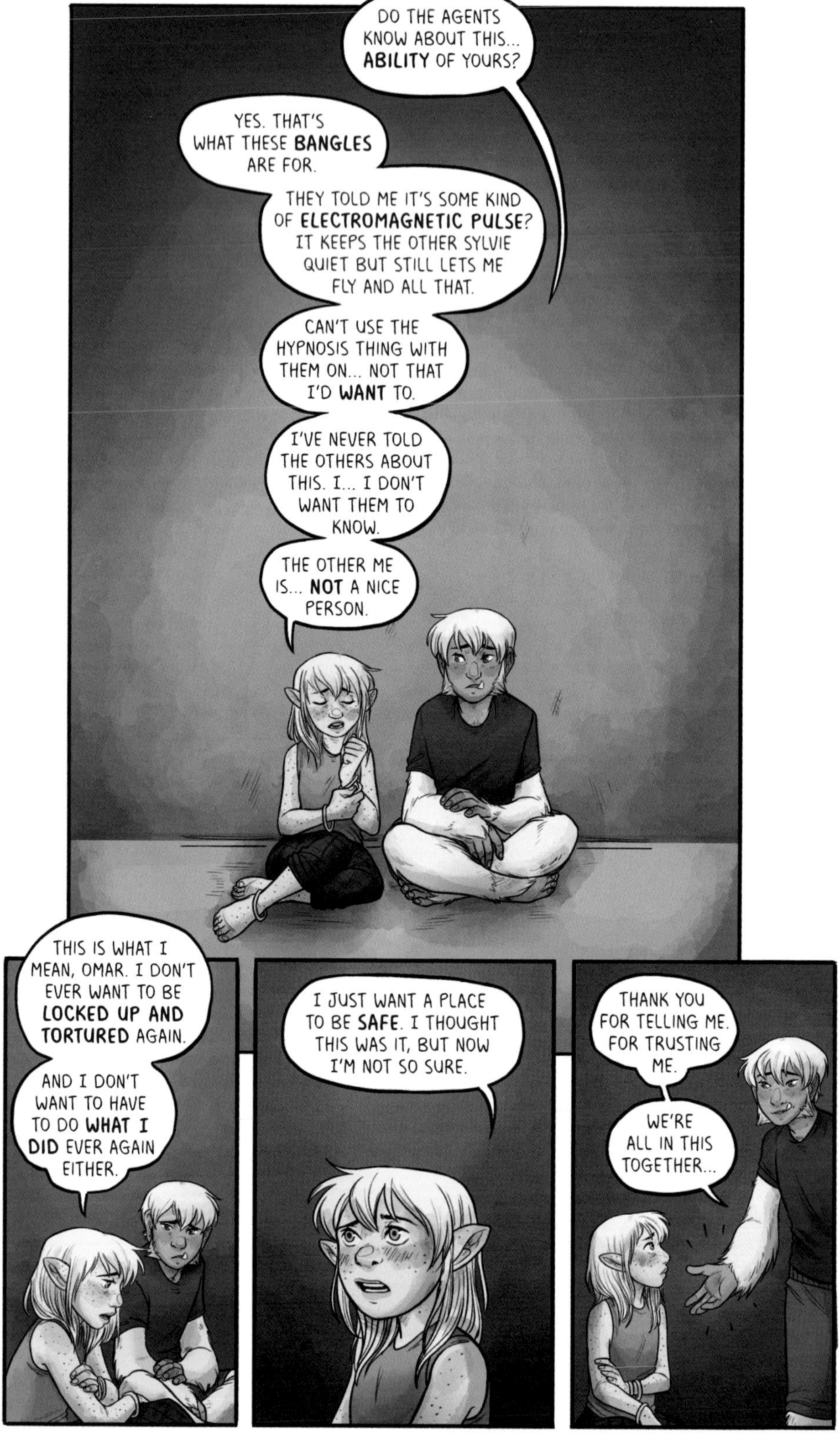
DO THE AGENTS KNOW ABOUT THIS... ABILITY OF YOURS?
YES. THAT'S WHAT THESE BANGLES ARE FOR.
THEY TOLD ME IT'S SOME KIND OF ELECTROMAGNETIC PULSE? IT KEEPS THE OTHER SYLVIE QUIET BUT STILL LETS ME FLY AND ALL THAT.
CAN'T USE THE HYPNOSIS THING WITH THEM ON... NOT THAT I'D WANT TO.
I'VE NEVER TOLD THE OTHERS ABOUT THIS. I... I DON'T WANT THEM TO KNOW.
THE OTHER ME IS... NOT A NICE PERSON.
THIS IS WHAT I MEAN, OMAR. I DON'T EVER WANT TO BE LOCKED UP AND TORTURED AGAIN.
AND I DON'T WANT TO HAVE TO DO WHAT I DID EVER AGAIN EITHER.
I JUST WANT A PLACE TO BE SAFE. I THOUGHT THIS WAS IT, BUT NOW I'M NOT SO SURE.
THANK YOU FOR TELLING ME. FOR TRUSTING ME.
WE'RE ALL IN THIS TOGETHER...

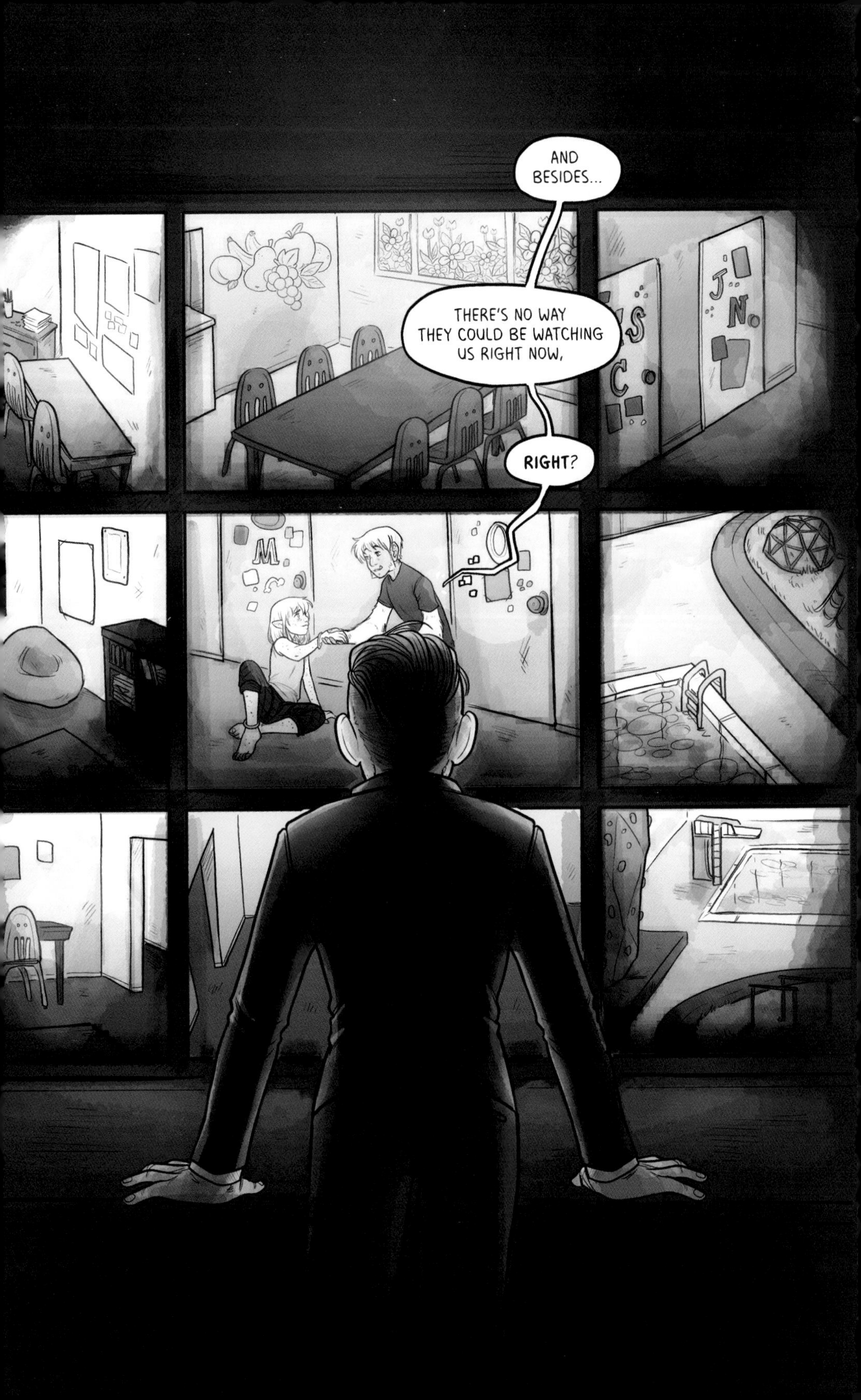
AND BESIDES...
THERE'S NO WAY THEY COULD BE WATCHING US RIGHT NOW,
RIGHT?

CHAPTER TWO

YOU CAN RUN BUT YOU CAN'T HIDE

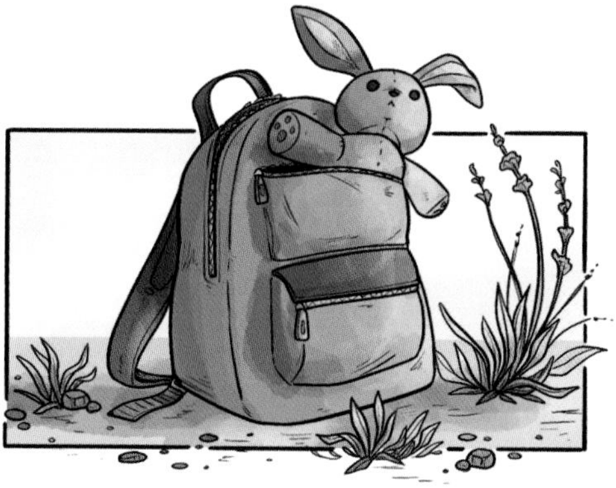

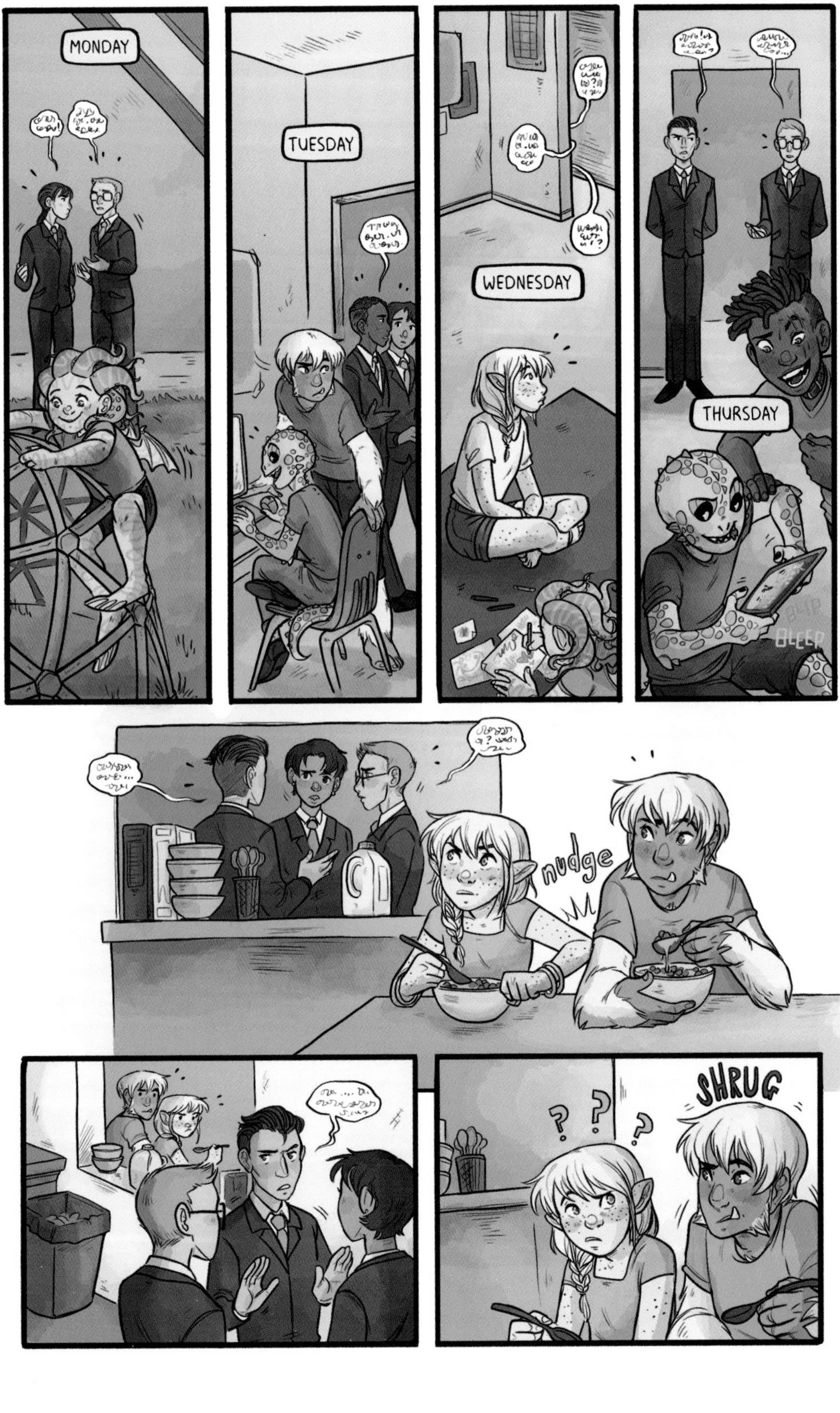
MONDAY
TUESDAY
WEDNESDAY
THURSDAY
nudge
SHRUG

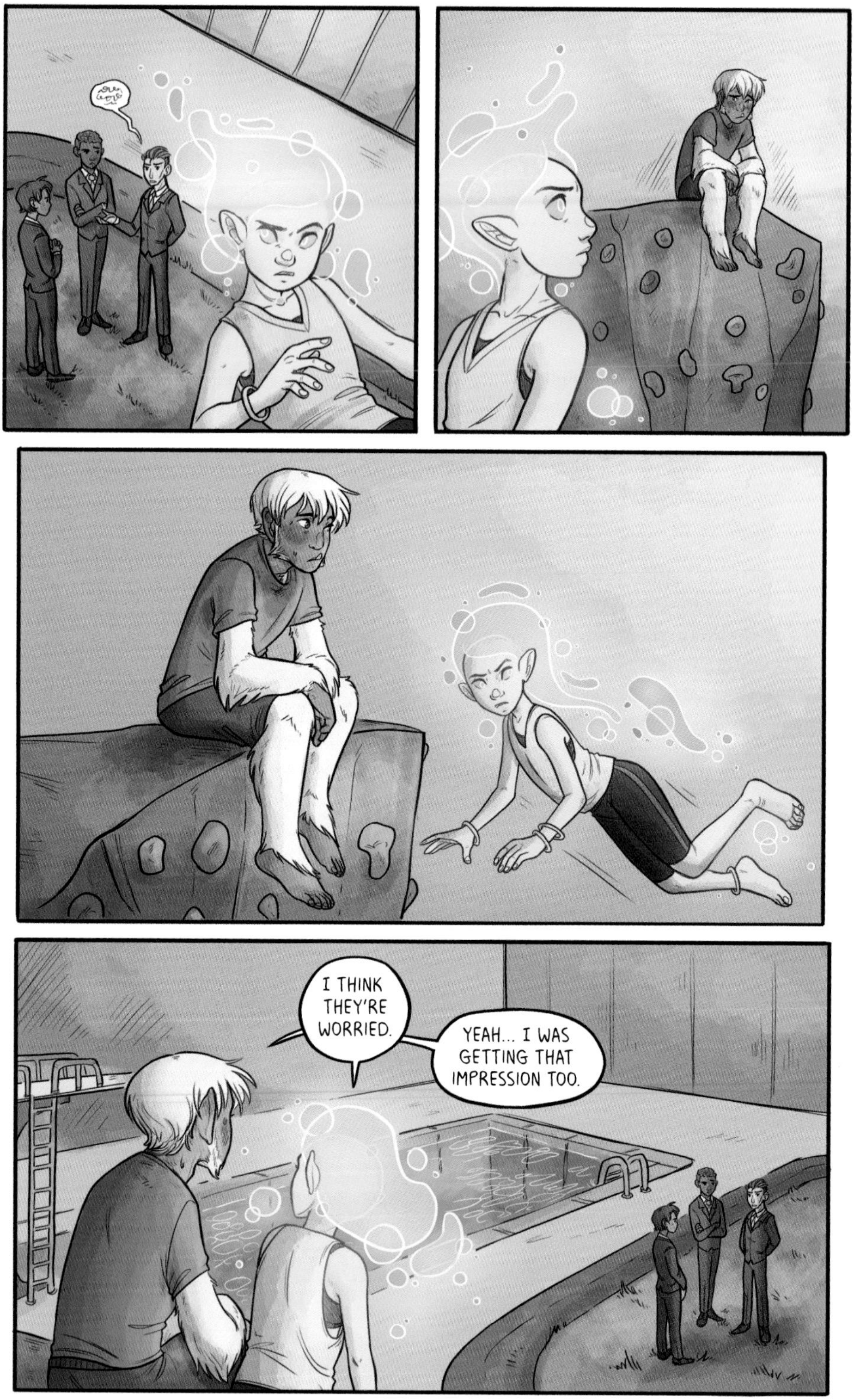
I THINK THEY'RE WORRIED.
YEAH... I WAS GETTING THAT IMPRESSION TOO.

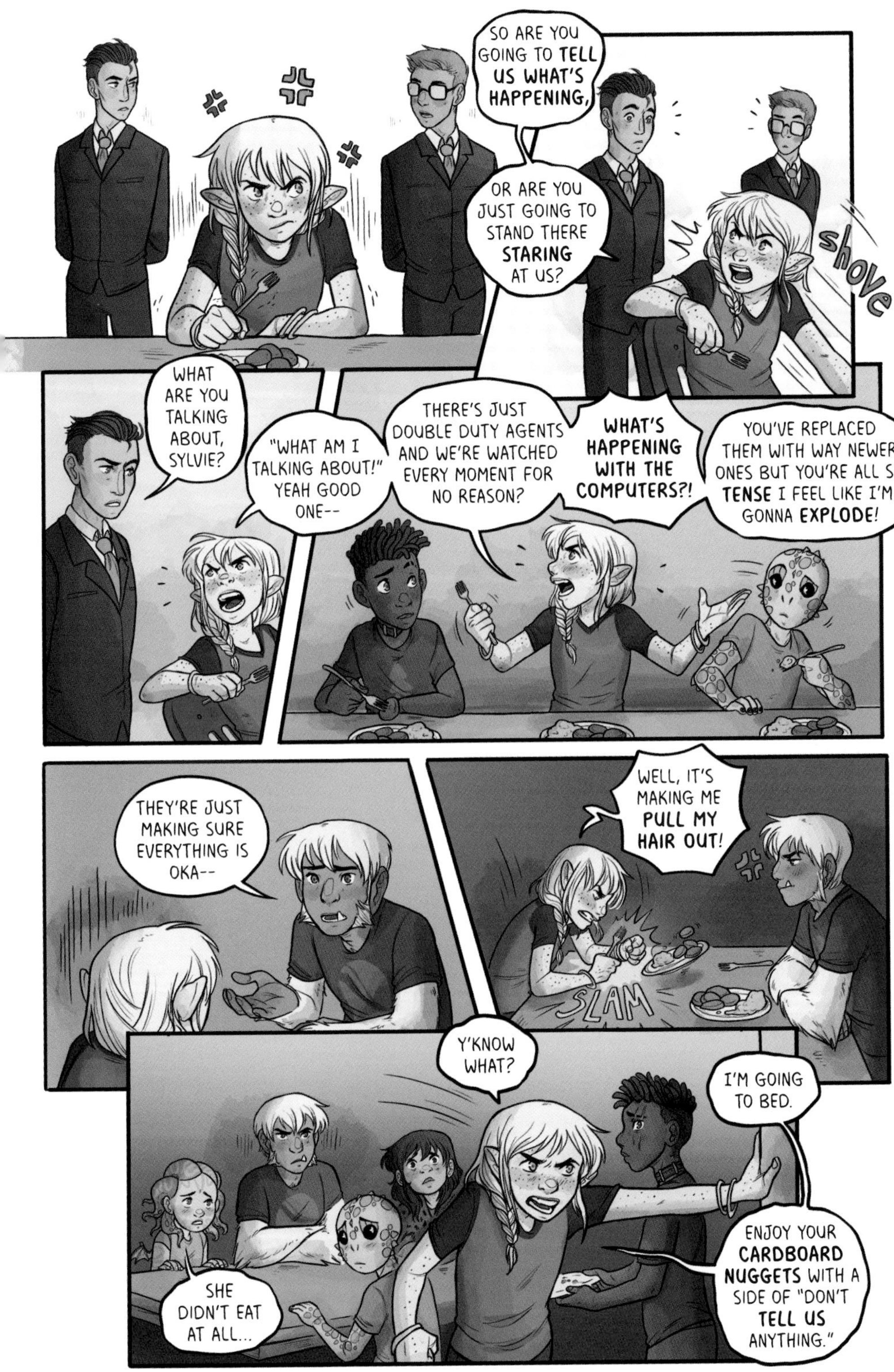
SO ARE YOU GOING TO TELL US WHAT'S HAPPENING,
OR ARE YOU JUST GOING TO STAND THERE STARING AT US?
shove
WHAT ARE YOU TALKING ABOUT, SYLVIE?
"WHAT AM I TALKING ABOUT!" YEAH GOOD ONE--
THERE'S JUST DOUBLE DUTY AGENTS AND WE'RE WATCHED EVERY MOMENT FOR NO REASON?
WHAT'S HAPPENING WITH THE COMPUTERS?!
YOU'VE REPLACED THEM WITH WAY NEWER ONES BUT YOU'RE ALL SO TENSE I FEEL LIKE I'M, GONNA EXPLODE!
THEY'RE JUST MAKING SURE EVERYTHING IS OKA--
WELL, IT'S MAKING ME PULL MY HAIR OUT!
SLAM
Y'KNOW WHAT?
I'M GOING TO BED.
ENJOY YOUR CARDBOARD NUGGETS WITH A SIDE OF "DON'T TELL US ANYTHING."
SHE DIDN'T EAT AT ALL...

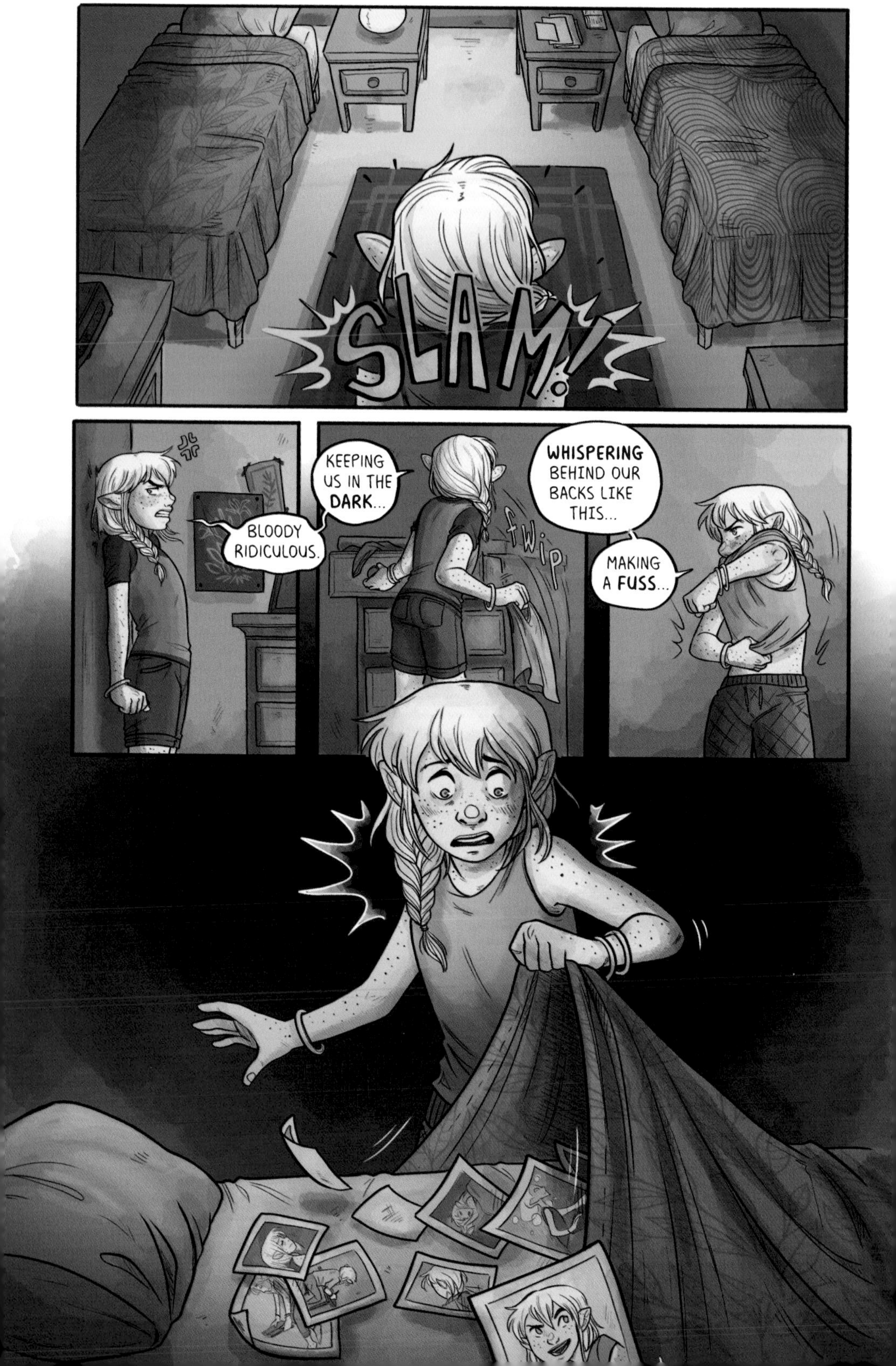
SLAM!
BLOODY RIDICULOUS.
KEEPING US IN THE DARK...
fwip
WHISPERING BEHIND OUR BACKS LIKE THIS...
MAKING A FUSS...

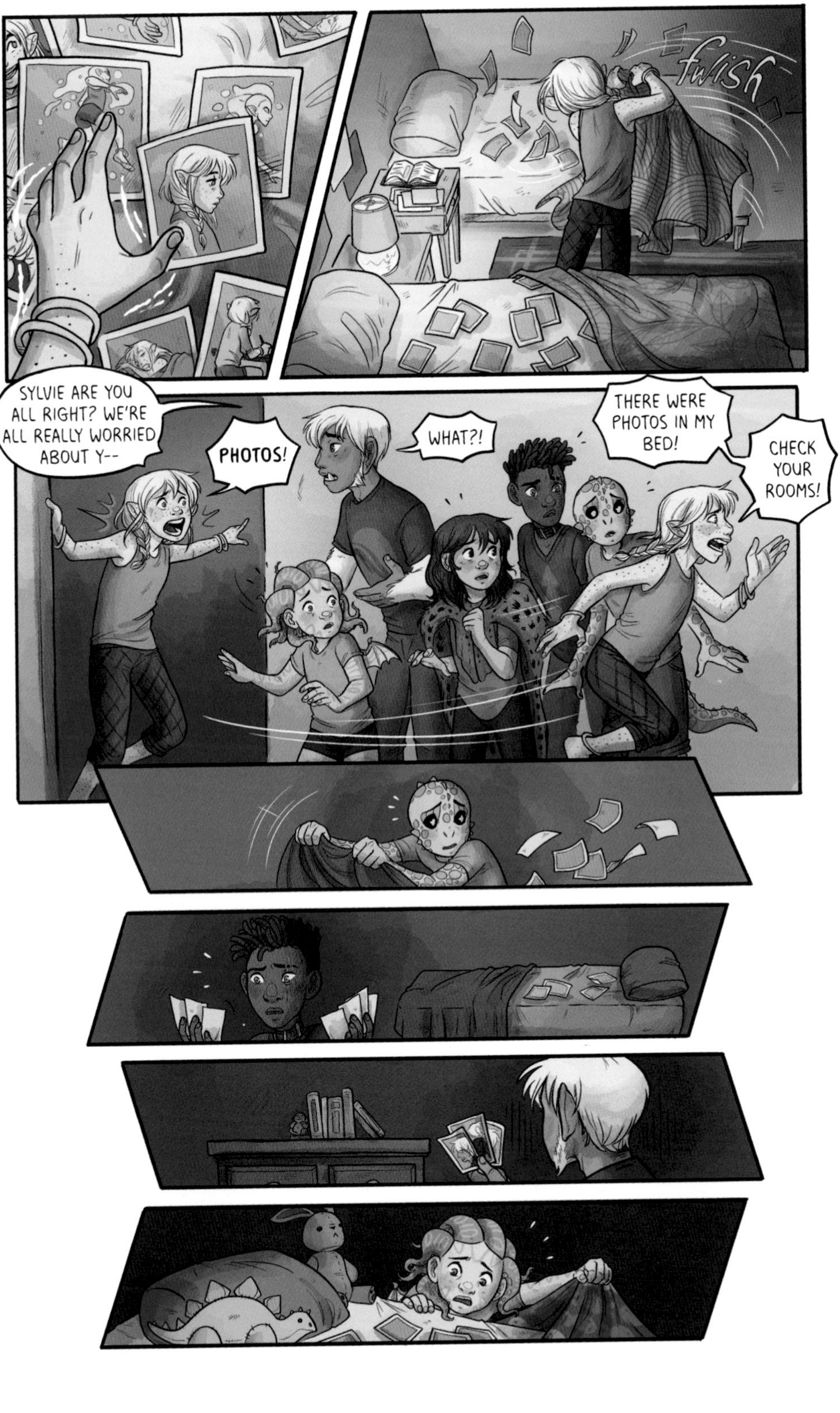
fwish
SYLVIE ARE YOU ALL RIGHT? WE'RE ALL REALLY WORRIED ABOUT Y--
PHOTOS!
WHAT?!
THERE WERE PHOTOS IN MY BED!
CHECK YOUR ROOMS!

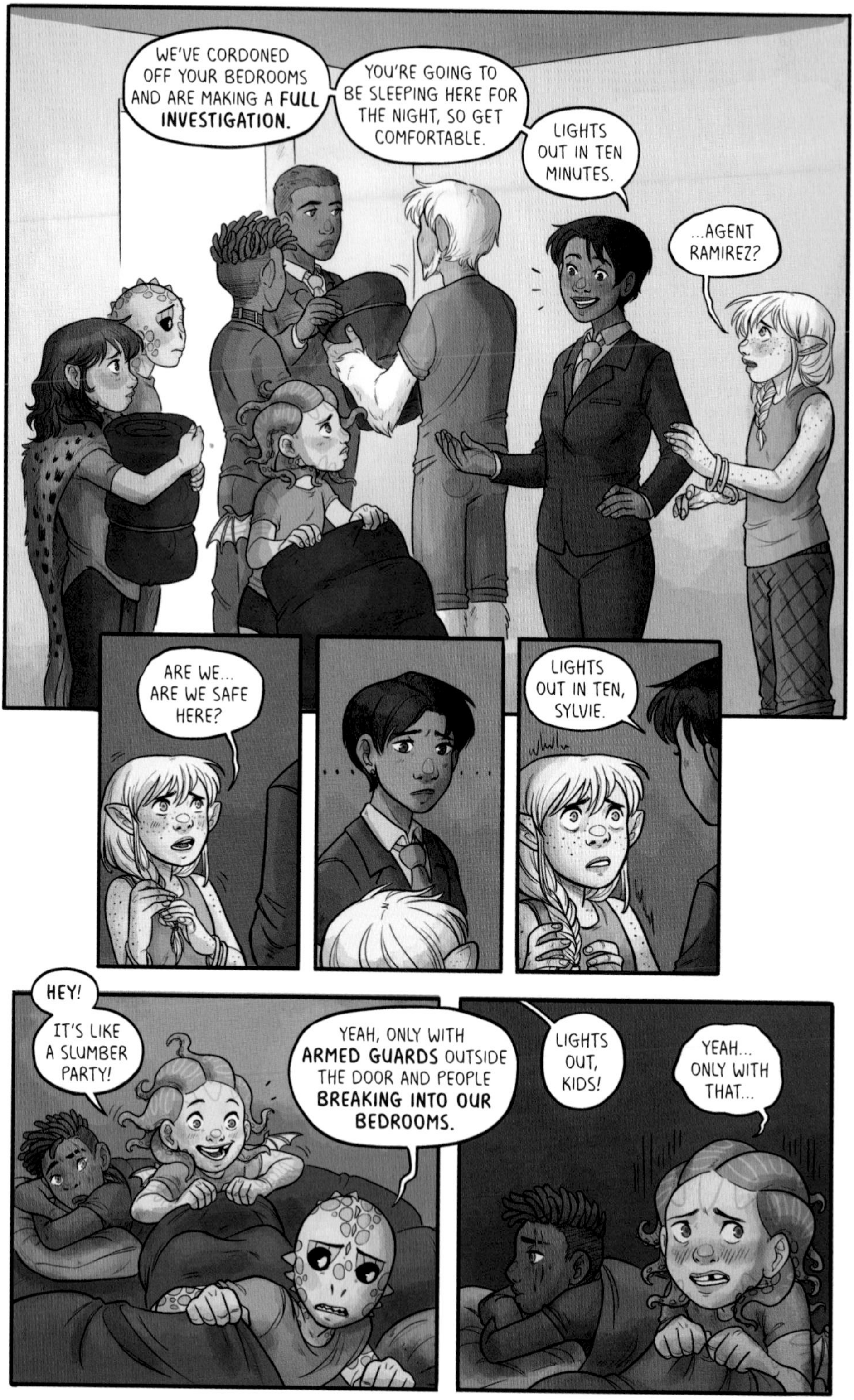
WE'VE CORDONED OFF YOUR BEDROOMS AND ARE MAKING A **FULL INVESTIGATION.**
YOU'RE GOING TO BE SLEEPING HERE FOR THE NIGHT, SO GET COMFORTABLE.
LIGHTS OUT IN TEN MINUTES.
...AGENT RAMIREZ?
ARE WE... ARE WE SAFE HERE?
. . .
LIGHTS OUT IN TEN, SYLVIE.
HEY!
IT'S LIKE A SLUMBER PARTY!
YEAH, ONLY WITH **ARMED GUARDS** OUTSIDE THE DOOR AND PEOPLE **BREAKING INTO OUR BEDROOMS.**
LIGHTS OUT, KIDS!
YEAH... ONLY WITH THAT...

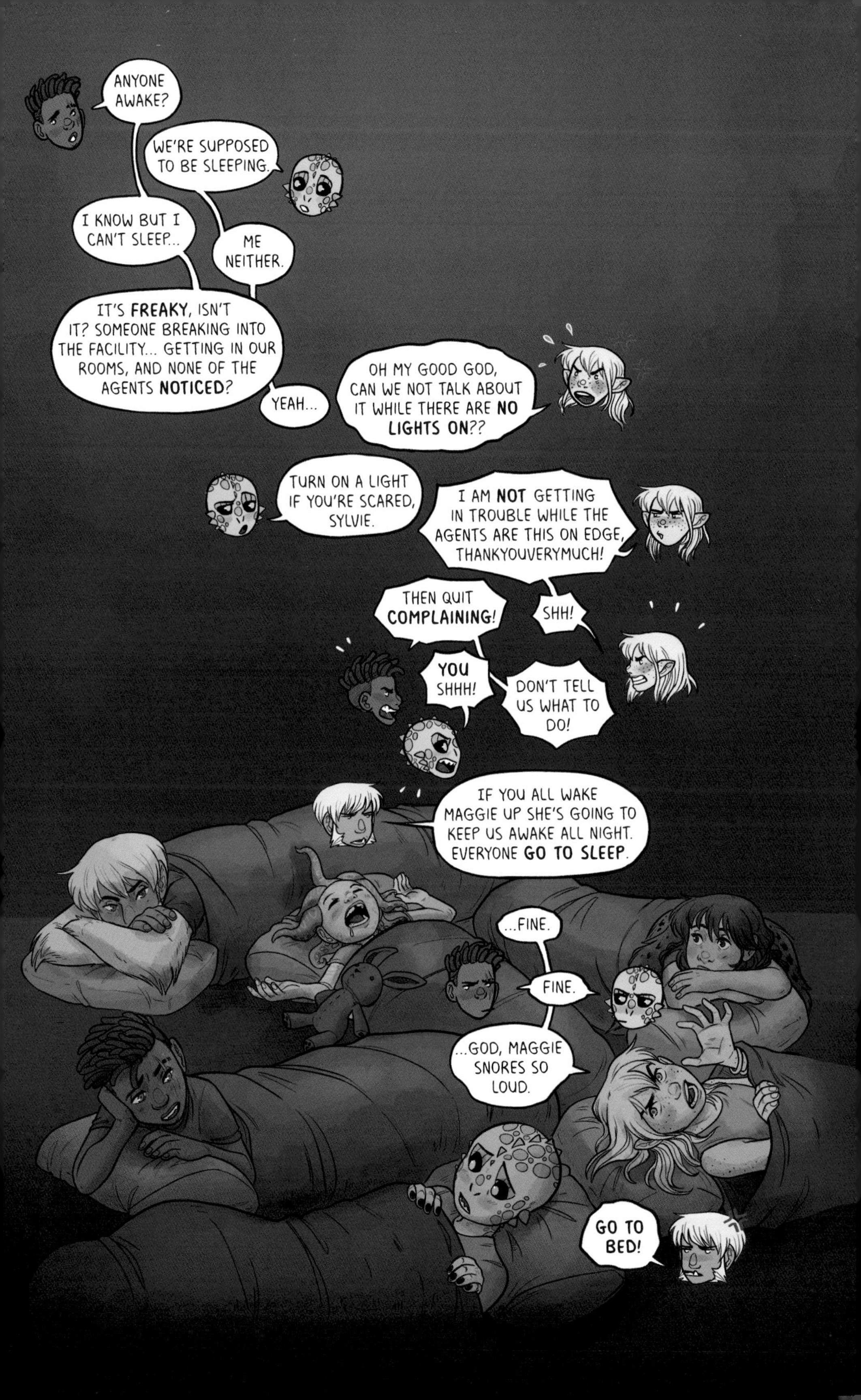
ANYONE AWAKE?
WE'RE SUPPOSED TO BE SLEEPING.
I KNOW BUT I CAN'T SLEEP...
ME NEITHER.
IT'S **FREAKY**, ISN'T IT? SOMEONE BREAKING INTO THE FACILITY... GETTING IN OUR ROOMS, AND NONE OF THE AGENTS **NOTICED**?
YEAH...
OH MY GOOD GOD, CAN WE NOT TALK ABOUT IT WHILE THERE ARE **NO LIGHTS ON**??
TURN ON A LIGHT IF YOU'RE SCARED, SYLVIE.
I AM **NOT** GETTING IN TROUBLE WHILE THE AGENTS ARE THIS ON EDGE, THANKYOUVERYMUCH!
THEN QUIT **COMPLAINING**!
SHH!
YOU SHHH!
DON'T TELL US WHAT TO DO!
IF YOU ALL WAKE MAGGIE UP SHE'S GOING TO KEEP US AWAKE ALL NIGHT. EVERYONE **GO TO SLEEP**.
...FINE.
FINE.
...GOD, MAGGIE SNORES SO LOUD.
GO TO BED!

WHAT ARE YOU DOING?

GOTTA MAKE SURE ALL MY STUFFIES FIT!

DID YOU PACK YOUR TOOTHBRUSH?

OH... OOPS.

THAT'S OKAY, I'VE GOT IT HERE. YOU'RE PRETTY EXCITED, HUH?

YUP!! I'VE ONLY BEEN OUTSIDE **ONCE** BEFORE!

AND I DON'T REALLY REMEMBER IT... BUT I BET IT WAS **GREAT!**

DO YOU THINK THERE'LL BE **TREES** AT THE NEW PLAYROOM?

MAYBE WE CAN PLAY OUTSIDE THERE!

DO YOU THINK THERE'LL BE **OTHER KIDS** AT THE NEW PLACE?

MAYBE WE'LL GET OUR OWN ROOMS!

THIS ROOM SMELLS TOO MUCH LIKE LIZARD.

HEYYY!

sigh

YOU'VE ONLY BEEN HERE A MONTH AND WE'RE MOVING ALREADY, HUH?

zzziiip!

tuck

WELL...

THE NEW PLACE WILL SURE BE BETTER THAN THIS ONE.

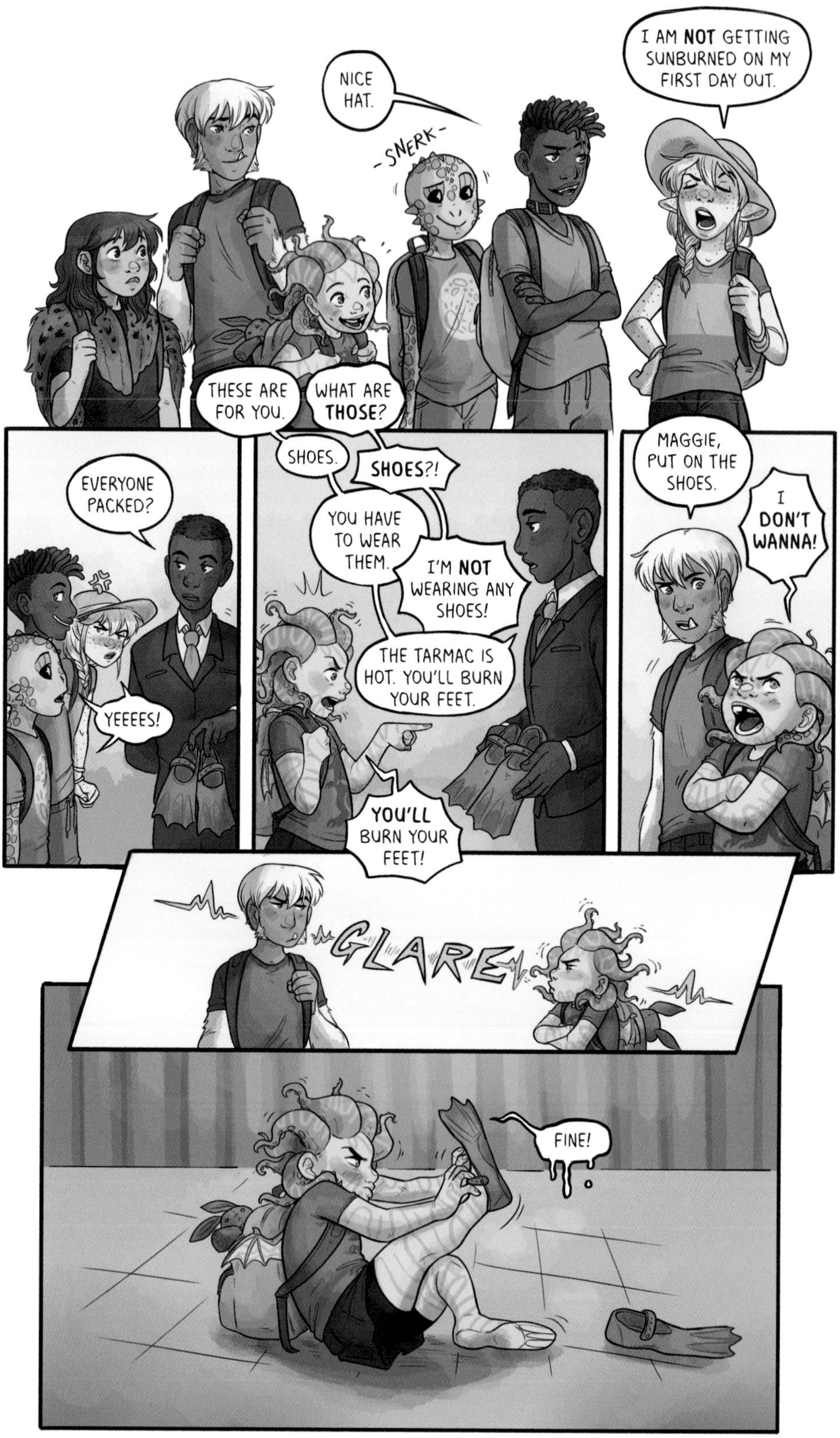
NICE HAT.
-SNERK-
I AM **NOT** GETTING SUNBURNED ON MY FIRST DAY OUT.
EVERYONE PACKED?
YEEEES!
THESE ARE FOR YOU.
WHAT ARE **THOSE**?
SHOES.
SHOES?!
YOU HAVE TO WEAR THEM.
I'M **NOT** WEARING ANY SHOES!
THE TARMAC IS HOT. YOU'LL BURN YOUR FEET.
YOU'LL BURN YOUR FEET!
MAGGIE, PUT ON THE SHOES.
I **DON'T WANNA!**
GLARE
FINE!

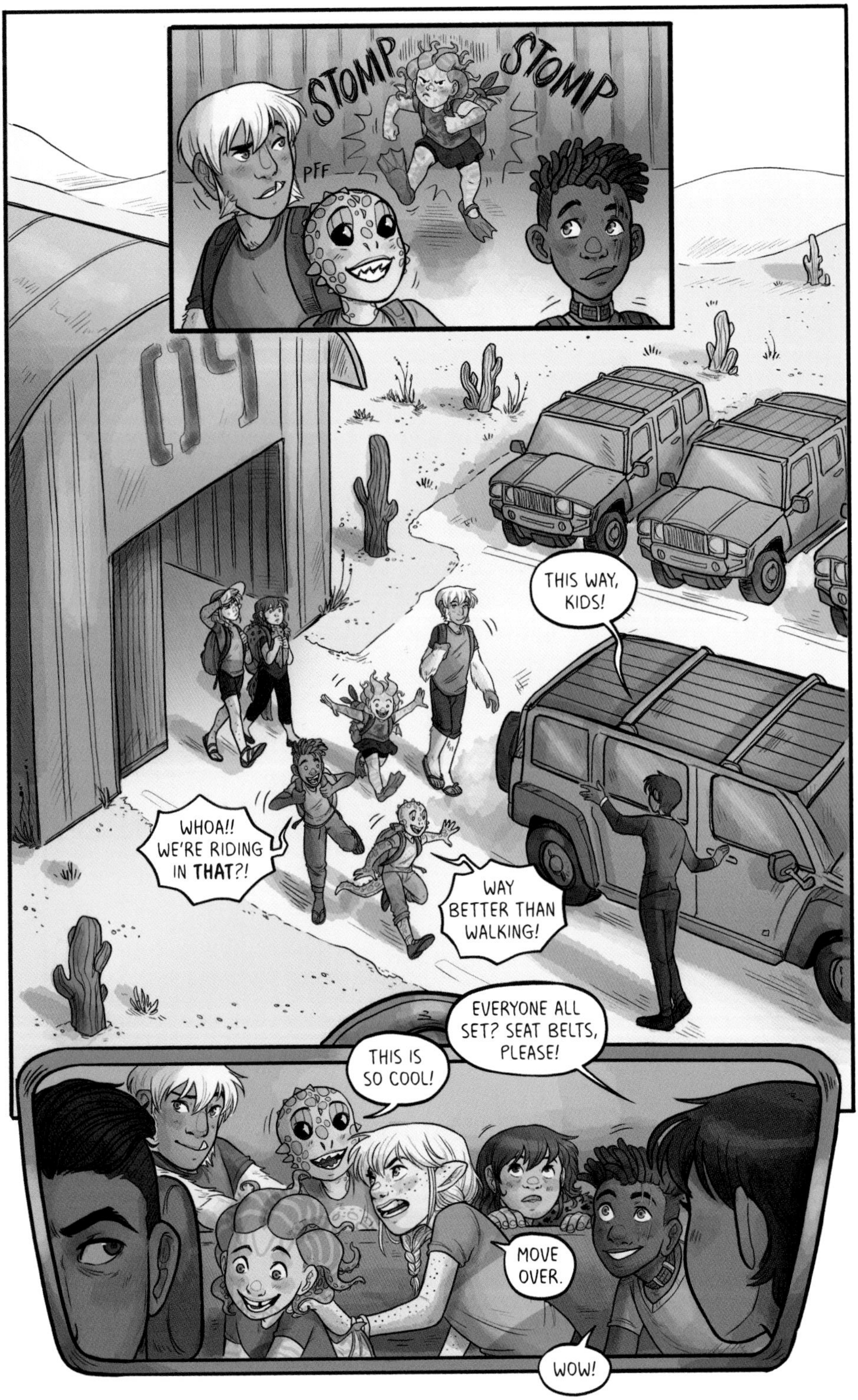
STOMP
STOMP
PFF
THIS WAY, KIDS!
WHOA!! WE'RE RIDING IN **THAT**?!
WAY BETTER THAN WALKING!
EVERYONE ALL SET? SEAT BELTS, PLEASE!
THIS IS SO COOL!
MOVE OVER.
WOW!

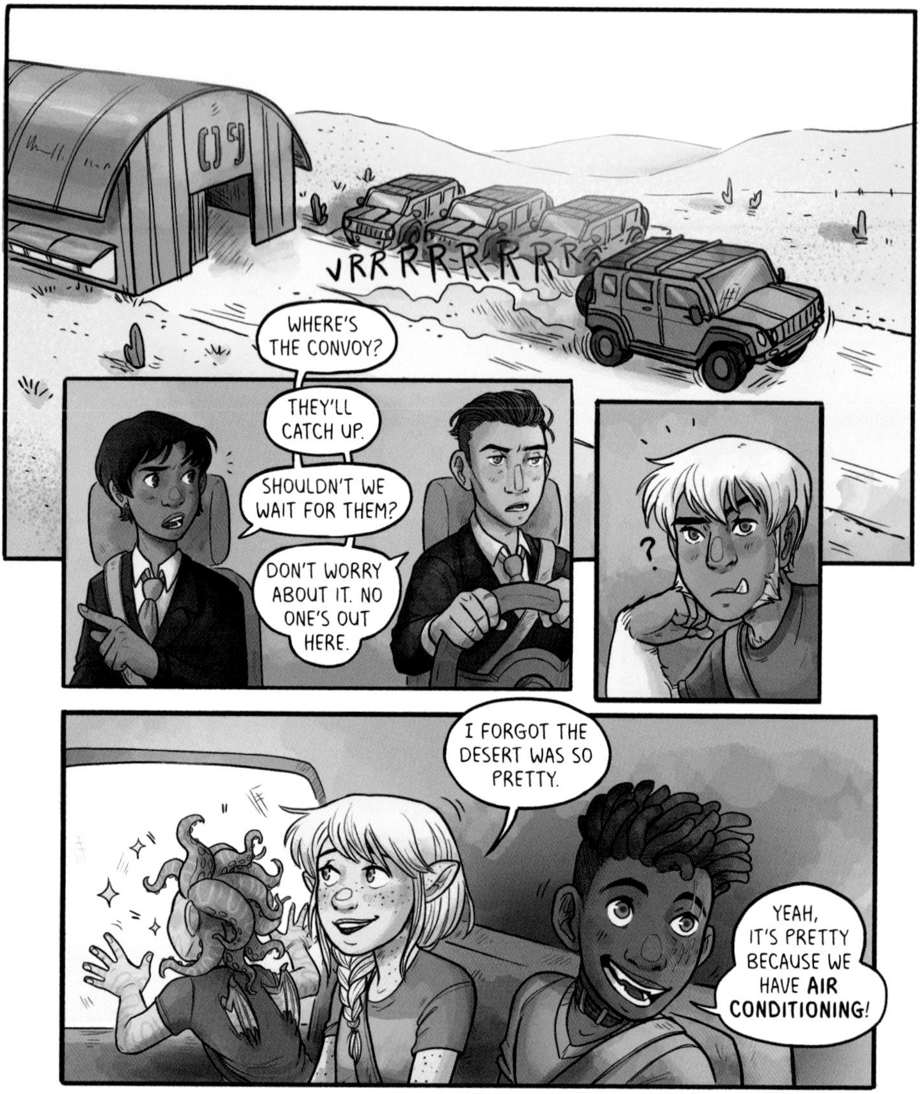
VRRRRRRRRRR
WHERE'S THE CONVOY?
THEY'LL CATCH UP.
SHOULDN'T WE WAIT FOR THEM?
DON'T WORRY ABOUT IT. NO ONE'S OUT HERE.
?
I FORGOT THE DESERT WAS SO PRETTY.
YEAH, IT'S PRETTY BECAUSE WE HAVE **AIR CONDITIONING**!

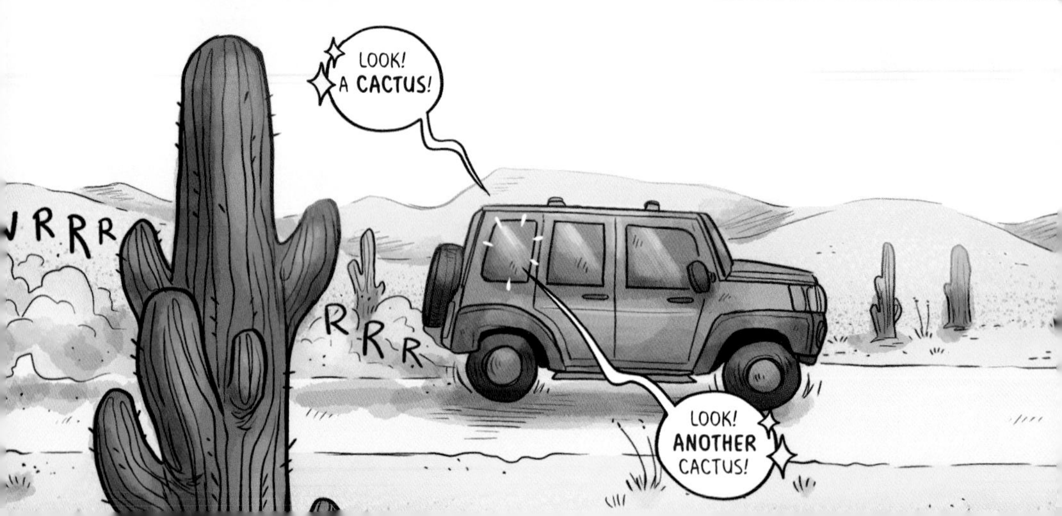
LOOK! A **CACTUS**!
VRRR
RRR
LOOK! **ANOTHER** CACTUS!

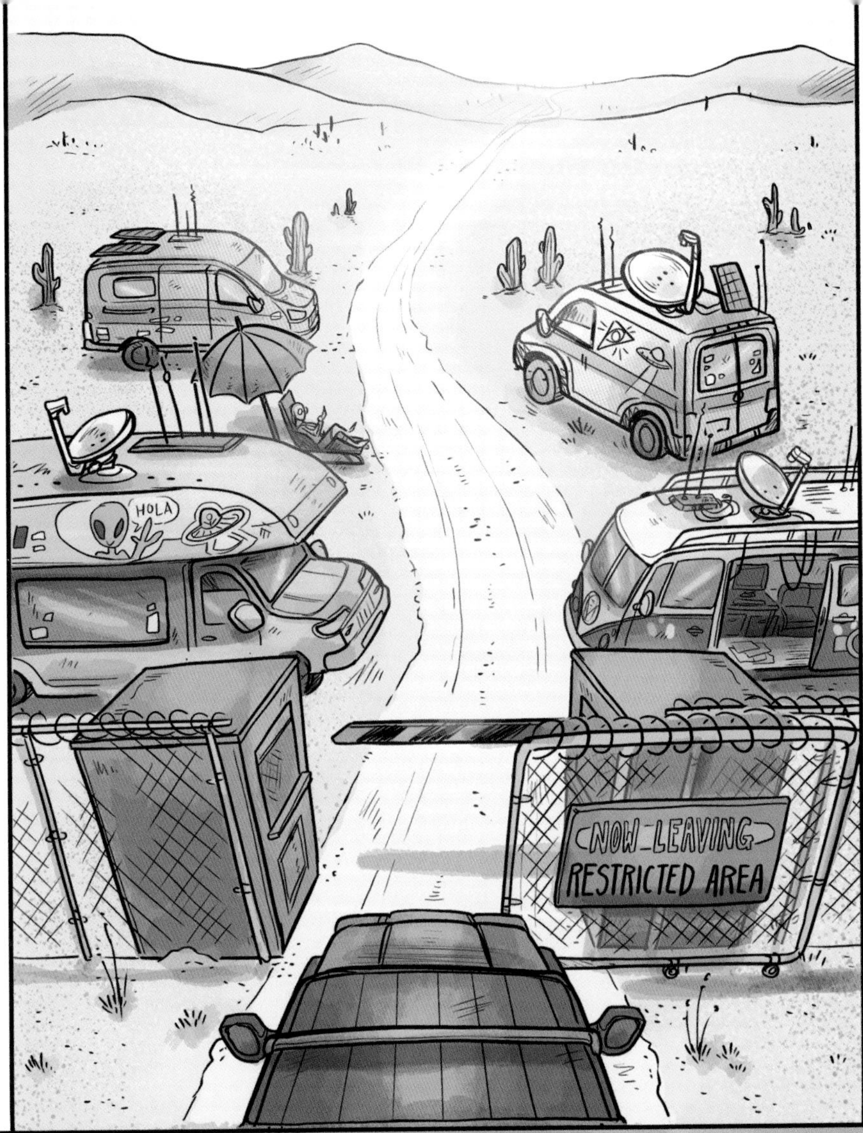
HOLA
NOW LEAVING
RESTRICTED AREA

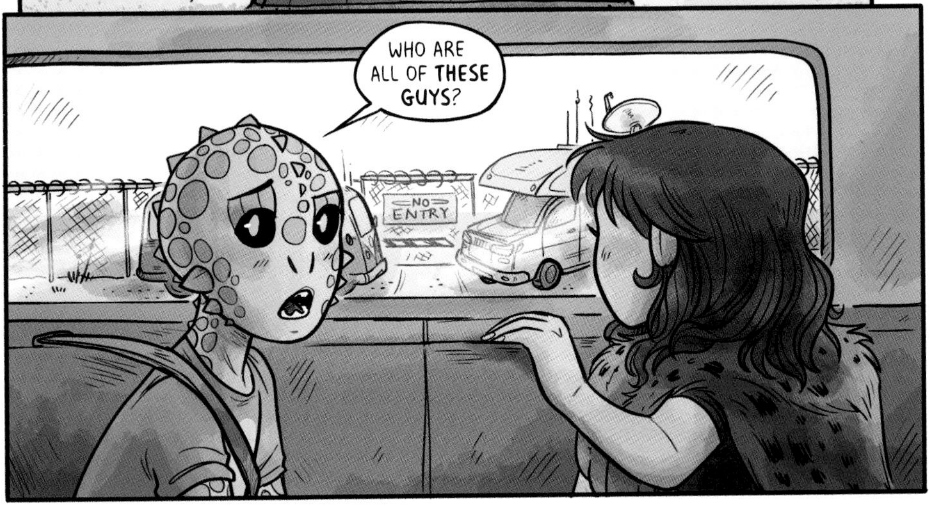
WHO ARE ALL OF THESE GUYS?
NO ENTRY

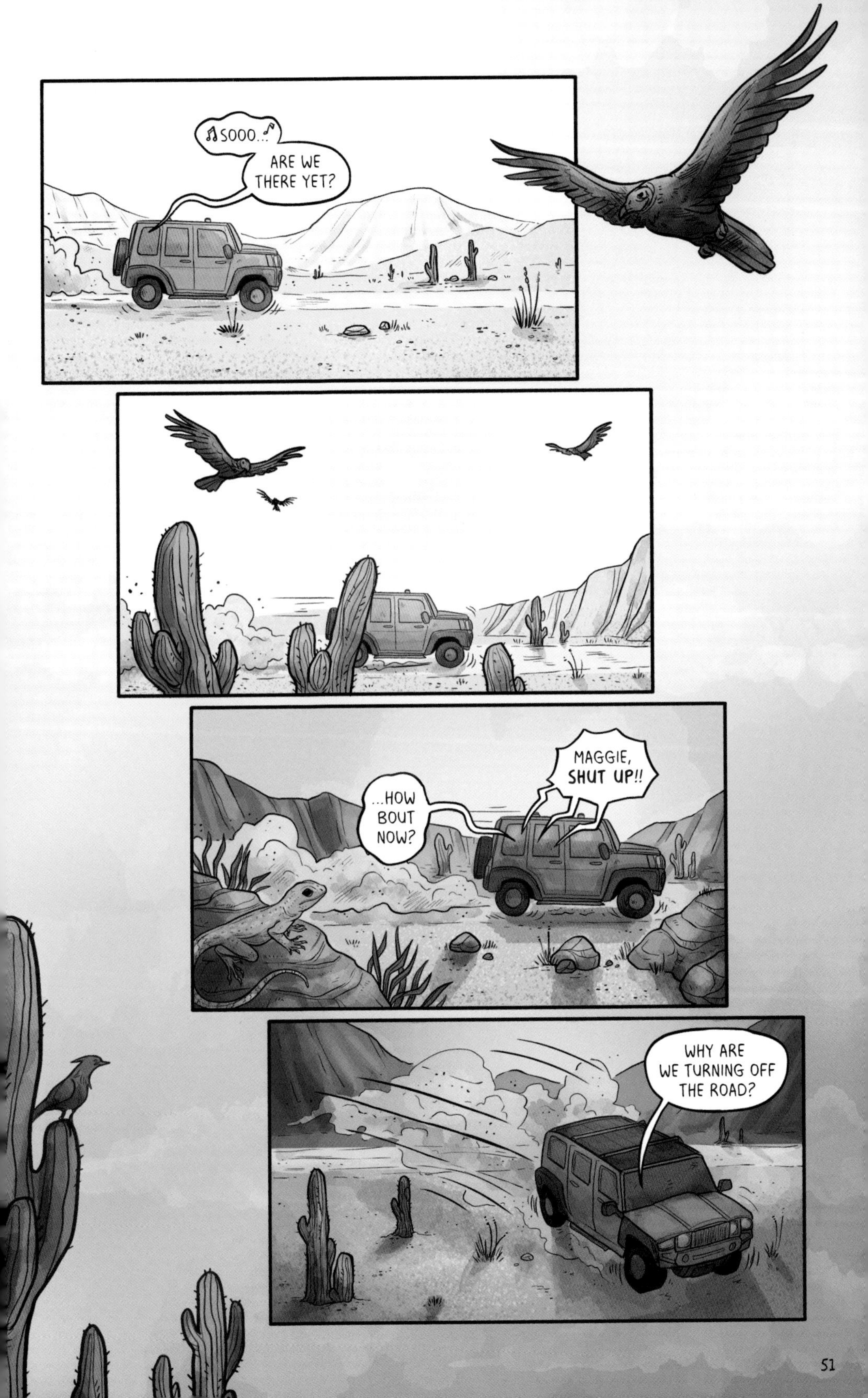
♫SOOO...♪
ARE WE THERE YET?
...HOW BOUT NOW?
MAGGIE, **SHUT UP!!**
WHY ARE WE TURNING OFF THE ROAD?

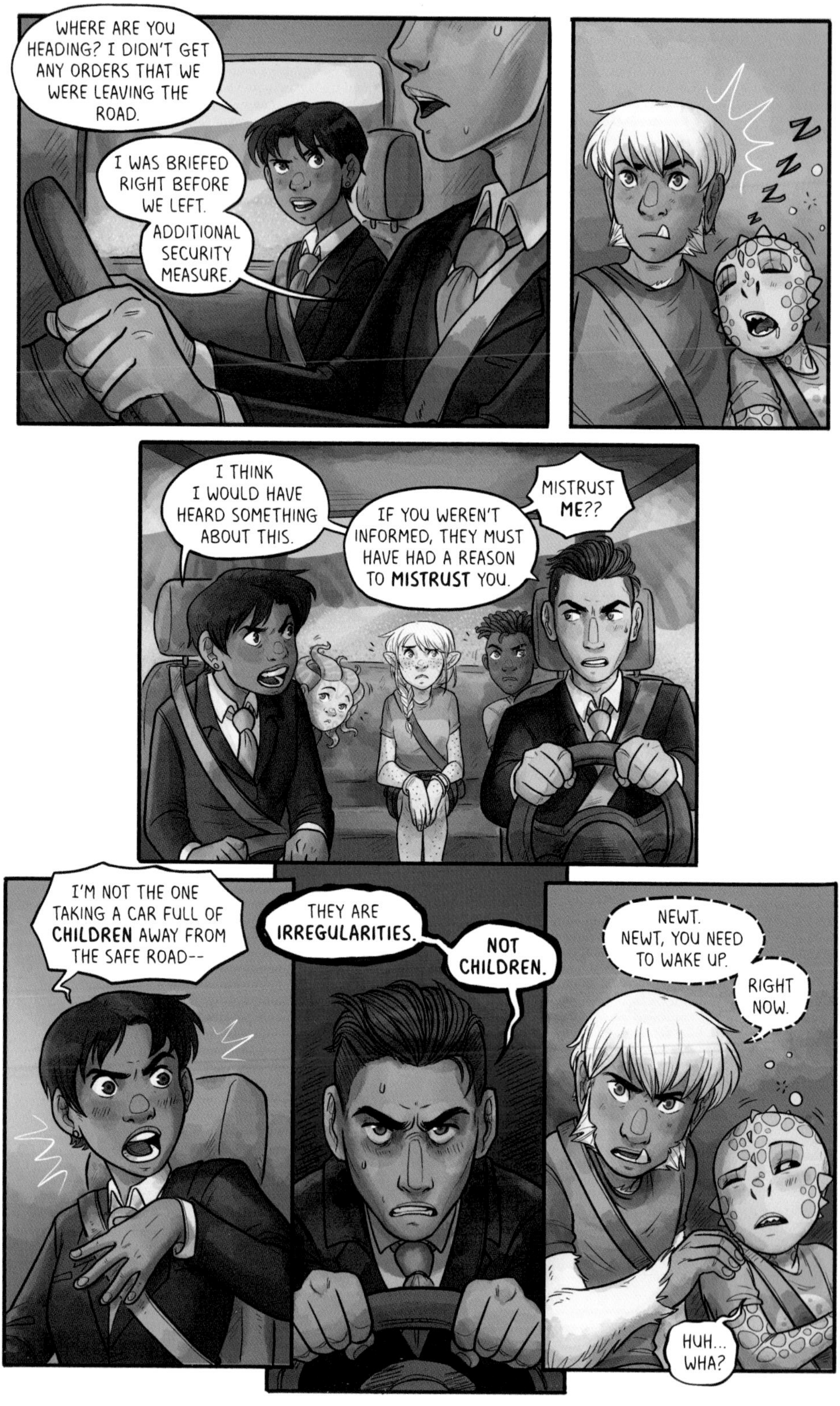
WHERE ARE YOU HEADING? I DIDN'T GET ANY ORDERS THAT WE WERE LEAVING THE ROAD.
I WAS BRIEFED RIGHT BEFORE WE LEFT.
ADDITIONAL SECURITY MEASURE.
I THINK I WOULD HAVE HEARD SOMETHING ABOUT THIS.
IF YOU WEREN'T INFORMED, THEY MUST HAVE HAD A REASON TO MISTRUST YOU.
MISTRUST ME??
I'M NOT THE ONE TAKING A CAR FULL OF CHILDREN AWAY FROM THE SAFE ROAD--
THEY ARE IRREGULARITIES.
NOT CHILDREN.
NEWT. NEWT, YOU NEED TO WAKE UP.
RIGHT NOW.
HUH... WHA?

53

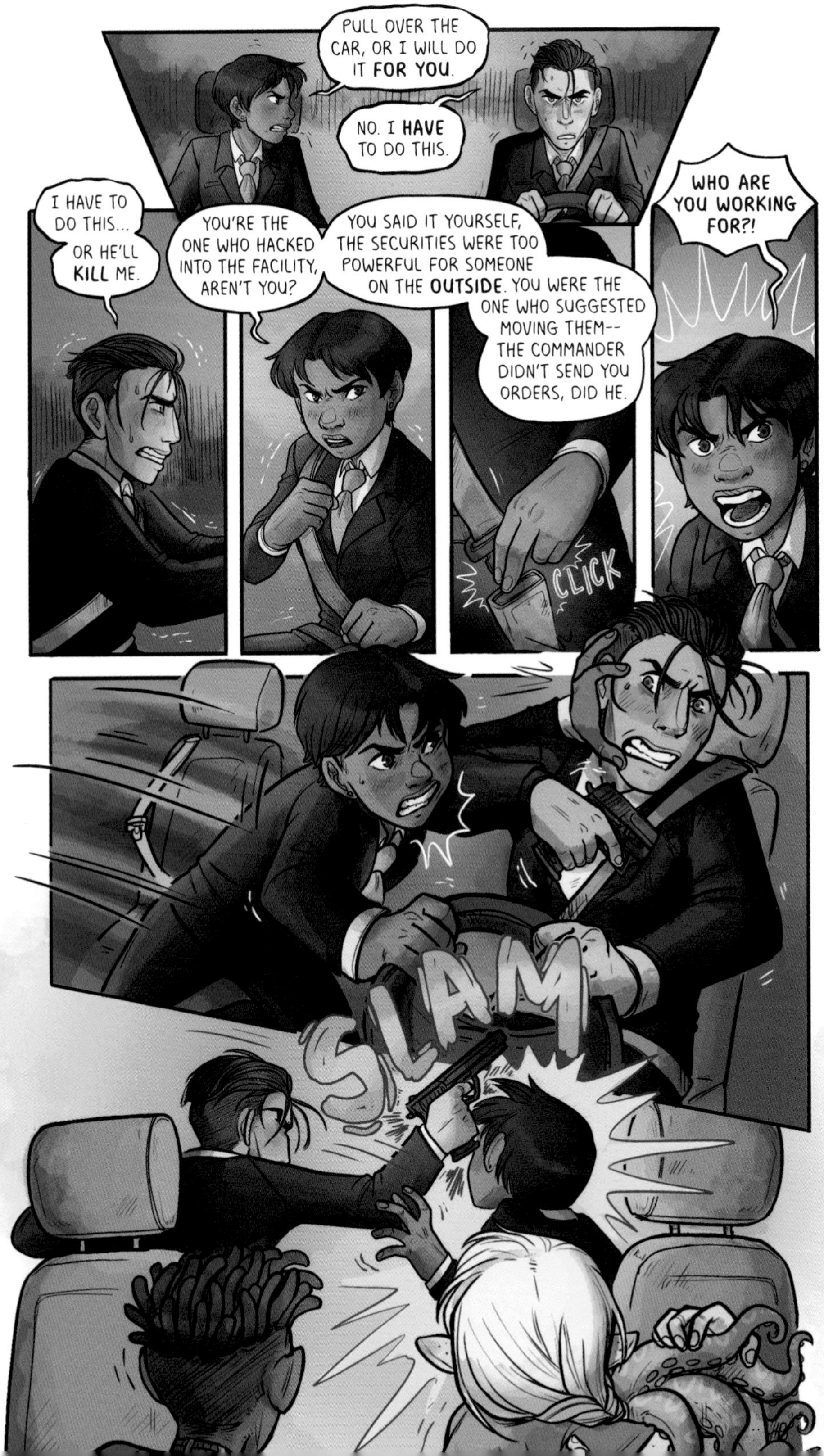
PULL OVER THE CAR, OR I WILL DO IT **FOR YOU**.
NO. I **HAVE** TO DO THIS.
I HAVE TO DO THIS...
OR HE'LL **KILL** ME.
YOU'RE THE ONE WHO HACKED INTO THE FACILITY, AREN'T YOU?
YOU SAID IT YOURSELF, THE SECURITIES WERE TOO POWERFUL FOR SOMEONE ON THE **OUTSIDE**. YOU WERE THE ONE WHO SUGGESTED MOVING THEM-- THE COMMANDER DIDN'T SEND YOU ORDERS, DID HE.
CLICK
WHO ARE YOU WORKING FOR?!
SLAM

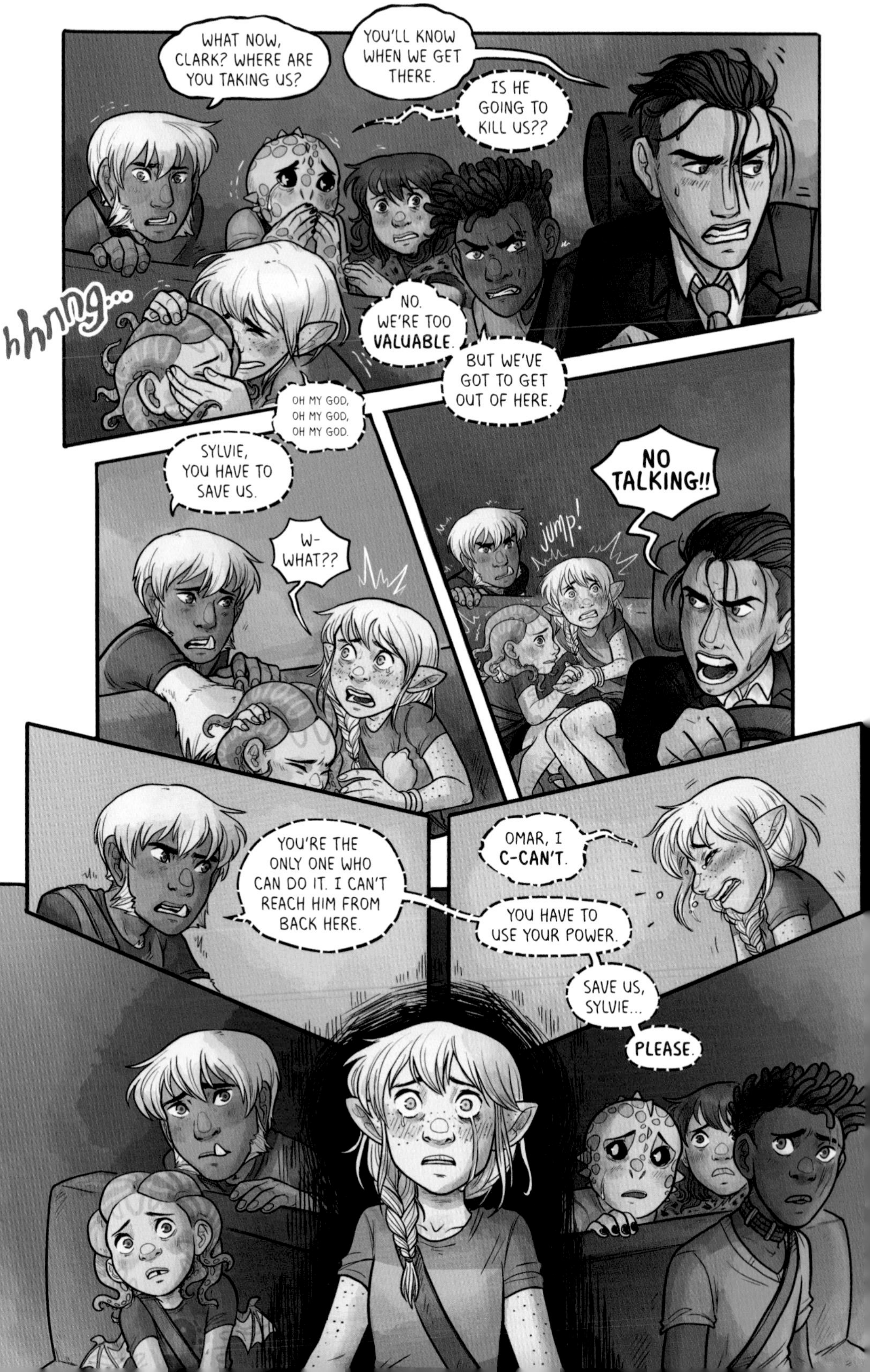
WHAT NOW, CLARK? WHERE ARE YOU TAKING US?
YOU'LL KNOW WHEN WE GET THERE.
IS HE GOING TO KILL US??
hhnng...
NO. WE'RE TOO **VALUABLE**.
BUT WE'VE GOT TO GET OUT OF HERE.
OH MY GOD, OH MY GOD, OH MY GOD.
SYLVIE, YOU HAVE TO SAVE US.
W- WHAT??
NO TALKING!!
jump!
YOU'RE THE ONLY ONE WHO CAN DO IT. I CAN'T REACH HIM FROM BACK HERE.
OMAR, I **C-CAN'T**.
YOU HAVE TO USE YOUR POWER.
SAVE US, SYLVIE...
PLEASE.

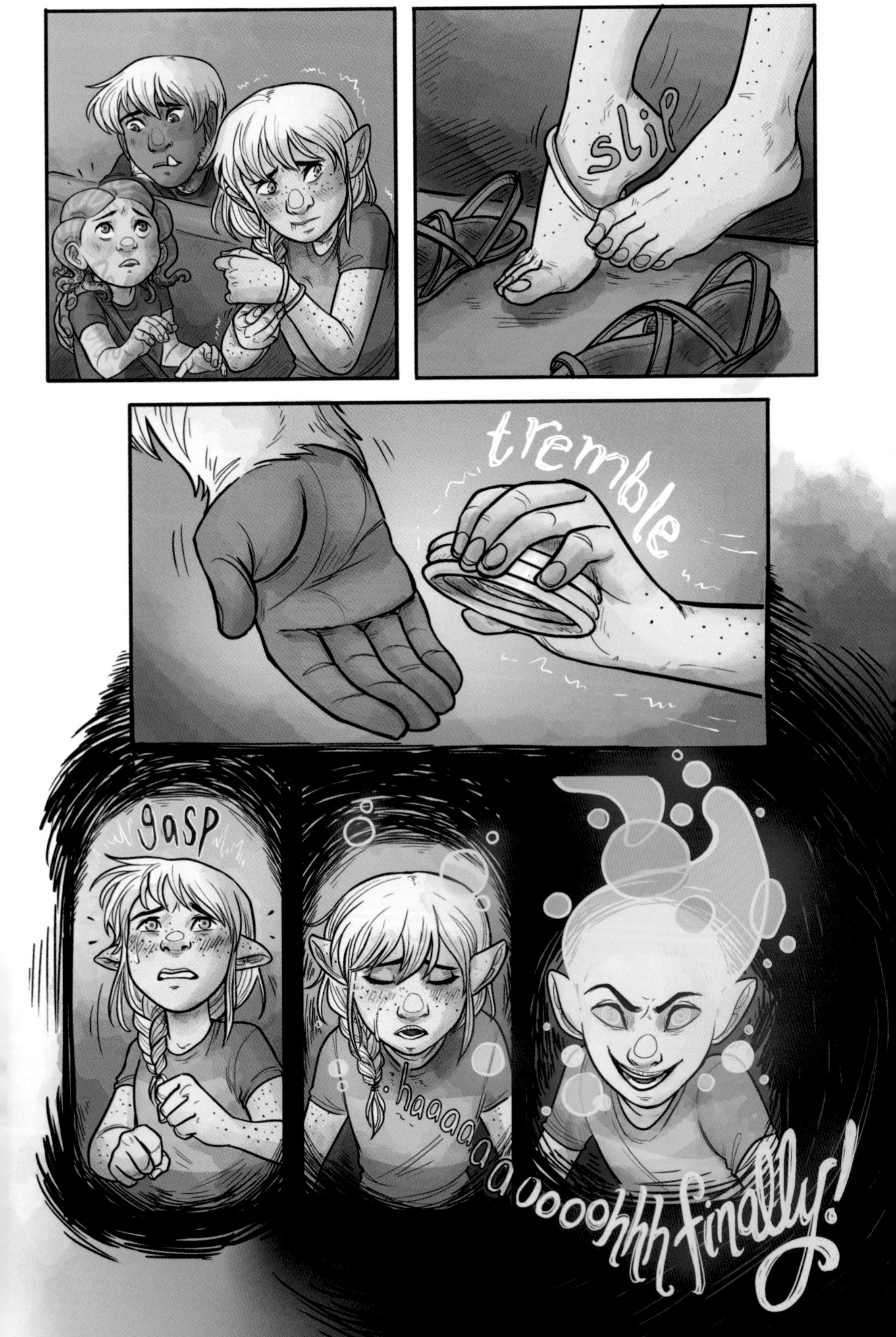
slip
tremble
gasp
haaaaaaaoooohhh finally!

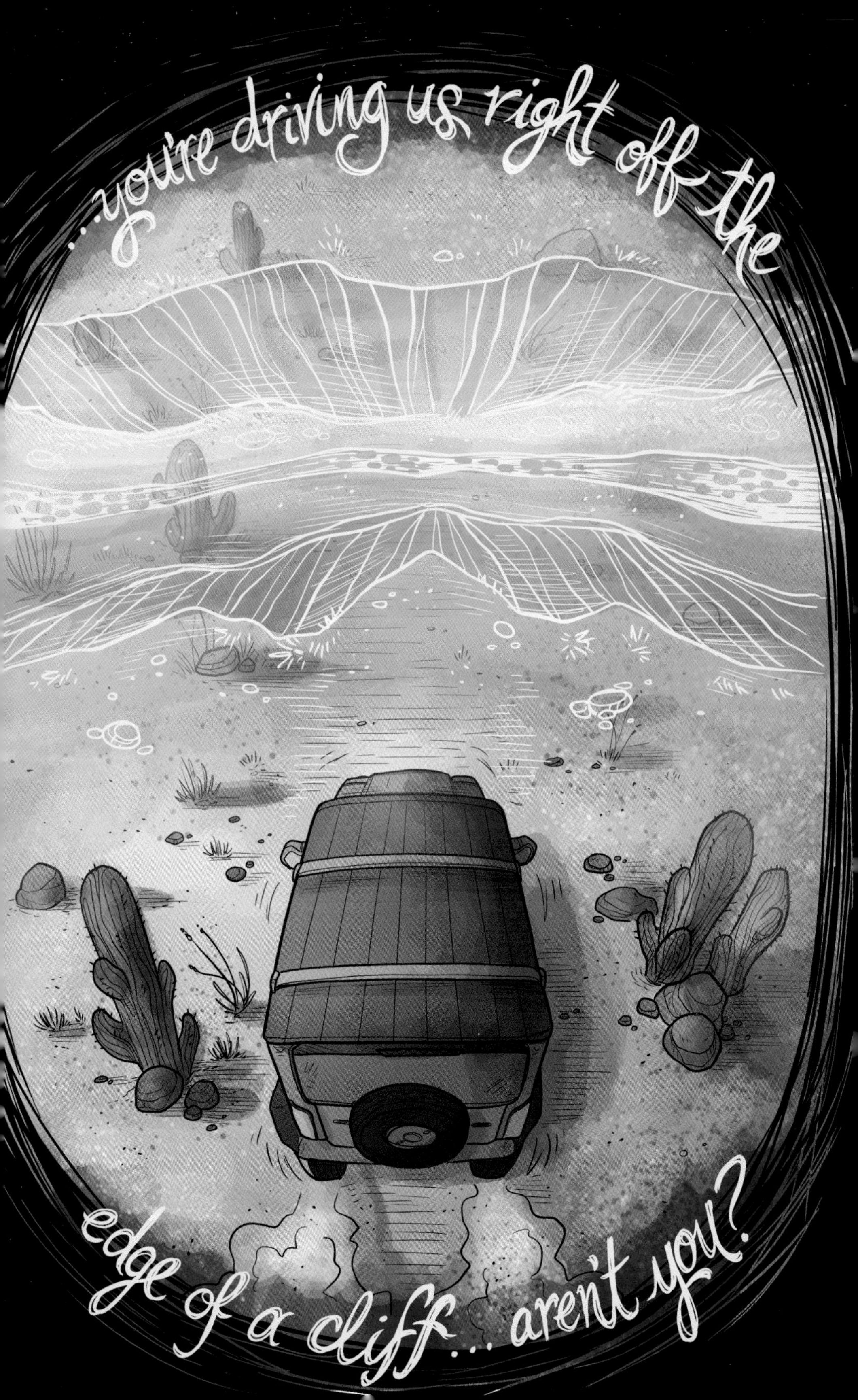
...you're driving us right off the
edge of a cliff... aren't you?

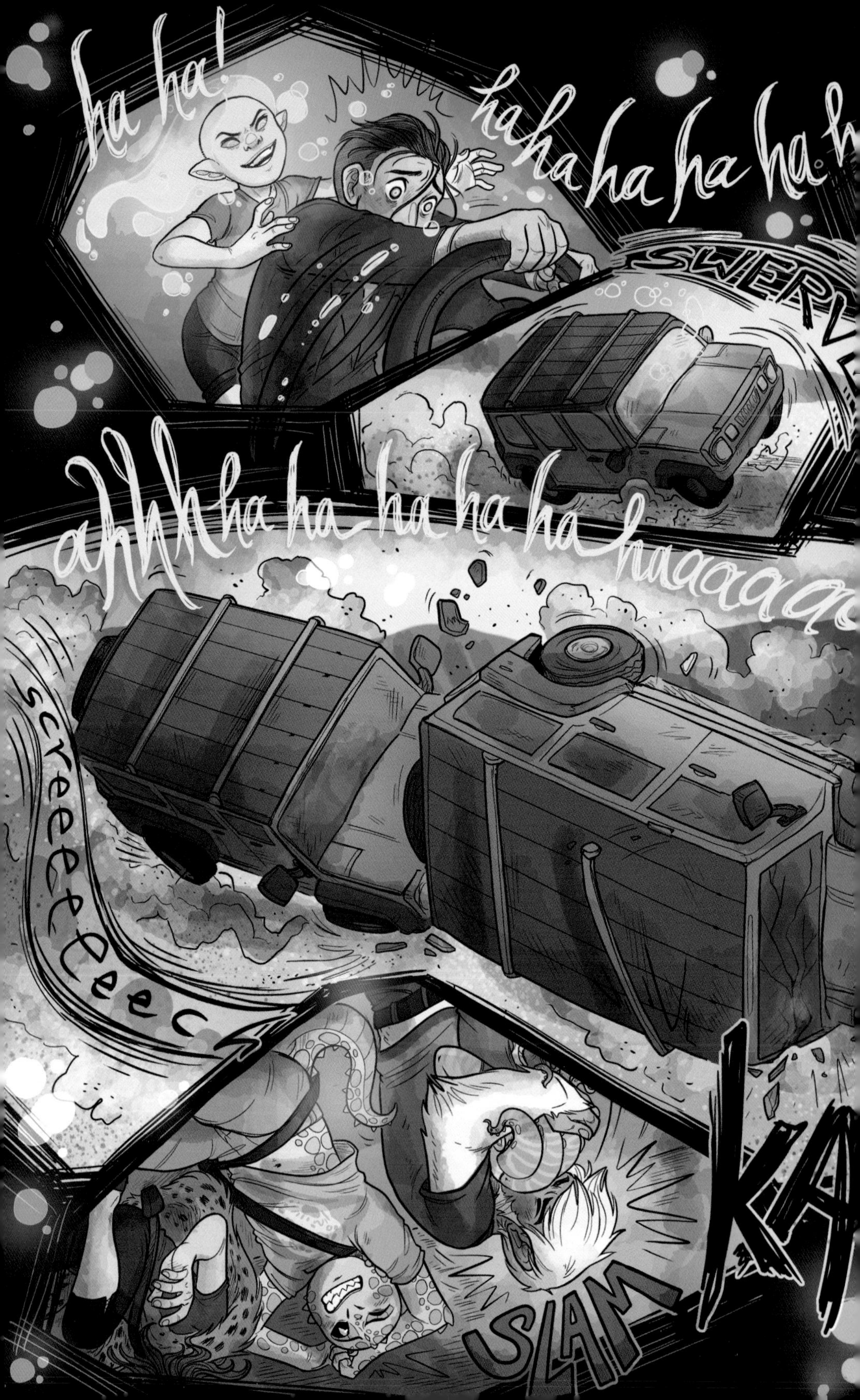
ha ha!
ha ha ha ha ha ha h
SWERVE
ahhh ha ha ha ha ha ha haaaaaa
screeeeeeech
SLAM
KA

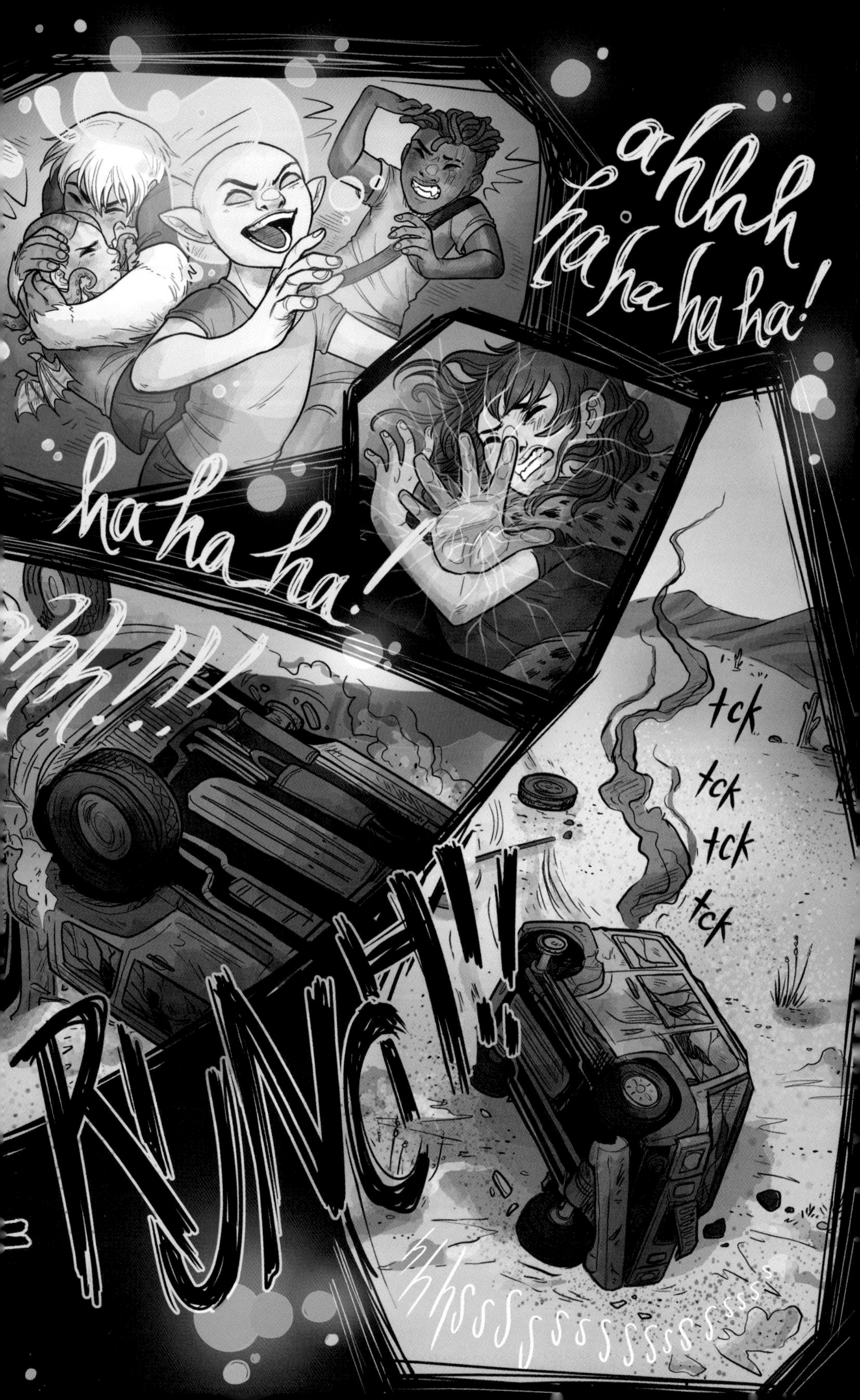

ahhh hahahaha!
hahaha!
tck
tck
tck
tck
RUNCH!!
shhssssssssssssss

CHAPTER THREE

WHITEOUT

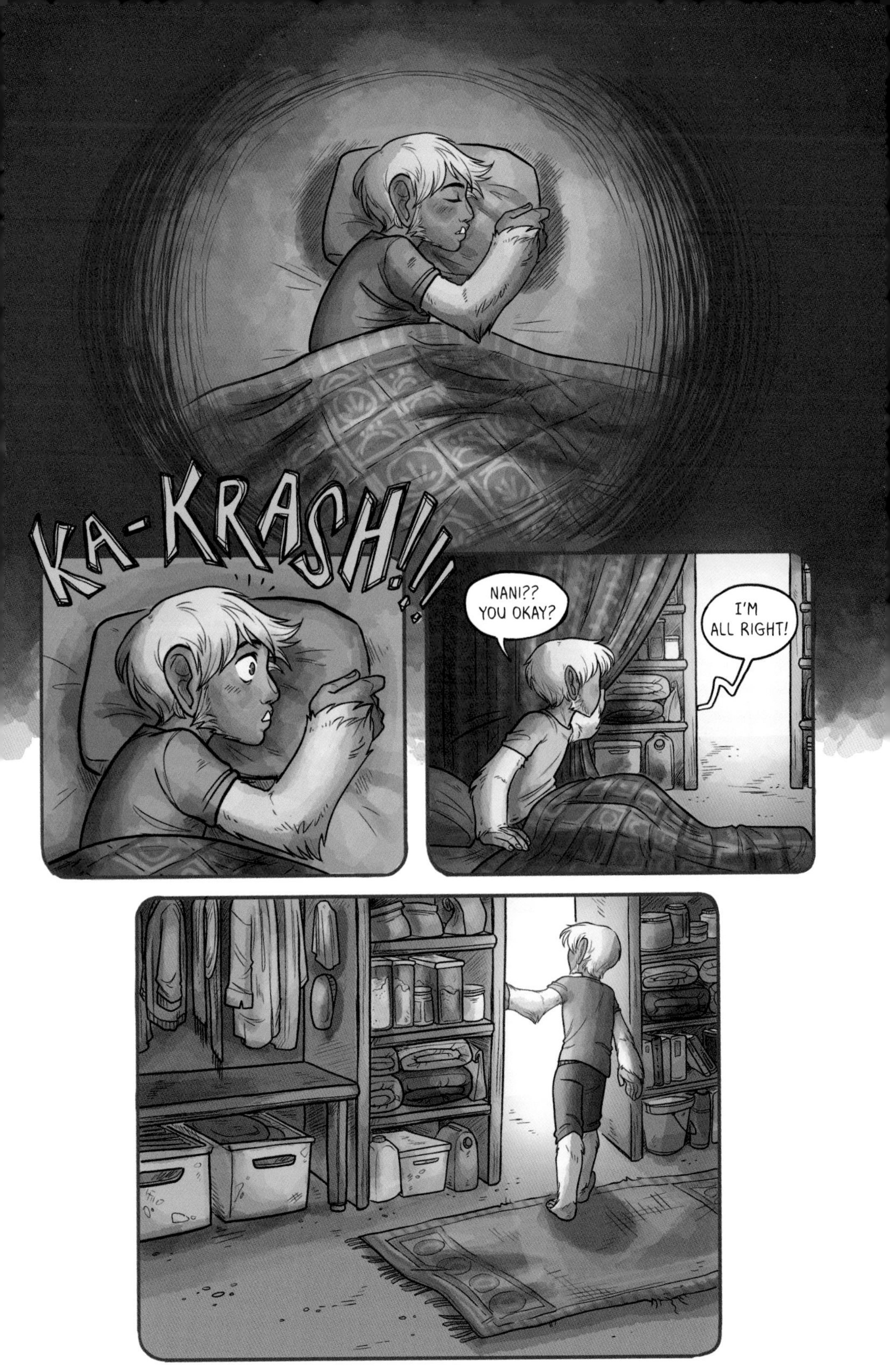
KA-KRASH!!!
NANI?? YOU OKAY?
I'M ALL RIGHT!

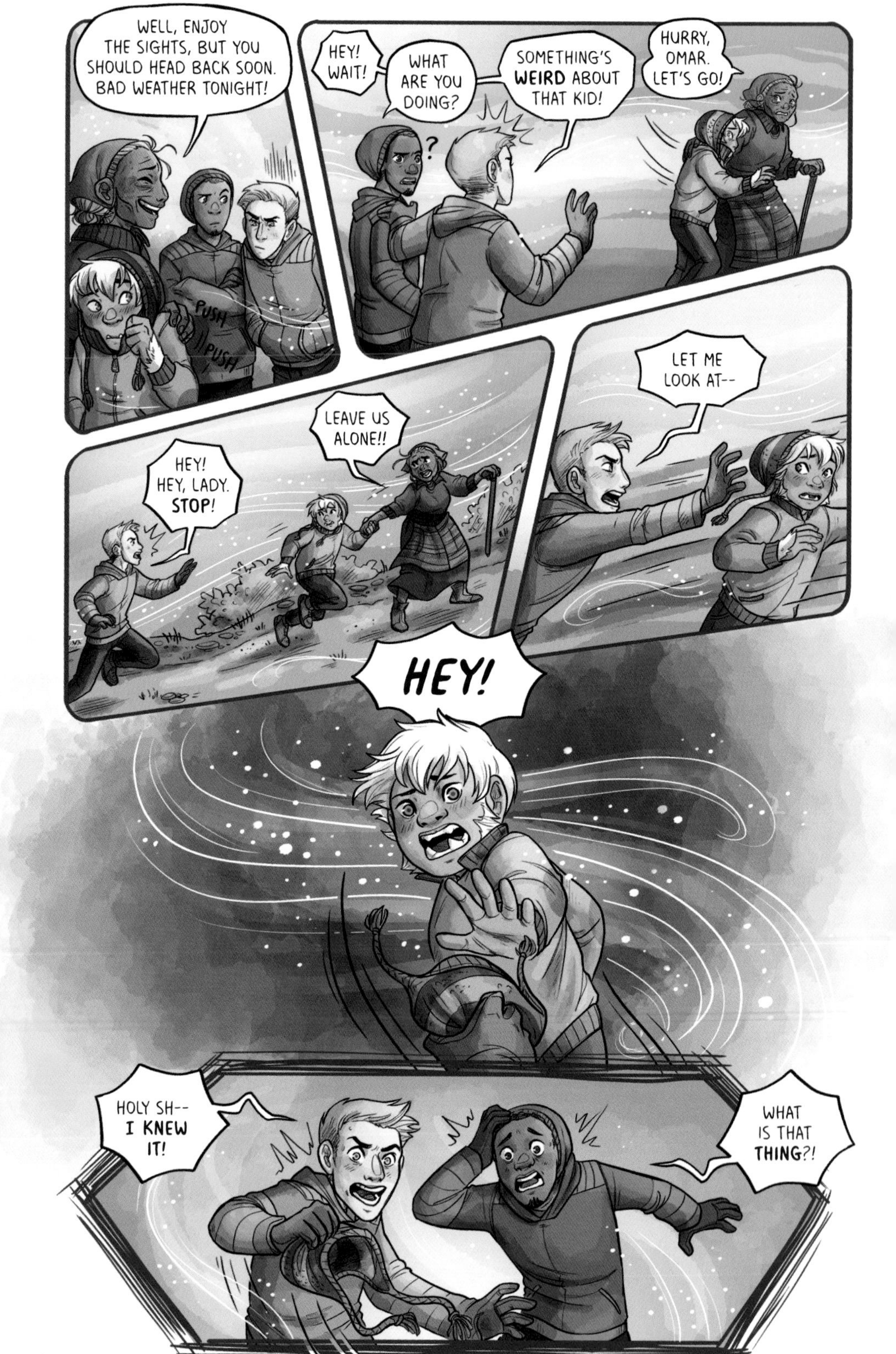
WELL, ENJOY THE SIGHTS, BUT YOU SHOULD HEAD BACK SOON. BAD WEATHER TONIGHT!
PUSH
PUSH
HEY! WAIT!
WHAT ARE YOU DOING?
?
SOMETHING'S **WEIRD** ABOUT THAT KID!
HURRY, OMAR. LET'S GO!
HEY! HEY, LADY. **STOP**!
LEAVE US ALONE!!
LET ME LOOK AT--
HEY!
HOLY SH-- **I KNEW IT!**
WHAT IS THAT **THING**?!

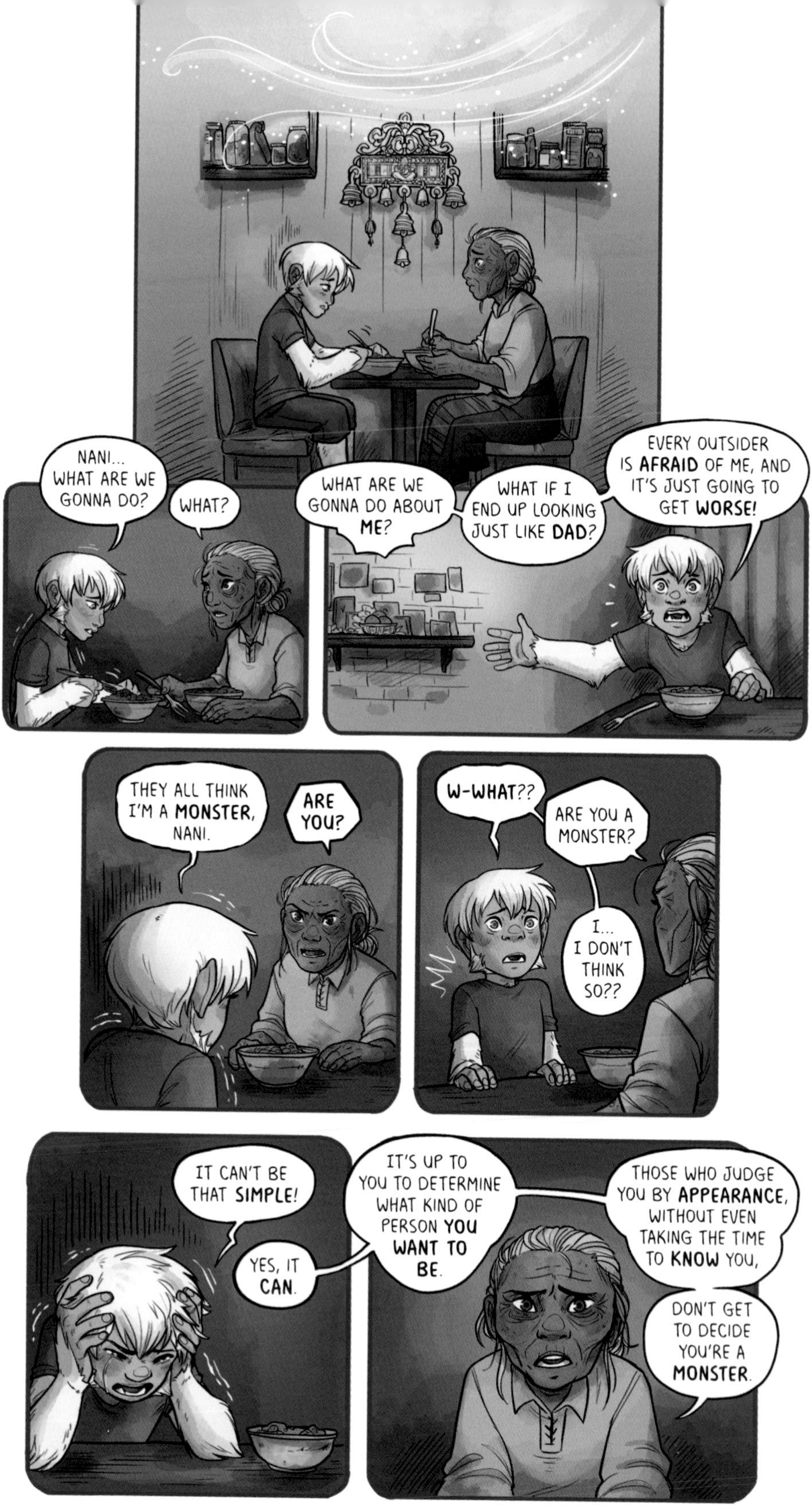
NANI... WHAT ARE WE GONNA DO?
WHAT?
WHAT ARE WE GONNA DO ABOUT **ME**?
WHAT IF I END UP LOOKING JUST LIKE **DAD**?
EVERY OUTSIDER IS **AFRAID** OF ME, AND IT'S JUST GOING TO GET **WORSE!**
THEY ALL THINK I'M A **MONSTER**, NANI.
ARE YOU?
W-WHAT??
ARE YOU A MONSTER?
I... I DON'T THINK SO??
IT CAN'T BE THAT **SIMPLE!**
YES, IT **CAN**.
IT'S UP TO YOU TO DETERMINE WHAT KIND OF PERSON **YOU WANT TO BE**.
THOSE WHO JUDGE YOU BY **APPEARANCE**, WITHOUT EVEN TAKING THE TIME TO **KNOW** YOU,
DON'T GET TO DECIDE YOU'RE A **MONSTER**.

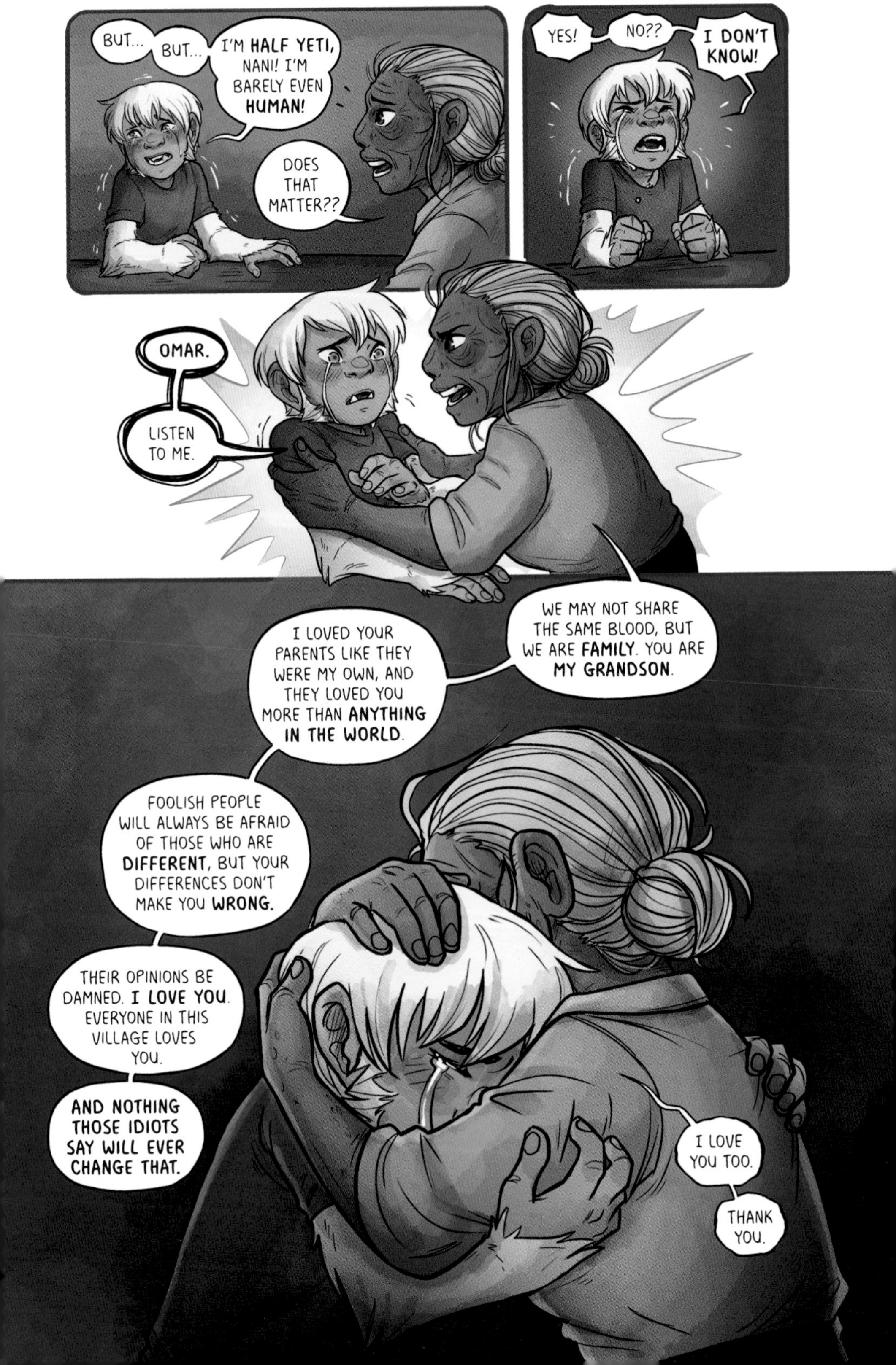
BUT...
BUT...
I'M HALF YETI, NANI! I'M BARELY EVEN HUMAN!
DOES THAT MATTER??
YES!
NO??
I DON'T KNOW!
OMAR.
LISTEN TO ME.
WE MAY NOT SHARE THE SAME BLOOD, BUT WE ARE FAMILY. YOU ARE MY GRANDSON.
I LOVED YOUR PARENTS LIKE THEY WERE MY OWN, AND THEY LOVED YOU MORE THAN ANYTHING IN THE WORLD.
FOOLISH PEOPLE WILL ALWAYS BE AFRAID OF THOSE WHO ARE DIFFERENT, BUT YOUR DIFFERENCES DON'T MAKE YOU WRONG.
THEIR OPINIONS BE DAMNED. I LOVE YOU. EVERYONE IN THIS VILLAGE LOVES YOU.
AND NOTHING THOSE IDIOTS SAY WILL EVER CHANGE THAT.
I LOVE YOU TOO.
THANK YOU.

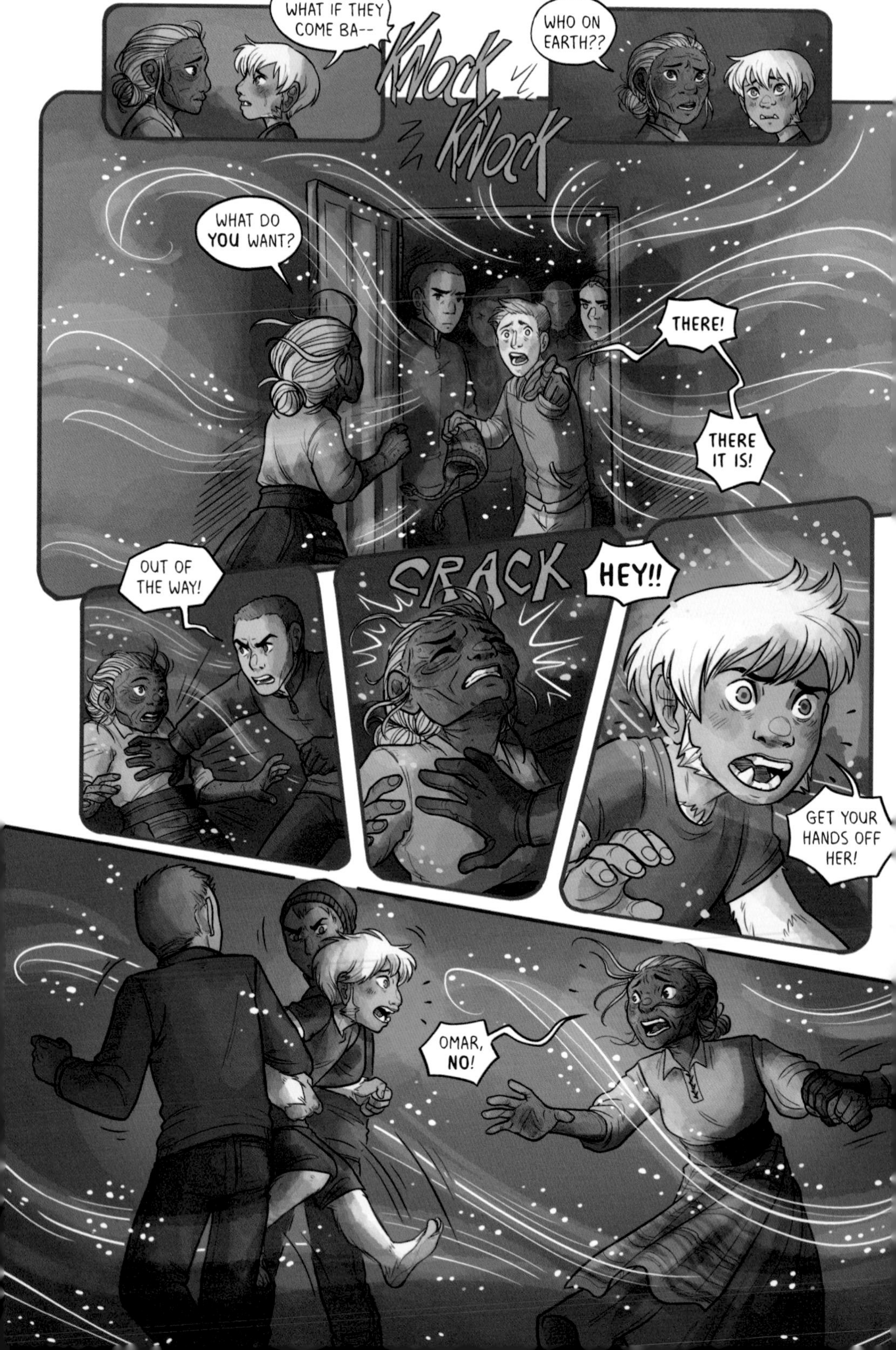
BUT... NANI, WHAT IF THEY COME BA--
KNOCK KNOCK
WHO ON EARTH??
WHAT DO YOU WANT?
THERE!
THERE IT IS!
OUT OF THE WAY!
CRACK
HEY!!
GET YOUR HANDS OFF HER!
OMAR, NO!

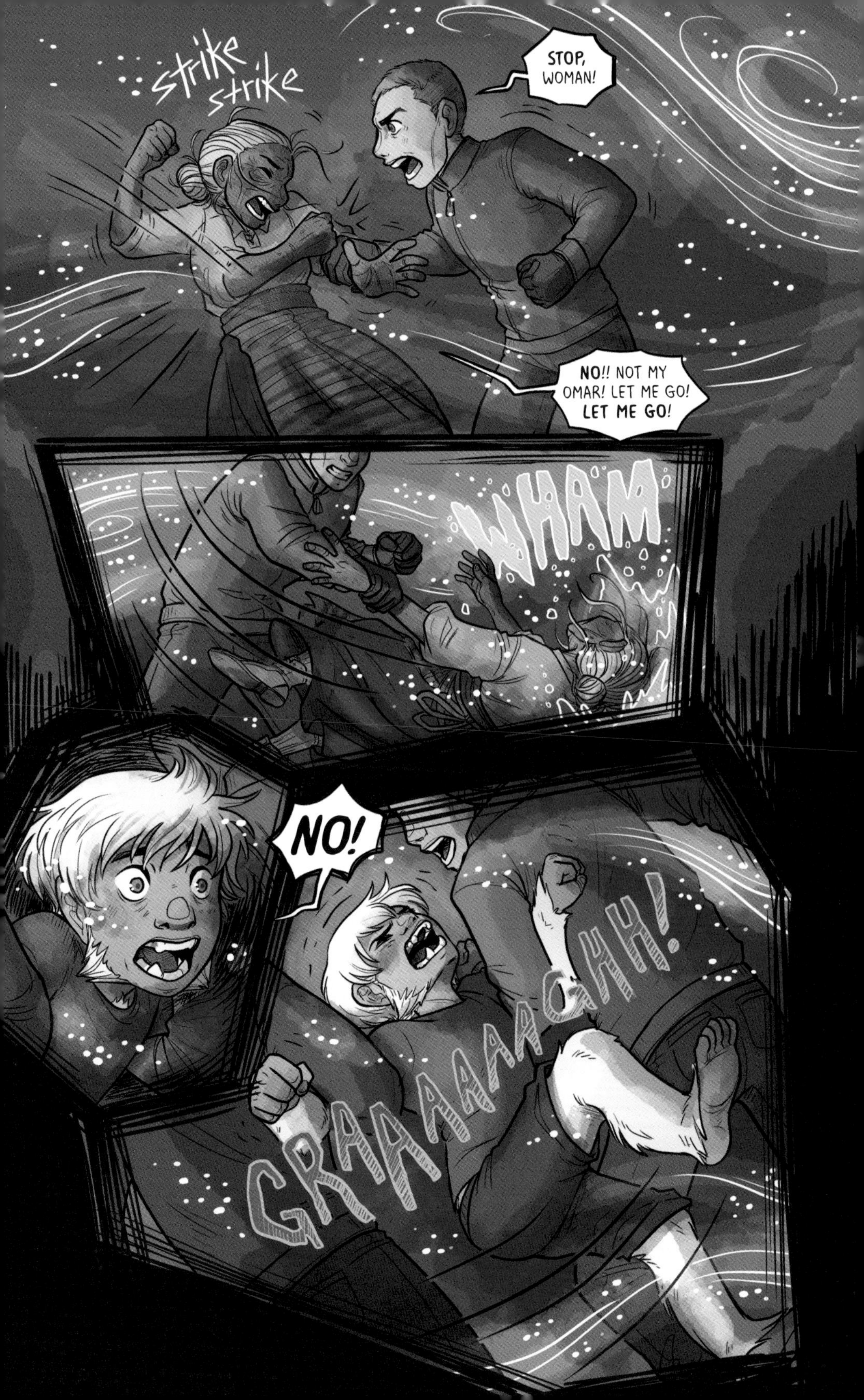
strike
strike
STOP, WOMAN!
NO!! NOT MY OMAR! LET ME GO! LET ME GO!
WHAM
NO!
GRAAAAAAGHH!

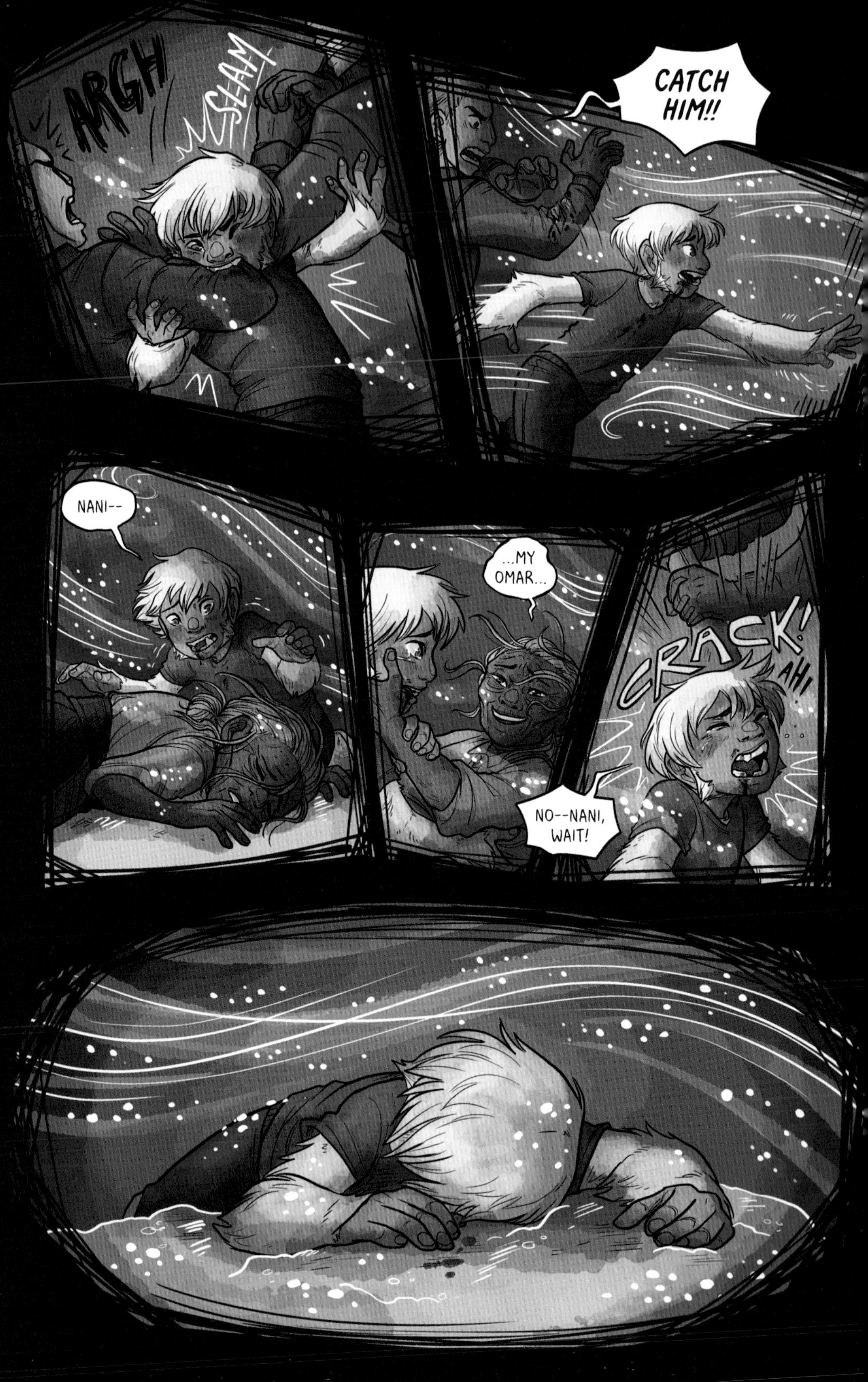
ARGH
SLAM
CATCH HIM!!
NANI--
...MY OMAR...
CRACK!
AH!
NO--NANI, WAIT!

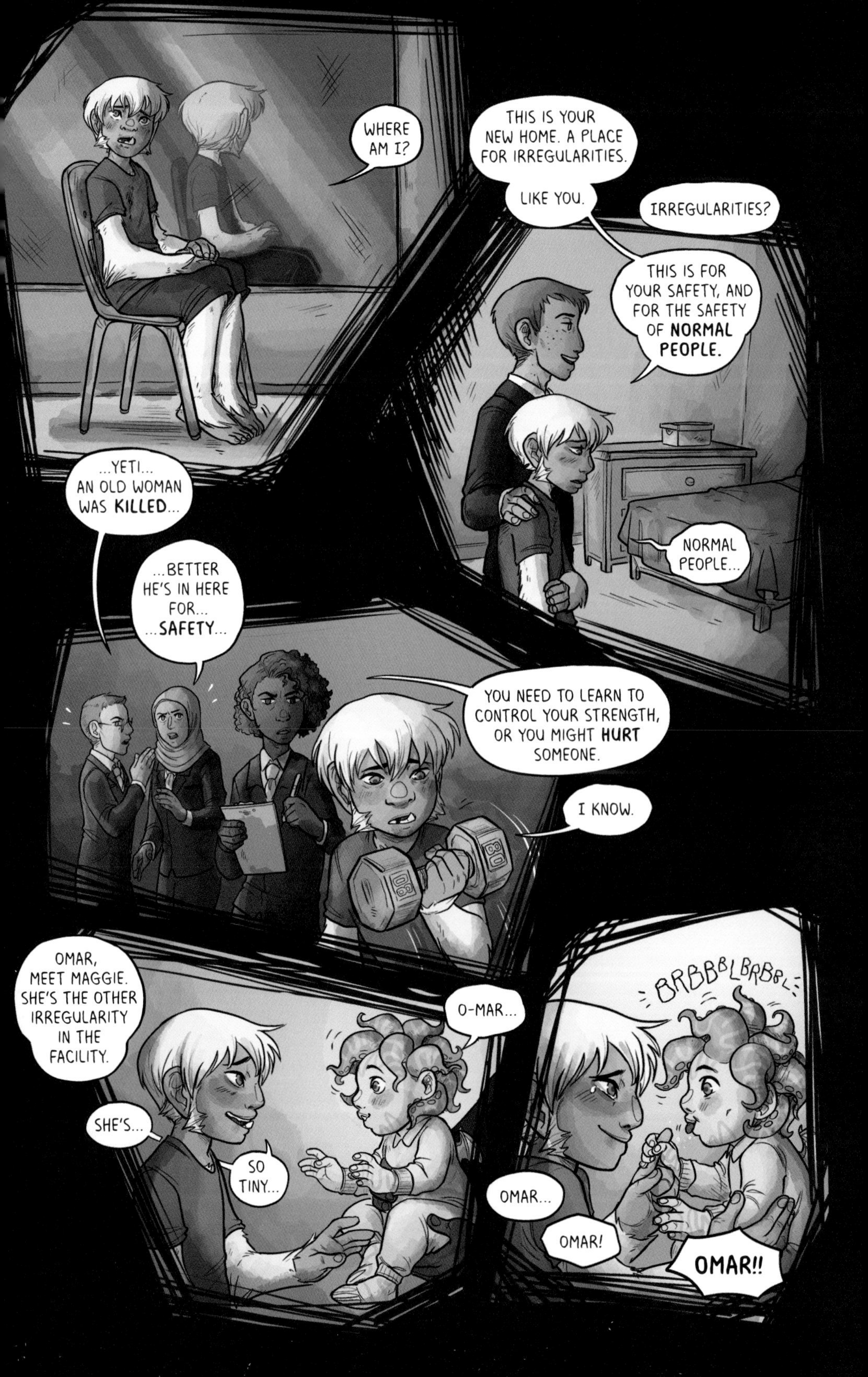
WHERE AM I?
THIS IS YOUR NEW HOME. A PLACE FOR IRREGULARITIES.
LIKE YOU.
IRREGULARITIES?
THIS IS FOR YOUR SAFETY, AND FOR THE SAFETY OF NORMAL PEOPLE.
NORMAL PEOPLE...
...YETI... AN OLD WOMAN WAS KILLED...
...BETTER HE'S IN HERE FOR... ...SAFETY...
YOU NEED TO LEARN TO CONTROL YOUR STRENGTH, OR YOU MIGHT HURT SOMEONE.
I KNOW.
80
80
OMAR, MEET MAGGIE. SHE'S THE OTHER IRREGULARITY IN THE FACILITY.
O-MAR...
SHE'S...
SO TINY...
BRBBBLBRBBL
OMAR...
OMAR!
OMAR!!

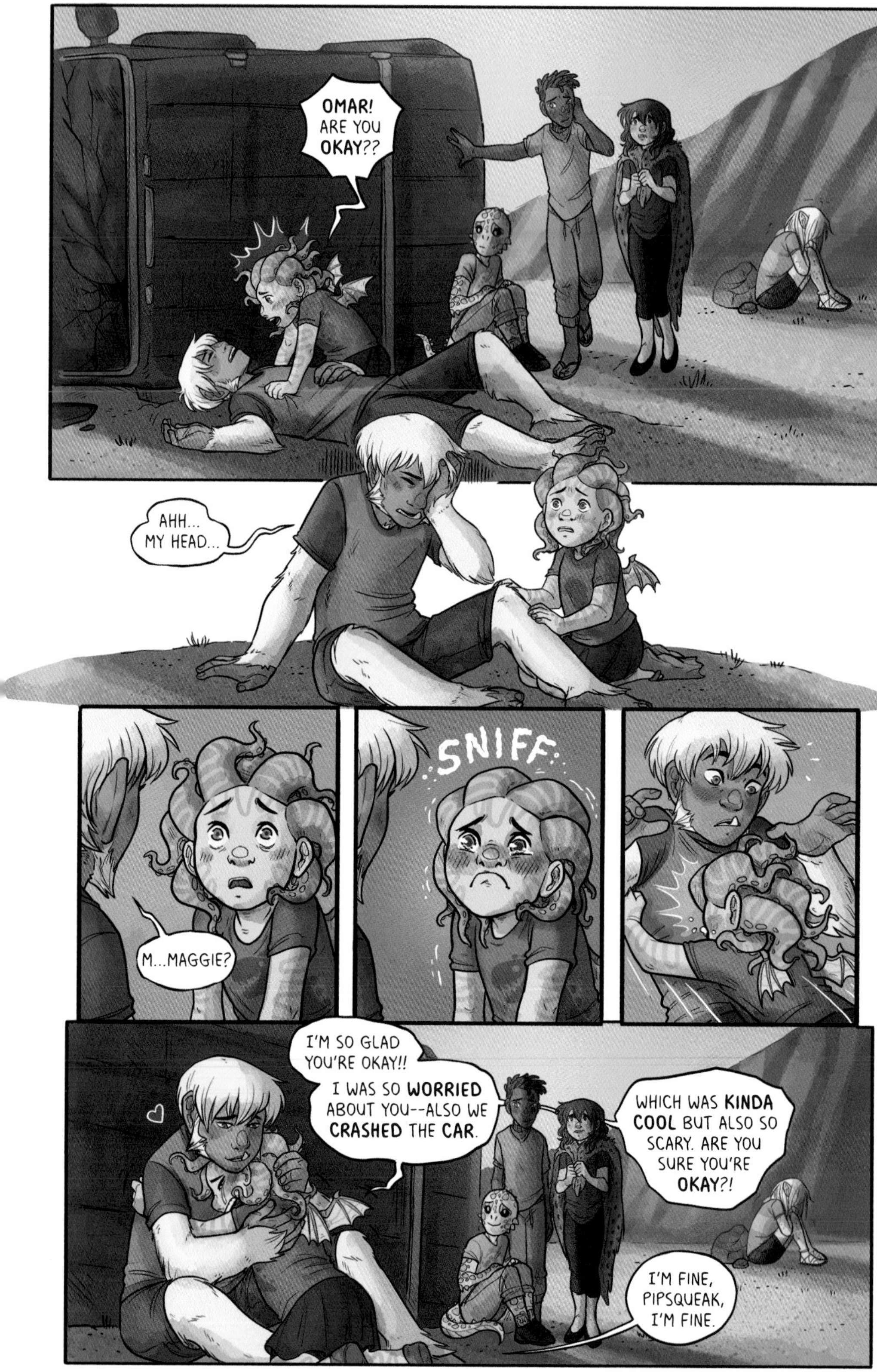
OMAR! ARE YOU OKAY??
AHH... MY HEAD...
M...MAGGIE?
SNIFF
I'M SO GLAD YOU'RE OKAY!!
I WAS SO WORRIED ABOUT YOU--ALSO WE CRASHED THE CAR.
WHICH WAS KINDA COOL BUT ALSO SO SCARY. ARE YOU SURE YOU'RE OKAY?!
I'M FINE, PIPSQUEAK, I'M FINE.

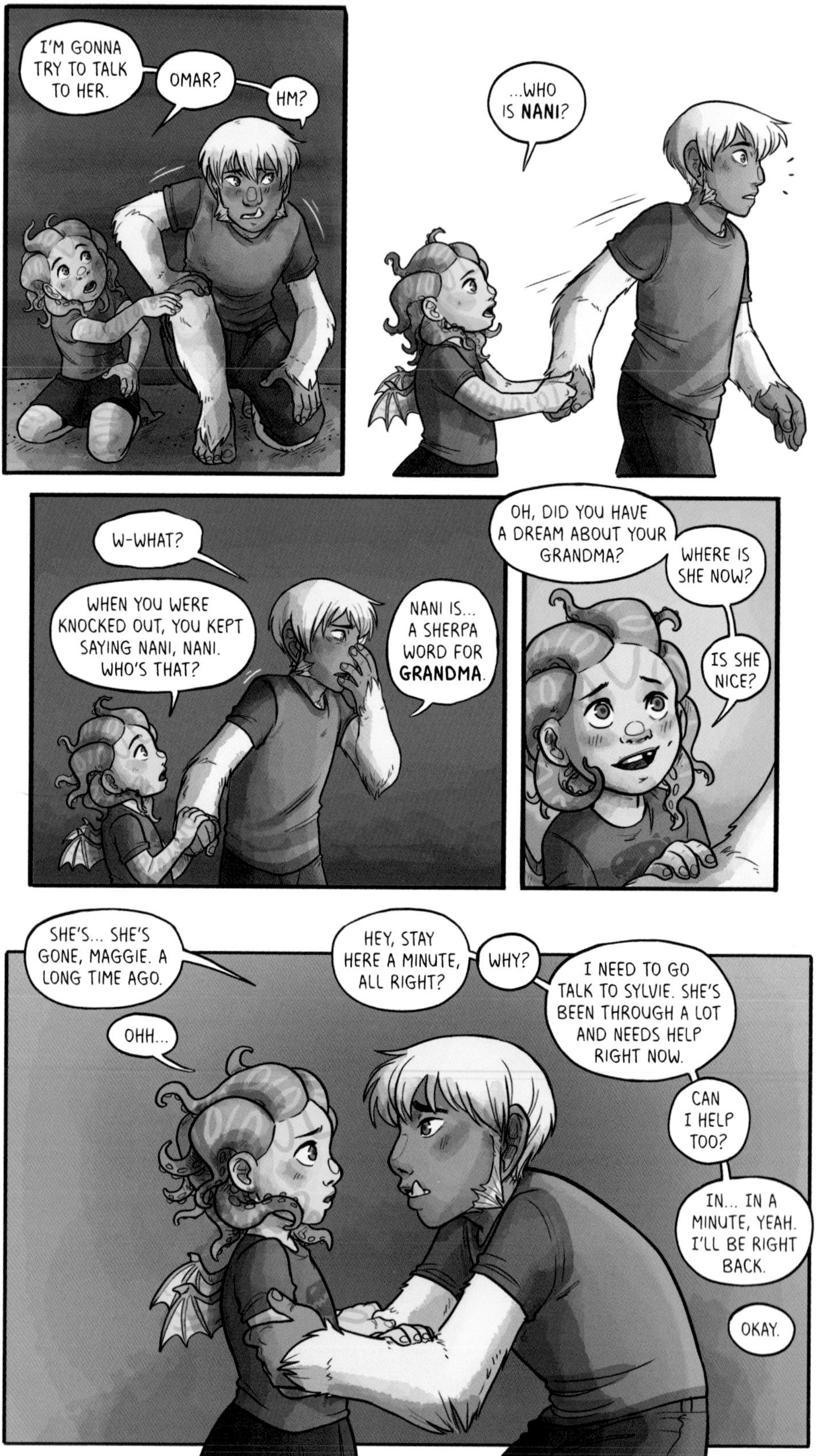
I'M GONNA TRY TO TALK TO HER.
OMAR?
HM?
...WHO IS **NANI**?
W-WHAT?
WHEN YOU WERE KNOCKED OUT, YOU KEPT SAYING NANI, NANI. WHO'S THAT?
NANI IS... A SHERPA WORD FOR **GRANDMA**.
OH, DID YOU HAVE A DREAM ABOUT YOUR GRANDMA?
WHERE IS SHE NOW?
IS SHE NICE?
SHE'S... SHE'S GONE, MAGGIE. A LONG TIME AGO.
OHH...
HEY, STAY HERE A MINUTE, ALL RIGHT?
WHY?
I NEED TO GO TALK TO SYLVIE. SHE'S BEEN THROUGH A LOT AND NEEDS HELP RIGHT NOW.
CAN I HELP TOO?
IN... IN A MINUTE, YEAH. I'LL BE RIGHT BACK.
OKAY.

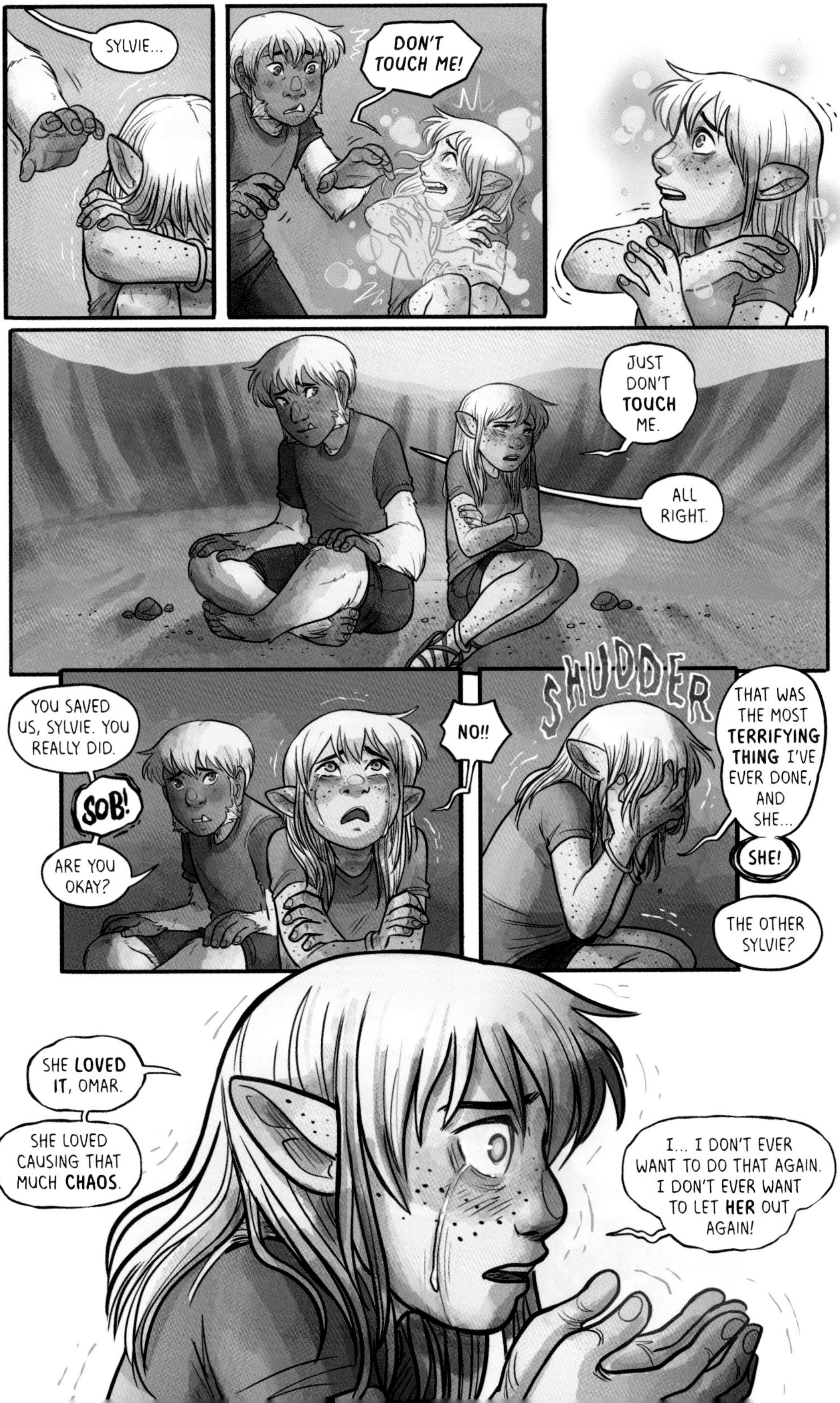
SYLVIE...
DON'T TOUCH ME!
JUST DON'T TOUCH ME.
ALL RIGHT.
YOU SAVED US, SYLVIE. YOU REALLY DID.
SOB!
ARE YOU OKAY?
NO!!
SHUDDER
THAT WAS THE MOST TERRIFYING THING I'VE EVER DONE, AND SHE...
SHE!
THE OTHER SYLVIE?
SHE LOVED IT, OMAR.
SHE LOVED CAUSING THAT MUCH CHAOS.
I... I DON'T EVER WANT TO DO THAT AGAIN. I DON'T EVER WANT TO LET HER OUT AGAIN!

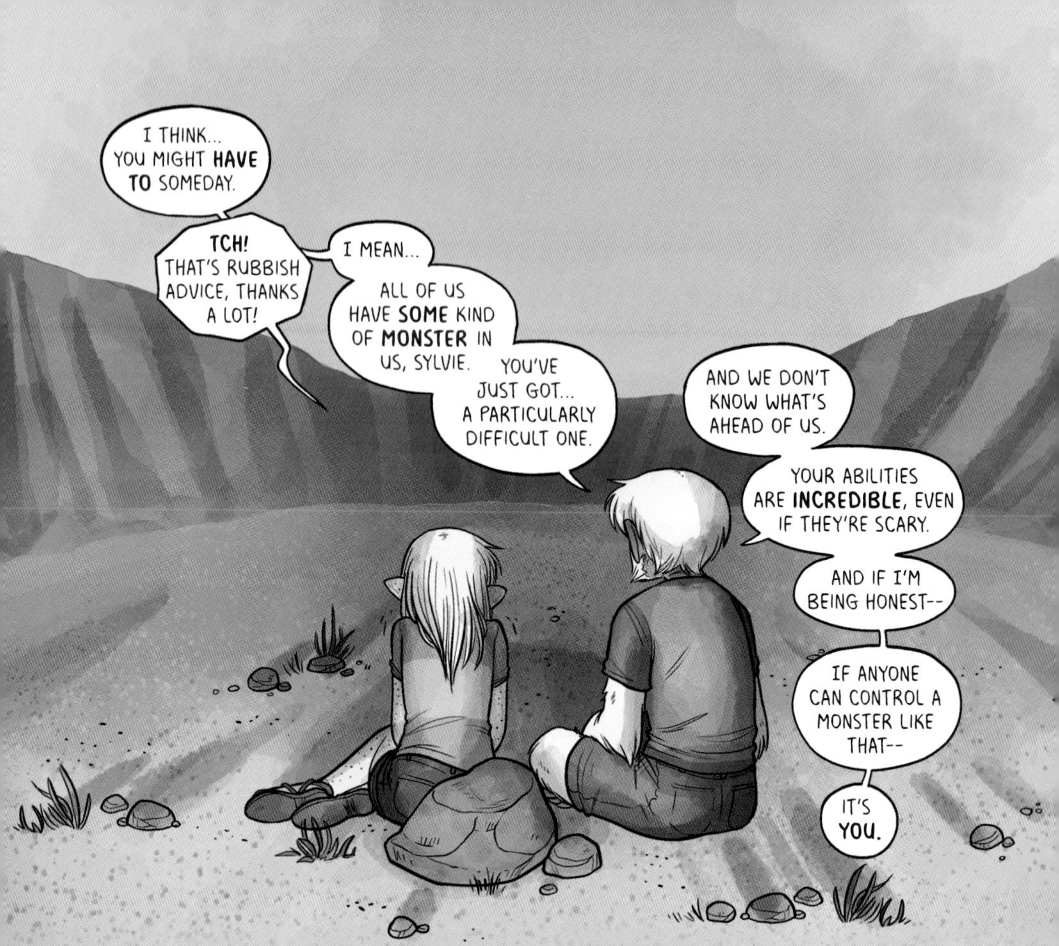
I THINK... YOU MIGHT **HAVE TO** SOMEDAY.
TCH! THAT'S RUBBISH ADVICE, THANKS A LOT!
I MEAN...
ALL OF US HAVE **SOME** KIND OF **MONSTER** IN US, SYLVIE.
YOU'VE JUST GOT... A PARTICULARLY DIFFICULT ONE.
AND WE DON'T KNOW WHAT'S AHEAD OF US.
YOUR ABILITIES ARE **INCREDIBLE**, EVEN IF THEY'RE SCARY.
AND IF I'M BEING HONEST--
IF ANYONE CAN CONTROL A MONSTER LIKE THAT--
IT'S **YOU.**

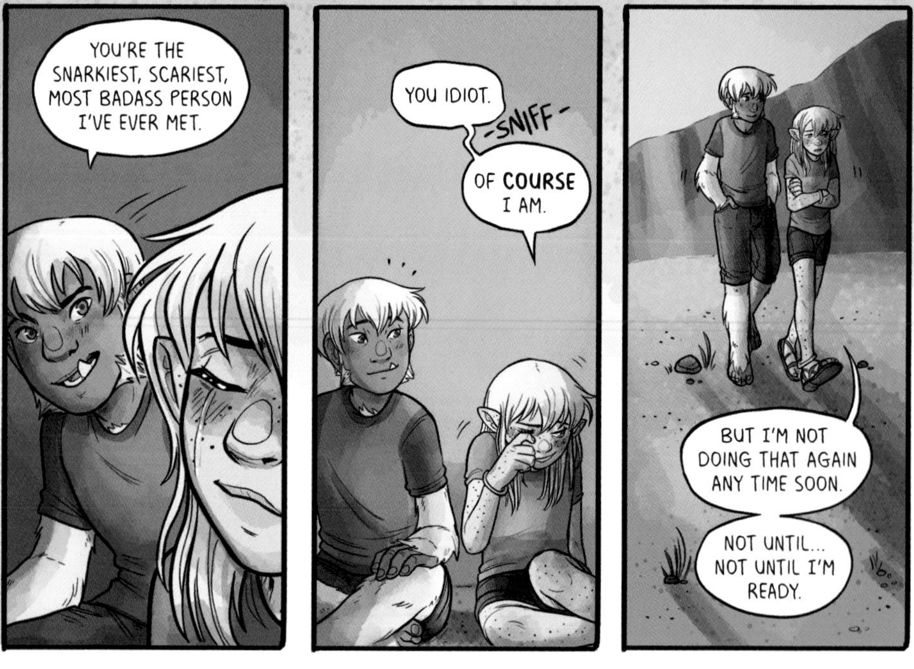
YOU'RE THE SNARKIEST, SCARIEST, MOST BADASS PERSON I'VE EVER MET.
YOU IDIOT.
-SNIFF-
OF **COURSE** I AM.
BUT I'M NOT DOING THAT AGAIN ANY TIME SOON.
NOT UNTIL... NOT UNTIL I'M READY.

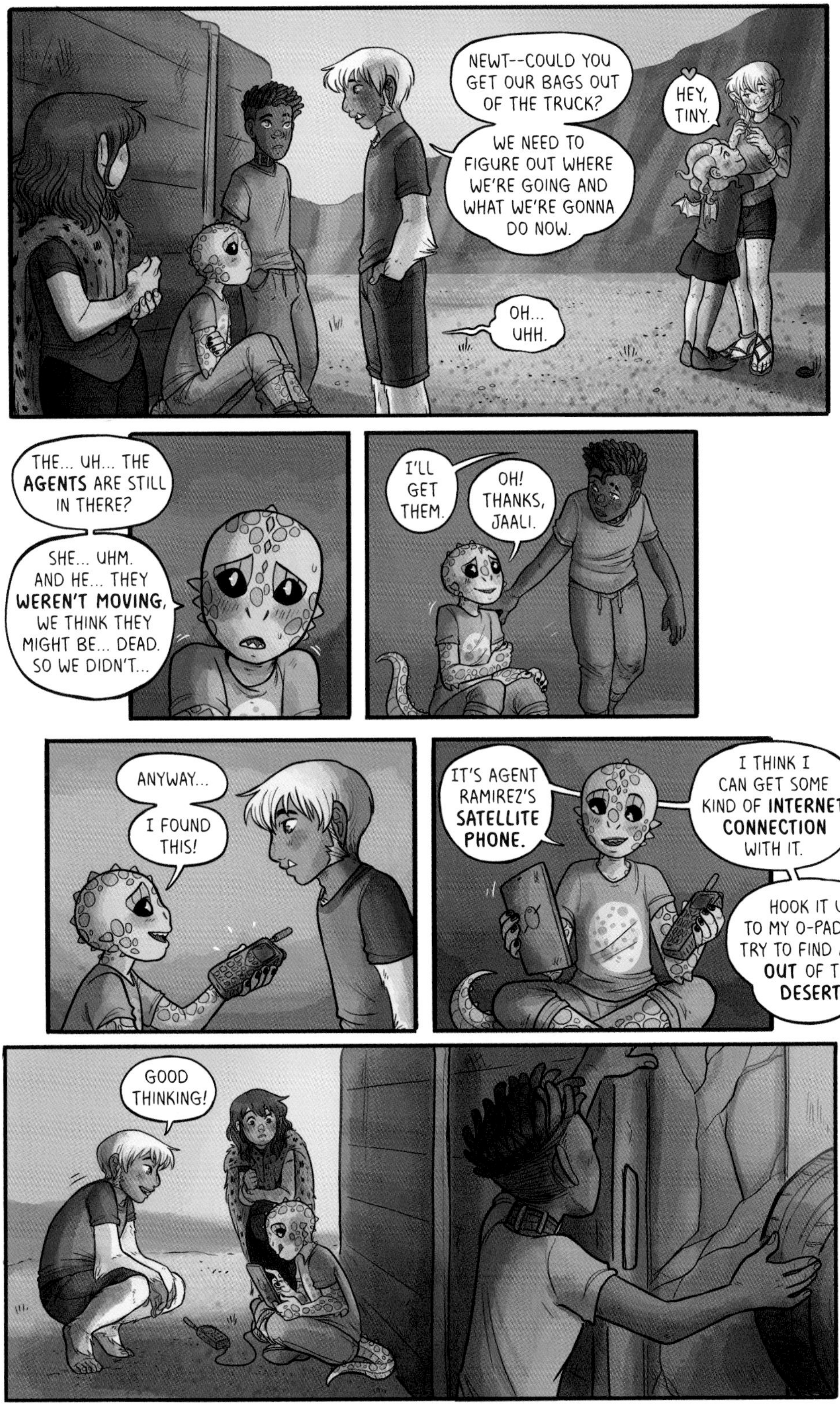
NEWT--COULD YOU GET OUR BAGS OUT OF THE TRUCK?
WE NEED TO FIGURE OUT WHERE WE'RE GOING AND WHAT WE'RE GONNA DO NOW.
HEY, TINY.
OH... UHH.
THE... UH... THE **AGENTS** ARE STILL IN THERE?
SHE... UHM. AND HE... THEY **WEREN'T MOVING**, WE THINK THEY MIGHT BE... DEAD. SO WE DIDN'T...
I'LL GET THEM.
OH! THANKS, JAALI.
ANYWAY...
I FOUND THIS!
IT'S AGENT RAMIREZ'S **SATELLITE PHONE.**
I THINK I CAN GET SOME KIND OF **INTERNET CONNECTION** WITH IT.
HOOK IT UP TO MY O-PAD AND TRY TO FIND A WAY **OUT** OF THIS **DESERT**!
GOOD THINKING!

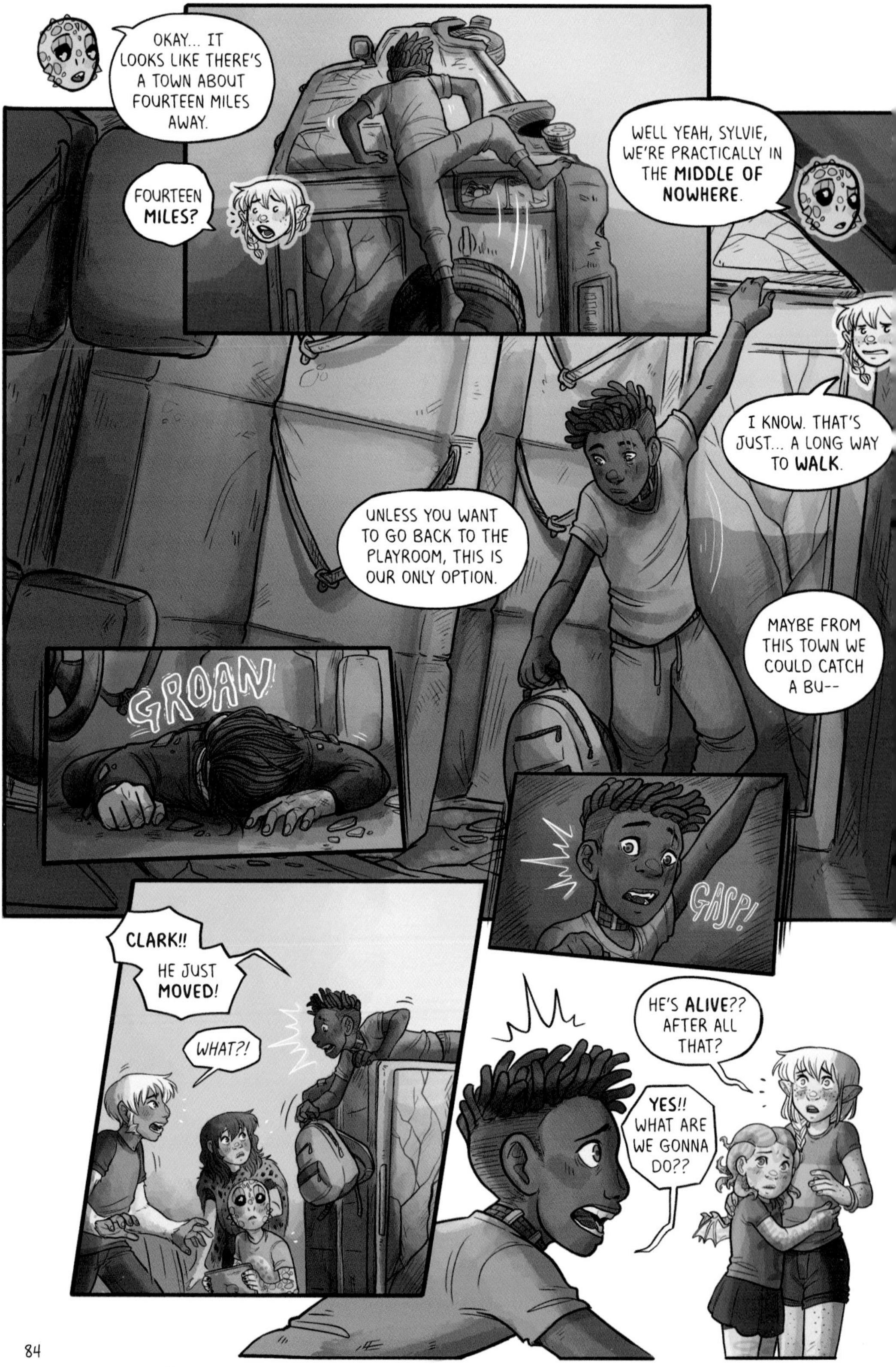
OKAY... IT LOOKS LIKE THERE'S A TOWN ABOUT FOURTEEN MILES AWAY.
FOURTEEN MILES?
WELL YEAH, SYLVIE, WE'RE PRACTICALLY IN THE MIDDLE OF NOWHERE.
I KNOW. THAT'S JUST... A LONG WAY TO WALK.
UNLESS YOU WANT TO GO BACK TO THE PLAYROOM, THIS IS OUR ONLY OPTION.
MAYBE FROM THIS TOWN WE COULD CATCH A BU--
GROAN
GASP!
CLARK!!
HE JUST MOVED!
WHAT?!
HE'S ALIVE?? AFTER ALL THAT?
YES!! WHAT ARE WE GONNA DO??

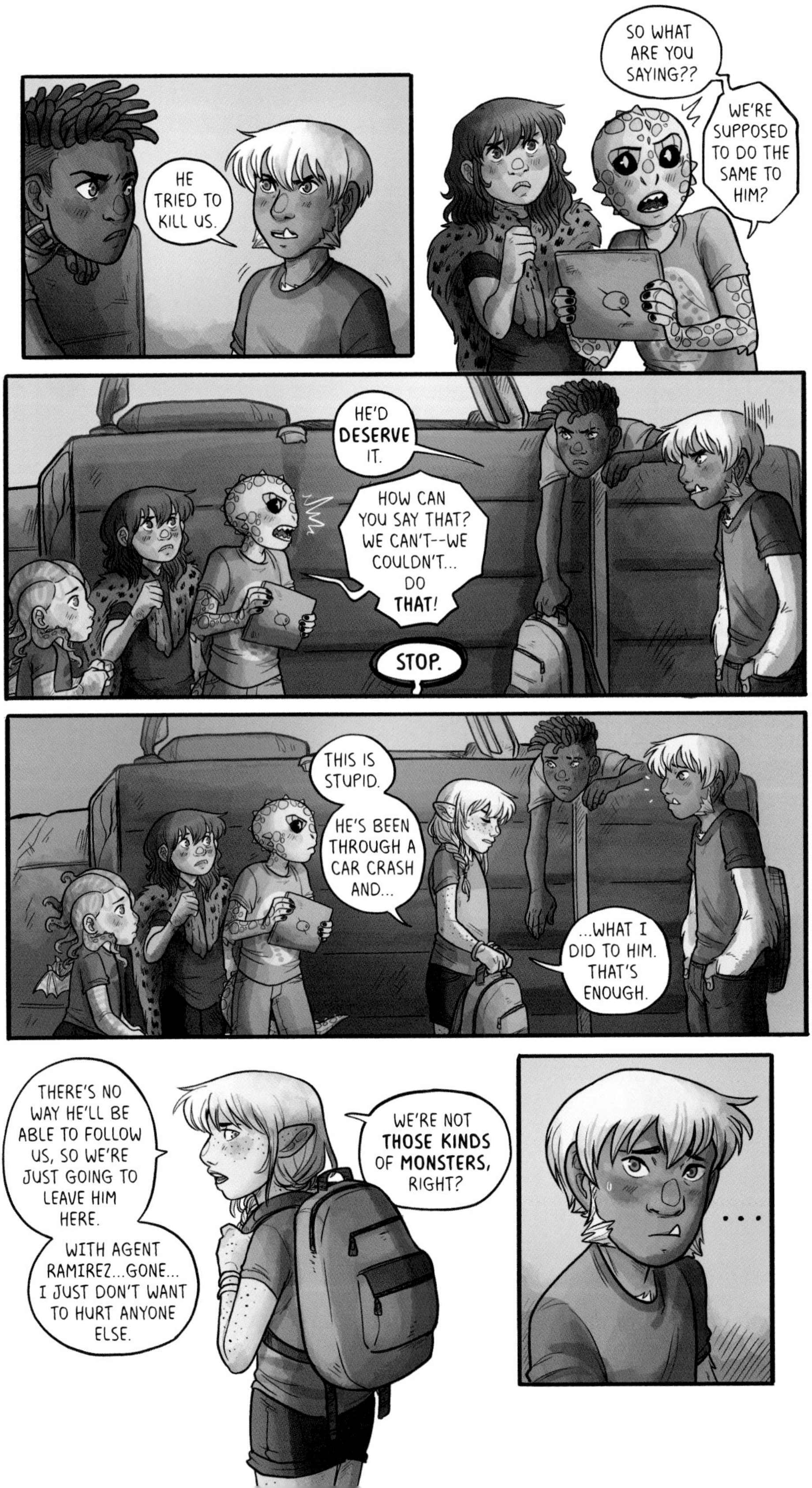
HE TRIED TO KILL US.
SO WHAT ARE YOU SAYING??
WE'RE SUPPOSED TO DO THE SAME TO HIM?
HE'D **DESERVE** IT.
HOW CAN YOU SAY THAT? WE CAN'T--WE COULDN'T... DO **THAT**!
STOP.
THIS IS STUPID.
HE'S BEEN THROUGH A CAR CRASH AND...
...WHAT I DID TO HIM. THAT'S ENOUGH.
THERE'S NO WAY HE'LL BE ABLE TO FOLLOW US, SO WE'RE JUST GOING TO LEAVE HIM HERE.
WITH AGENT RAMIREZ...GONE... I JUST DON'T WANT TO HURT ANYONE ELSE.
WE'RE NOT **THOSE KINDS** OF **MONSTERS**, RIGHT?
...

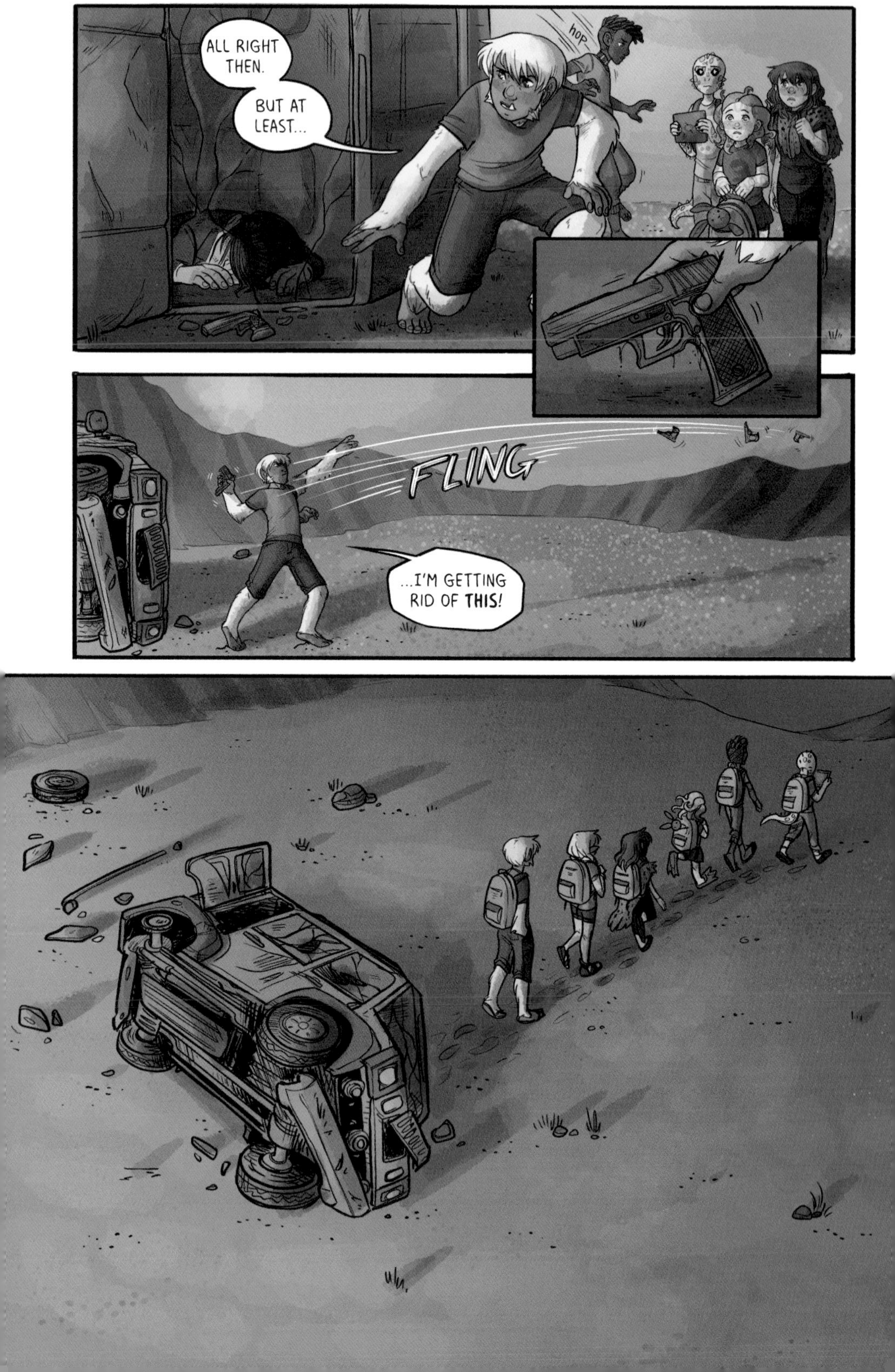
ALL RIGHT THEN.
BUT AT LEAST...
hop
FLING
...I'M GETTING RID OF THIS!

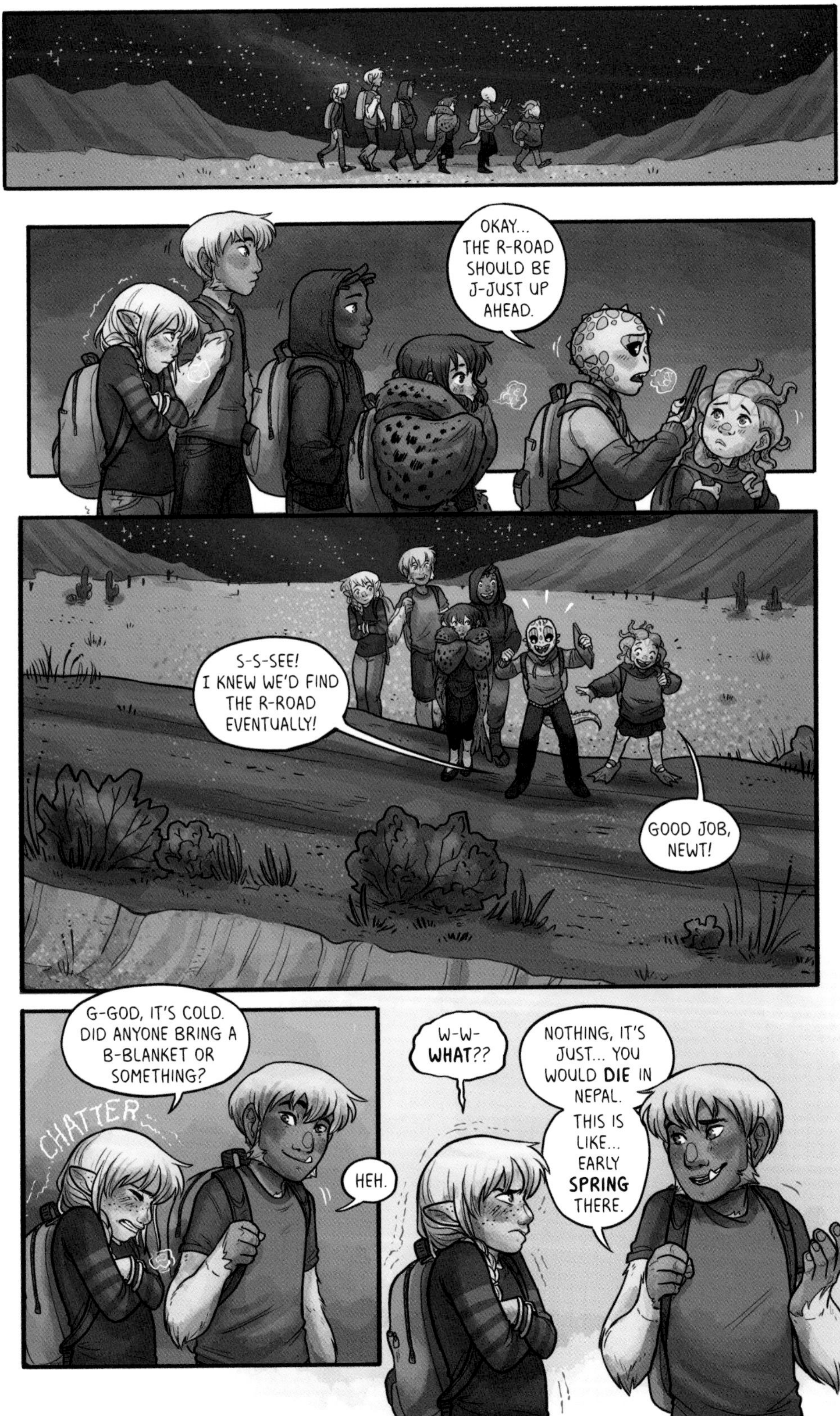

OKAY... THE R-ROAD SHOULD BE J-JUST UP AHEAD.
S-S-SEE! I KNEW WE'D FIND THE R-ROAD EVENTUALLY!
GOOD JOB, NEWT!
G-GOD, IT'S COLD. DID ANYONE BRING A B-BLANKET OR SOMETHING?
CHATTER
HEH.
W-W-**WHAT**??
NOTHING, IT'S JUST... YOU WOULD **DIE** IN NEPAL.
THIS IS LIKE... EARLY **SPRING** THERE.

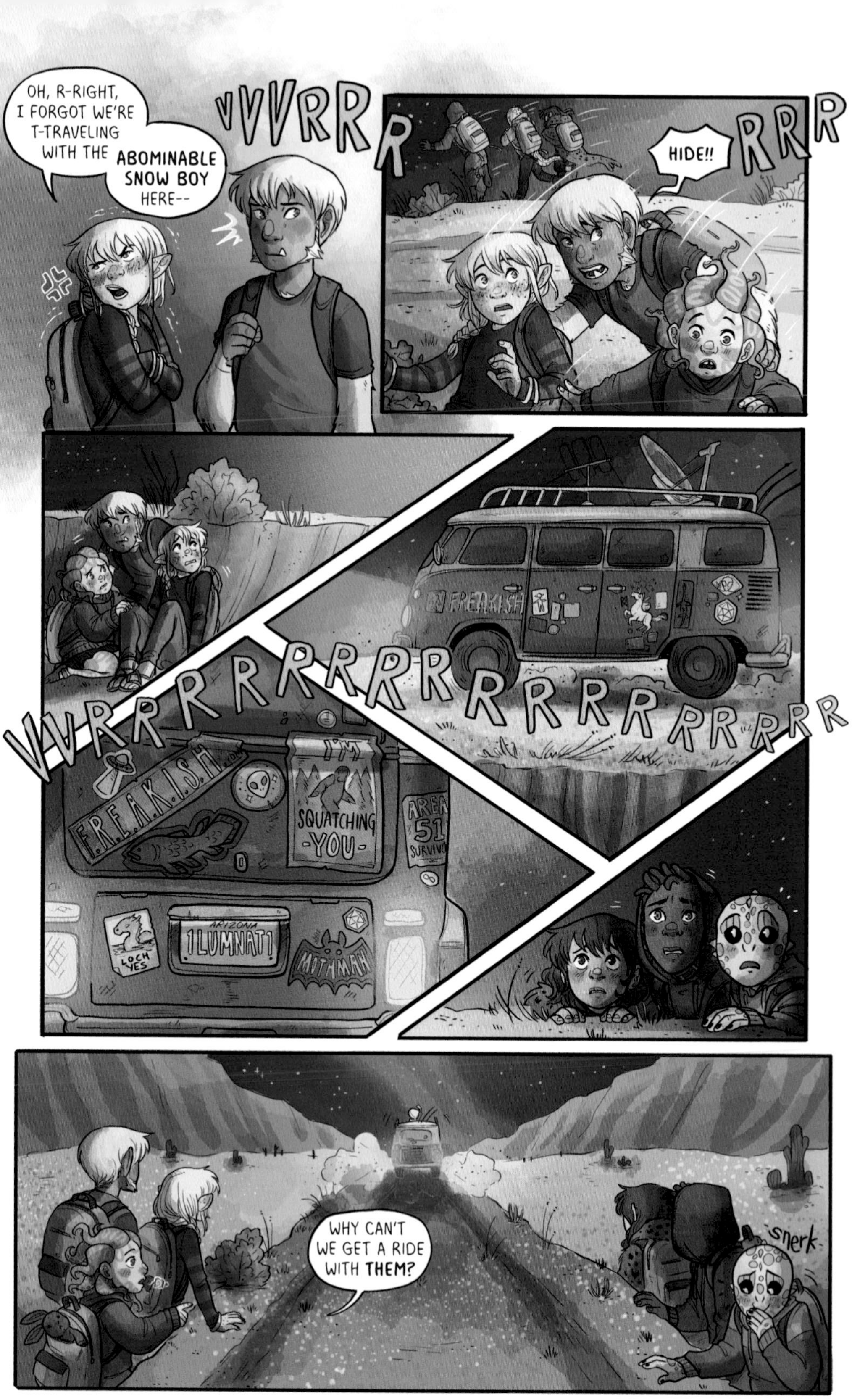

OH, R-RIGHT, I FORGOT WE'RE T-TRAVELING WITH THE ABOMINABLE SNOW BOY HERE--
VVVRRR
RRR
HIDE!!
FREAKISH
VVRRRRRRRRRRRRRRRRR
F.R.E.A.K.I.S.H.
I'M SQUATCHING -YOU-
AREA 51 SURVIVO
ARIZONA
1LUMNAT1
LOCH YES
MITHMAH
WHY CAN'T WE GET A RIDE WITH THEM?
snerk

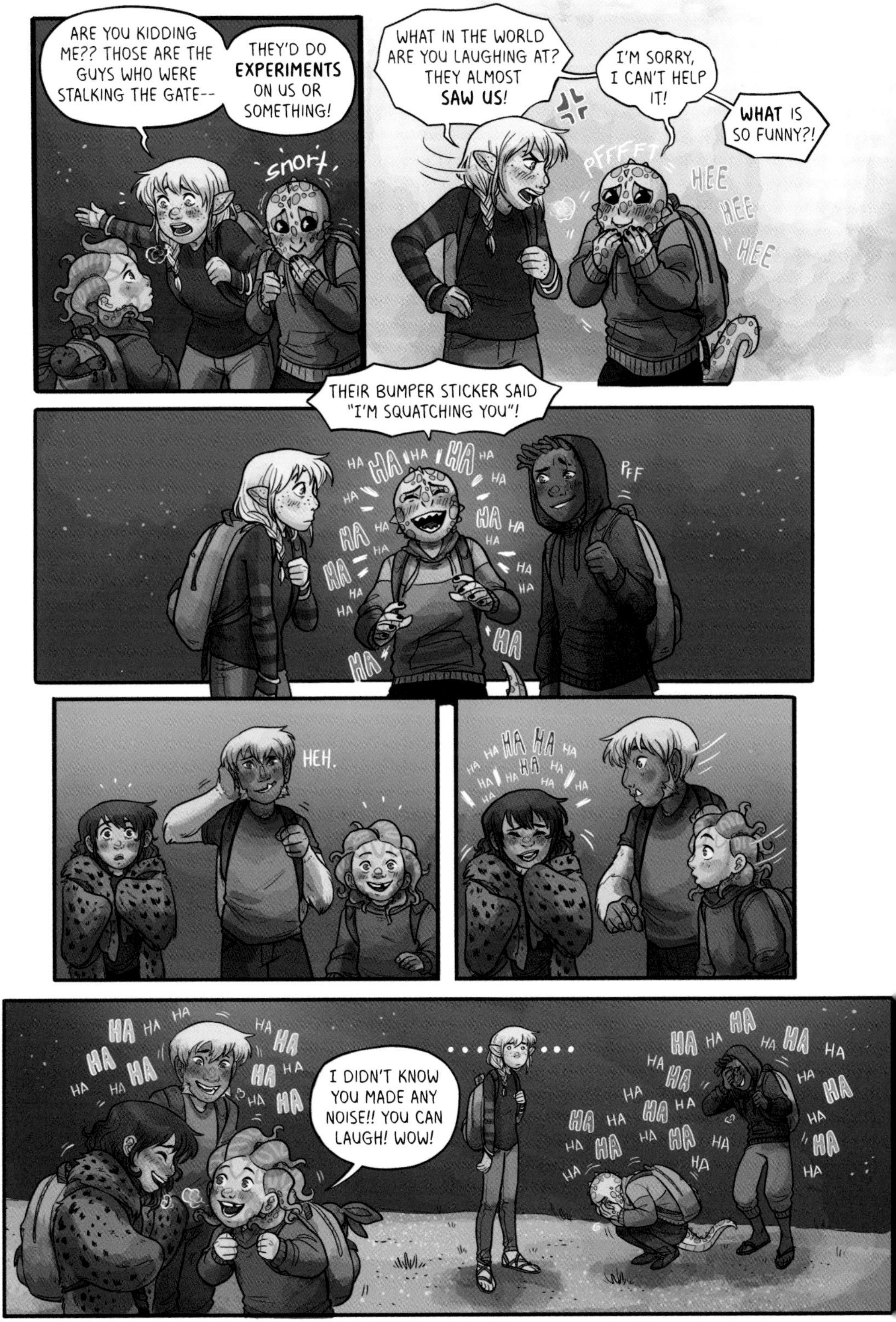
ARE YOU KIDDING ME?? THOSE ARE THE GUYS WHO WERE STALKING THE GATE--
THEY'D DO **EXPERIMENTS** ON US OR SOMETHING!
snort
WHAT IN THE WORLD ARE YOU LAUGHING AT? THEY ALMOST **SAW US**!
I'M SORRY, I CAN'T HELP IT!
WHAT IS SO FUNNY?!
PFFFFT
HEE HEE HEE
THEIR BUMPER STICKER SAID "I'M SQUATCHING YOU"!
HA HA HA HA HA HA HA HA HA HA HA HA HA HA HA HA HA HA HA HA HA
PFF
HEH.
HA HA HA HA HA HA HA HA HA HA HA HA HA
HA HA HA HA HA HA HA HA HA HA HA HA HA
I DIDN'T KNOW YOU MADE ANY NOISE!! YOU CAN LAUGH! WOW!
. . . . . .
HA HA HA HA HA HA HA HA HA HA HA HA HA HA HA HA HA HA HA HA HA HA HA HA HA HA HA HA

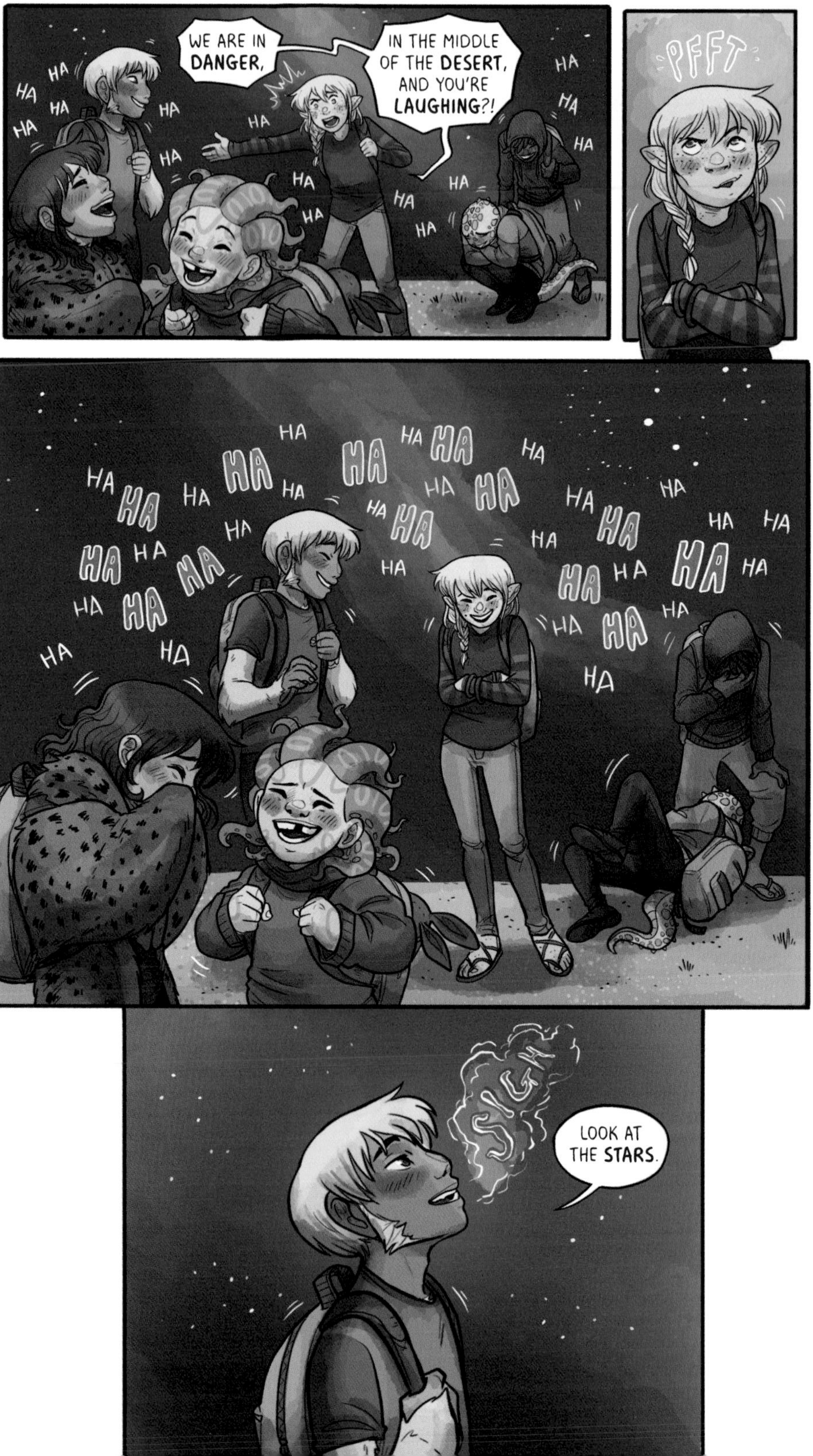
WE ARE IN DANGER,
IN THE MIDDLE OF THE DESERT, AND YOU'RE LAUGHING?!
HA HA HA HA HA HA HA HA HA HA HA HA HA
PFFT
HA HA HA HA HA HA HA HA HA HA HA HA HA HA HA HA HA HA HA HA HA HA HA HA HA HA HA HA HA HA HA HA HA HA HA HA
SIGH
LOOK AT THE STARS.

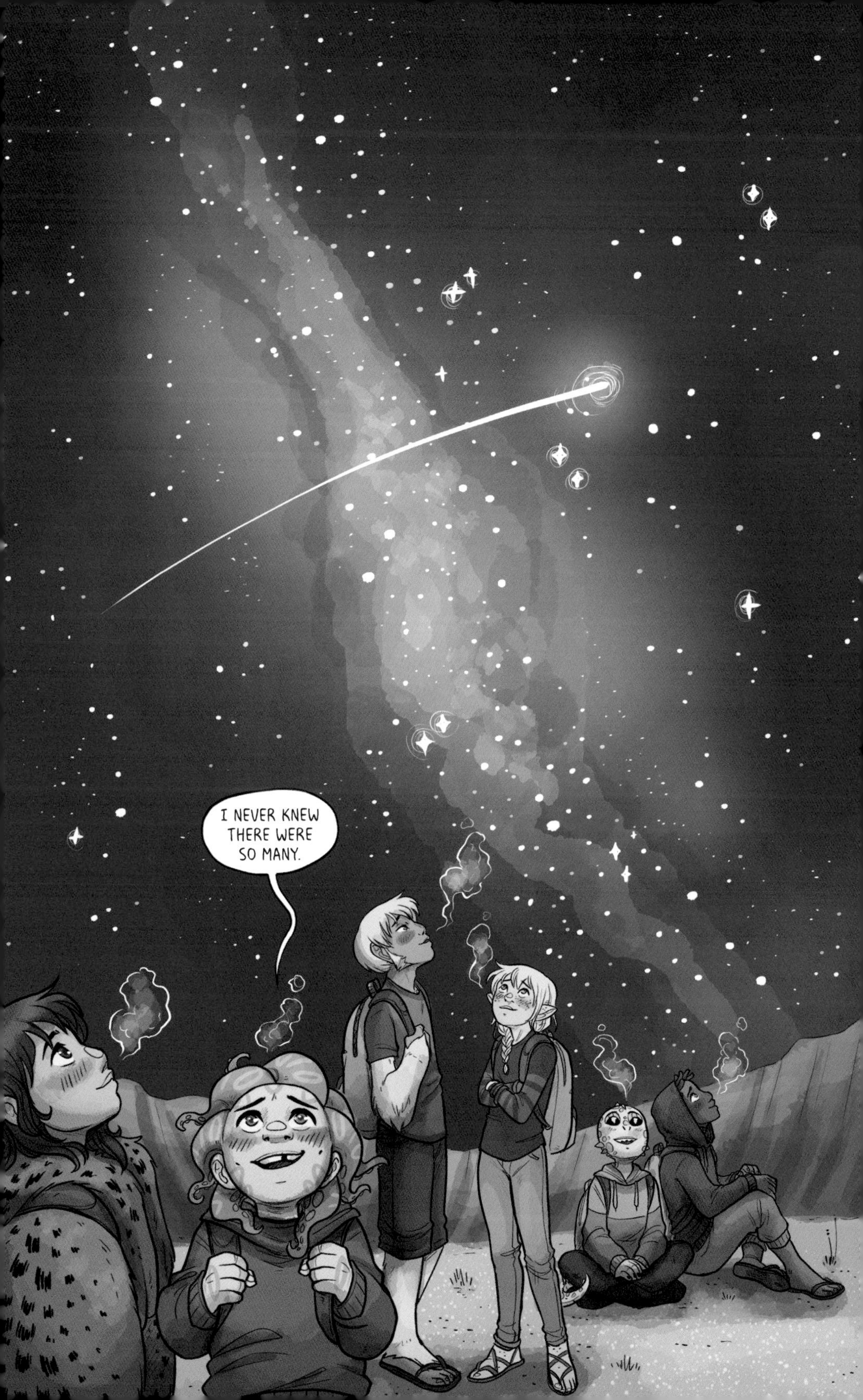
I NEVER KNEW THERE WERE SO MANY.

CHAPTER FOUR

HEAT WAVES

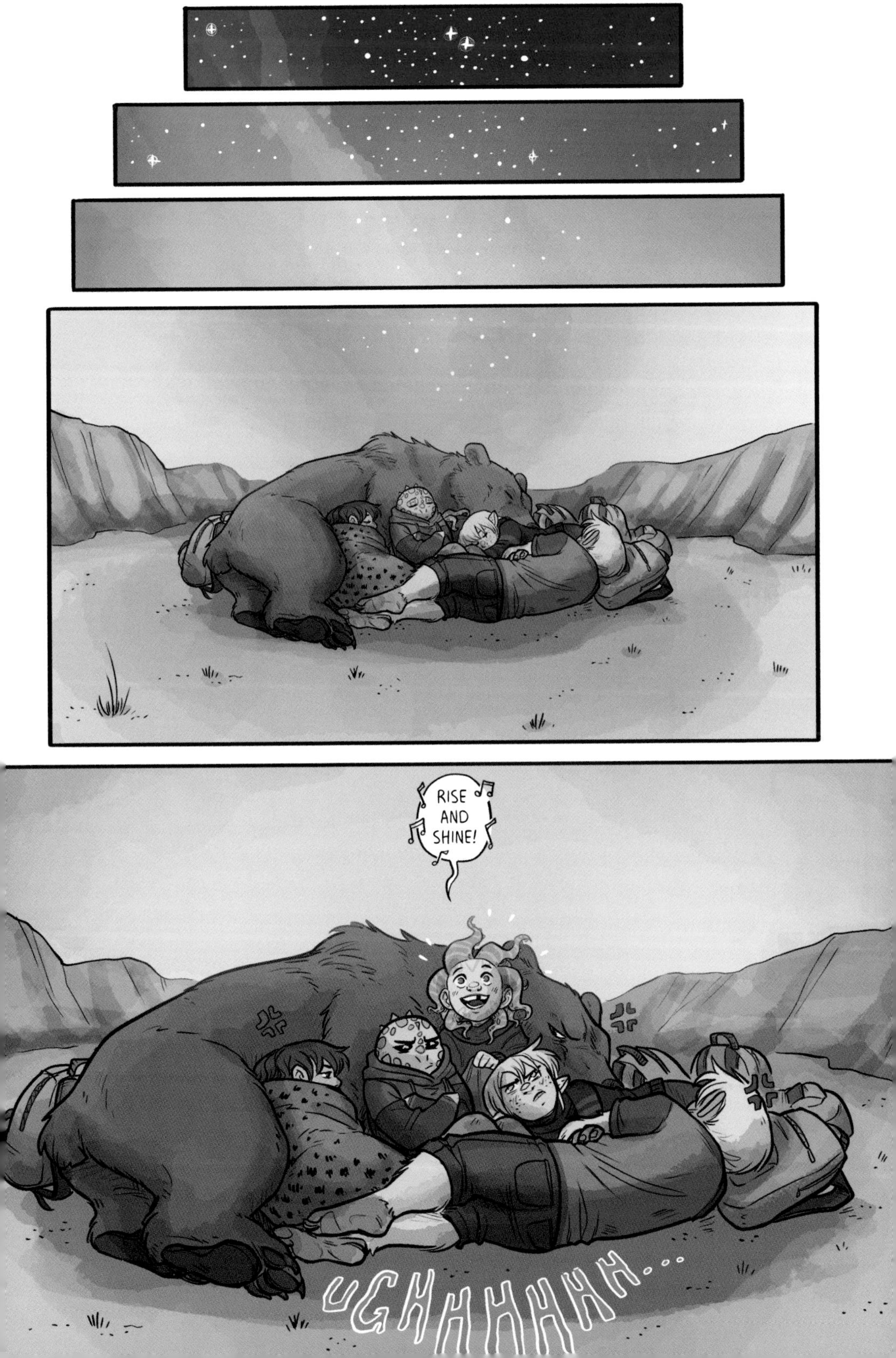
RISE AND SHINE!
UGHHHHHH...

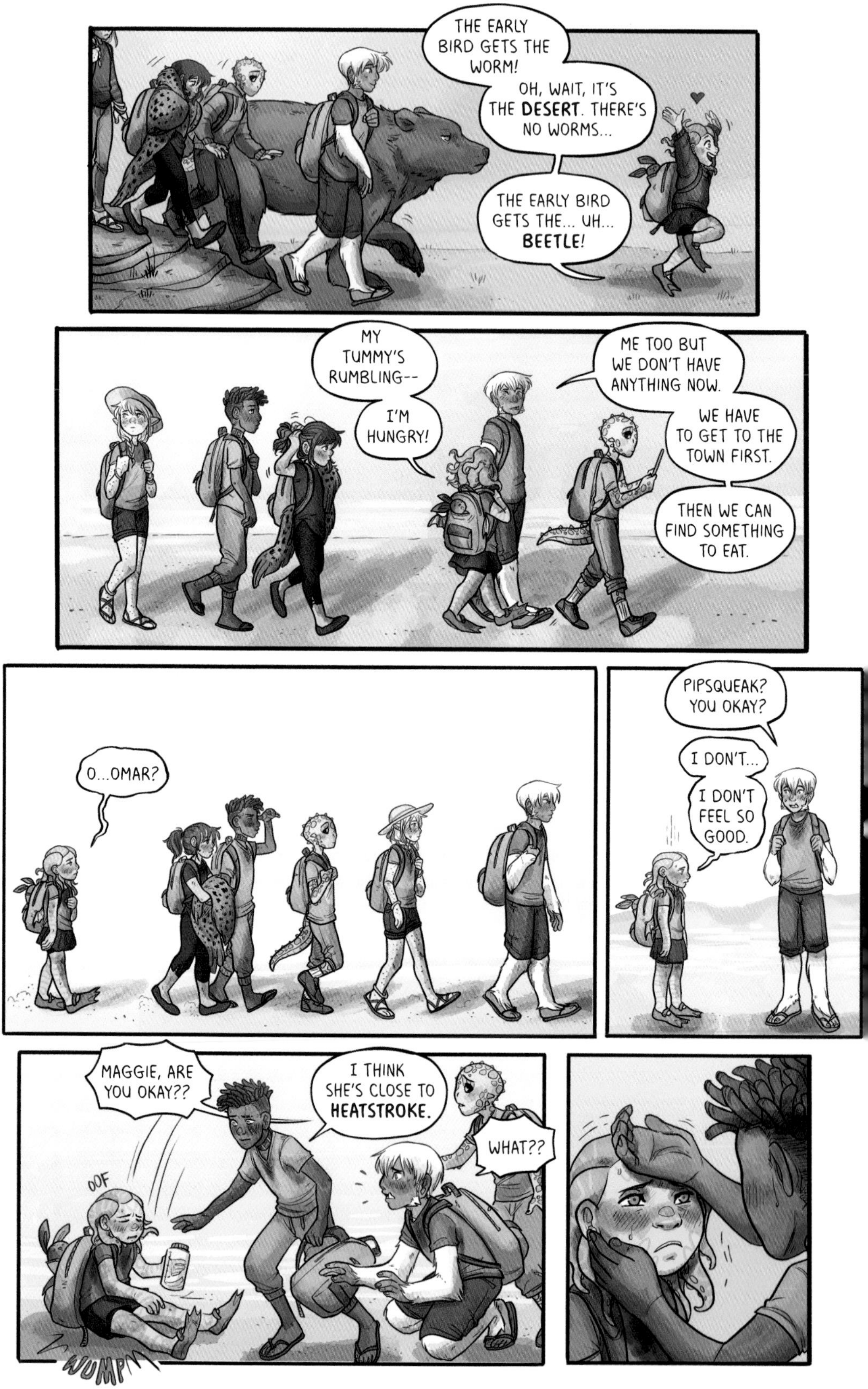
THE EARLY BIRD GETS THE WORM!
OH, WAIT, IT'S THE **DESERT**. THERE'S NO WORMS...
THE EARLY BIRD GETS THE... UH... **BEETLE**!
MY TUMMY'S RUMBLING--
I'M HUNGRY!
ME TOO BUT WE DON'T HAVE ANYTHING NOW.
WE HAVE TO GET TO THE TOWN FIRST.
THEN WE CAN FIND SOMETHING TO EAT.
O...OMAR?
PIPSQUEAK? YOU OKAY?
I DON'T...
I DON'T FEEL SO GOOD.
MAGGIE, ARE YOU OKAY??
I THINK SHE'S CLOSE TO **HEATSTROKE**.
WHAT??
OOF
WUMP

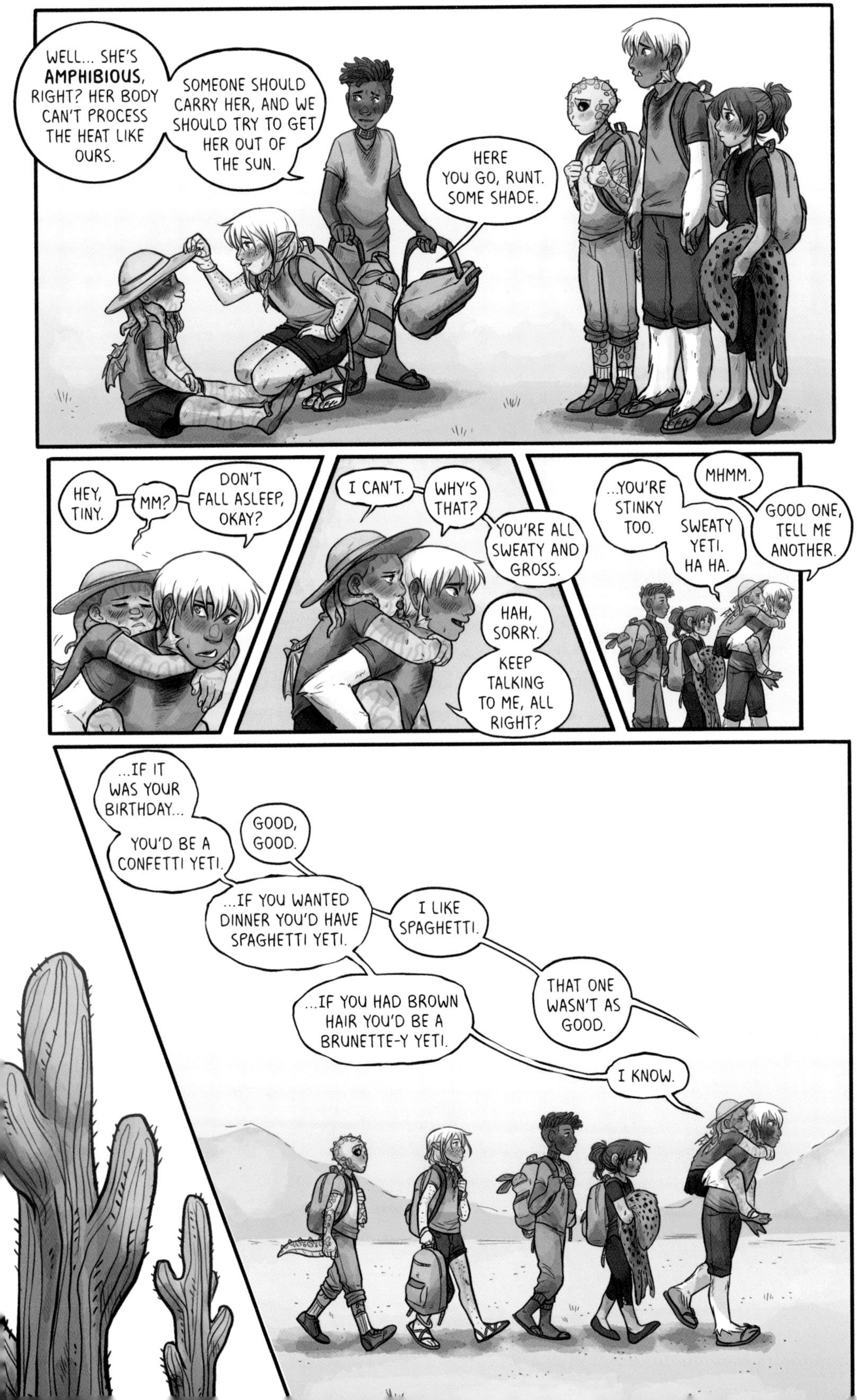
WELL... SHE'S **AMPHIBIOUS**, RIGHT? HER BODY CAN'T PROCESS THE HEAT LIKE OURS.
SOMEONE SHOULD CARRY HER, AND WE SHOULD TRY TO GET HER OUT OF THE SUN.
HERE YOU GO, RUNT. SOME SHADE.
HEY, TINY.
MM?
DON'T FALL ASLEEP, OKAY?
I CAN'T.
WHY'S THAT?
YOU'RE ALL SWEATY AND GROSS.
HAH, SORRY.
KEEP TALKING TO ME, ALL RIGHT?
...YOU'RE STINKY TOO.
MHMM.
SWEATY YETI. HA HA.
GOOD ONE, TELL ME ANOTHER.
...IF IT WAS YOUR BIRTHDAY...
YOU'D BE A CONFETTI YETI.
GOOD, GOOD.
...IF YOU WANTED DINNER YOU'D HAVE SPAGHETTI YETI.
I LIKE SPAGHETTI.
...IF YOU HAD BROWN HAIR YOU'D BE A BRUNETTE-Y YETI.
THAT ONE WASN'T AS GOOD.
I KNOW.

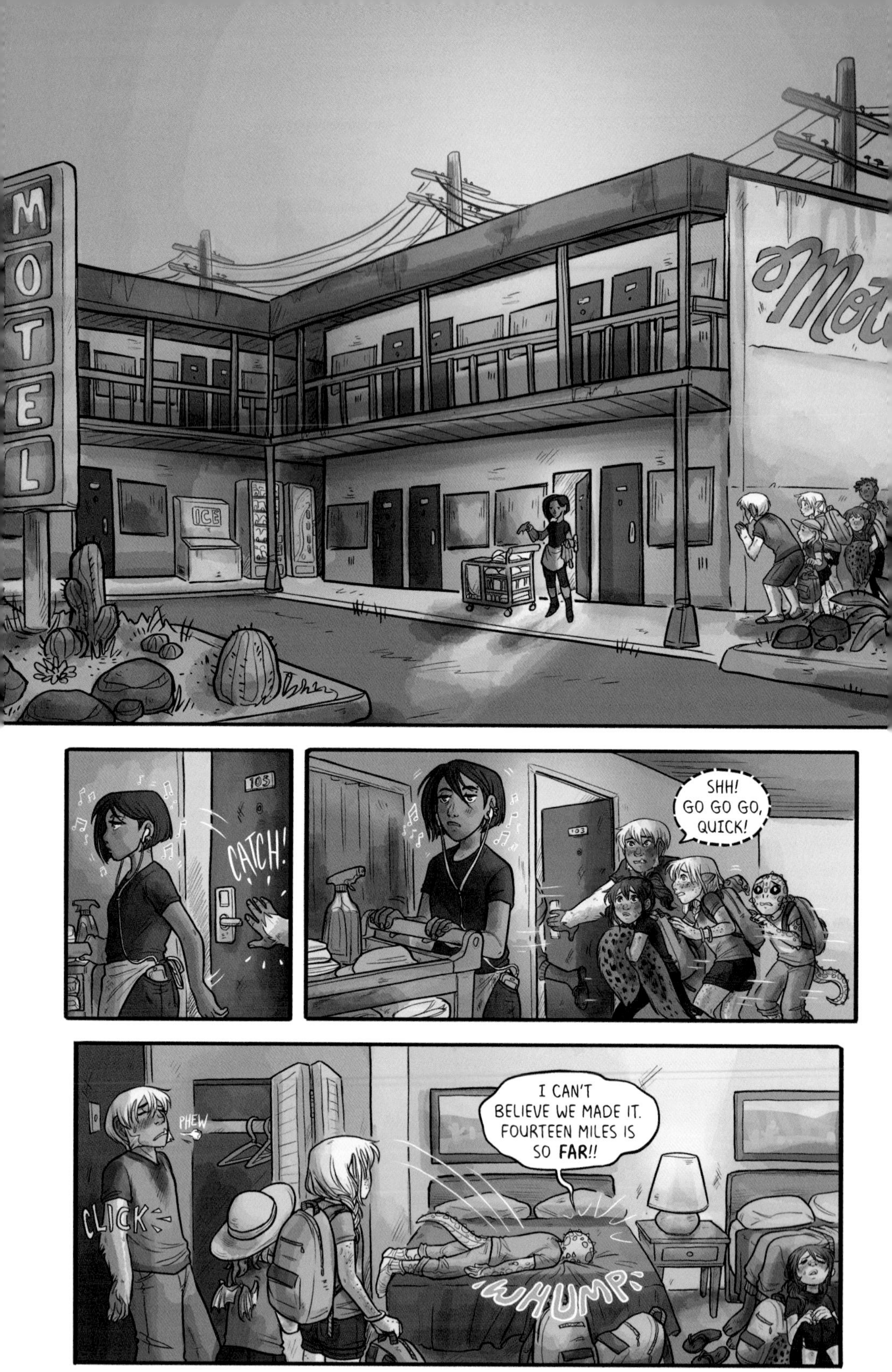

MOTEL
Motel
ICE
105
CATCH!
103
SHH! GO GO GO, QUICK!
PHEW
CLICK
I CAN'T BELIEVE WE MADE IT. FOURTEEN MILES IS SO **FAR**!!
WHUMP

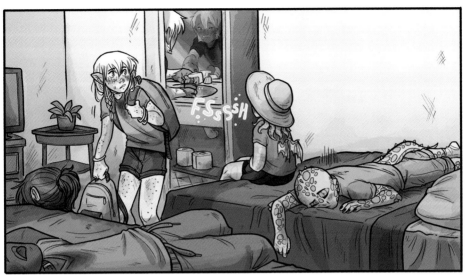

FSsssSH

HERE, TINY.

DON'T DRINK TOO FAST, OKAY?

gulp. gulp.

MHM.

HEY... ANYONE NEED THE BATHROOM OR CAN I GO?

NAH.

GO FOR IT.

SO...

WHAT ARE WE GOING TO DO NOW?

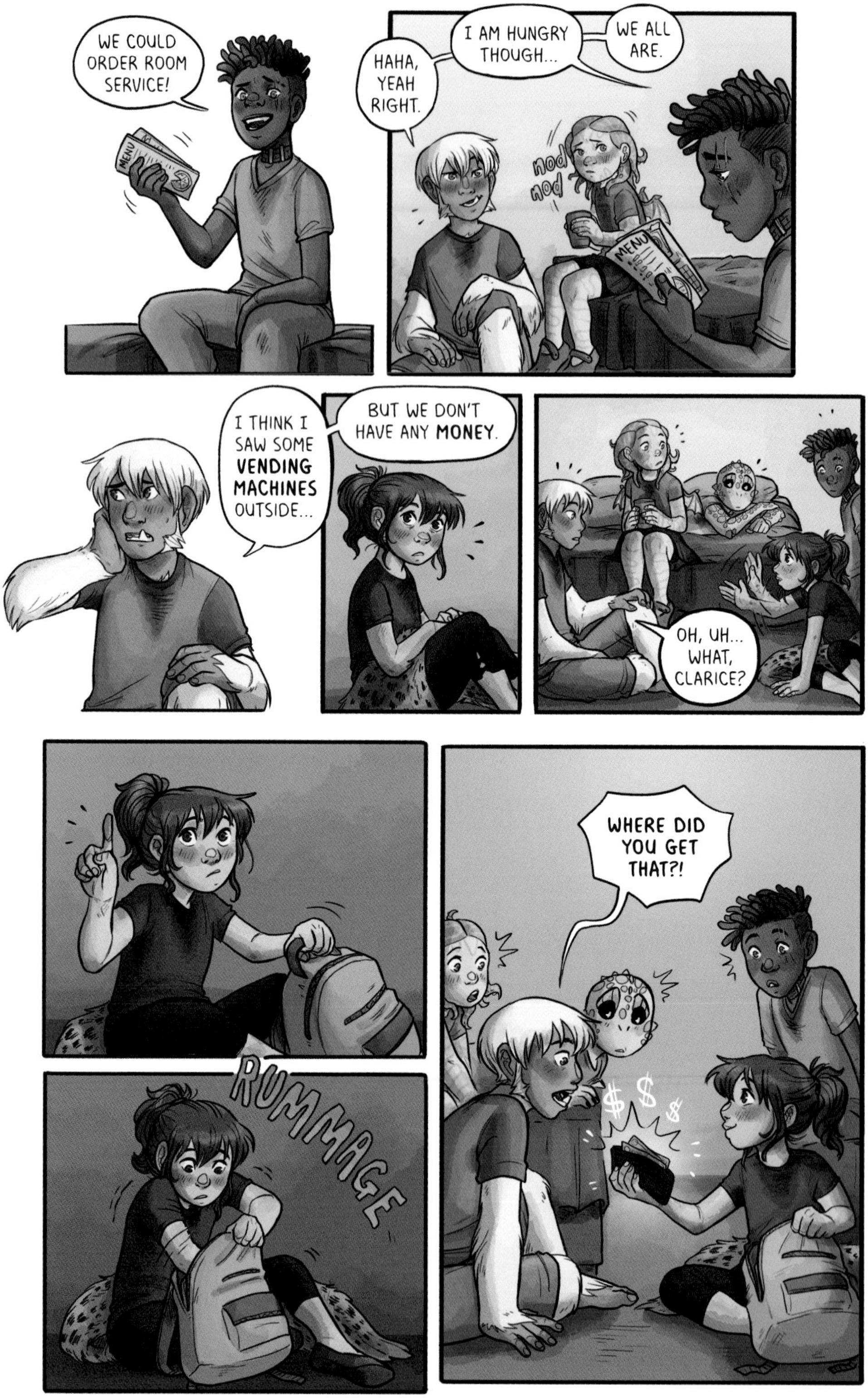
WE COULD ORDER ROOM SERVICE!
MENU
HAHA, YEAH RIGHT.
I AM HUNGRY THOUGH...
WE ALL ARE.
nod nod
MENU
I THINK I SAW SOME VENDING MACHINES OUTSIDE...
BUT WE DON'T HAVE ANY MONEY.
OH, UH... WHAT, CLARICE?
RUMMAGE
WHERE DID YOU GET THAT?!
$ $ $

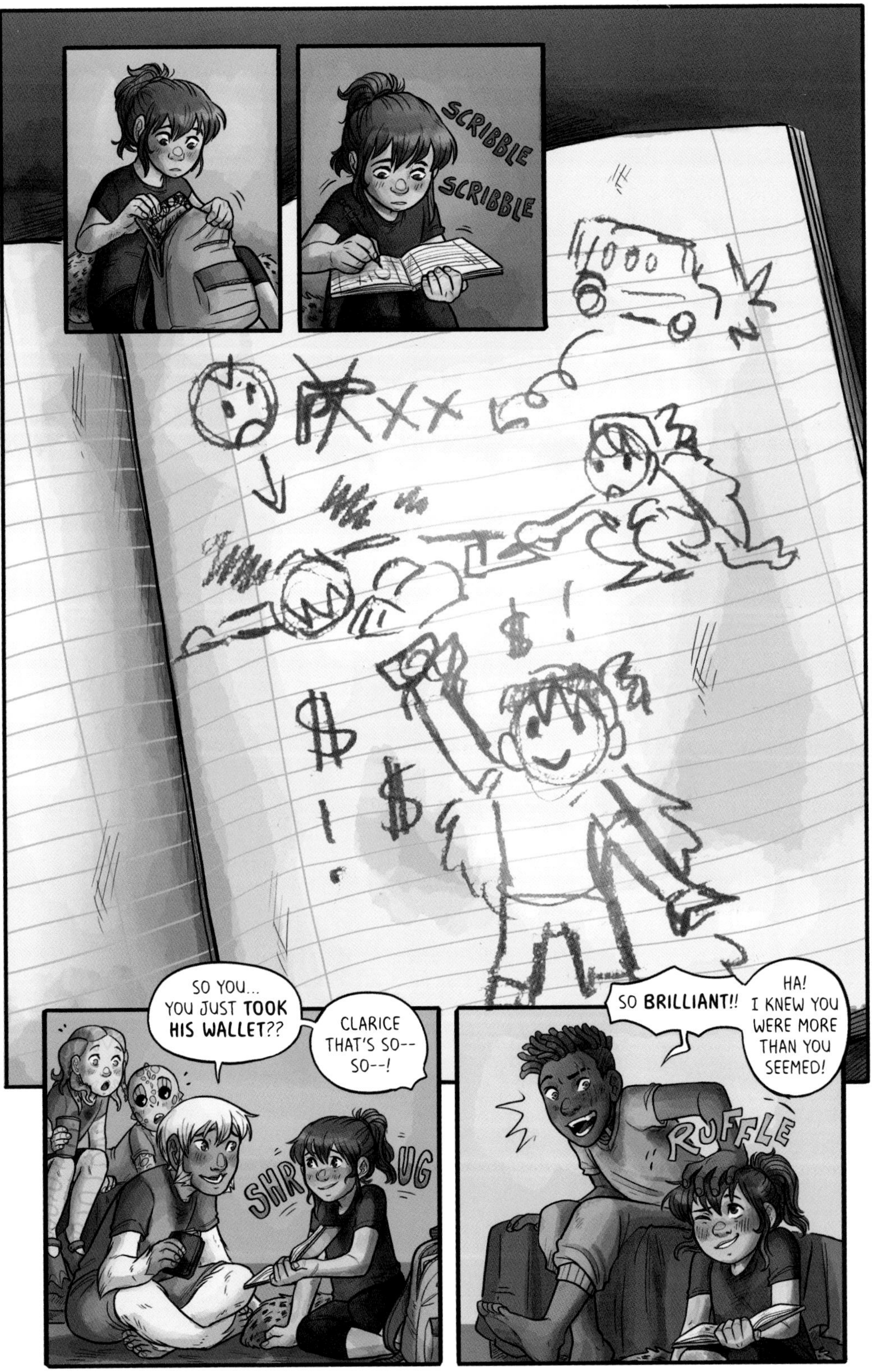
SCRIBBLE
SCRIBBLE
SO YOU... YOU JUST TOOK HIS WALLET??
CLARICE THAT'S SO-- SO--!
SHRUG
SO BRILLIANT!!
HA! I KNEW YOU WERE MORE THAN YOU SEEMED!
RUFFLE

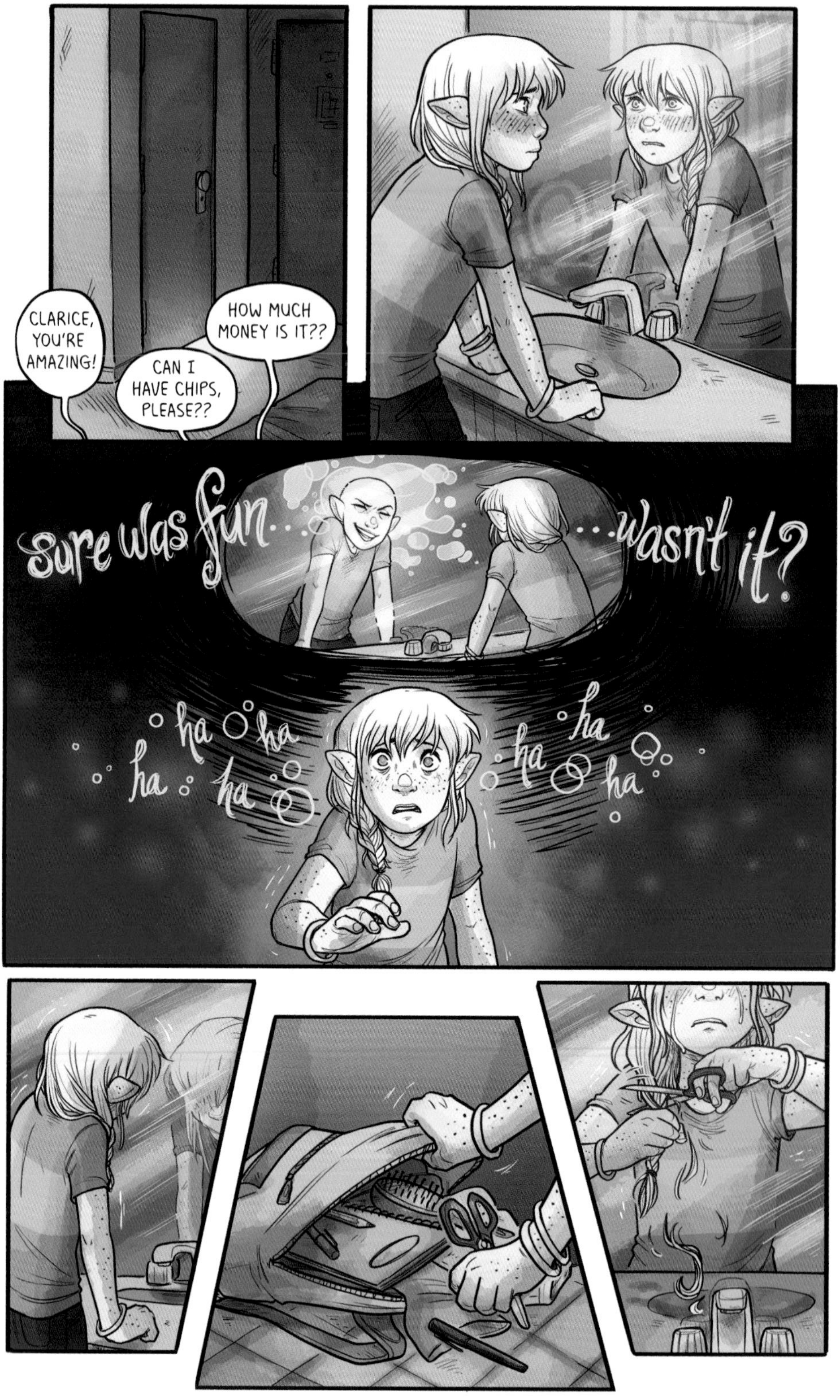

CLARICE, YOU'RE AMAZING!
HOW MUCH MONEY IS IT??
CAN I HAVE CHIPS, PLEASE??
sure was fun...
...wasn't it?
ha ha ha ha
ha ha ha ha

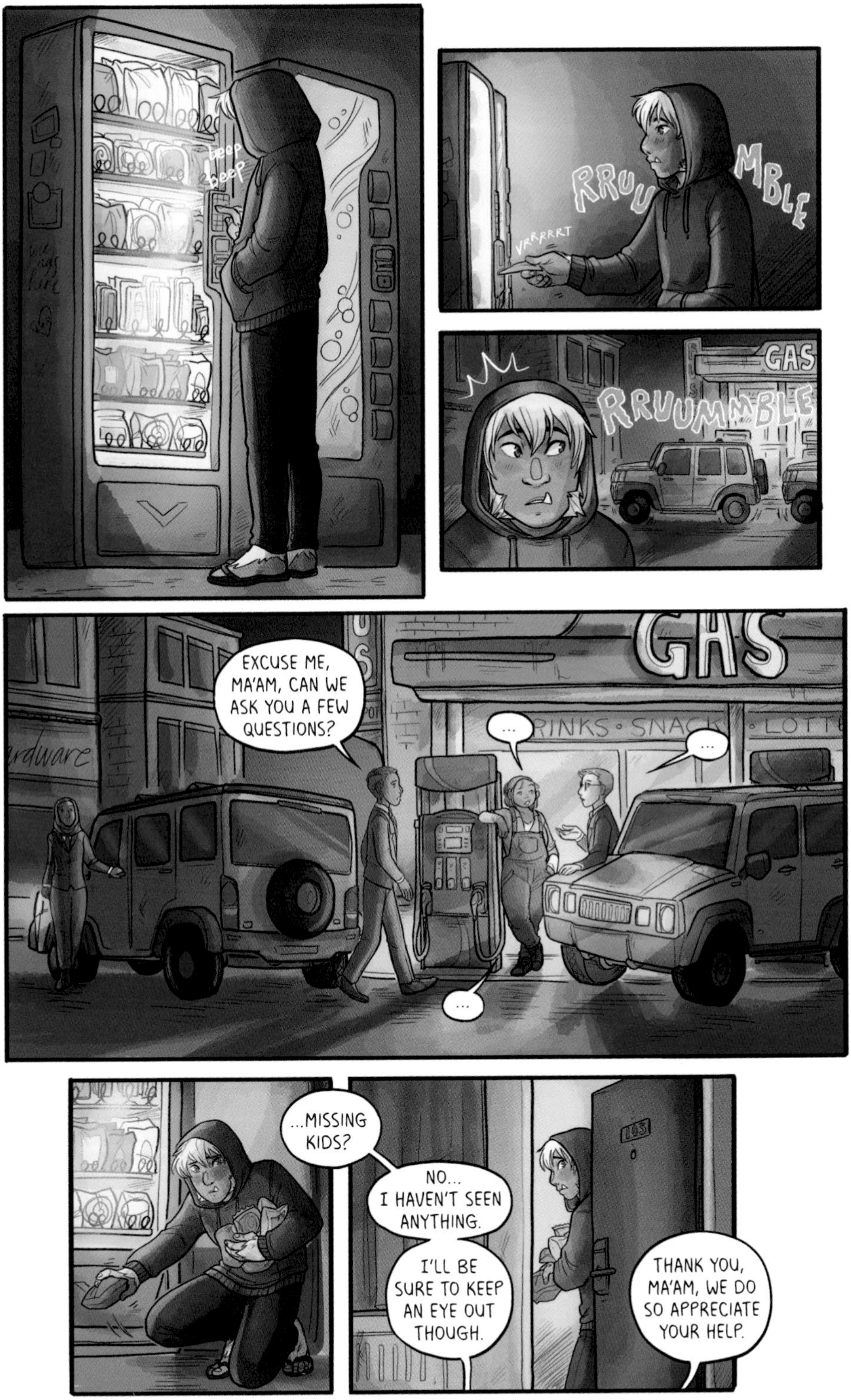
beep
beep
RRUU
MBLE
VRRRRRT
GAS
RRUUMMBLE
GAS
EXCUSE ME, MA'AM, CAN WE ASK YOU A FEW QUESTIONS?
...
...
...
...MISSING KIDS?
NO... I HAVEN'T SEEN ANYTHING.
I'LL BE SURE TO KEEP AN EYE OUT THOUGH.
THANK YOU, MA'AM, WE DO SO APPRECIATE YOUR HELP.

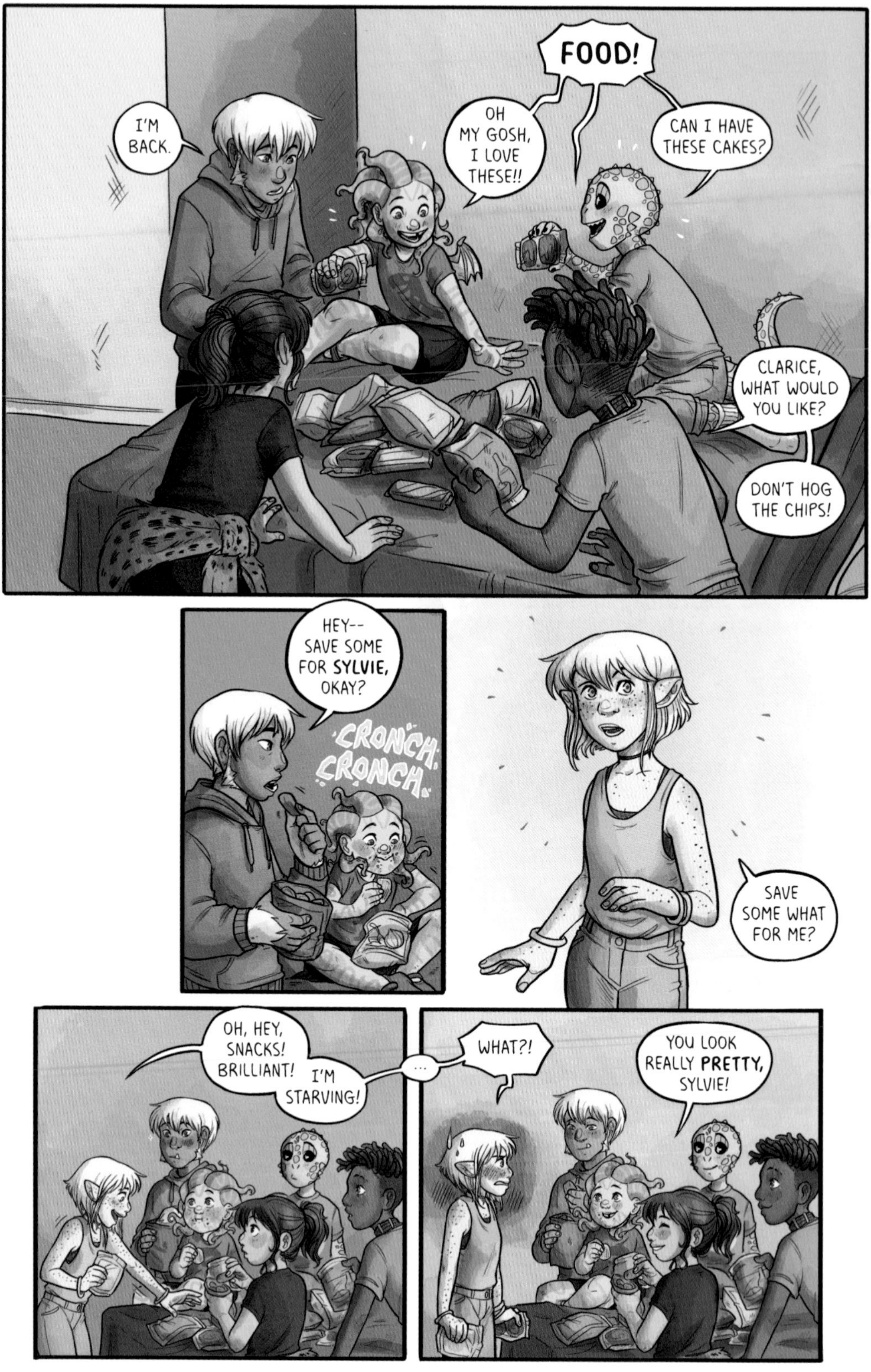
I'M BACK.
FOOD!
OH MY GOSH, I LOVE THESE!!
CAN I HAVE THESE CAKES?
CLARICE, WHAT WOULD YOU LIKE?
DON'T HOG THE CHIPS!
HEY-- SAVE SOME FOR SYLVIE, OKAY?
CRONCH CRONCH
SAVE SOME WHAT FOR ME?
OH, HEY, SNACKS! BRILLIANT!
I'M STARVING!
...
WHAT?!
YOU LOOK REALLY PRETTY, SYLVIE!

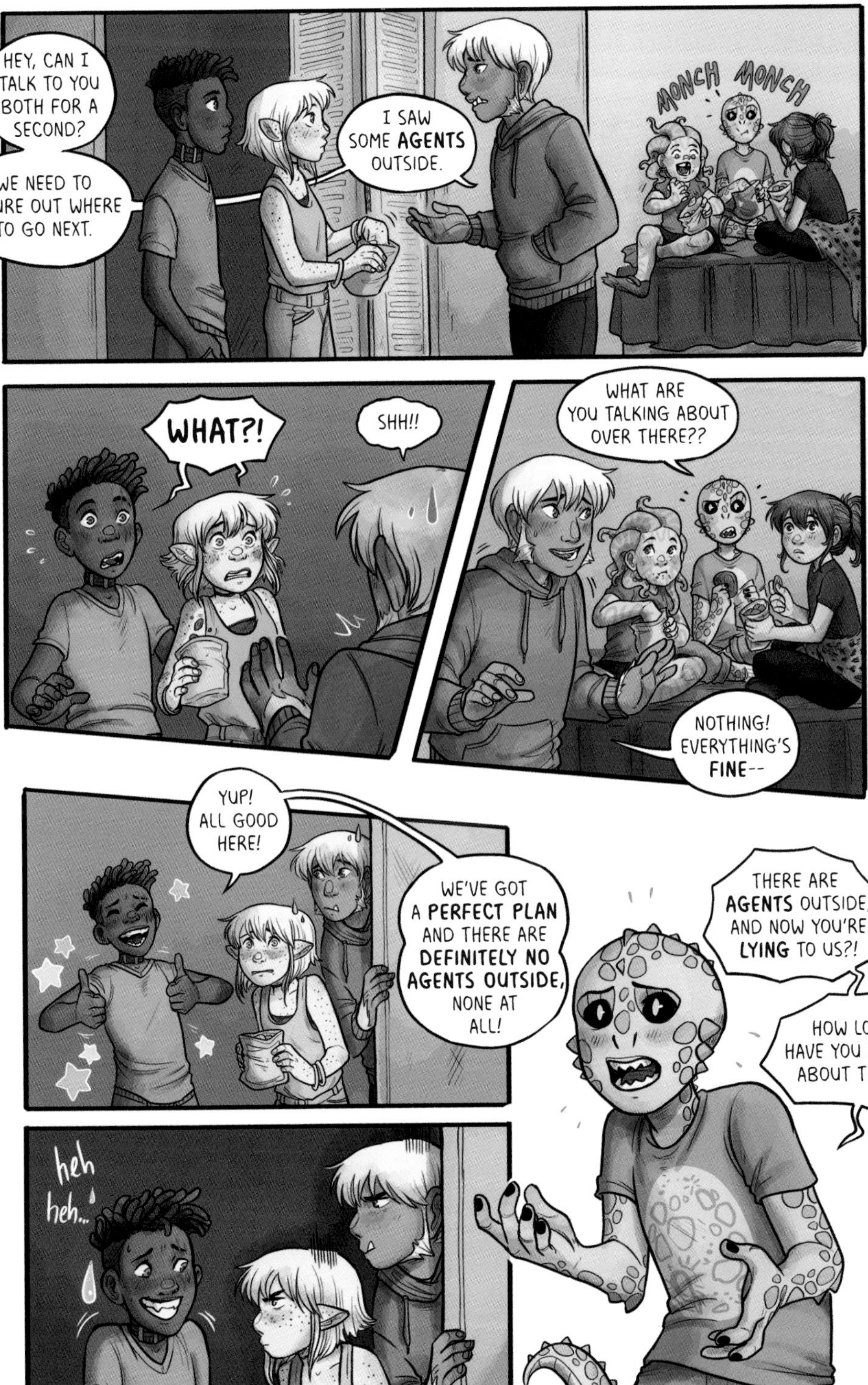
HEY, CAN I TALK TO YOU BOTH FOR A SECOND?
WE NEED TO FIGURE OUT WHERE TO GO NEXT.
I SAW SOME AGENTS OUTSIDE.
MONCH MONCH
WHAT?!
SHH!!
WHAT ARE YOU TALKING ABOUT OVER THERE??
NOTHING! EVERYTHING'S FINE--
YUP! ALL GOOD HERE!
WE'VE GOT A PERFECT PLAN AND THERE ARE DEFINITELY NO AGENTS OUTSIDE, NONE AT ALL!
heh heh...
THERE ARE AGENTS OUTSIDE, AND NOW YOU'RE LYING TO US?!
HOW LONG HAVE YOU KNOWN ABOUT THIS??

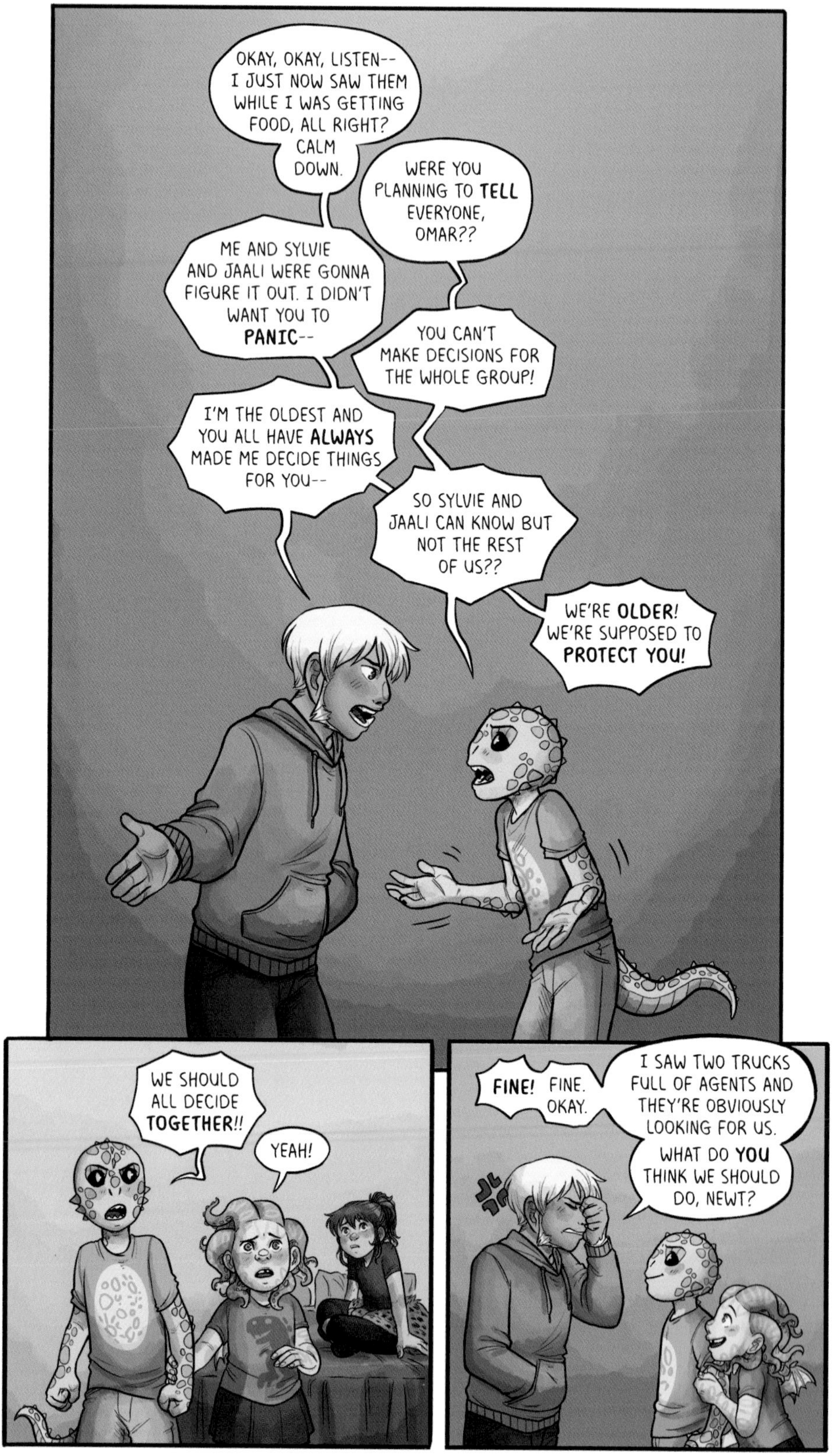
OKAY, OKAY, LISTEN-- I JUST NOW SAW THEM WHILE I WAS GETTING FOOD, ALL RIGHT? CALM DOWN.
WERE YOU PLANNING TO **TELL** EVERYONE, OMAR??
ME AND SYLVIE AND JAALI WERE GONNA FIGURE IT OUT. I DIDN'T WANT YOU TO **PANIC**--
YOU CAN'T MAKE DECISIONS FOR THE WHOLE GROUP!
I'M THE OLDEST AND YOU ALL HAVE **ALWAYS** MADE ME DECIDE THINGS FOR YOU--
SO SYLVIE AND JAALI CAN KNOW BUT NOT THE REST OF US??
WE'RE **OLDER!** WE'RE SUPPOSED TO **PROTECT YOU!**
WE SHOULD ALL DECIDE **TOGETHER!!**
YEAH!
FINE!
FINE. OKAY.
I SAW TWO TRUCKS FULL OF AGENTS AND THEY'RE OBVIOUSLY LOOKING FOR US.
WHAT DO **YOU** THINK WE SHOULD DO, NEWT?

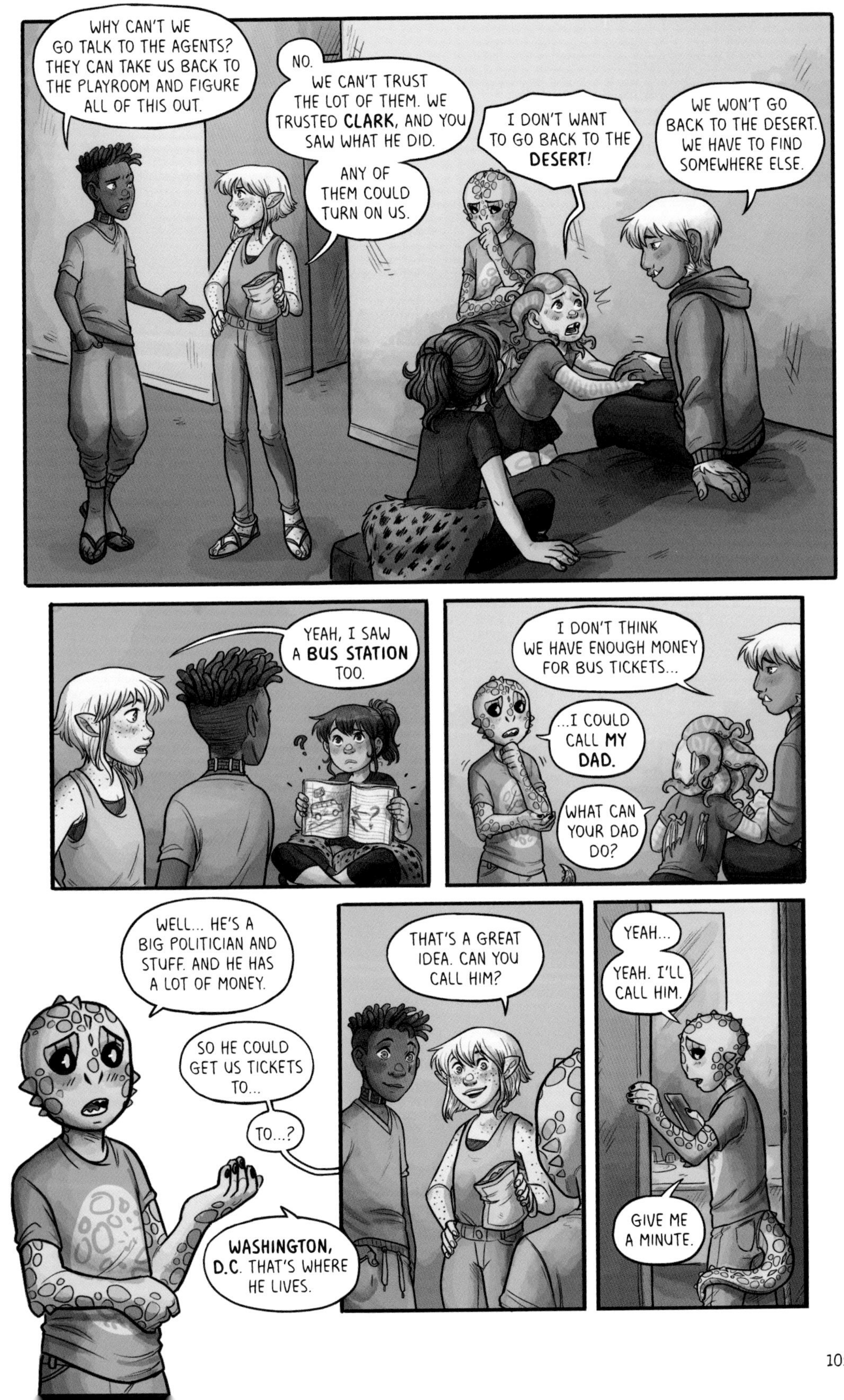

WHY CAN'T WE GO TALK TO THE AGENTS? THEY CAN TAKE US BACK TO THE PLAYROOM AND FIGURE ALL OF THIS OUT.
NO.
WE CAN'T TRUST THE LOT OF THEM. WE TRUSTED **CLARK**, AND YOU SAW WHAT HE DID.
ANY OF THEM COULD TURN ON US.
I DON'T WANT TO GO BACK TO THE **DESERT**!
WE WON'T GO BACK TO THE DESERT. WE HAVE TO FIND SOMEWHERE ELSE.
YEAH, I SAW A **BUS STATION** TOO.
I DON'T THINK WE HAVE ENOUGH MONEY FOR BUS TICKETS...
...I COULD CALL **MY DAD.**
WHAT CAN YOUR DAD DO?
WELL... HE'S A BIG POLITICIAN AND STUFF. AND HE HAS A LOT OF MONEY.
SO HE COULD GET US TICKETS TO...
TO...?
WASHINGTON, D.C. THAT'S WHERE HE LIVES.
THAT'S A GREAT IDEA. CAN YOU CALL HIM?
YEAH...
YEAH. I'LL CALL HIM.
GIVE ME A MINUTE.

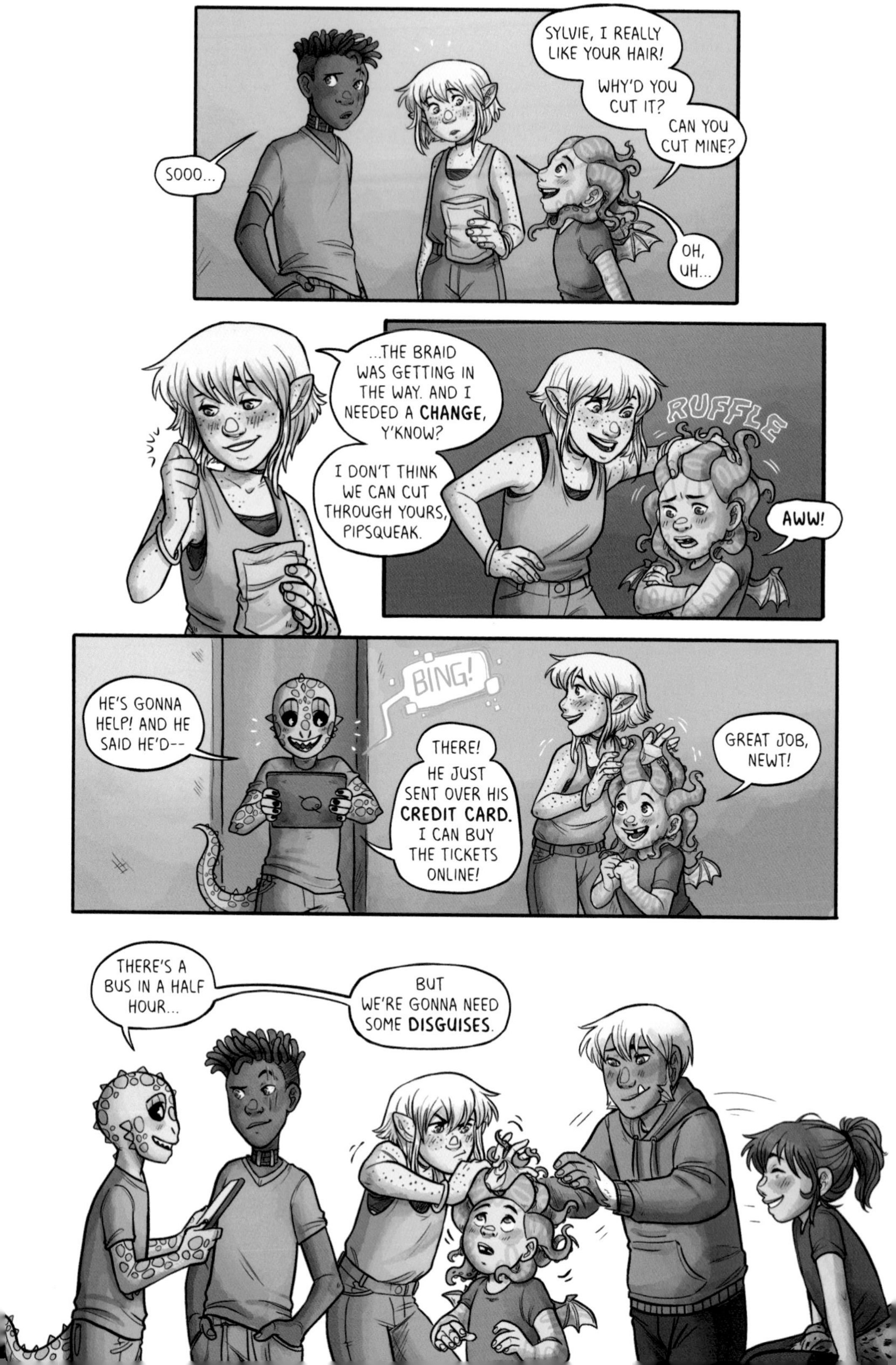

SYLVIE, I REALLY LIKE YOUR HAIR!
WHY'D YOU CUT IT?
CAN YOU CUT MINE?
SOOO...
OH, UH...
...THE BRAID WAS GETTING IN THE WAY. AND I NEEDED A **CHANGE**, Y'KNOW?
I DON'T THINK WE CAN CUT THROUGH YOURS, PIPSQUEAK.
RUFFLE
AWW!
HE'S GONNA HELP! AND HE SAID HE'D--
BING!
THERE! HE JUST SENT OVER HIS **CREDIT CARD.** I CAN BUY THE TICKETS ONLINE!
GREAT JOB, NEWT!
THERE'S A BUS IN A HALF HOUR...
BUT WE'RE GONNA NEED SOME **DISGUISES**.

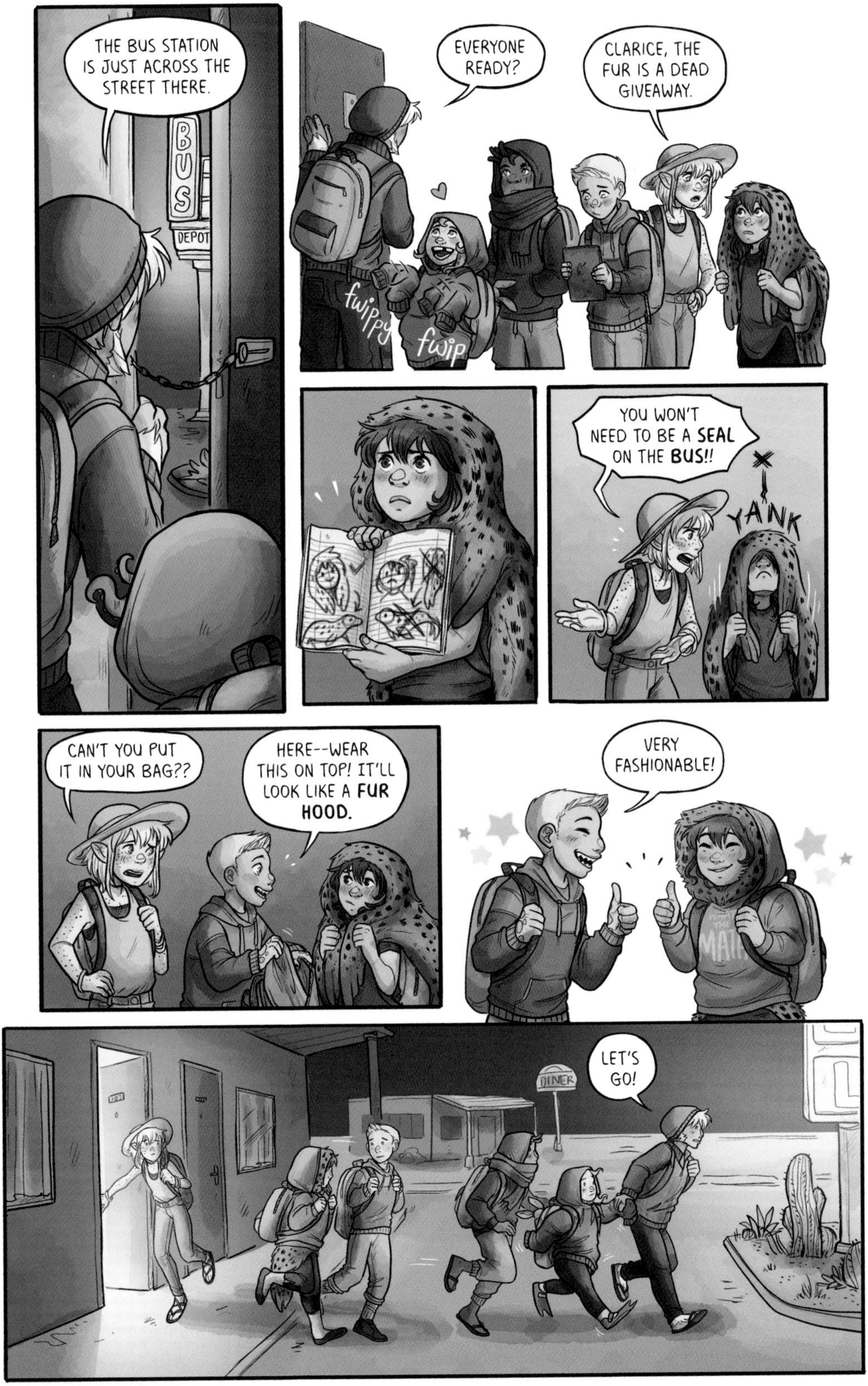
THE BUS STATION IS JUST ACROSS THE STREET THERE.
BUS
DEPOT
EVERYONE READY?
CLARICE, THE FUR IS A DEAD GIVEAWAY.
fwippy
fwip
YOU WON'T NEED TO BE A SEAL ON THE BUS!!
YANK
CAN'T YOU PUT IT IN YOUR BAG??
HERE--WEAR THIS ON TOP! IT'LL LOOK LIKE A FUR HOOD.
VERY FASHIONABLE!
DINER
LET'S GO!

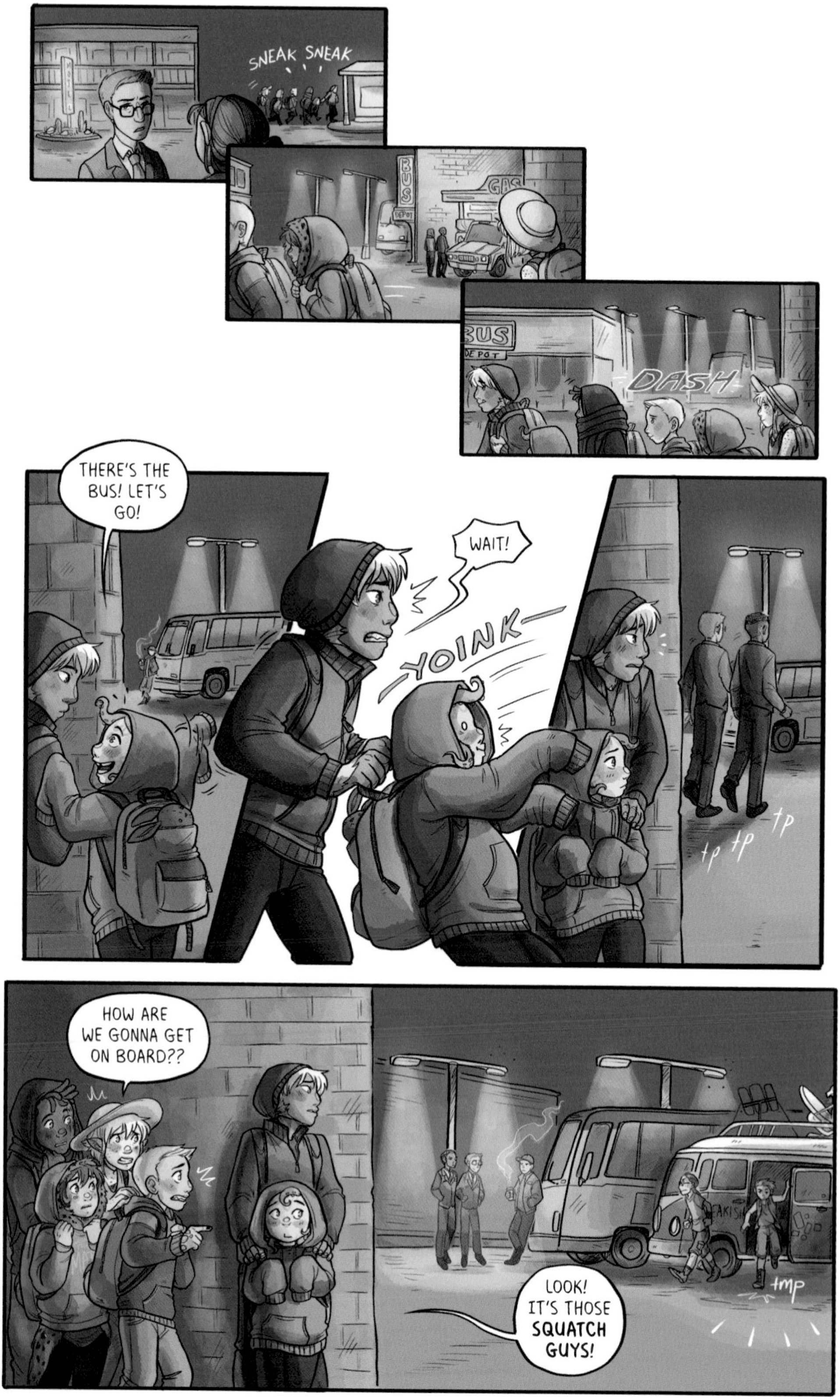
SNEAK SNEAK
BUS
DEPOT
GAS
DASH
THERE'S THE BUS! LET'S GO!
WAIT!
YOINK
tp tp tp
HOW ARE WE GONNA GET ON BOARD??
LOOK! IT'S THOSE **SQUATCH GUYS!**
tmp

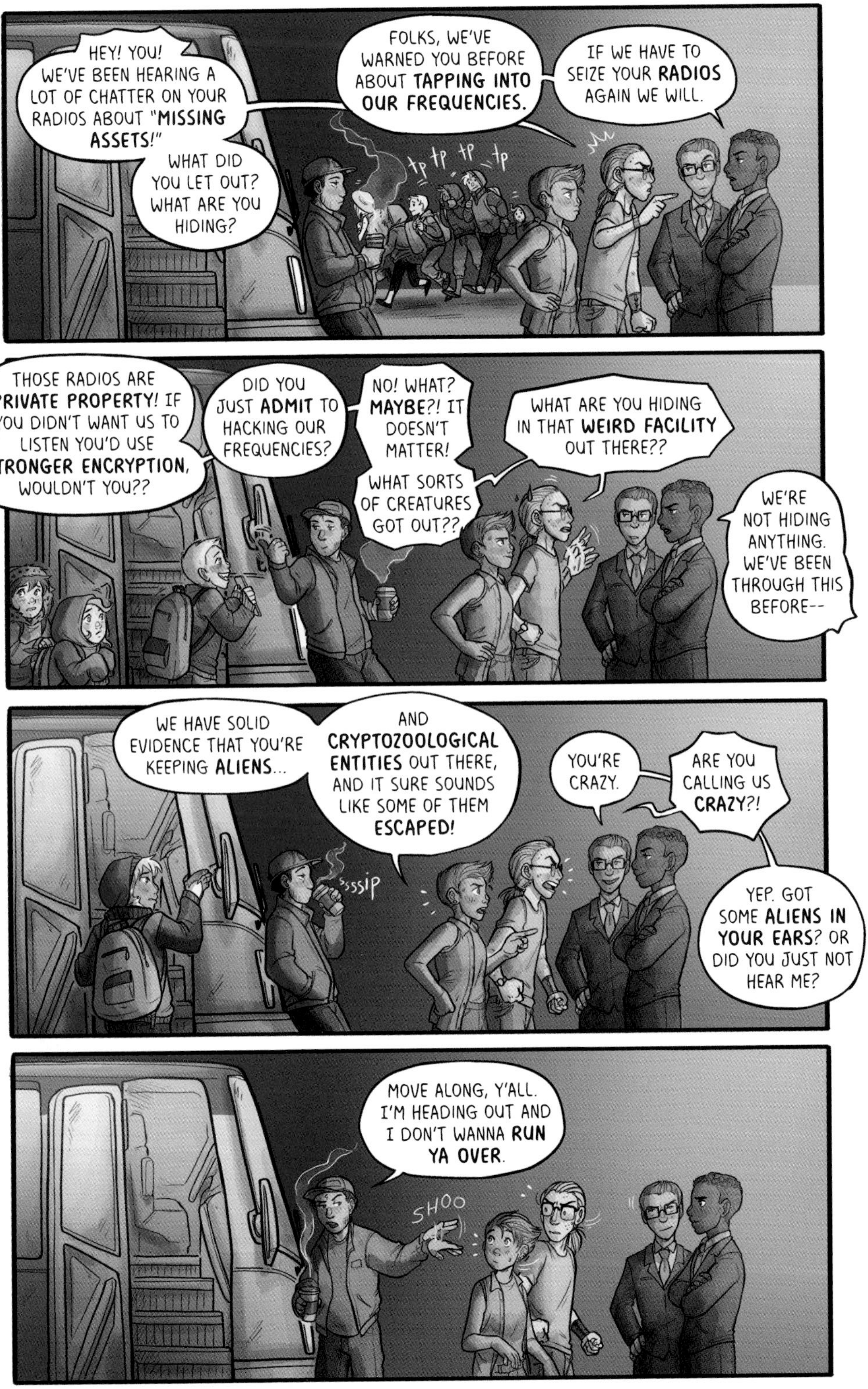
HEY! YOU! WE'VE BEEN HEARING A LOT OF CHATTER ON YOUR RADIOS ABOUT "MISSING ASSETS!"
WHAT DID YOU LET OUT? WHAT ARE YOU HIDING?
FOLKS, WE'VE WARNED YOU BEFORE ABOUT TAPPING INTO OUR FREQUENCIES.
IF WE HAVE TO SEIZE YOUR RADIOS AGAIN WE WILL.
tp tp tp tp
THOSE RADIOS ARE PRIVATE PROPERTY! IF YOU DIDN'T WANT US TO LISTEN YOU'D USE STRONGER ENCRYPTION, WOULDN'T YOU??
DID YOU JUST ADMIT TO HACKING OUR FREQUENCIES?
NO! WHAT? MAYBE?! IT DOESN'T MATTER!
WHAT SORTS OF CREATURES GOT OUT??
WHAT ARE YOU HIDING IN THAT WEIRD FACILITY OUT THERE??
WE'RE NOT HIDING ANYTHING. WE'VE BEEN THROUGH THIS BEFORE--
WE HAVE SOLID EVIDENCE THAT YOU'RE KEEPING ALIENS...
AND CRYPTOZOOLOGICAL ENTITIES OUT THERE, AND IT SURE SOUNDS LIKE SOME OF THEM ESCAPED!
sssSIP
YOU'RE CRAZY.
ARE YOU CALLING US CRAZY?!
YEP. GOT SOME ALIENS IN YOUR EARS? OR DID YOU JUST NOT HEAR ME?
MOVE ALONG, Y'ALL. I'M HEADING OUT AND I DON'T WANNA RUN YA OVER.
SHOO

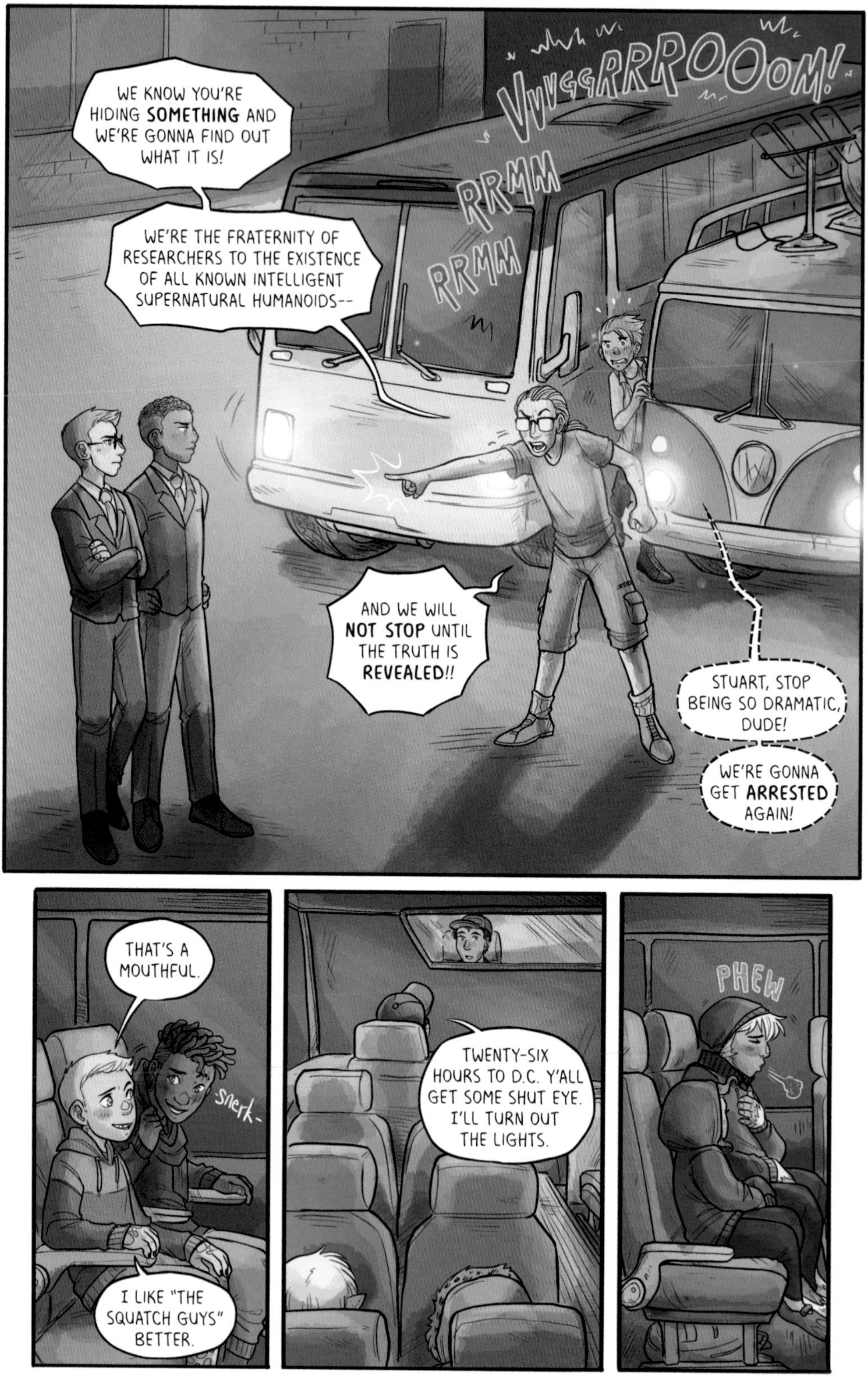
VVVGGRRROOoOM!
RRMM
RRMM
WE KNOW YOU'RE HIDING **SOMETHING** AND WE'RE GONNA FIND OUT WHAT IT IS!
WE'RE THE FRATERNITY OF RESEARCHERS TO THE EXISTENCE OF ALL KNOWN INTELLIGENT SUPERNATURAL HUMANOIDS--
AND WE WILL **NOT STOP** UNTIL THE TRUTH IS **REVEALED**!!
STUART, STOP BEING SO DRAMATIC, DUDE!
WE'RE GONNA GET **ARRESTED** AGAIN!
THAT'S A MOUTHFUL.
-SNERK-
I LIKE "THE SQUATCH GUYS" BETTER.
TWENTY-SIX HOURS TO D.C. Y'ALL GET SOME SHUT EYE. I'LL TURN OUT THE LIGHTS.
PHEW

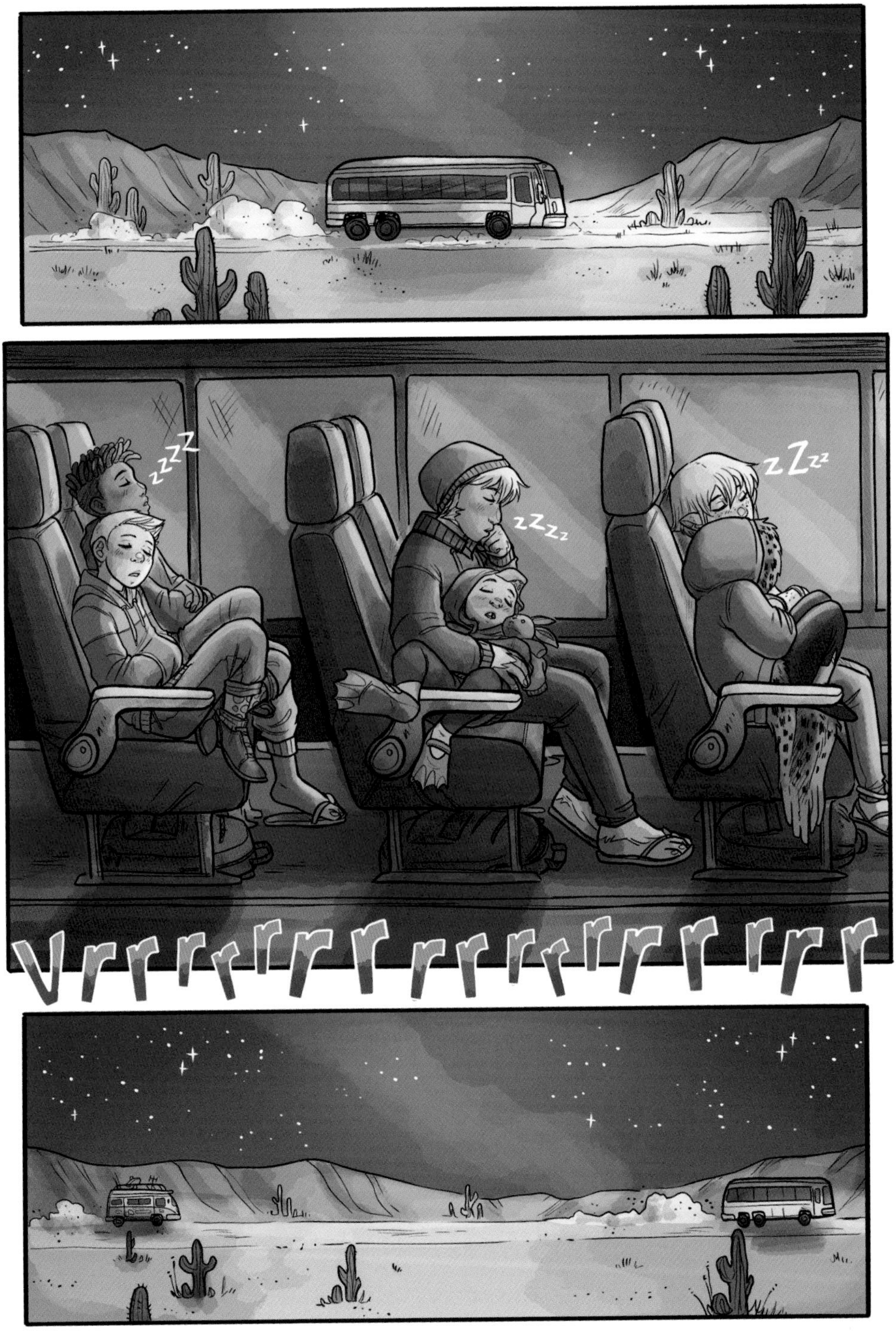
zzzZ
zZzz
zZzz
Vrrrrrrrrrrrrrrrrr

CHAPTER FIVE

HIGHLY IRREGULAR

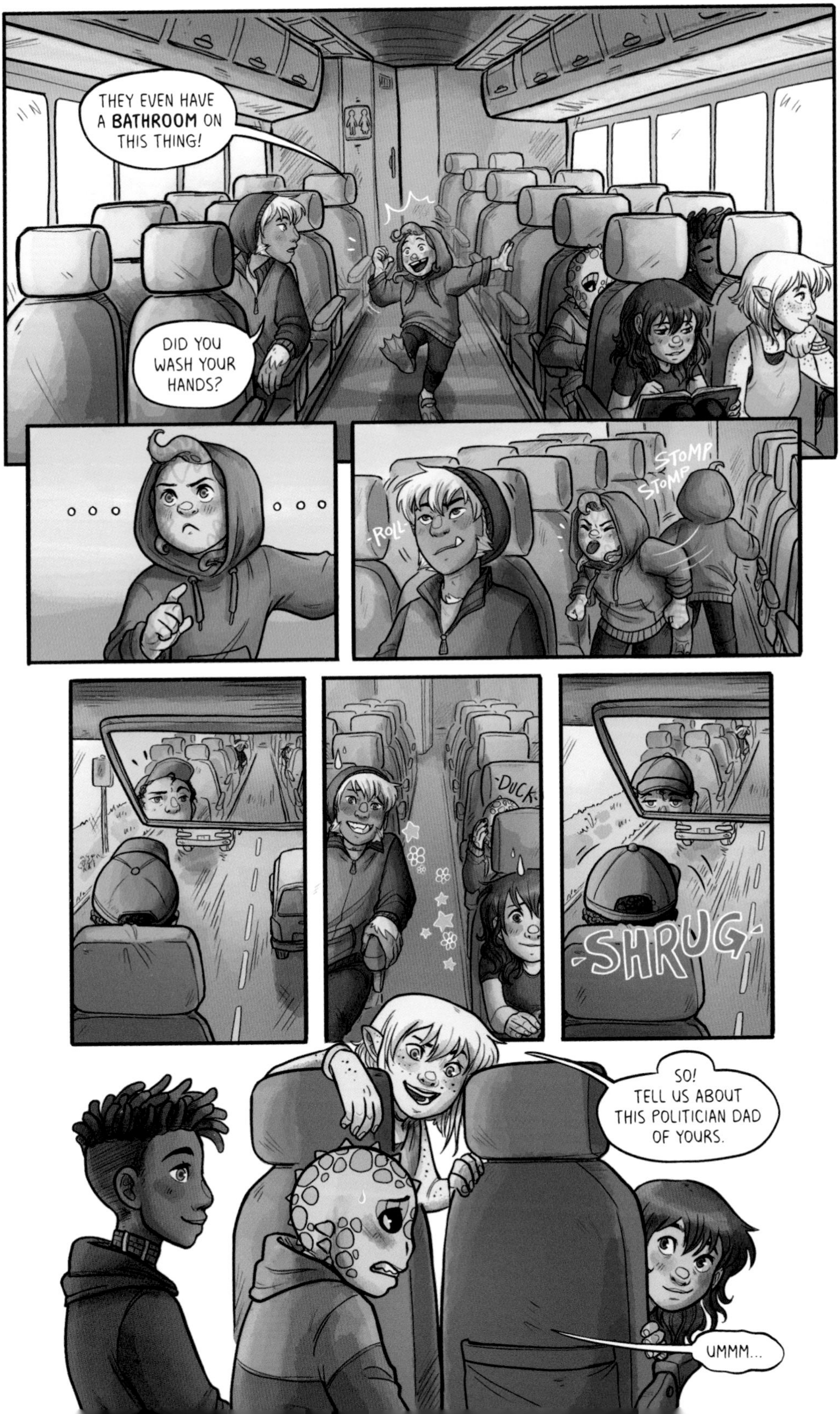
THEY EVEN HAVE A BATHROOM ON THIS THING!
DID YOU WASH YOUR HANDS?
ROLL
STOMP
STOMP
DUCK
SHRUG
SO! TELL US ABOUT THIS POLITICIAN DAD OF YOURS.
UMMM...

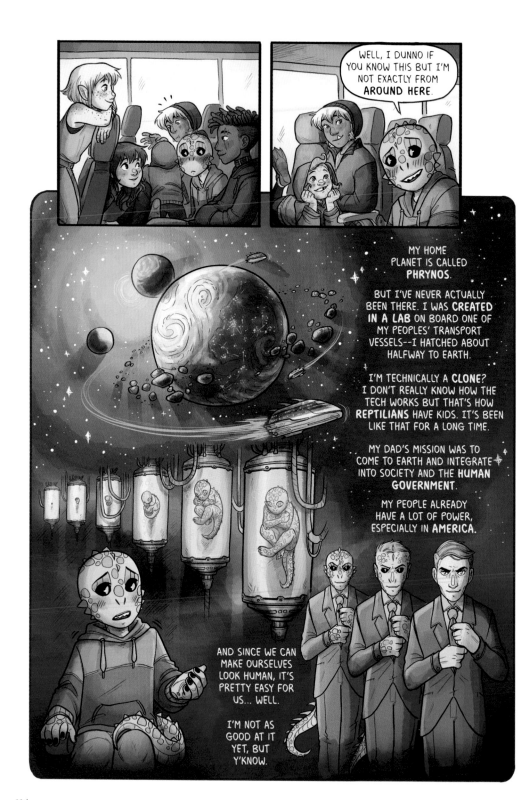

WELL, I DUNNO IF YOU KNOW THIS BUT I'M NOT EXACTLY FROM **AROUND HERE**.

MY HOME PLANET IS CALLED **PHRYNOS**.

BUT I'VE NEVER ACTUALLY BEEN THERE. I WAS **CREATED IN A LAB** ON BOARD ONE OF MY PEOPLES' TRANSPORT VESSELS--I HATCHED ABOUT HALFWAY TO EARTH.

I'M TECHNICALLY A **CLONE**? I DON'T REALLY KNOW HOW THE TECH WORKS BUT THAT'S HOW **REPTILIANS** HAVE KIDS. IT'S BEEN LIKE THAT FOR A LONG TIME.

MY DAD'S MISSION WAS TO COME TO EARTH AND INTEGRATE INTO SOCIETY AND THE **HUMAN GOVERNMENT**.

MY PEOPLE ALREADY HAVE A LOT OF POWER, ESPECIALLY IN **AMERICA**.

AND SINCE WE CAN MAKE OURSELVES LOOK HUMAN, IT'S PRETTY EASY FOR US... WELL.

I'M NOT AS GOOD AT IT YET, BUT Y'KNOW.

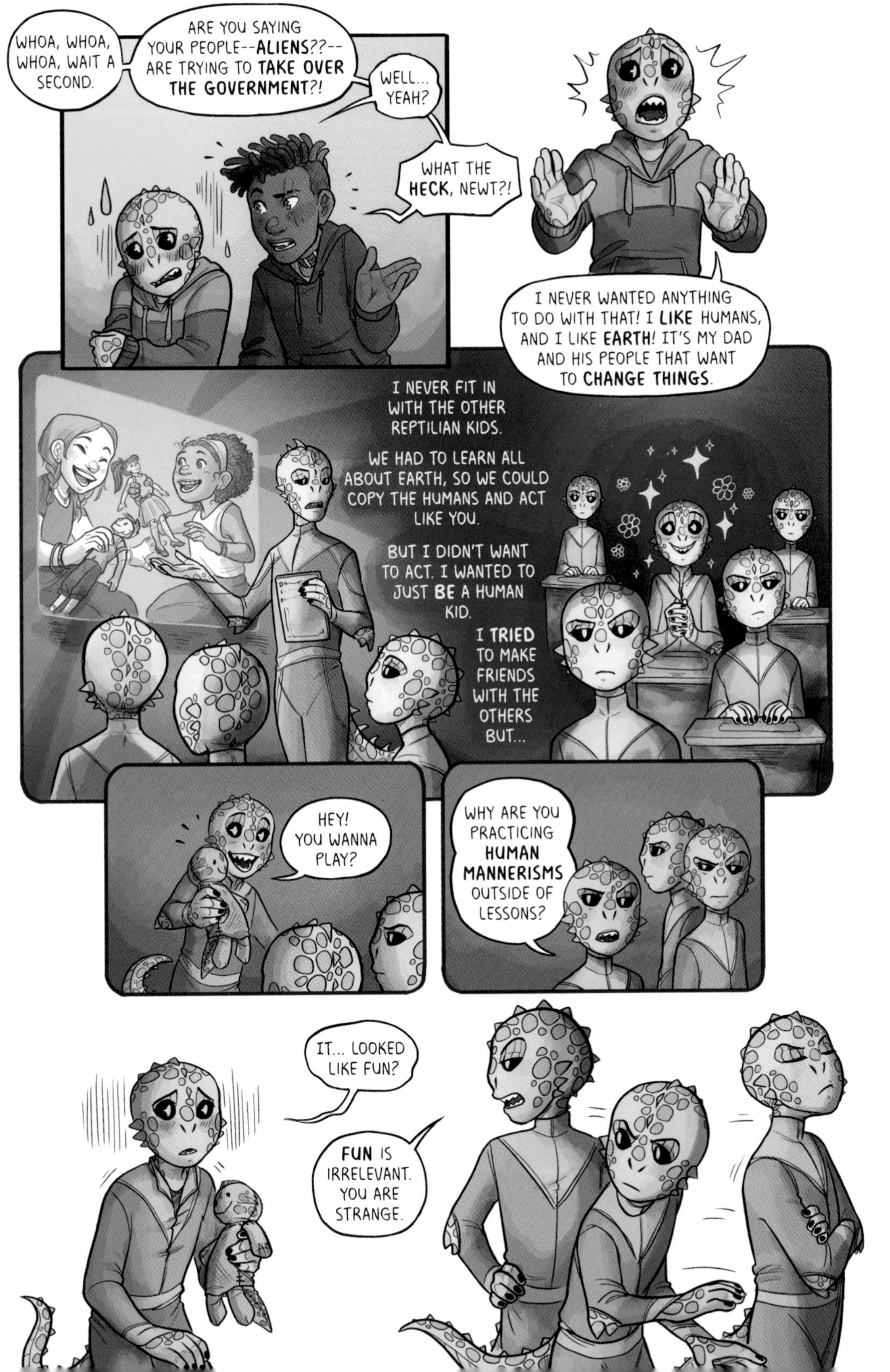
WHOA, WHOA, WHOA, WAIT A SECOND.
ARE YOU SAYING YOUR PEOPLE--ALIENS??--ARE TRYING TO TAKE OVER THE GOVERNMENT?!
WELL... YEAH?
WHAT THE HECK, NEWT?!
I NEVER WANTED ANYTHING TO DO WITH THAT! I LIKE HUMANS, AND I LIKE EARTH! IT'S MY DAD AND HIS PEOPLE THAT WANT TO CHANGE THINGS.
I NEVER FIT IN WITH THE OTHER REPTILIAN KIDS.
WE HAD TO LEARN ALL ABOUT EARTH, SO WE COULD COPY THE HUMANS AND ACT LIKE YOU.
BUT I DIDN'T WANT TO ACT. I WANTED TO JUST BE A HUMAN KID.
I TRIED TO MAKE FRIENDS WITH THE OTHERS BUT...
HEY! YOU WANNA PLAY?
WHY ARE YOU PRACTICING HUMAN MANNERISMS OUTSIDE OF LESSONS?
IT... LOOKED LIKE FUN?
FUN IS IRRELEVANT. YOU ARE STRANGE.

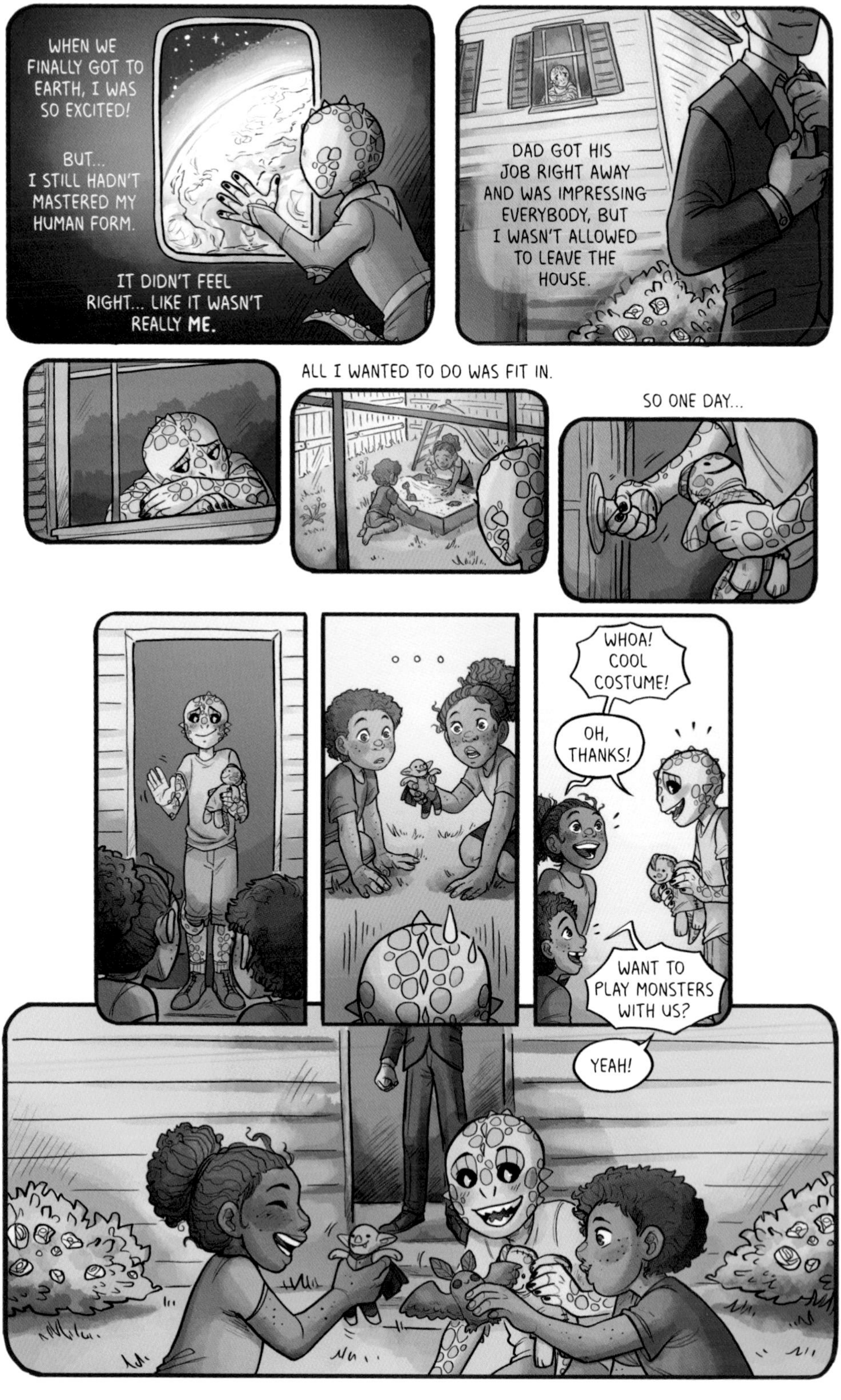
WHEN WE FINALLY GOT TO EARTH, I WAS SO EXCITED!
BUT... I STILL HADN'T MASTERED MY HUMAN FORM.
IT DIDN'T FEEL RIGHT... LIKE IT WASN'T REALLY ME.
DAD GOT HIS JOB RIGHT AWAY AND WAS IMPRESSING EVERYBODY, BUT I WASN'T ALLOWED TO LEAVE THE HOUSE.
ALL I WANTED TO DO WAS FIT IN.
SO ONE DAY...
...
WHOA! COOL COSTUME!
OH, THANKS!
WANT TO PLAY MONSTERS WITH US?
YEAH!

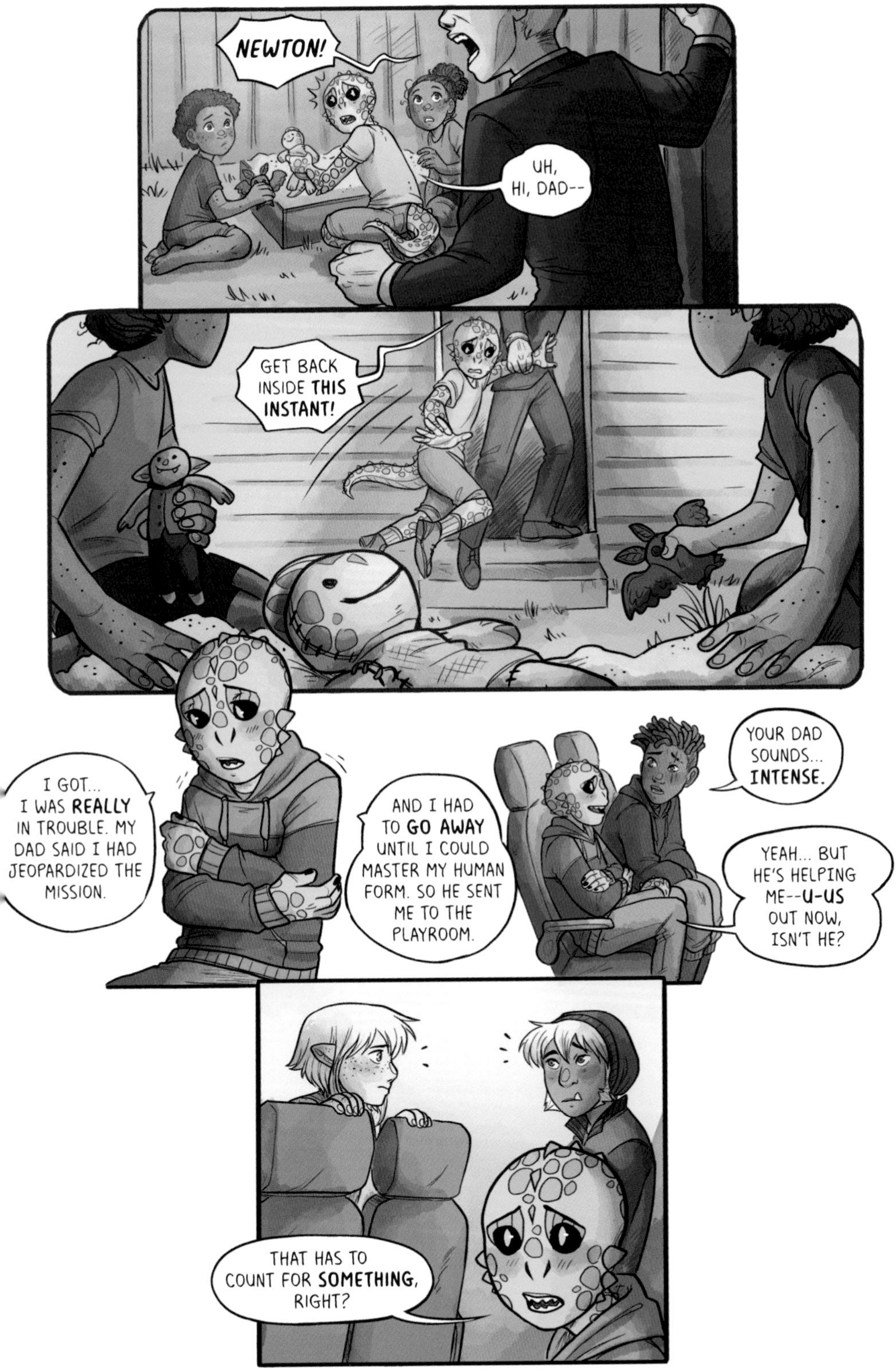
NEWTON!
UH, HI, DAD--
GET BACK INSIDE THIS INSTANT!
I GOT... I WAS REALLY IN TROUBLE. MY DAD SAID I HAD JEOPARDIZED THE MISSION.
AND I HAD TO GO AWAY UNTIL I COULD MASTER MY HUMAN FORM. SO HE SENT ME TO THE PLAYROOM.
YOUR DAD SOUNDS... INTENSE.
YEAH... BUT HE'S HELPING ME--U-US OUT NOW, ISN'T HE?
THAT HAS TO COUNT FOR SOMETHING, RIGHT?

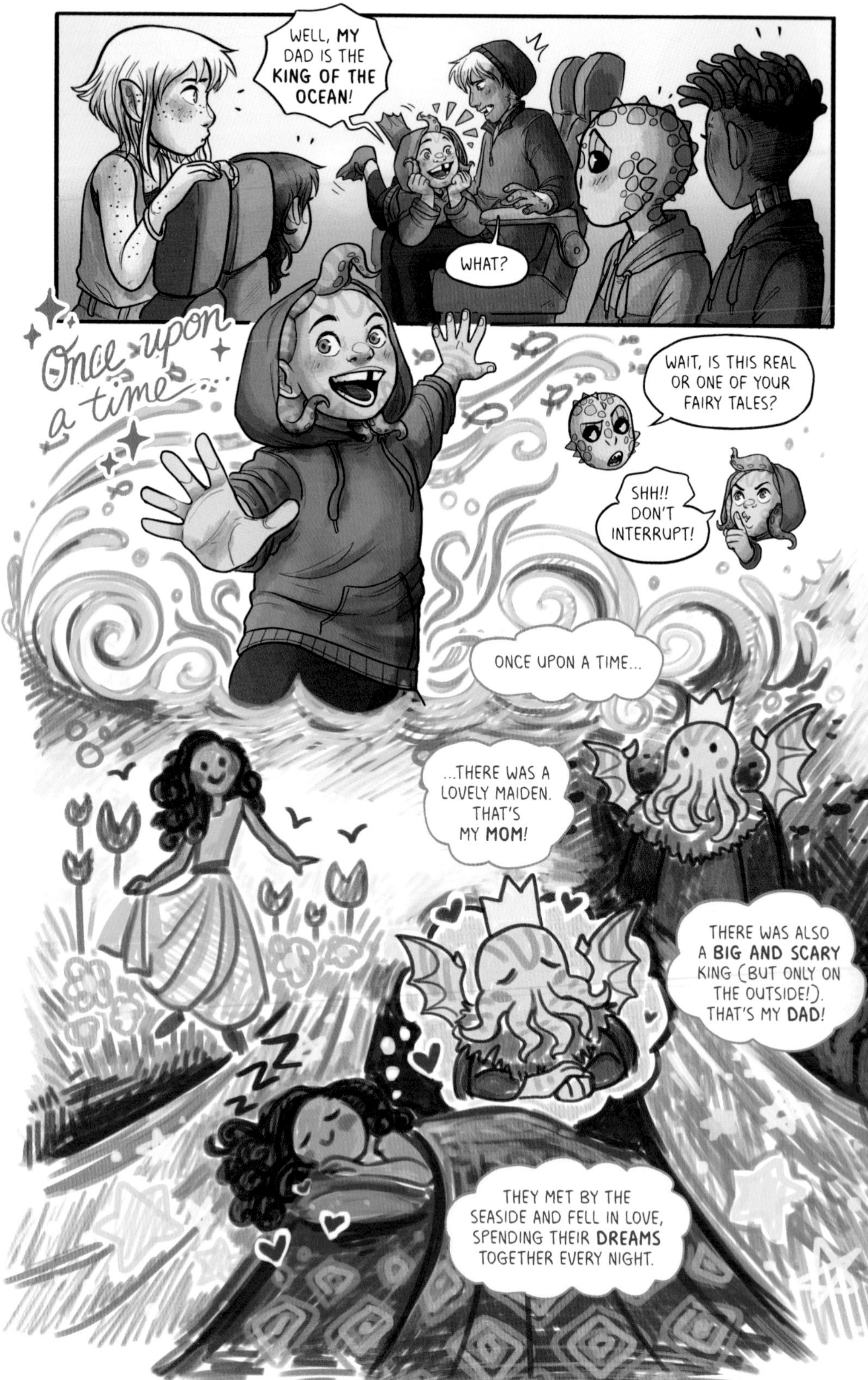
WELL, MY DAD IS THE KING OF THE OCEAN!
WHAT?
Once upon a time
WAIT, IS THIS REAL OR ONE OF YOUR FAIRY TALES?
SHH!! DON'T INTERRUPT!
ONCE UPON A TIME...
...THERE WAS A LOVELY MAIDEN. THAT'S MY MOM!
THERE WAS ALSO A BIG AND SCARY KING (BUT ONLY ON THE OUTSIDE!). THAT'S MY DAD!
THEY MET BY THE SEASIDE AND FELL IN LOVE, SPENDING THEIR DREAMS TOGETHER EVERY NIGHT.

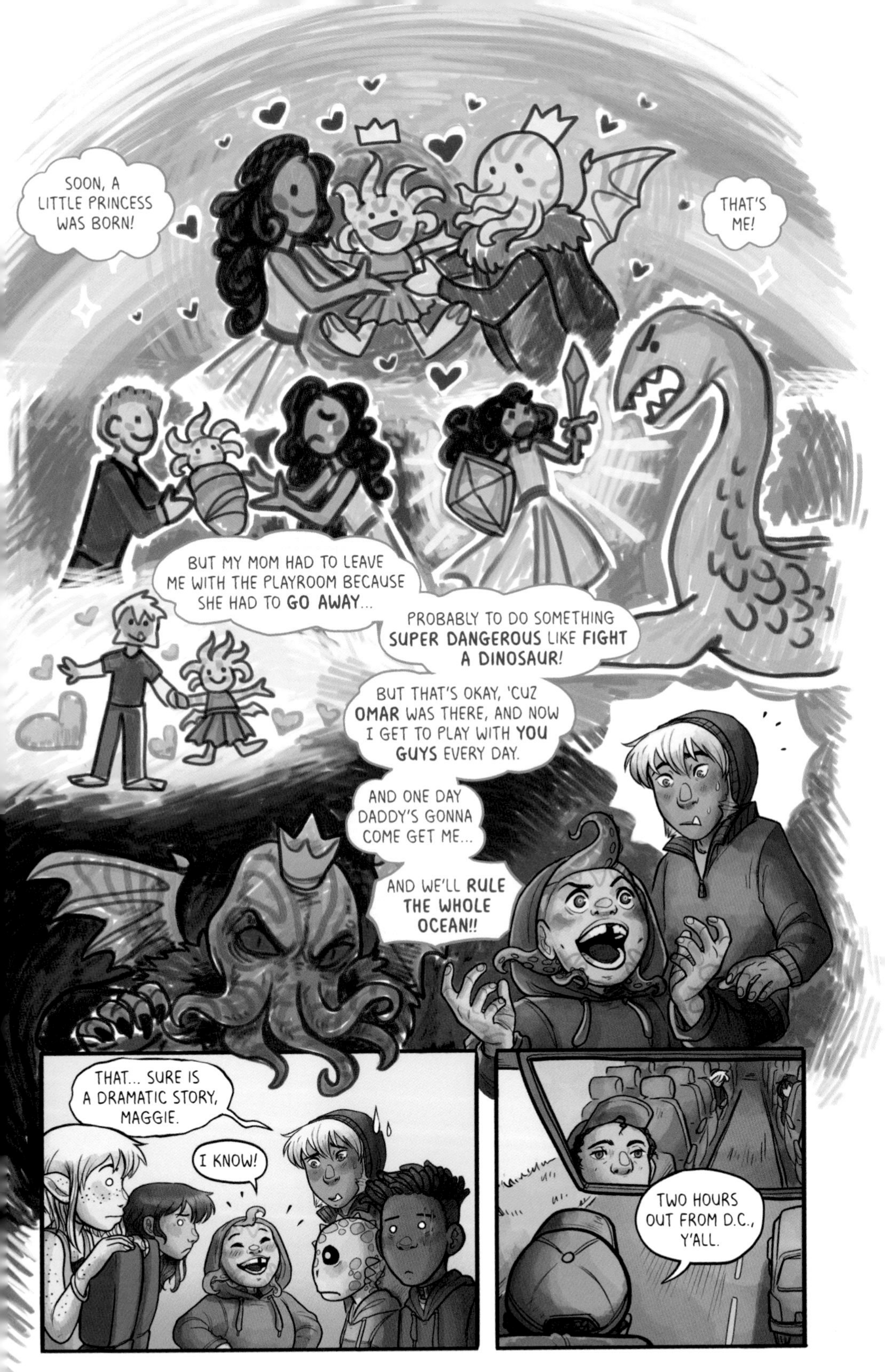
SOON, A LITTLE PRINCESS WAS BORN!
THAT'S ME!
BUT MY MOM HAD TO LEAVE ME WITH THE PLAYROOM BECAUSE SHE HAD TO GO AWAY...
PROBABLY TO DO SOMETHING SUPER DANGEROUS LIKE FIGHT A DINOSAUR!
BUT THAT'S OKAY, 'CUZ OMAR WAS THERE, AND NOW I GET TO PLAY WITH YOU GUYS EVERY DAY.
AND ONE DAY DADDY'S GONNA COME GET ME...
AND WE'LL RULE THE WHOLE OCEAN!!
THAT... SURE IS A DRAMATIC STORY, MAGGIE.
I KNOW!
TWO HOURS OUT FROM D.C., Y'ALL.

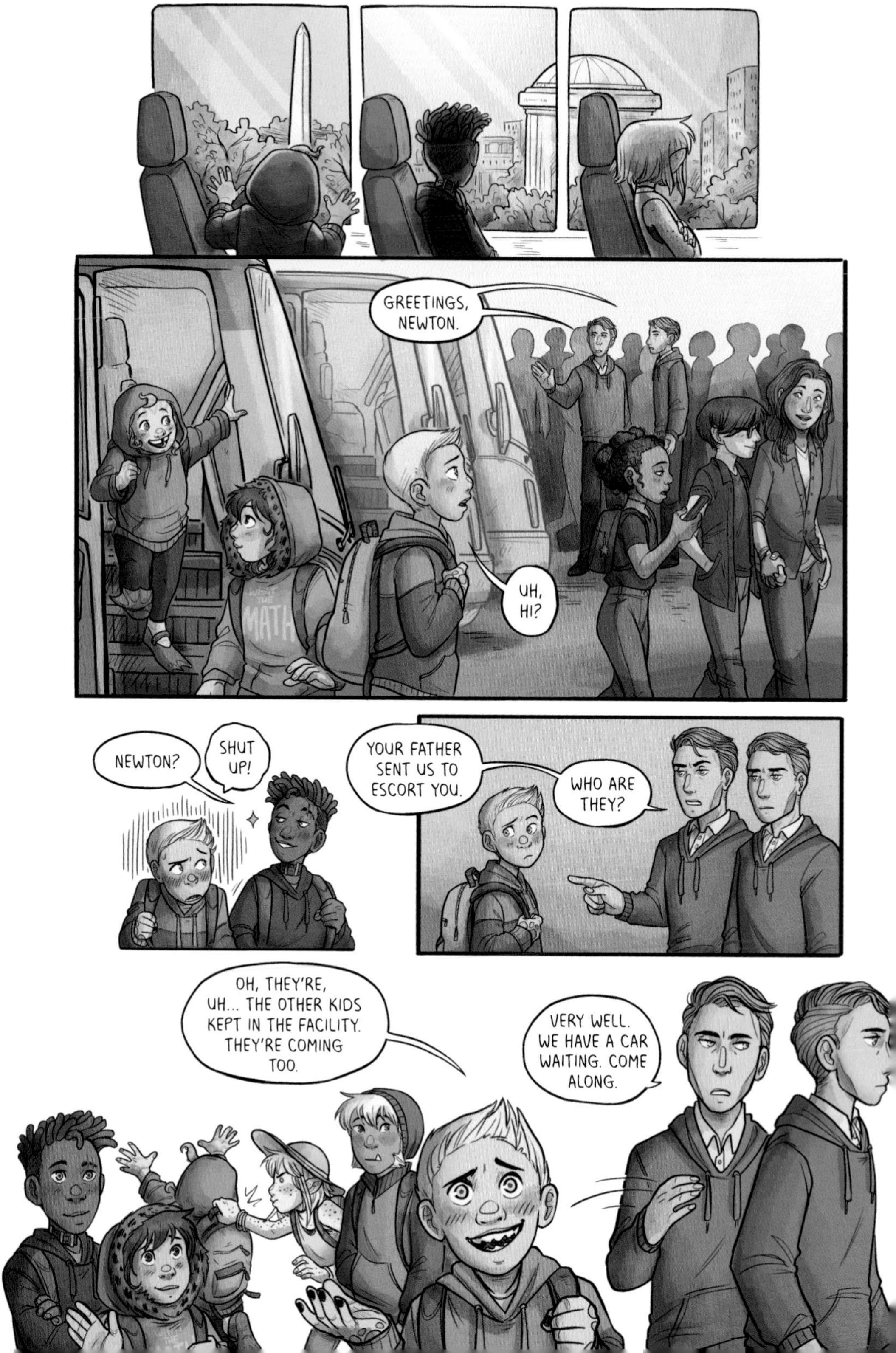
GREETINGS, NEWTON.
MATH
UH, HI?
NEWTON?
SHUT UP!
YOUR FATHER SENT US TO ESCORT YOU.
WHO ARE THEY?
OH, THEY'RE, UH... THE OTHER KIDS KEPT IN THE FACILITY. THEY'RE COMING TOO.
VERY WELL. WE HAVE A CAR WAITING. COME ALONG.

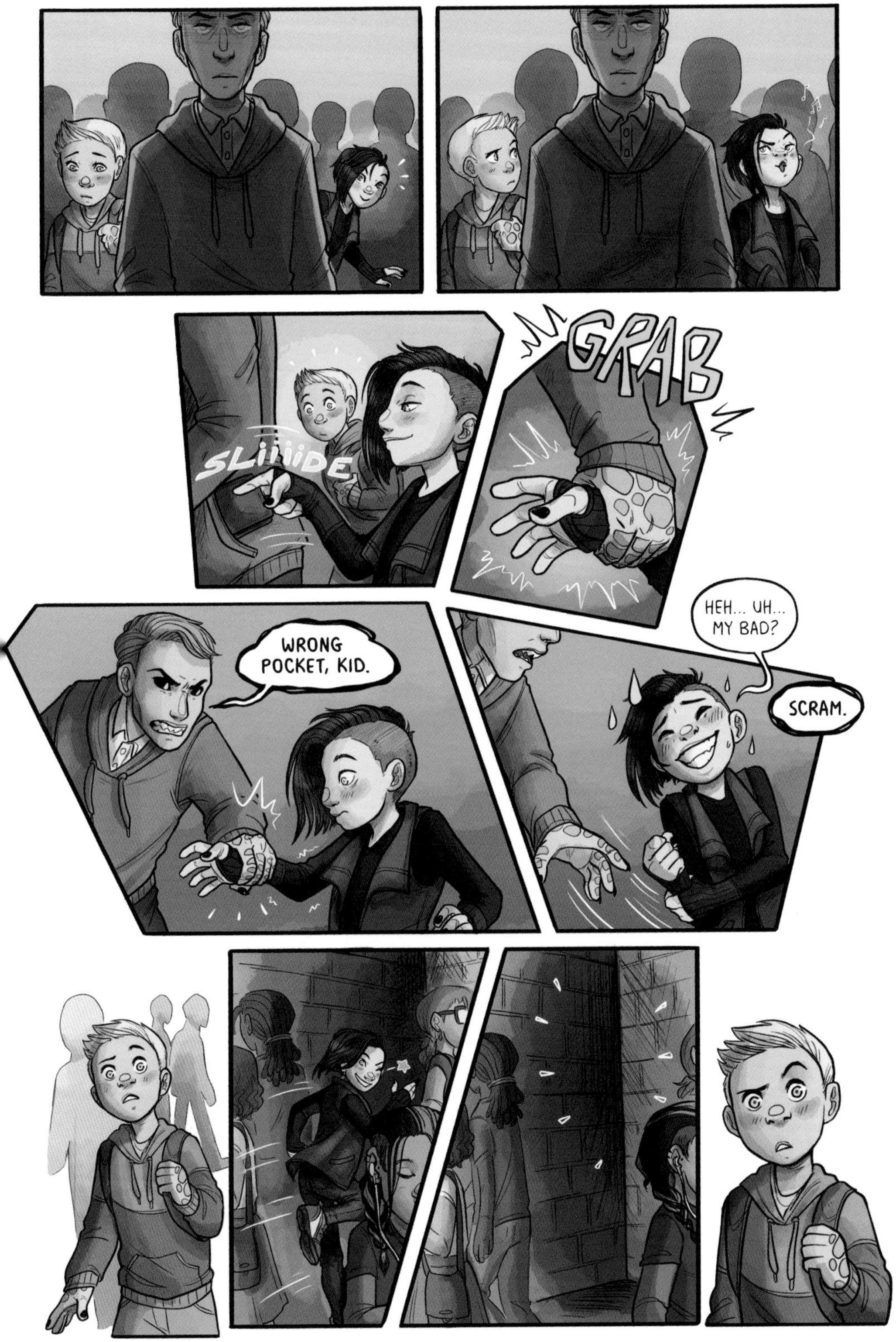
SLIIIIDE
GRAB
WRONG POCKET, KID.
HEH... UH... MY BAD?
SCRAM.

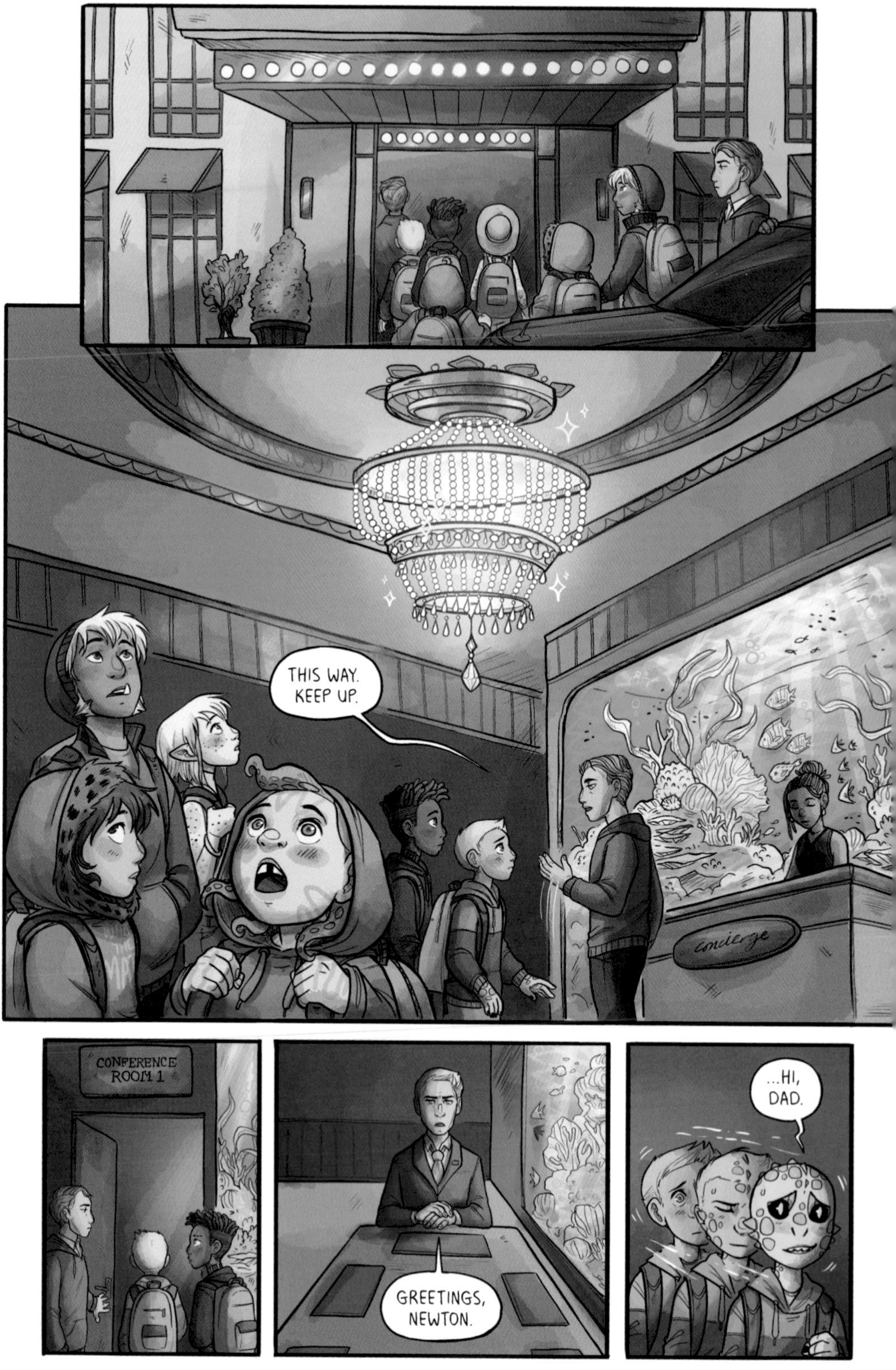
THIS WAY. KEEP UP.
concierge
CONFERENCE ROOM 1
GREETINGS, NEWTON.
...HI, DAD.

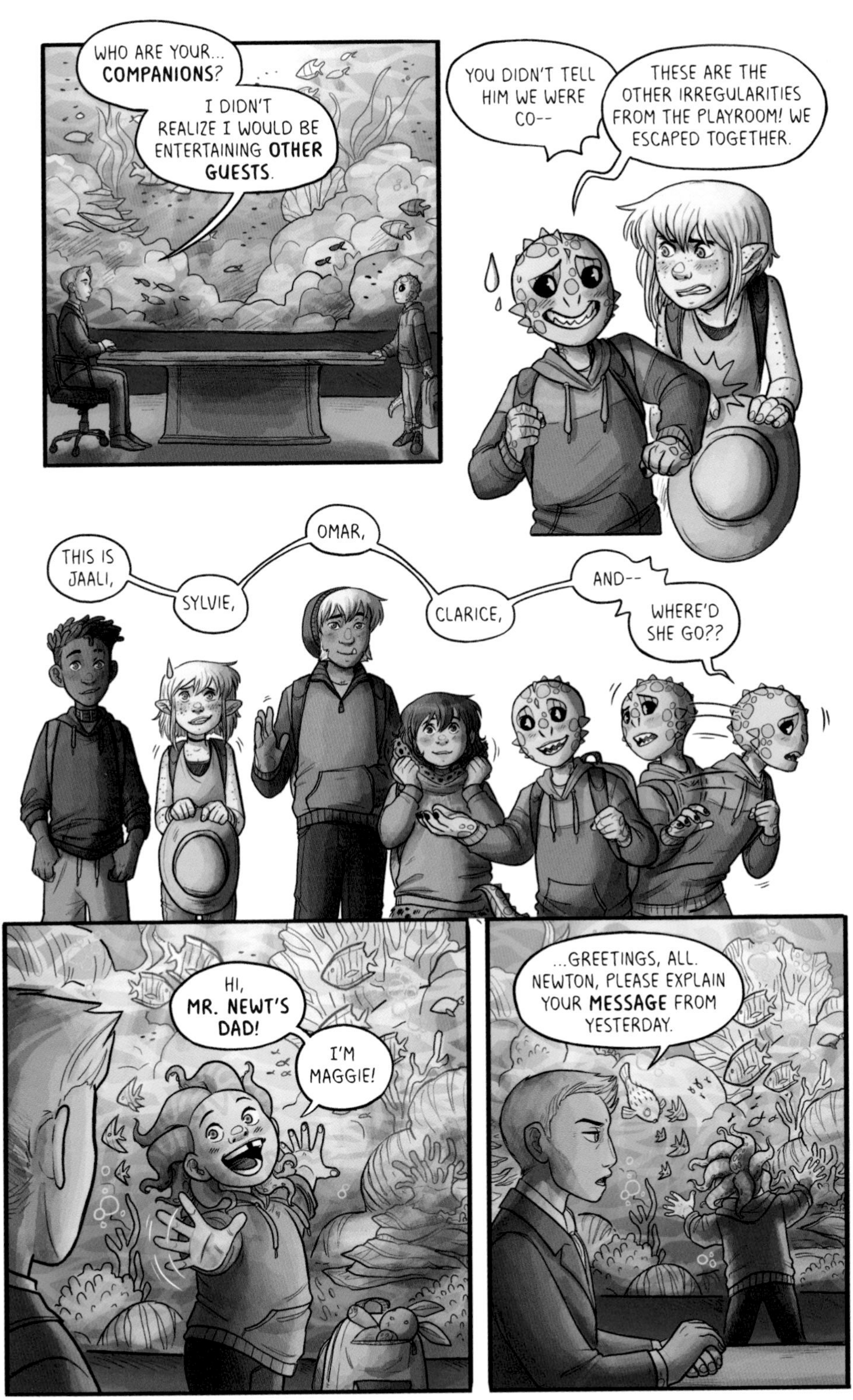
WHO ARE YOUR... **COMPANIONS**?
I DIDN'T REALIZE I WOULD BE ENTERTAINING **OTHER GUESTS**.
YOU DIDN'T TELL HIM WE WERE CO--
THESE ARE THE OTHER IRREGULARITIES FROM THE PLAYROOM! WE ESCAPED TOGETHER.
THIS IS JAALI,
SYLVIE,
OMAR,
CLARICE,
AND--
WHERE'D SHE GO??
HI, **MR. NEWT'S DAD!**
I'M MAGGIE!
...GREETINGS, ALL. NEWTON, PLEASE EXPLAIN YOUR **MESSAGE** FROM YESTERDAY.

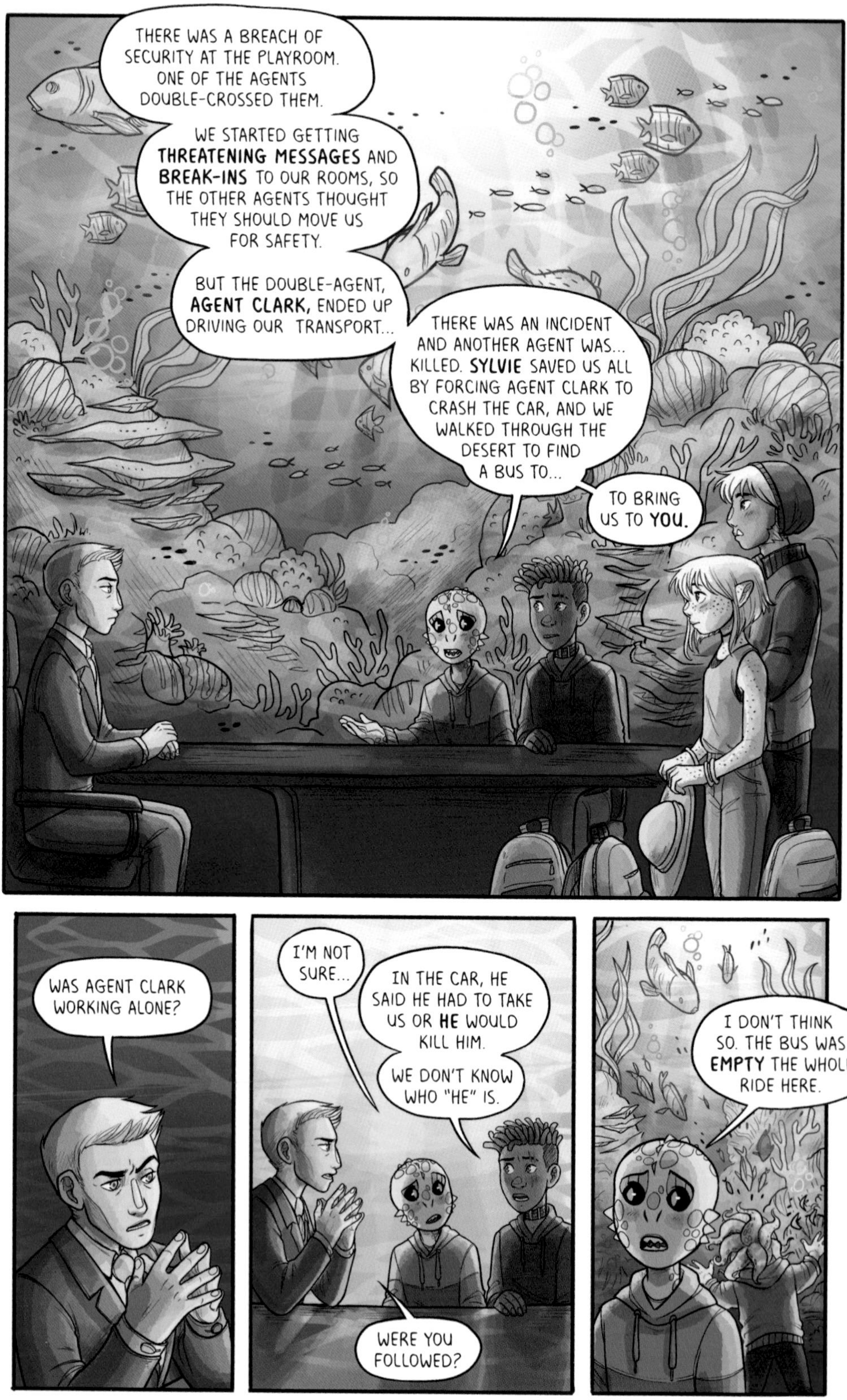
THERE WAS A BREACH OF SECURITY AT THE PLAYROOM. ONE OF THE AGENTS DOUBLE-CROSSED THEM.
WE STARTED GETTING **THREATENING MESSAGES** AND **BREAK-INS** TO OUR ROOMS, SO THE OTHER AGENTS THOUGHT THEY SHOULD MOVE US FOR SAFETY.
BUT THE DOUBLE-AGENT, **AGENT CLARK,** ENDED UP DRIVING OUR TRANSPORT...
THERE WAS AN INCIDENT AND ANOTHER AGENT WAS... KILLED. **SYLVIE** SAVED US ALL BY FORCING AGENT CLARK TO CRASH THE CAR, AND WE WALKED THROUGH THE DESERT TO FIND A BUS TO...
TO BRING US TO **YOU.**
WAS AGENT CLARK WORKING ALONE?
I'M NOT SURE...
IN THE CAR, HE SAID HE HAD TO TAKE US OR **HE** WOULD KILL HIM.
WE DON'T KNOW WHO "HE" IS.
WERE YOU FOLLOWED?
I DON'T THINK SO. THE BUS WAS **EMPTY** THE WHOLE RIDE HERE.

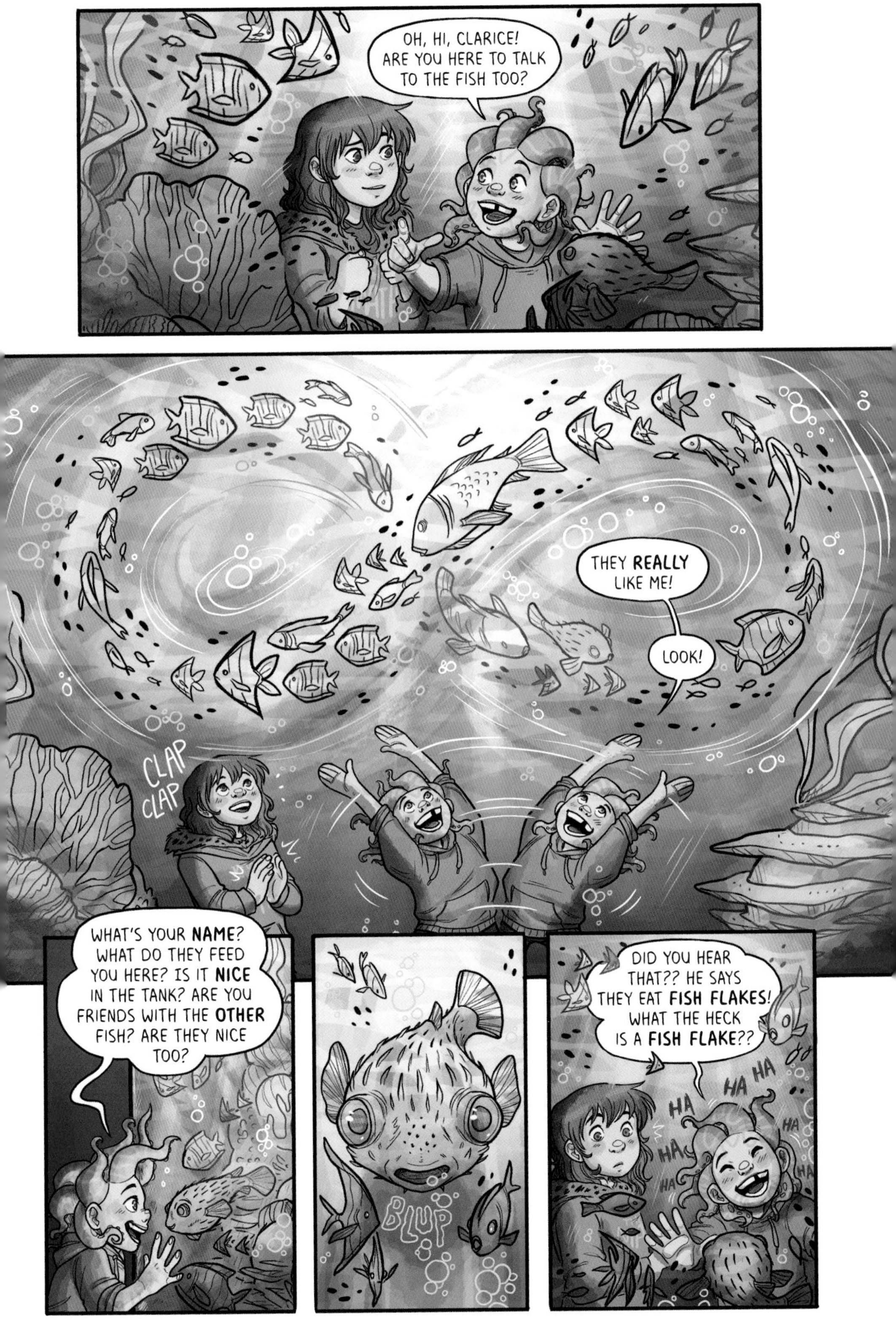

OH, HI, CLARICE! ARE YOU HERE TO TALK TO THE FISH TOO?
THEY **REALLY** LIKE ME!
LOOK!
CLAP CLAP
WHAT'S YOUR **NAME**? WHAT DO THEY FEED YOU HERE? IS IT **NICE** IN THE TANK? ARE YOU FRIENDS WITH THE **OTHER** FISH? ARE THEY NICE TOO?
BLUP
DID YOU HEAR THAT?? HE SAYS THEY EAT **FISH FLAKES**! WHAT THE HECK IS A **FISH FLAKE**??
HA HA HA HA HA HA HA

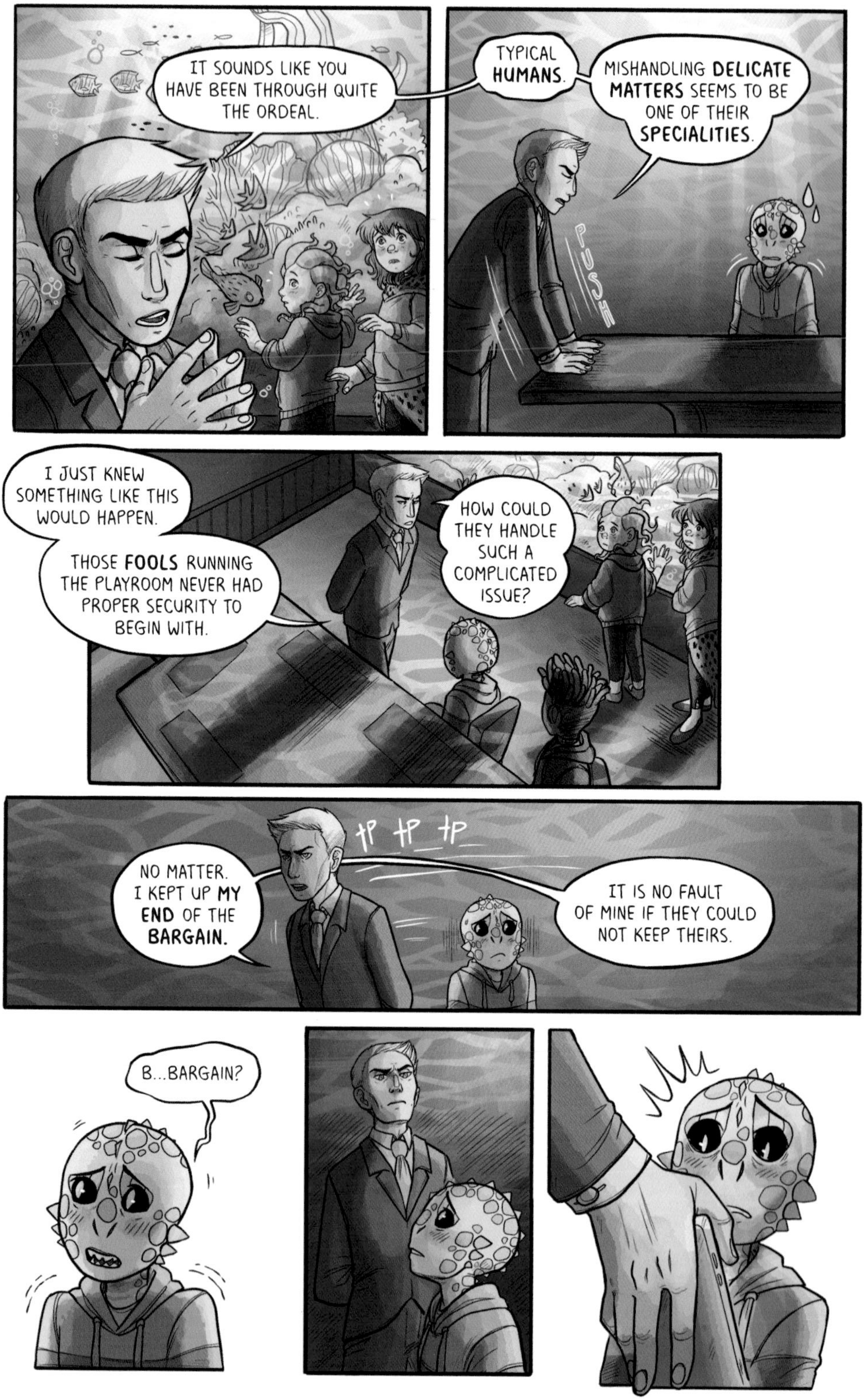
IT SOUNDS LIKE YOU HAVE BEEN THROUGH QUITE THE ORDEAL.
TYPICAL HUMANS.
MISHANDLING DELICATE MATTERS SEEMS TO BE ONE OF THEIR SPECIALITIES.
PUSH
I JUST KNEW SOMETHING LIKE THIS WOULD HAPPEN.
THOSE FOOLS RUNNING THE PLAYROOM NEVER HAD PROPER SECURITY TO BEGIN WITH.
HOW COULD THEY HANDLE SUCH A COMPLICATED ISSUE?
TP TP TP
NO MATTER. I KEPT UP MY END OF THE BARGAIN.
IT IS NO FAULT OF MINE IF THEY COULD NOT KEEP THEIRS.
B...BARGAIN?

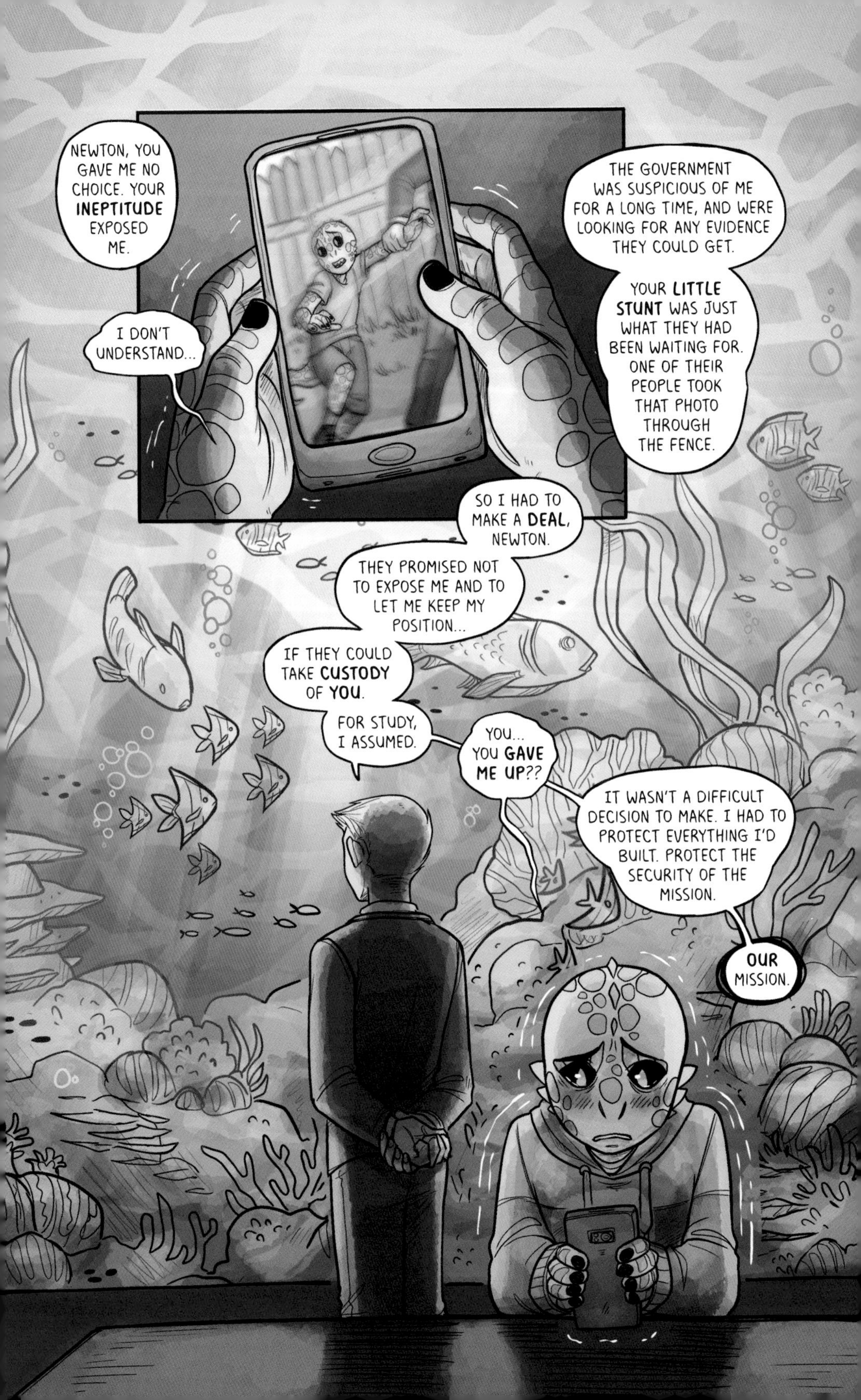
NEWTON, YOU GAVE ME NO CHOICE. YOUR **INEPTITUDE** EXPOSED ME.
THE GOVERNMENT WAS SUSPICIOUS OF ME FOR A LONG TIME, AND WERE LOOKING FOR ANY EVIDENCE THEY COULD GET.
YOUR **LITTLE STUNT** WAS JUST WHAT THEY HAD BEEN WAITING FOR. ONE OF THEIR PEOPLE TOOK THAT PHOTO THROUGH THE FENCE.
I DON'T UNDERSTAND...
SO I HAD TO MAKE A **DEAL**, NEWTON.
THEY PROMISED NOT TO EXPOSE ME AND TO LET ME KEEP MY POSITION...
IF THEY COULD TAKE **CUSTODY** OF **YOU**.
FOR STUDY, I ASSUMED.
YOU... YOU **GAVE ME UP**??
IT WASN'T A DIFFICULT DECISION TO MAKE. I HAD TO PROTECT EVERYTHING I'D BUILT. PROTECT THE SECURITY OF THE MISSION.
OUR MISSION.

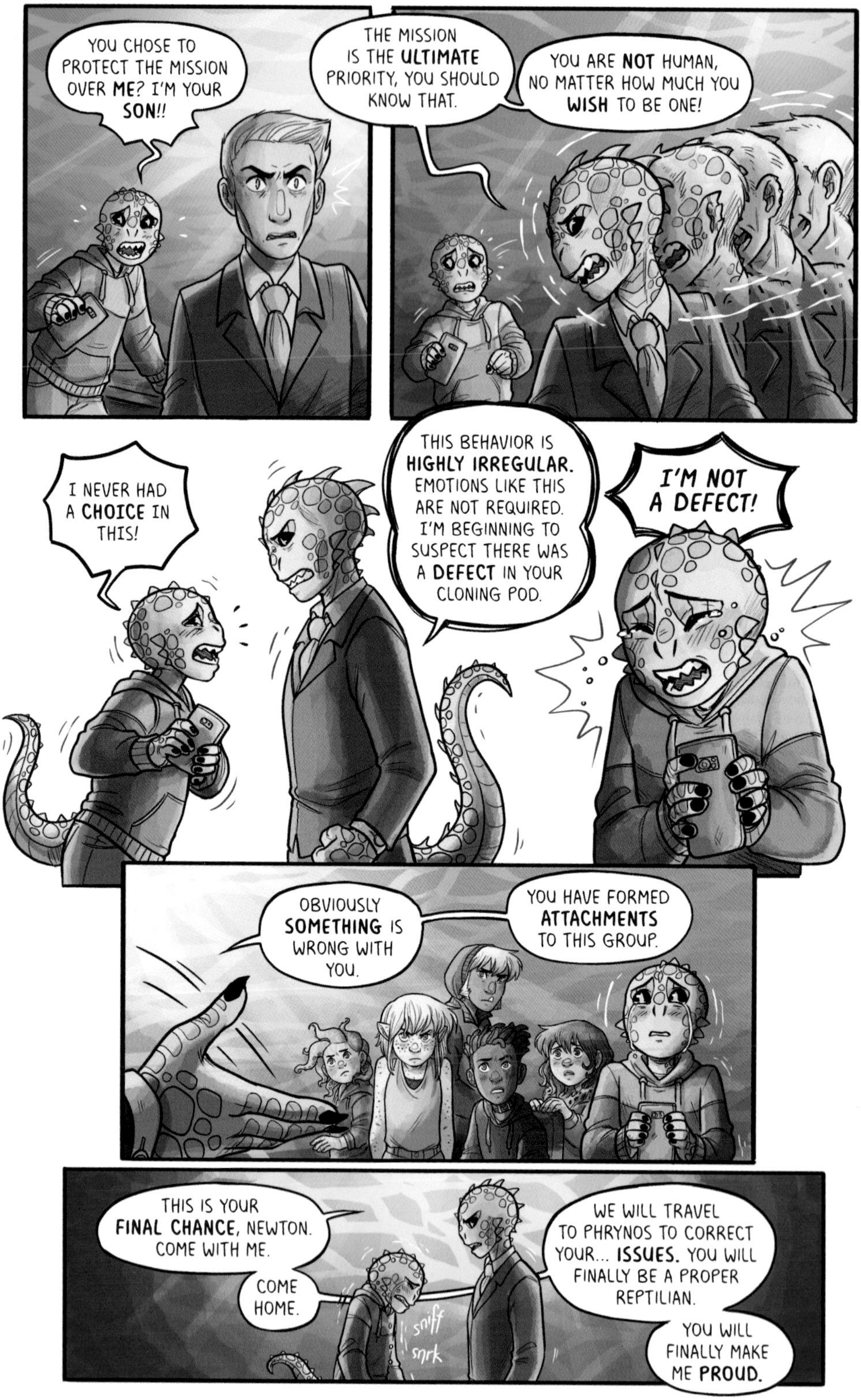
YOU CHOSE TO PROTECT THE MISSION OVER **ME**? I'M YOUR **SON**!!
THE MISSION IS THE **ULTIMATE** PRIORITY, YOU SHOULD KNOW THAT.
YOU ARE **NOT** HUMAN, NO MATTER HOW MUCH YOU **WISH** TO BE ONE!
I NEVER HAD A **CHOICE** IN THIS!
THIS BEHAVIOR IS **HIGHLY IRREGULAR.** EMOTIONS LIKE THIS ARE NOT REQUIRED. I'M BEGINNING TO SUSPECT THERE WAS A **DEFECT** IN YOUR CLONING POD.
I'M NOT A DEFECT!
YOU HAVE FORMED **ATTACHMENTS** TO THIS GROUP.
OBVIOUSLY **SOMETHING** IS WRONG WITH YOU.
THIS IS YOUR **FINAL CHANCE,** NEWTON. COME WITH ME.
COME HOME.
sniff
snrk
WE WILL TRAVEL TO PHRYNOS TO CORRECT YOUR... **ISSUES.** YOU WILL FINALLY BE A PROPER REPTILIAN.
YOU WILL FINALLY MAKE ME **PROUD.**

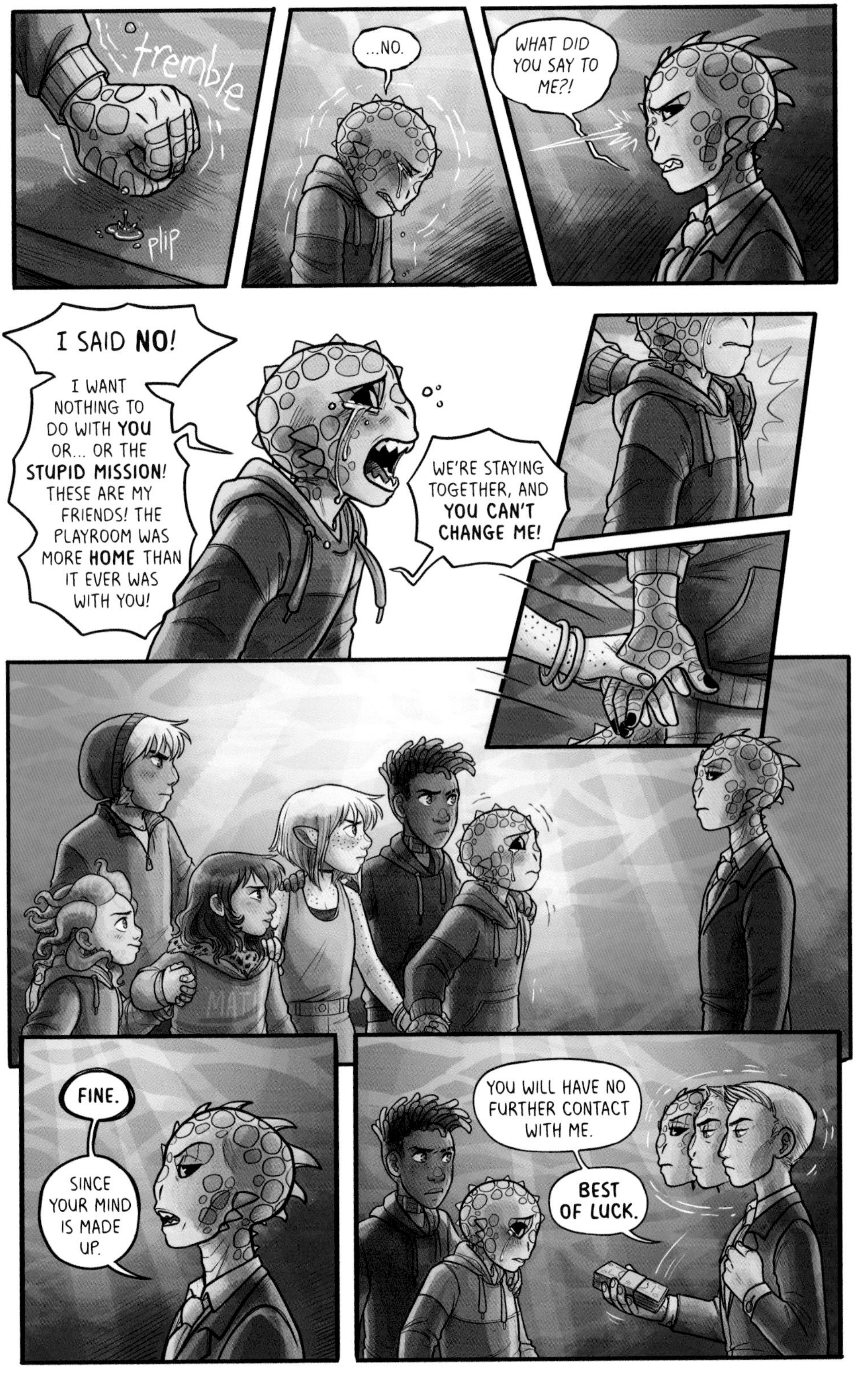
tremble
plip
...NO.
WHAT DID YOU SAY TO ME?!
I SAID **NO**!
I WANT NOTHING TO DO WITH **YOU** OR... OR THE **STUPID MISSION**! THESE ARE MY FRIENDS! THE PLAYROOM WAS MORE **HOME** THAN IT EVER WAS WITH YOU!
WE'RE STAYING TOGETHER, AND **YOU CAN'T CHANGE ME!**
MATH
FINE.
SINCE YOUR MIND IS MADE UP.
YOU WILL HAVE NO FURTHER CONTACT WITH ME.
BEST OF LUCK.

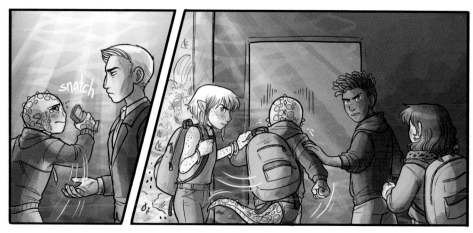

snatch

TIME TO GO, MAGGIE.

OKAY.

fwip

BYE!

STOMP STOMP

...NEWT?

I'M SO SORRY.

I'M SO SORRY I DRAGGED YOU INTO THIS--AND NOW WE HAVE **NOWHERE TO GO!**

IT'S OKAY, WE'LL FIGURE SOMETHING OUT.

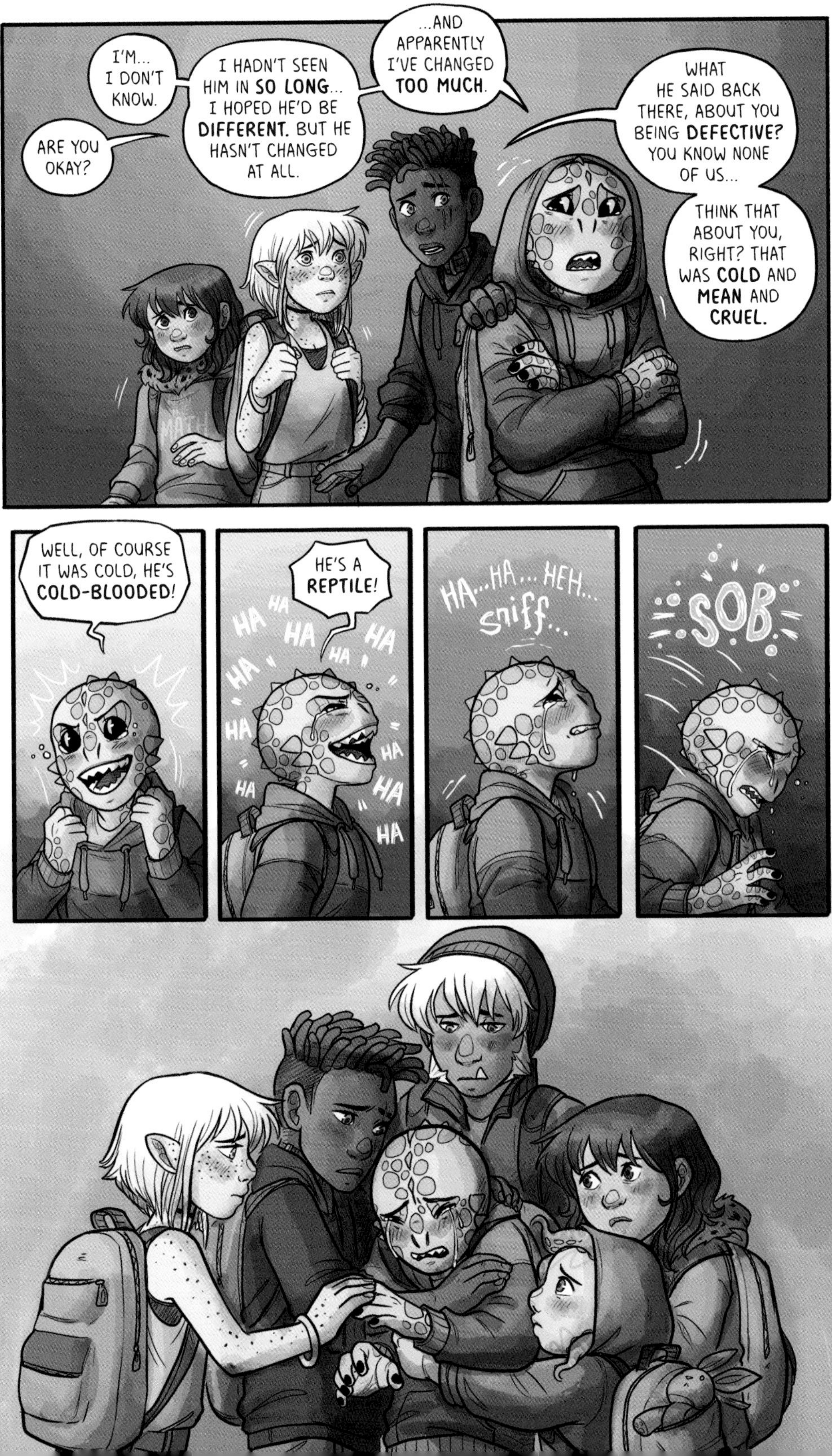
ARE YOU OKAY?
I'M... I DON'T KNOW.
I HADN'T SEEN HIM IN SO LONG... I HOPED HE'D BE DIFFERENT. BUT HE HASN'T CHANGED AT ALL.
...AND APPARENTLY I'VE CHANGED TOO MUCH.
WHAT HE SAID BACK THERE, ABOUT YOU BEING DEFECTIVE? YOU KNOW NONE OF US...
THINK THAT ABOUT YOU, RIGHT? THAT WAS COLD AND MEAN AND CRUEL.
MATH
WELL, OF COURSE IT WAS COLD, HE'S COLD-BLOODED!
HE'S A REPTILE!
HA HA HA HA HA HA HA HA HA HA HA HA
HA...HA... HEH... sniff...
SOB

CHAPTER SIX

TWO
HOUSES

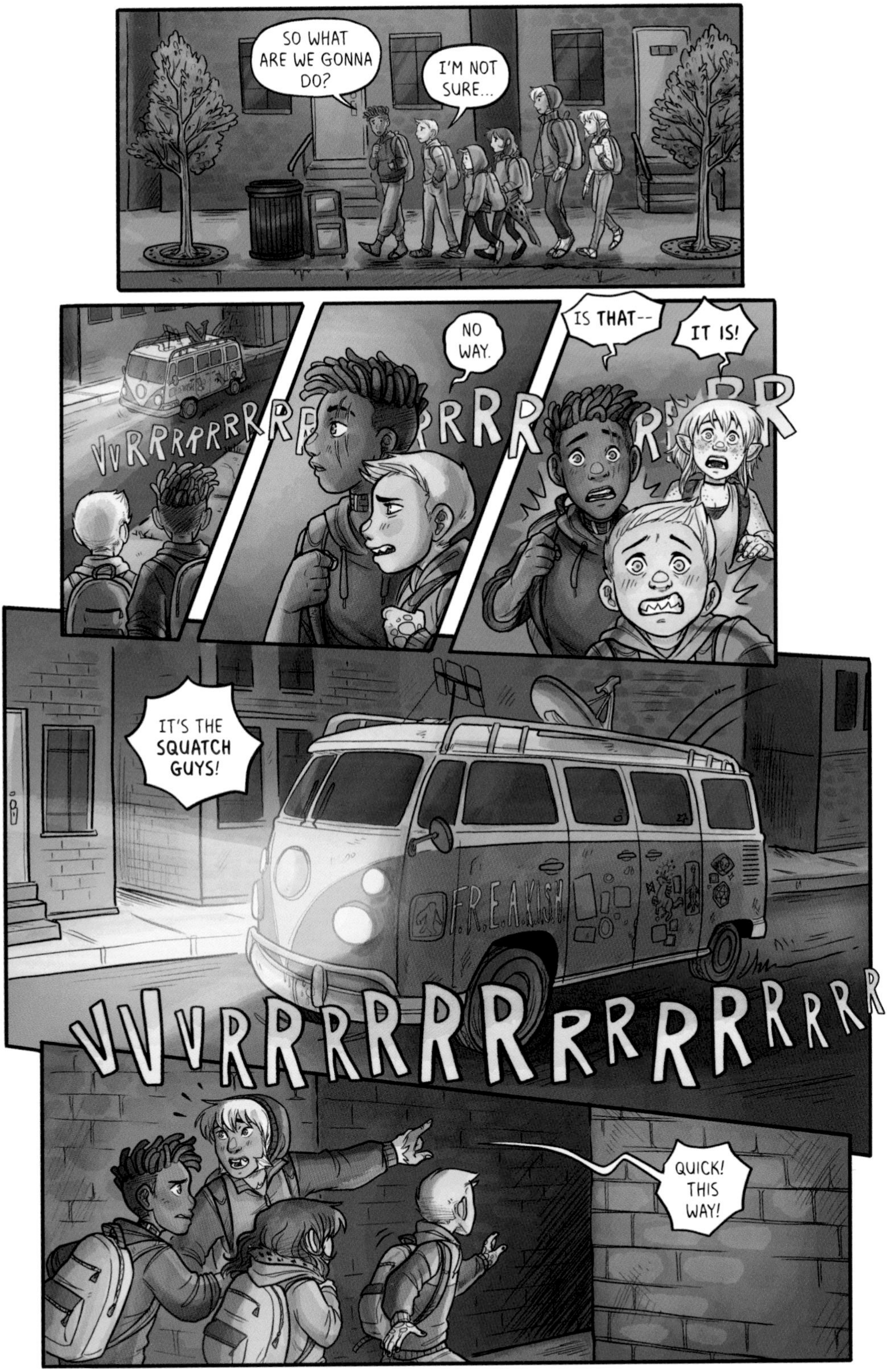

SO WHAT ARE WE GONNA DO?
I'M NOT SURE...
VVRRRRRRRRRRR
NO WAY.
IS THAT--
IT IS!
IT'S THE SQUATCH GUYS!
F.R.E.A.K.I.S.H.
VVVRRRRRRRRRRRRRR
QUICK! THIS WAY!

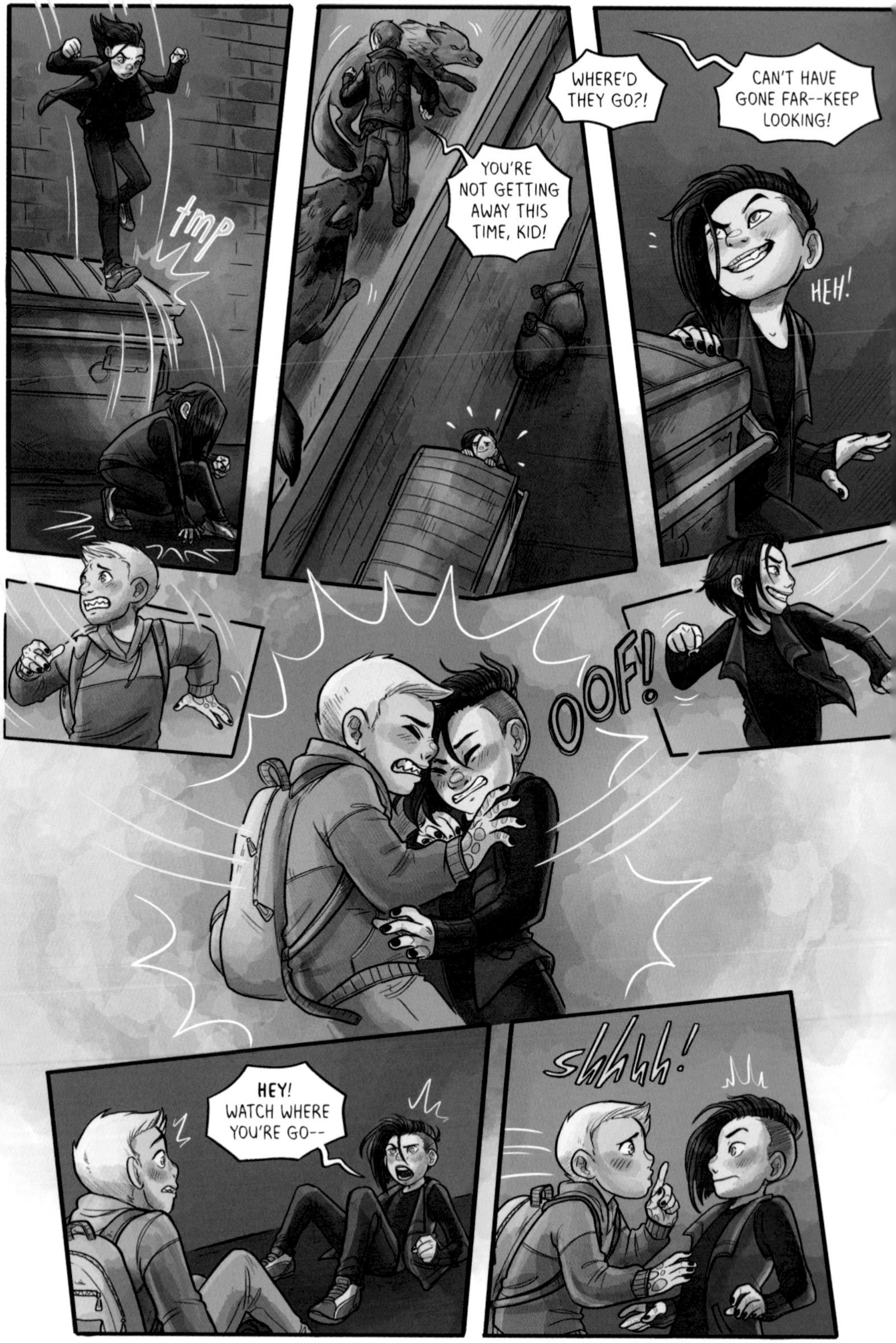
tmp
YOU'RE NOT GETTING AWAY THIS TIME, KID!
WHERE'D THEY GO?!
CAN'T HAVE GONE FAR--KEEP LOOKING!
HEH!
OOF!
HEY! WATCH WHERE YOU'RE GO--
shhhh!

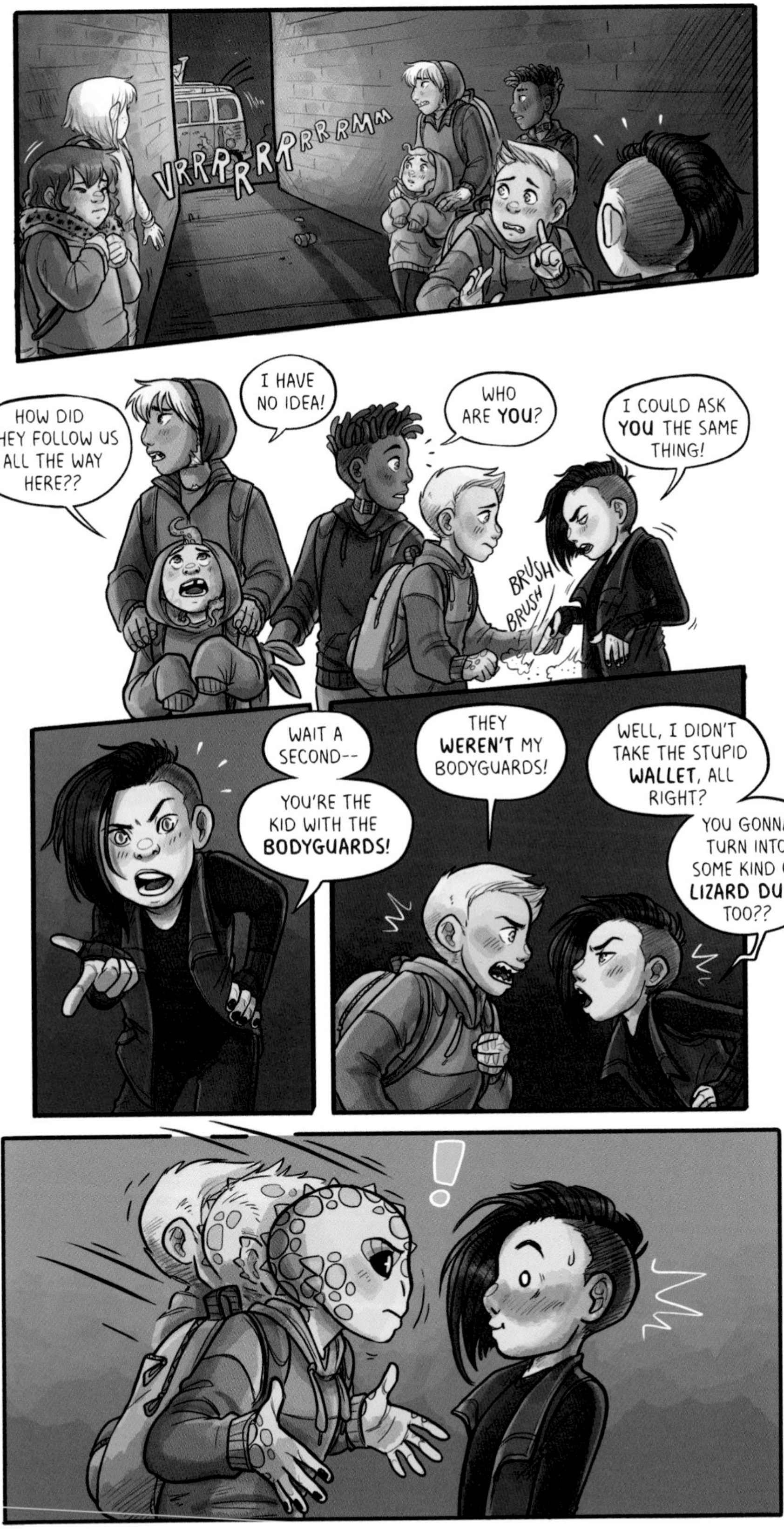
VRRRRRRRRRRRMM
HOW DID THEY FOLLOW US ALL THE WAY HERE??
I HAVE NO IDEA!
WHO ARE YOU?
I COULD ASK YOU THE SAME THING!
BRUSH BRUSH
WAIT A SECOND--
YOU'RE THE KID WITH THE BODYGUARDS!
THEY WEREN'T MY BODYGUARDS!
WELL, I DIDN'T TAKE THE STUPID WALLET, ALL RIGHT?
YOU GONNA TURN INTO SOME KIND OF LIZARD DUDE TOO??
!

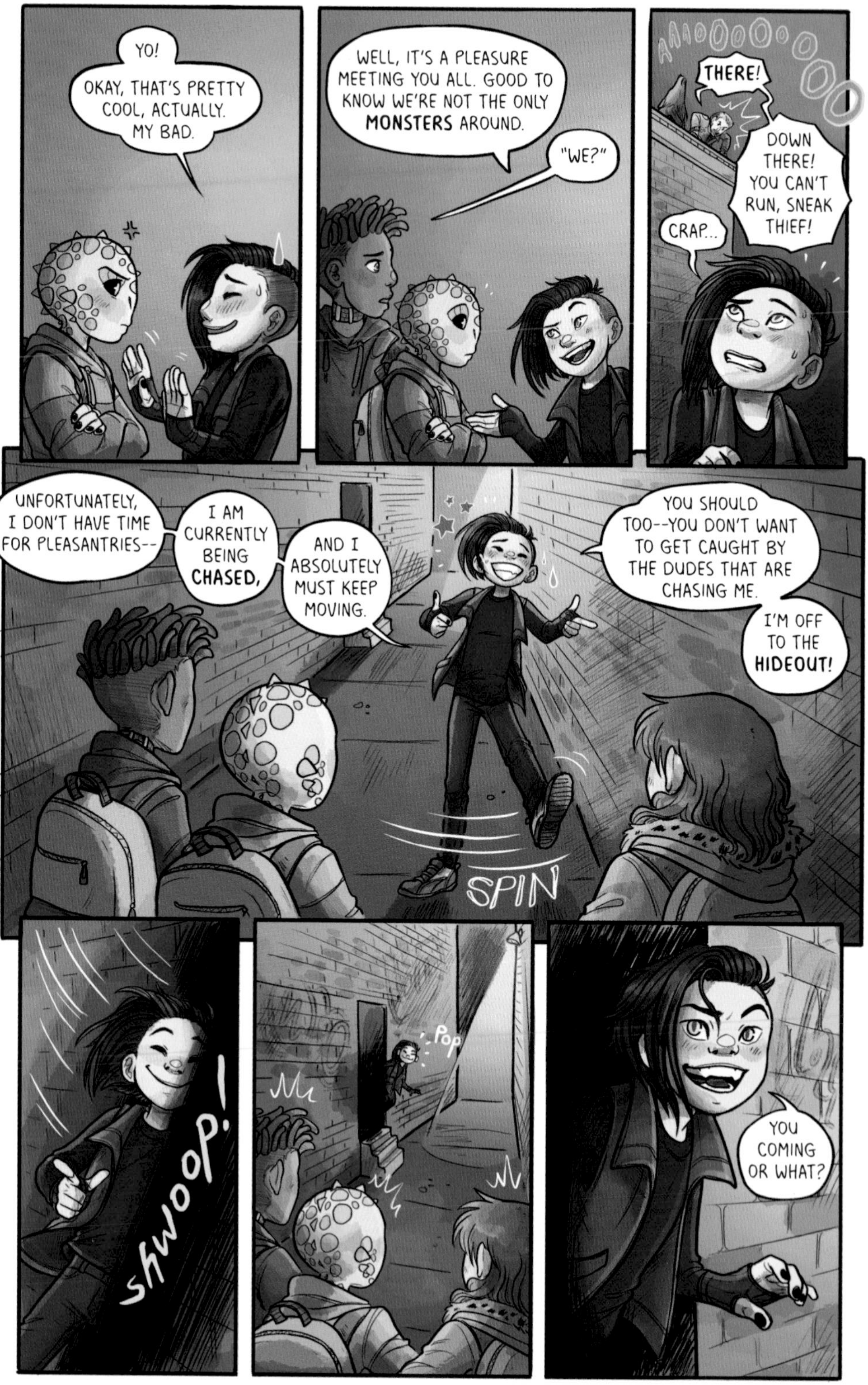
YO!
OKAY, THAT'S PRETTY COOL, ACTUALLY. MY BAD.
WELL, IT'S A PLEASURE MEETING YOU ALL. GOOD TO KNOW WE'RE NOT THE ONLY MONSTERS AROUND.
"WE?"
AAAOOOOOOOO
THERE!
DOWN THERE! YOU CAN'T RUN, SNEAK THIEF!
CRAP...
UNFORTUNATELY, I DON'T HAVE TIME FOR PLEASANTRIES--
I AM CURRENTLY BEING CHASED,
AND I ABSOLUTELY MUST KEEP MOVING.
YOU SHOULD TOO--YOU DON'T WANT TO GET CAUGHT BY THE DUDES THAT ARE CHASING ME.
I'M OFF TO THE HIDEOUT!
SPIN
SHWOOP!
POP
YOU COMING OR WHAT?

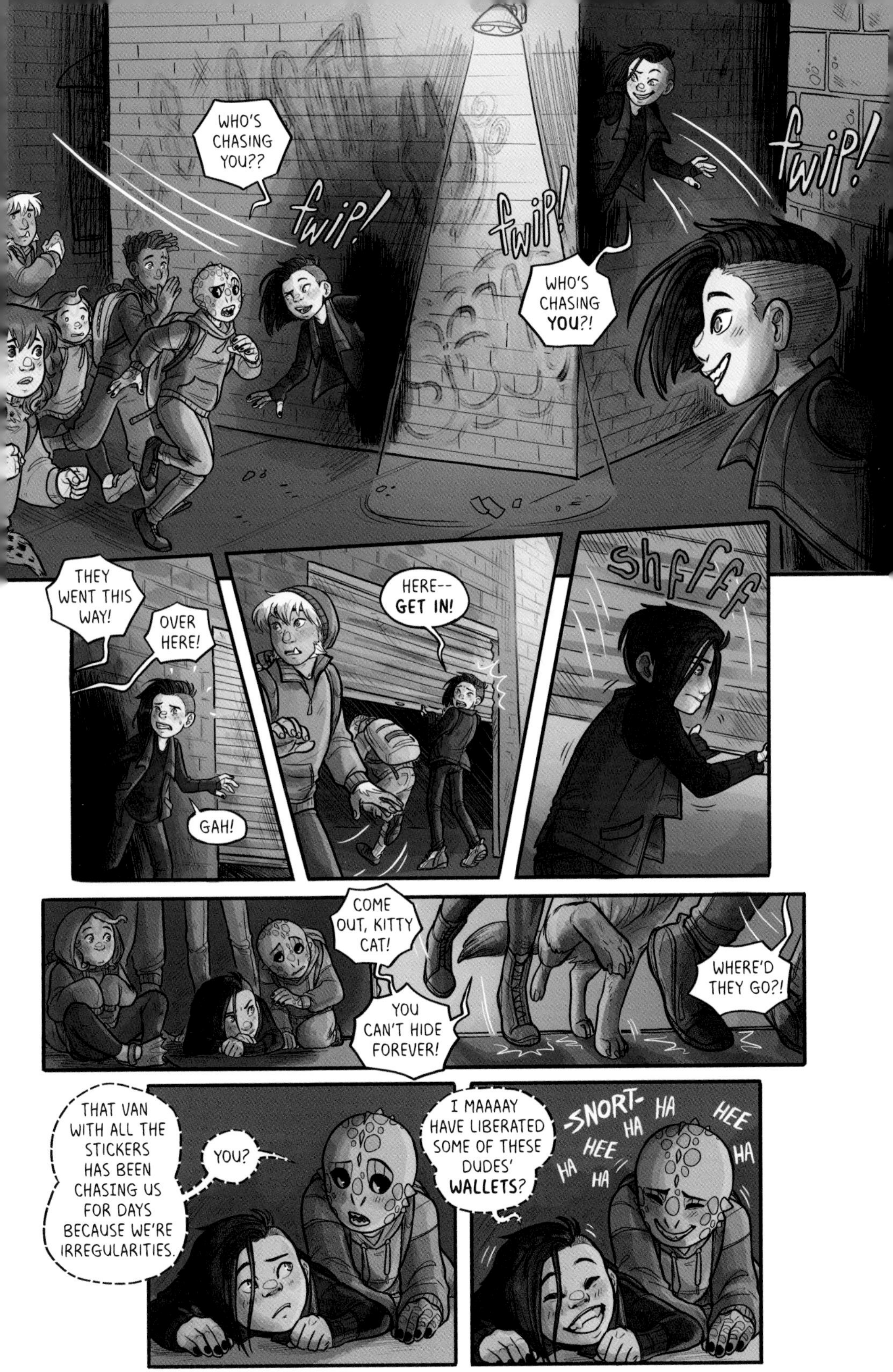
WHO'S CHASING YOU??
fwip!
fwip!
WHO'S CHASING YOU?!
fwip!
THEY WENT THIS WAY!
OVER HERE!
GAH!
HERE-- GET IN!
shffff
COME OUT, KITTY CAT!
YOU CAN'T HIDE FOREVER!
WHERE'D THEY GO?!
THAT VAN WITH ALL THE STICKERS HAS BEEN CHASING US FOR DAYS BECAUSE WE'RE IRREGULARITIES.
YOU?
I MAAAAY HAVE LIBERATED SOME OF THESE DUDES' WALLETS?
-SNORT- HA HA HEE HA HEE HA HA HEE HA

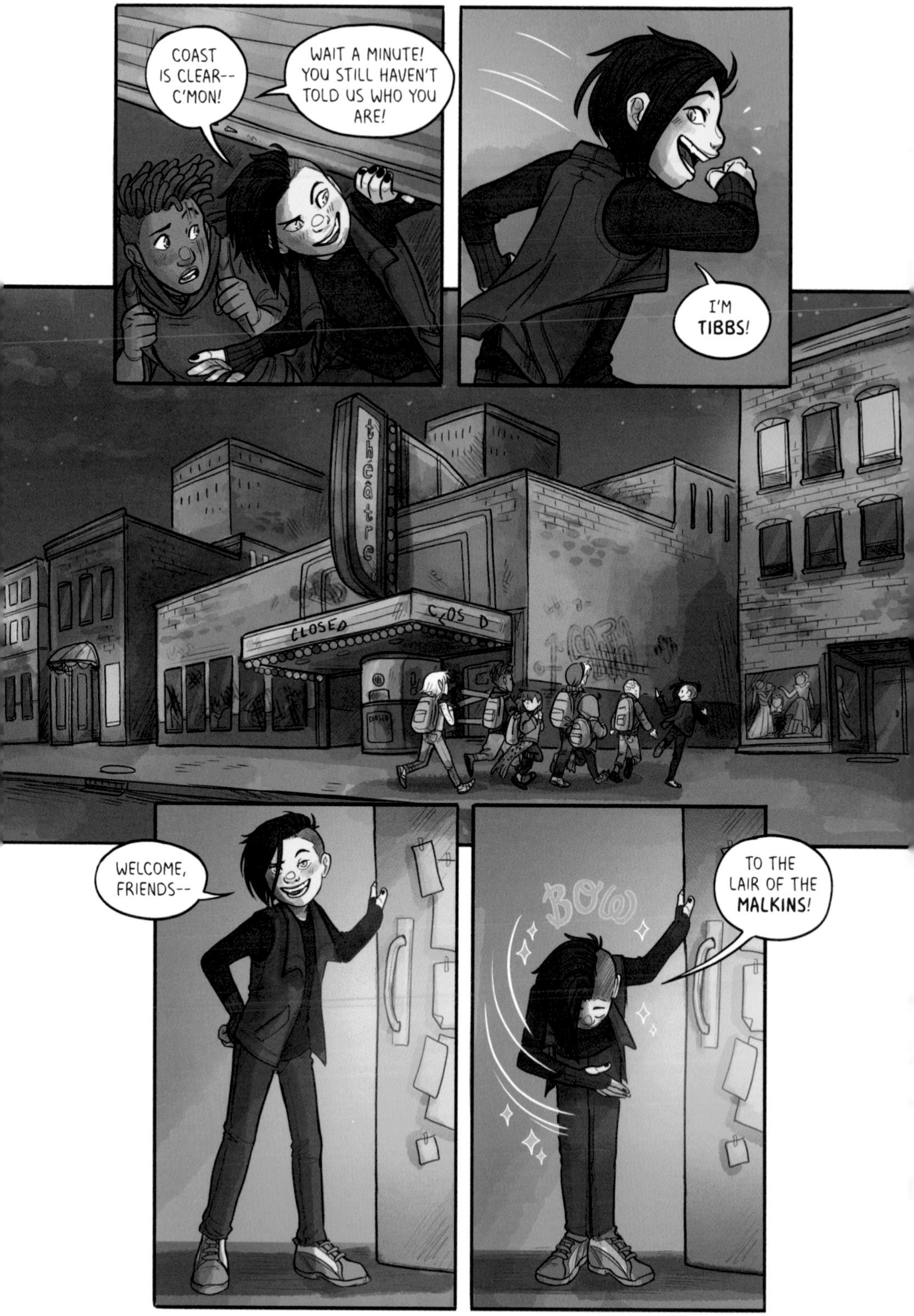
COAST IS CLEAR-- C'MON!
WAIT A MINUTE! YOU STILL HAVEN'T TOLD US WHO YOU ARE!
I'M TIBBS!
théâtre
CLOSED
WELCOME, FRIENDS--
BOW
TO THE LAIR OF THE MALKINS!

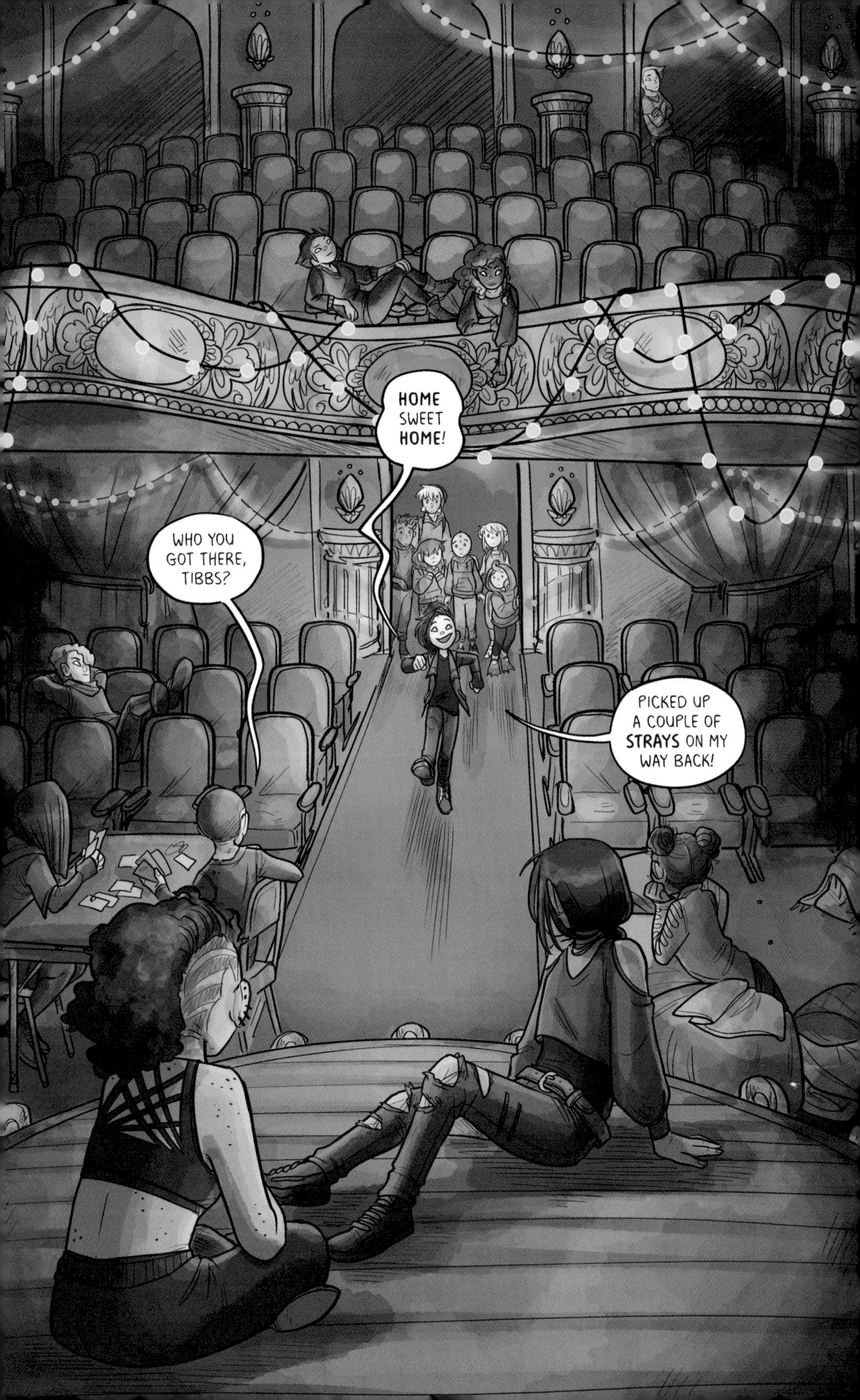
HOME SWEET HOME!
WHO YOU GOT THERE, TIBBS?
PICKED UP A COUPLE OF STRAYS ON MY WAY BACK!

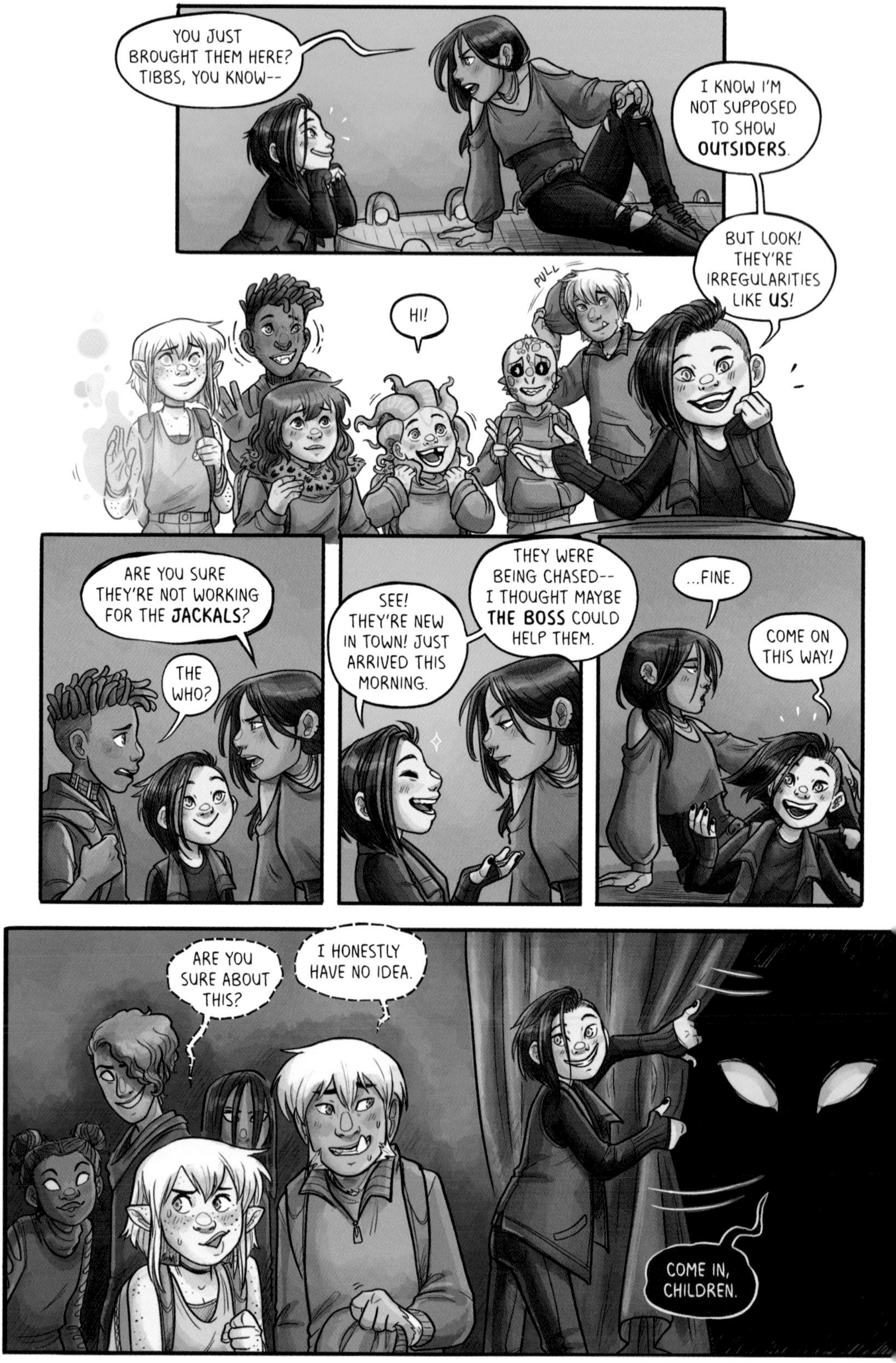
YOU JUST BROUGHT THEM HERE? TIBBS, YOU KNOW--
I KNOW I'M NOT SUPPOSED TO SHOW OUTSIDERS.
BUT LOOK! THEY'RE IRREGULARITIES LIKE US!
PULL
HI!
ARE YOU SURE THEY'RE NOT WORKING FOR THE JACKALS?
THE WHO?
SEE! THEY'RE NEW IN TOWN! JUST ARRIVED THIS MORNING.
THEY WERE BEING CHASED-- I THOUGHT MAYBE THE BOSS COULD HELP THEM.
...FINE.
COME ON THIS WAY!
ARE YOU SURE ABOUT THIS?
I HONESTLY HAVE NO IDEA.
COME IN, CHILDREN.

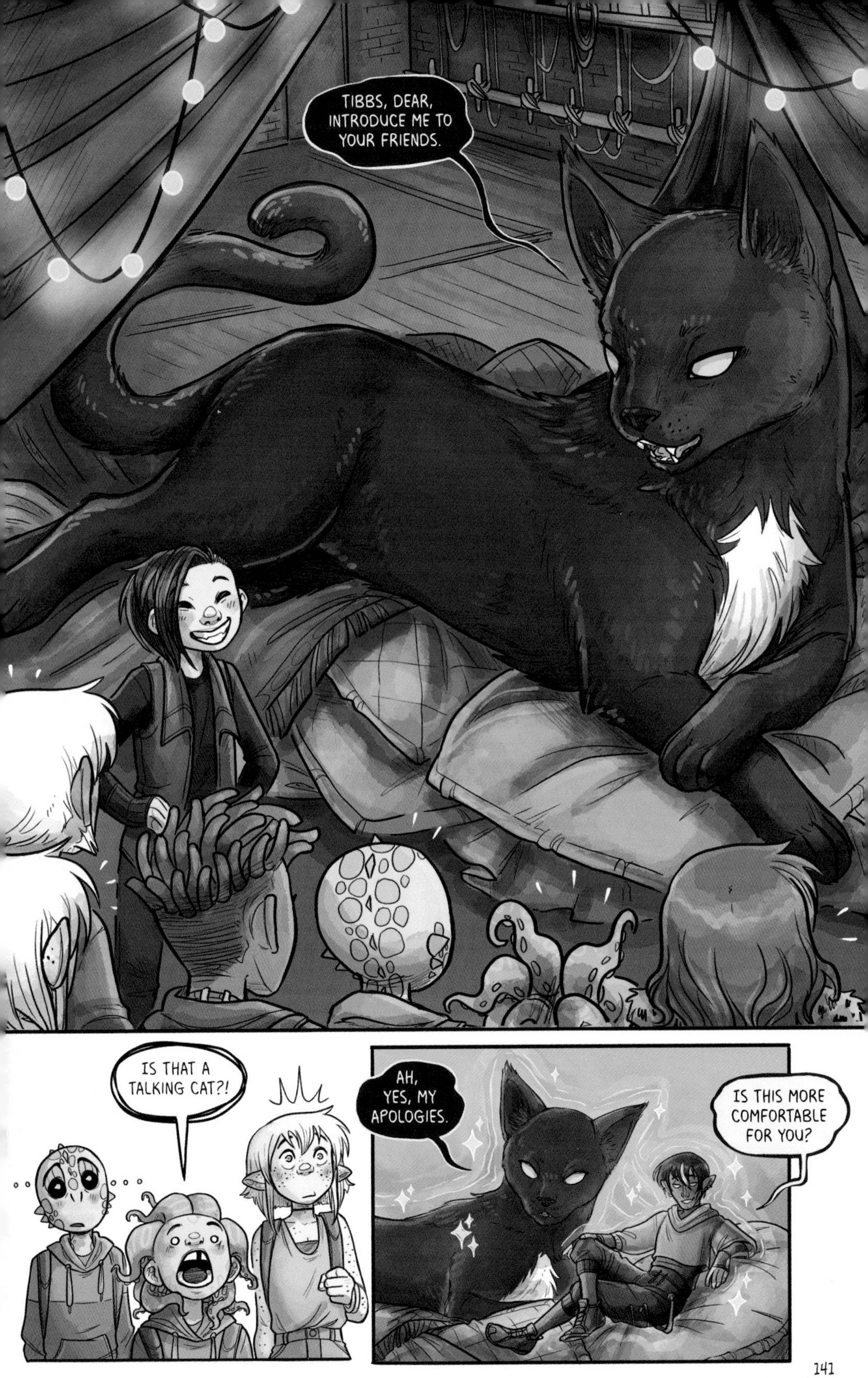
TIBBS, DEAR, INTRODUCE ME TO YOUR FRIENDS.
IS THAT A TALKING CAT?!
AH, YES, MY APOLOGIES.
IS THIS MORE COMFORTABLE FOR YOU?

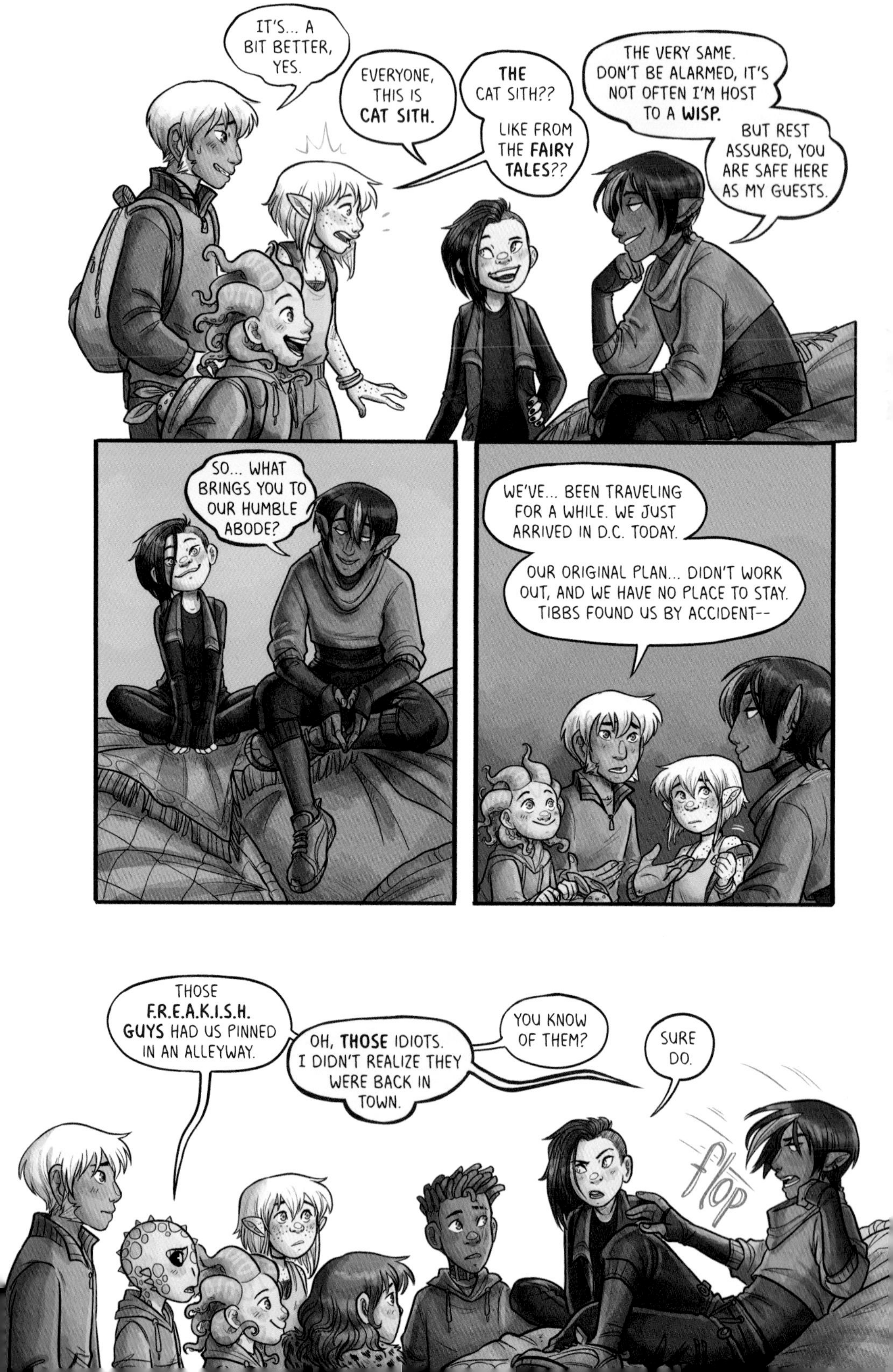
IT'S... A BIT BETTER, YES.
EVERYONE, THIS IS CAT SITH.
THE CAT SITH??
LIKE FROM THE FAIRY TALES??
THE VERY SAME. DON'T BE ALARMED, IT'S NOT OFTEN I'M HOST TO A WISP.
BUT REST ASSURED, YOU ARE SAFE HERE AS MY GUESTS.
SO... WHAT BRINGS YOU TO OUR HUMBLE ABODE?
WE'VE... BEEN TRAVELING FOR A WHILE. WE JUST ARRIVED IN D.C. TODAY.
OUR ORIGINAL PLAN... DIDN'T WORK OUT, AND WE HAVE NO PLACE TO STAY. TIBBS FOUND US BY ACCIDENT--
THOSE F.R.E.A.K.I.S.H. GUYS HAD US PINNED IN AN ALLEYWAY.
OH, THOSE IDIOTS. I DIDN'T REALIZE THEY WERE BACK IN TOWN.
YOU KNOW OF THEM?
SURE DO.
flop

AND AS **REVENGE**, THEY'VE TAKEN ONE OF OURS. **JAYLA**.

BUT YOU **DIDN'T** KIDNAP THEIR FRIEND?

OF COURSE NOT!

WHAT REASON WOULD WE HAVE?

BESIDES, OUR METHODS ARE MUCH **QUIETER** AND **MORE SUBTLE**.

IN RETURN FOR ROOM AND BOARD HERE, I WOULD ASK THAT YOU RESCUE OUR MISSING MALKIN.

THE JACKALS KNOW TO WATCH OUT FOR US, BUT THEY WILL NEVER SEE YOU COMING.

TIBBS CAN GIVE YOU MORE INFORMATION AND LEAD YOU TO THE JACKAL HIDEOUT TOMORROW.

THEY KNOW THIS CITY LIKE THE BACK OF THEIR HAND.

FOR TONIGHT, EAT, SLEEP, REST.

THANK YOU, SIR.

THANKS, MR. KITTY!

YOU'RE WELCOME, MY DEAR.

TOSS

CATCH

THANKS!

ISN'T THIS **AMAZING**?? ALL THESE IRREGULARITIES LIVING RIGHT UNDER THE CITY'S NOSE!

IT IS IMPRESSIVE.

munch munch

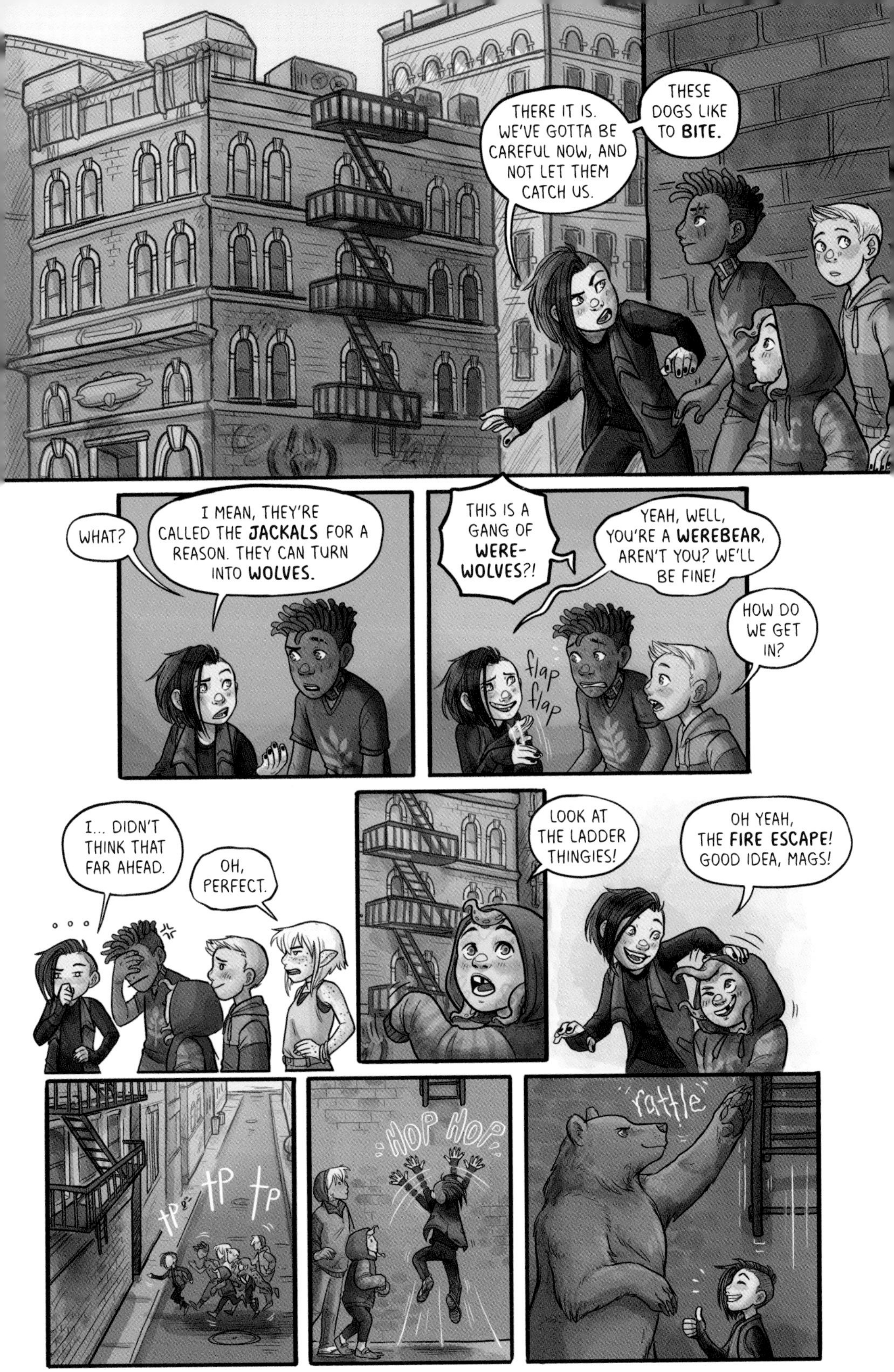
THERE IT IS. WE'VE GOTTA BE CAREFUL NOW, AND NOT LET THEM CATCH US.
THESE DOGS LIKE TO **BITE.**
WHAT?
I MEAN, THEY'RE CALLED THE **JACKALS** FOR A REASON. THEY CAN TURN INTO **WOLVES.**
THIS IS A GANG OF **WERE-WOLVES**?!
YEAH, WELL, YOU'RE A **WEREBEAR**, AREN'T YOU? WE'LL BE FINE!
flap flap
HOW DO WE GET IN?
I... DIDN'T THINK THAT FAR AHEAD.
OH, PERFECT.
LOOK AT THE LADDER THINGIES!
OH YEAH, THE **FIRE ESCAPE**! GOOD IDEA, MAGS!
TP TP TP
HOP HOP
rattle

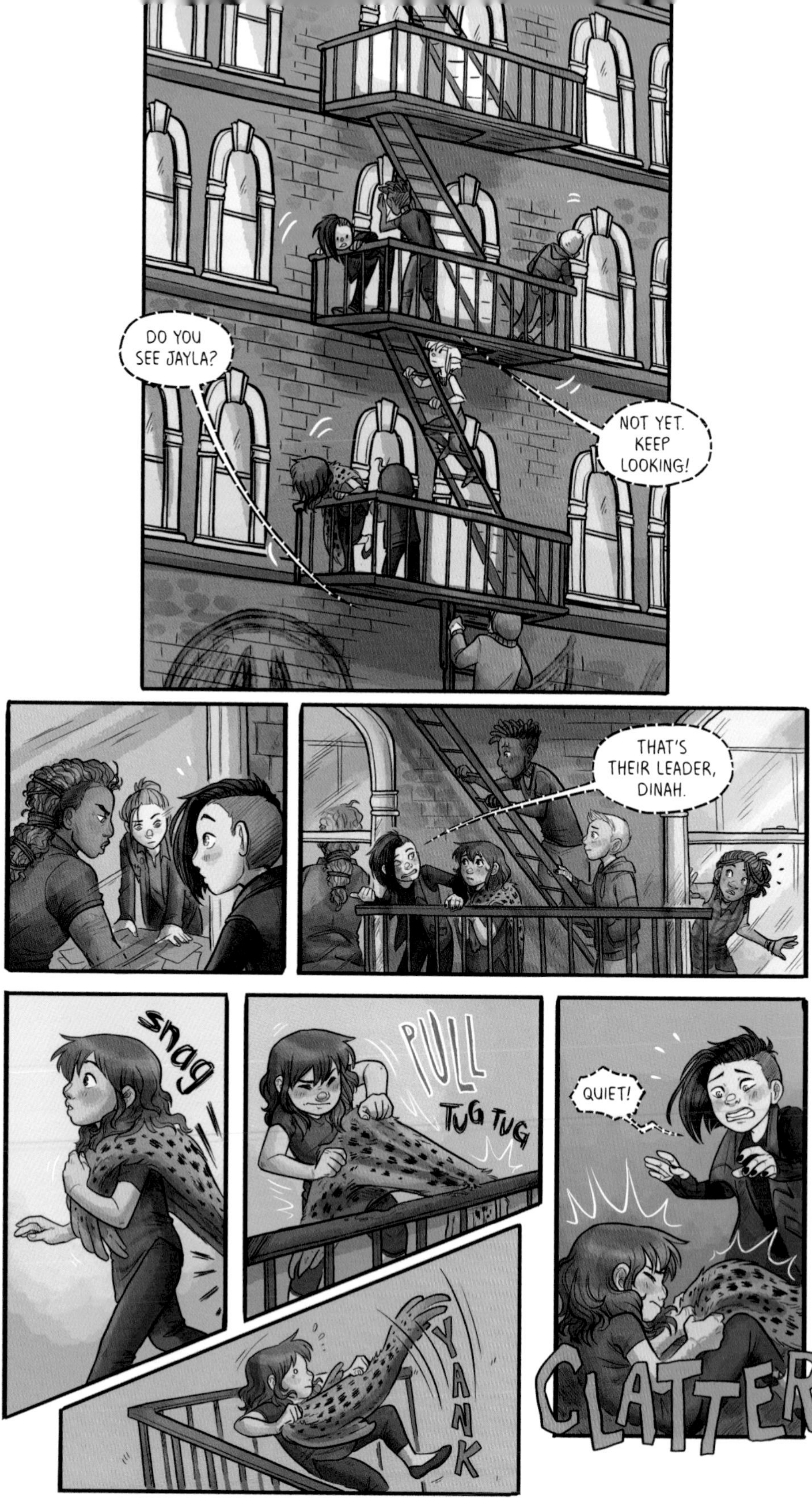
DO YOU SEE JAYLA?
NOT YET. KEEP LOOKING!
THAT'S THEIR LEADER, DINAH.
snag
PULL
TUG TUG
YANK
QUIET!
CLATTER

W—WHAT??

HE NEVER TOLD ME ABOUT—

THEY WERE **TOGETHER**??

YEAH.

DO THE TEXTS SAY WHERE THEY WENT?

THEY KEEP TALKING ABOUT **"THE SANCTUARY"**?

IT COMES UP A BUNCH OF TIMES. AND... HERE! THEY PLANNED TO RUN AWAY!

THEY LEFT A WEEK AGO. HE MUST HAVE FORGOTTEN HIS PHONE.

WHAT'S THE SANCTUARY?

IT SOUNDS LIKE IT'S A SAFE HAVEN FOR IRREGULARITIES... OUT WEST IN WASHINGTON STATE.

HE JUST LEFT?! WITHOUT SAYING GOODBYE?! **QUÉ IMBÉCIL!**

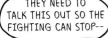
WHUMP

SO BOTH SIDES THINK THEIR MEMBER WAS KIDNAPPED, BUT THEY LEFT TOGETHER WITHOUT TELLING ANYONE.

THEY WERE SO AFRAID OF THE GANGS TRYING TO **BREAK THEM UP.**

THIS IS **SO** MESSED UP.

THEY NEED TO TALK THIS OUT SO THE FIGHTING CAN STOP—

BUT HOW DO WE GET THEM IN THE SAME PLACE? WILL THEY **TRUST** EACH OTHER?

NO. THE MALKINS WILL THINK THE JACKALS ARE SETTING UP A TRAP.

THE JACKALS WILL THINK THE SAME THING. THE ONLY WAY TO GET THEM TOGETHER WOULD BE TO **TRICK THEM** INTO IT.

I HAVE AN ABSOLUTELY HORRIBLE, WONDERFUL, **TERRIBLE** IDEA...

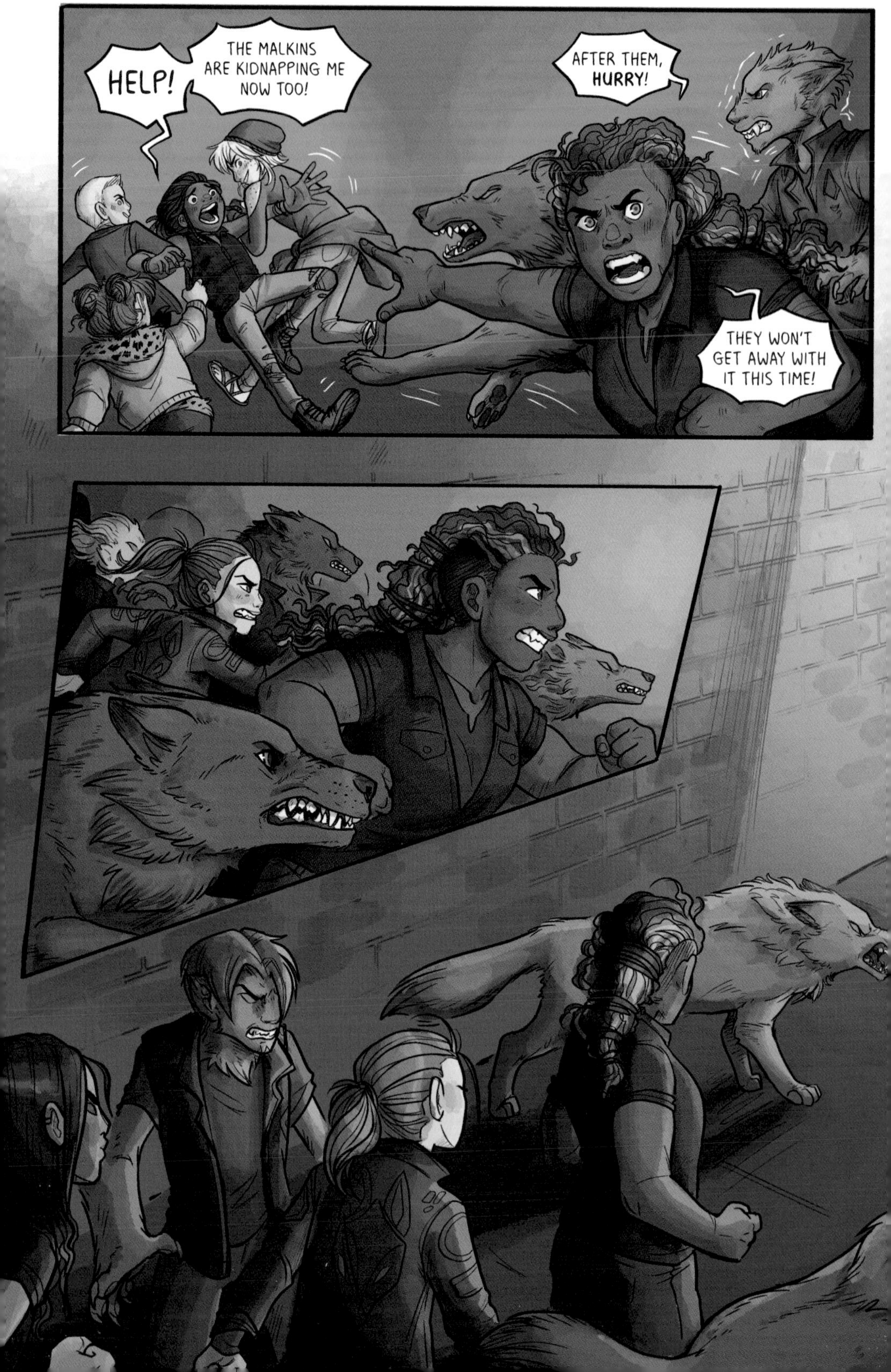
HELP!
THE MALKINS ARE KIDNAPPING ME NOW TOO!
AFTER THEM, **HURRY**!
THEY WON'T GET AWAY WITH IT THIS TIME!

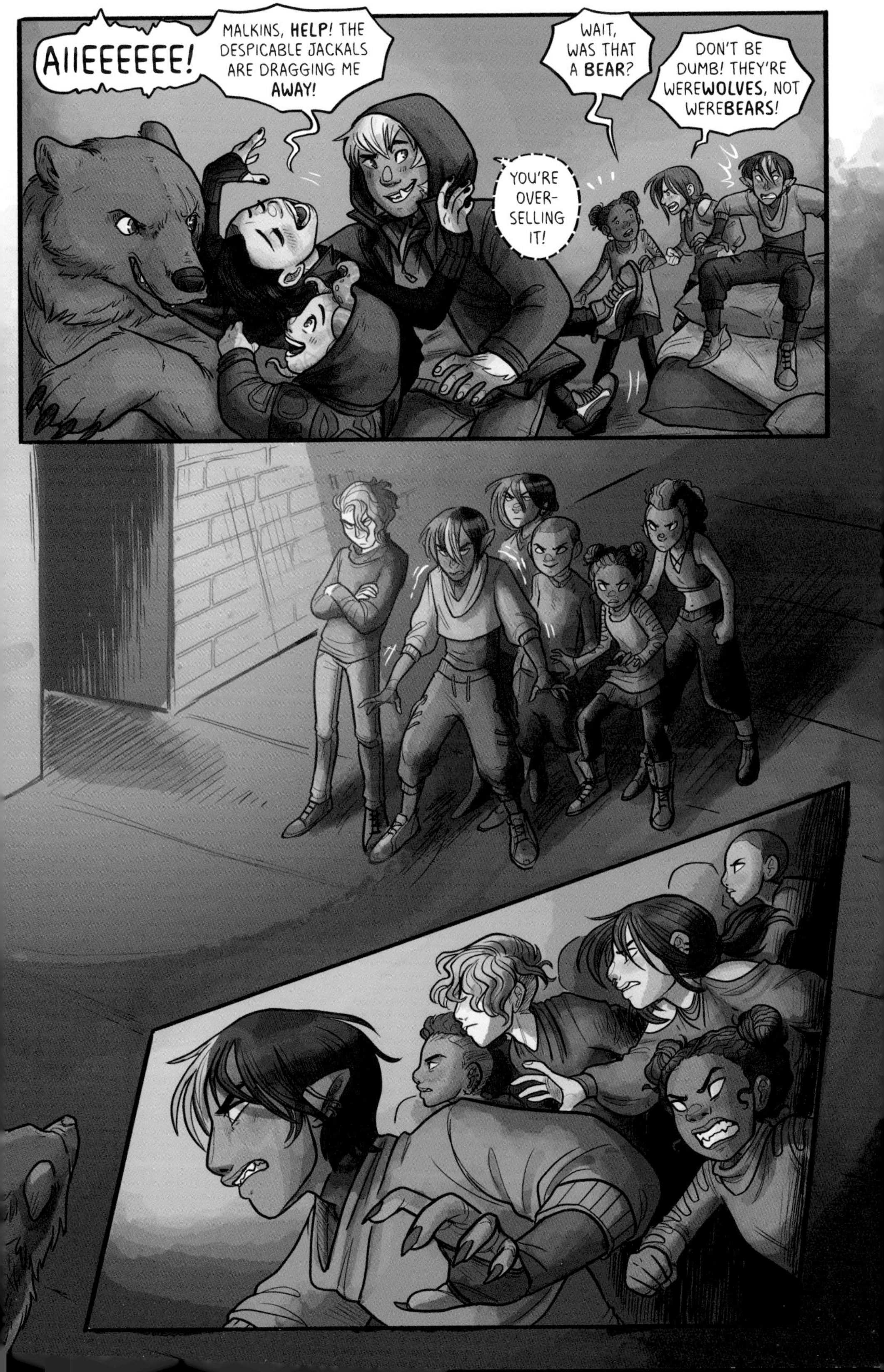
AIIEEEEEE!
MALKINS, HELP! THE DESPICABLE JACKALS ARE DRAGGING ME AWAY!
YOU'RE OVER-SELLING IT!
WAIT, WAS THAT A BEAR?
DON'T BE DUMB! THEY'RE WEREWOLVES, NOT WEREBEARS!

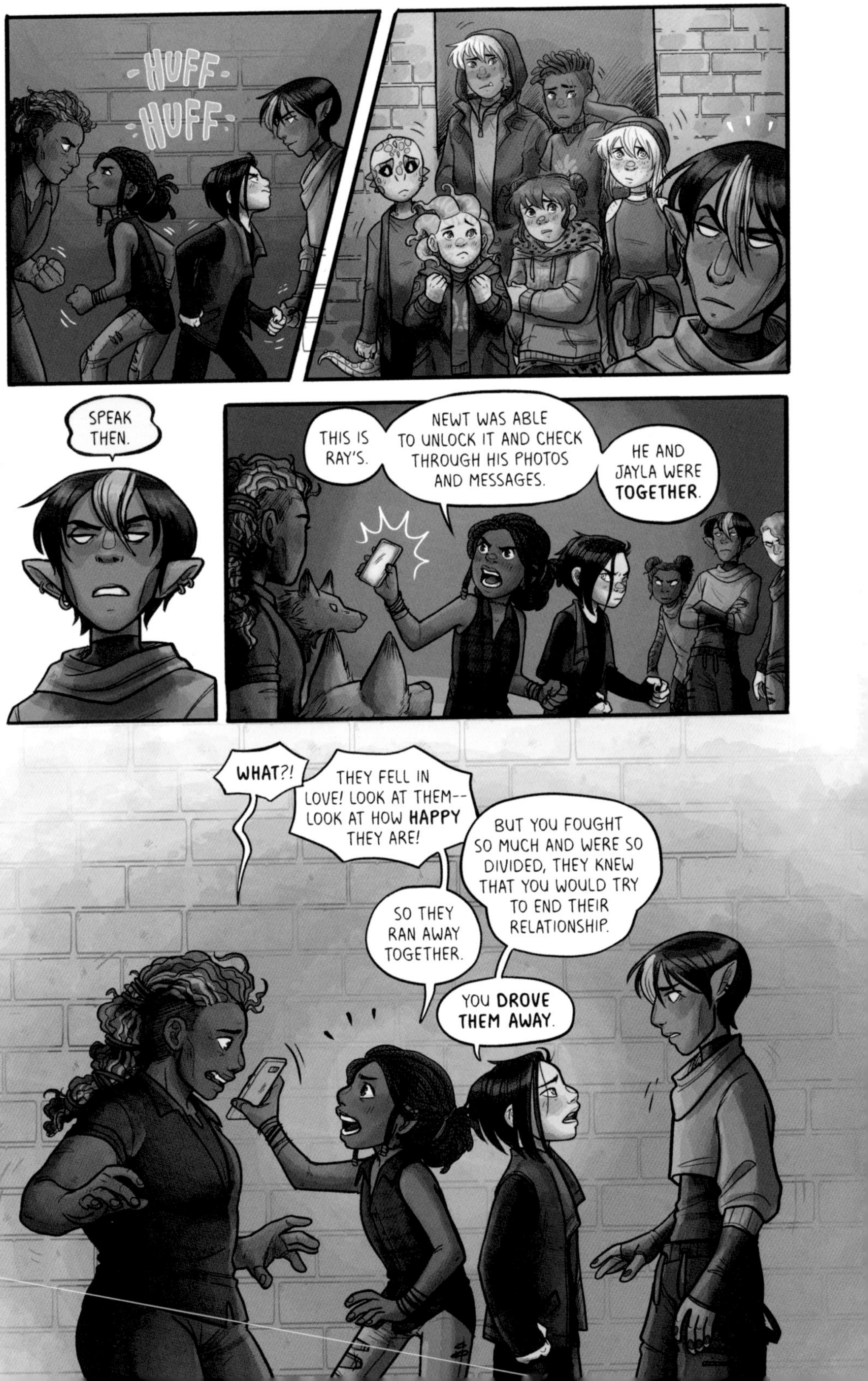
HUFF
HUFF
SPEAK THEN.
THIS IS RAY'S.
NEWT WAS ABLE TO UNLOCK IT AND CHECK THROUGH HIS PHOTOS AND MESSAGES.
HE AND JAYLA WERE **TOGETHER**.
WHAT?!
THEY FELL IN LOVE! LOOK AT THEM-- LOOK AT HOW **HAPPY** THEY ARE!
BUT YOU FOUGHT SO MUCH AND WERE SO DIVIDED, THEY KNEW THAT YOU WOULD TRY TO END THEIR RELATIONSHIP.
SO THEY RAN AWAY TOGETHER.
YOU **DROVE THEM AWAY**.

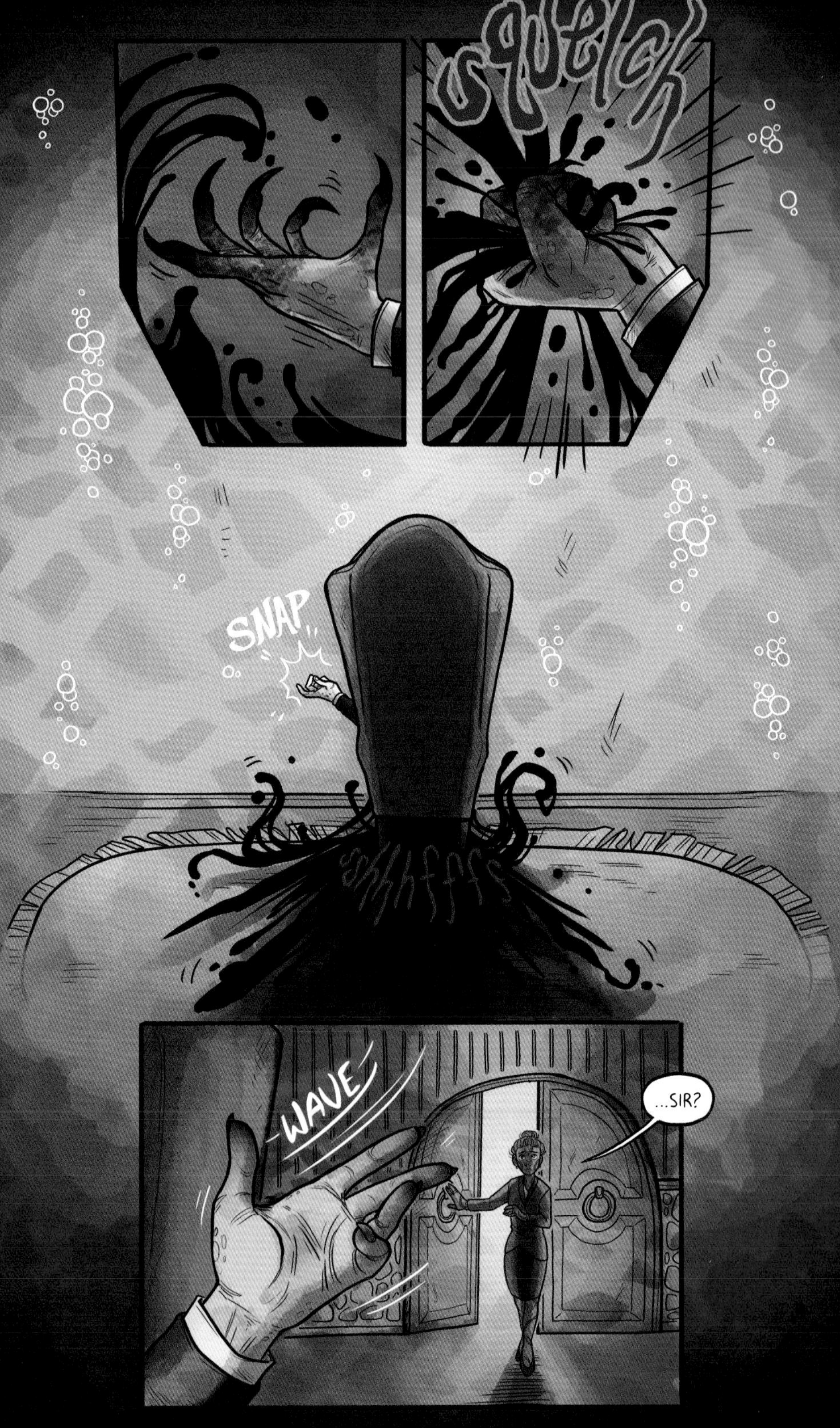
squelch
SNAP
shhhffff
WAVE
...SIR?

CHAPTER SEVEN

CROSS COUNTRY

-chatter-

-mumble-

-chatter-

-chatter-

SO I KNOW IT'S IN WASHINGTON STATE-- THAT'S WHERE RAY AND JAYLA WERE HEADED.

THEY HAVE A COUPLE OF MESSAGES BACK AND FORTH ABOUT BUS TICKETS AND STUFF...

BUT NO **ADDRESSES.**

CAN'T YOU JUST... LIKE... **GOOGLE** IT?

OH **SURE**, JUST SEARCH "HI, WHERE CAN A GROUP OF SIX **MONSTERS** THAT MAY OR MAY NOT INCLUDE...

A BEAR, A SELKIE, A YETI, AN ALIEN, A WILL-O-THE-WISP, AND **WHATEVER MAGGIE IS,** GO HIDE BECAUSE THE **GOVERNMENT** IS AFTER THEM?"

I'M SURE THAT WOULD WORK OUT **PERFECTLY.**

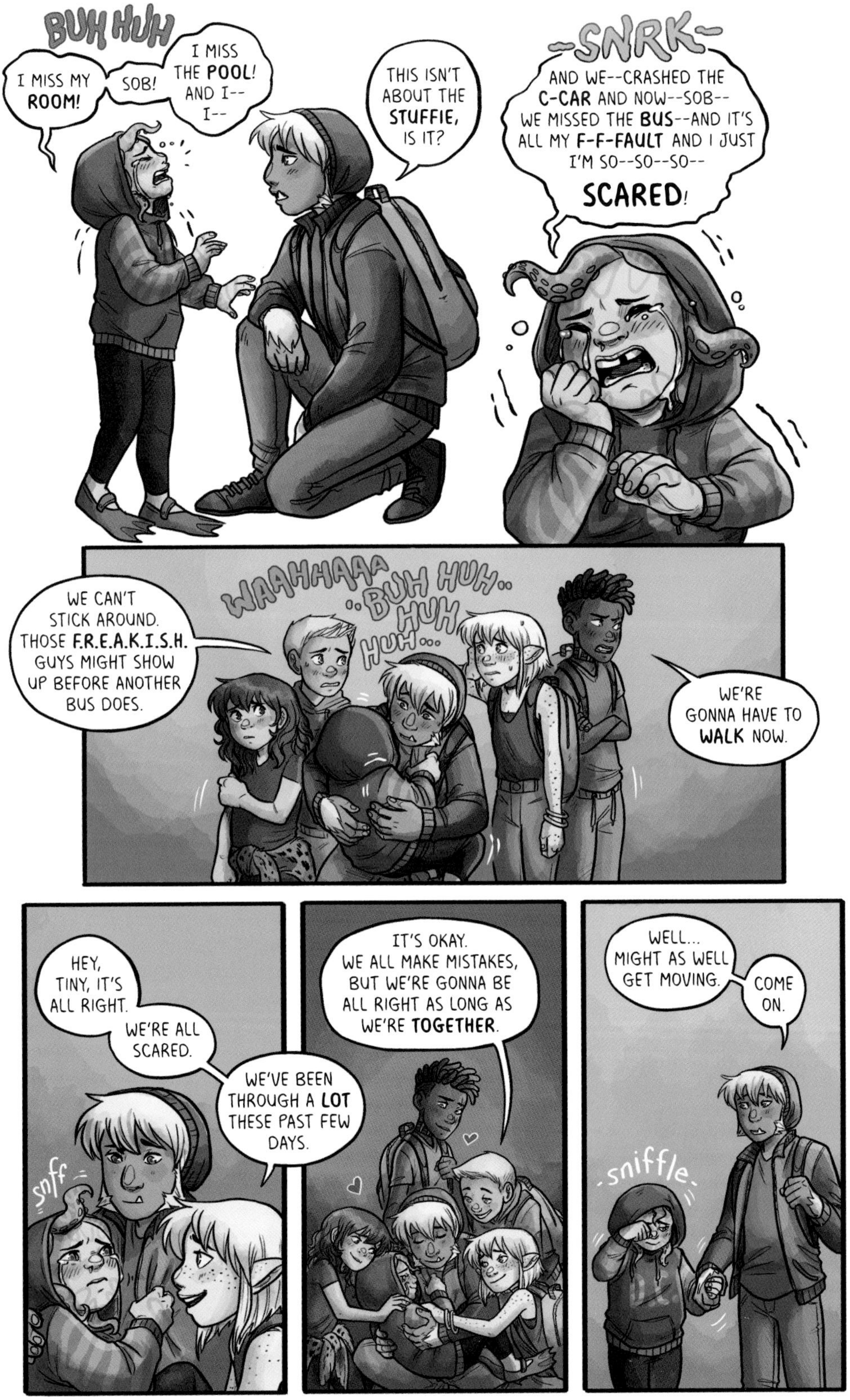
BUH HUH
I MISS MY ROOM!
SOB!
I MISS THE POOL! AND I-- I--
THIS ISN'T ABOUT THE STUFFIE, IS IT?
-SNRK-
AND WE--CRASHED THE C-CAR AND NOW--SOB-- WE MISSED THE BUS--AND IT'S ALL MY F-F-FAULT AND I JUST I'M SO--SO--SO-- SCARED!
WAAHHAAA
..BUH HUH..
HUH
HUH...
WE CAN'T STICK AROUND. THOSE F.R.E.A.K.I.S.H. GUYS MIGHT SHOW UP BEFORE ANOTHER BUS DOES.
WE'RE GONNA HAVE TO WALK NOW.
HEY, TINY, IT'S ALL RIGHT.
WE'RE ALL SCARED.
WE'VE BEEN THROUGH A LOT THESE PAST FEW DAYS.
snff
IT'S OKAY. WE ALL MAKE MISTAKES, BUT WE'RE GONNA BE ALL RIGHT AS LONG AS WE'RE TOGETHER.
WELL... MIGHT AS WELL GET MOVING.
COME ON.
-sniffle-

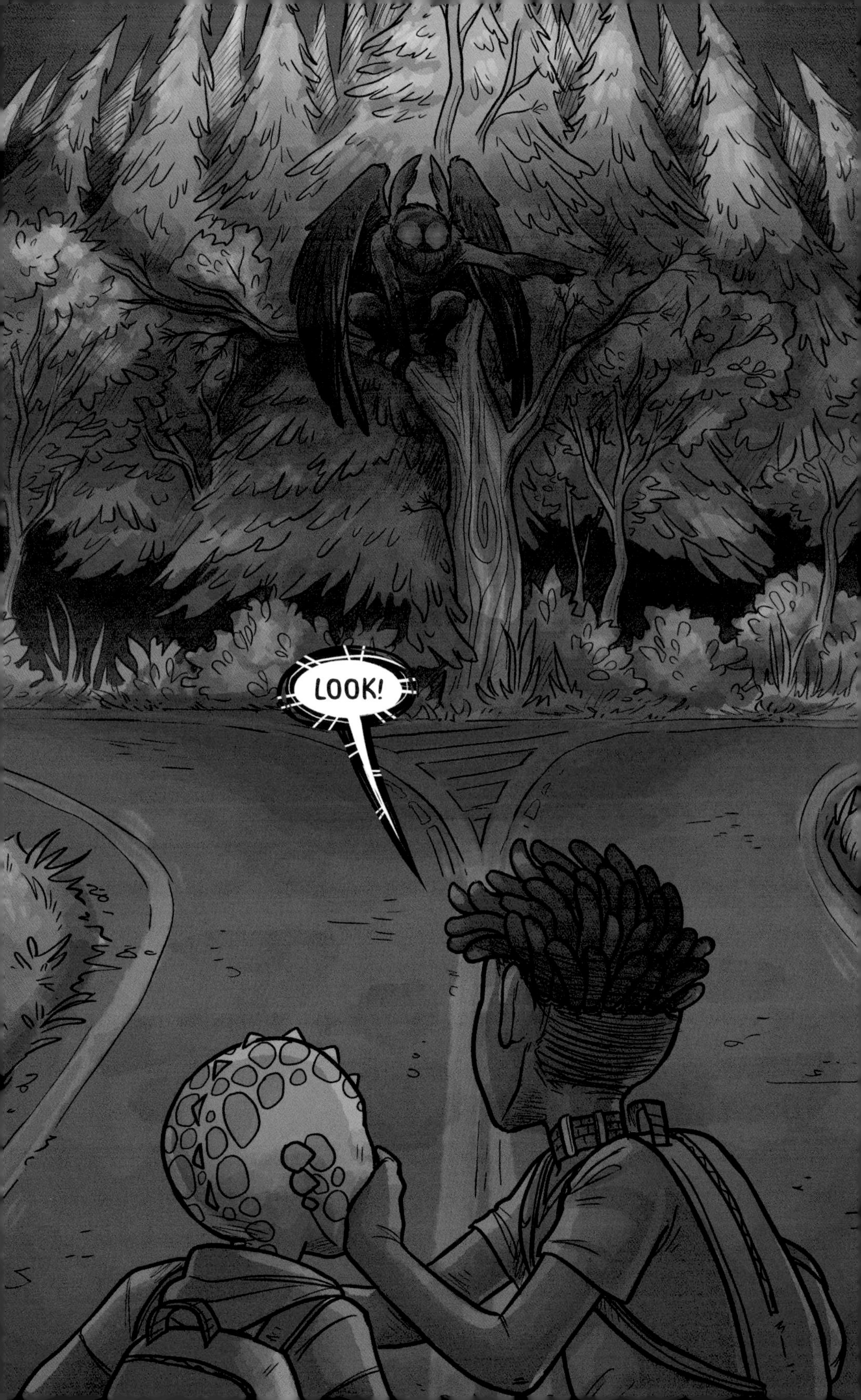
LOOK!

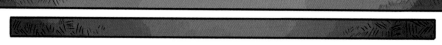

WHAT'S THAT LIGHT UP AHEAD?

LOOK! THERE'S THE BUS STATION!!

UGH

OH, THANK GOODNESS--

THERE'S **POWER** AND **WIFI** HERE.

tap tap

YAAAAWN

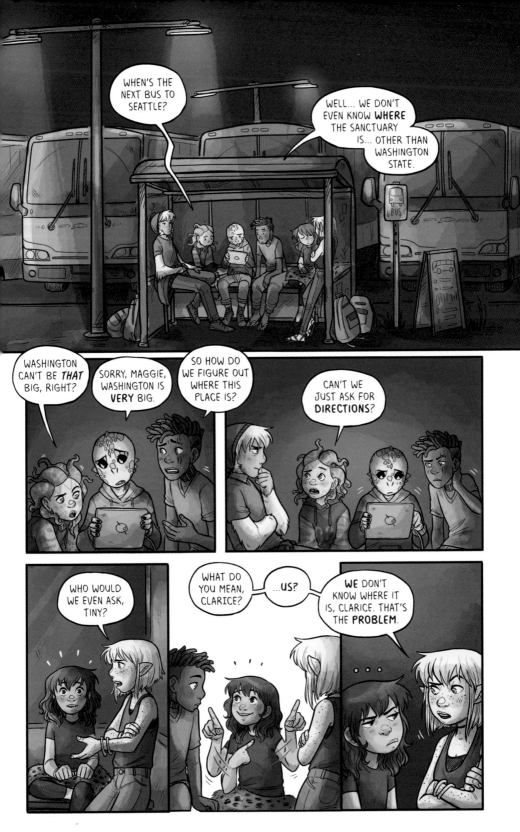

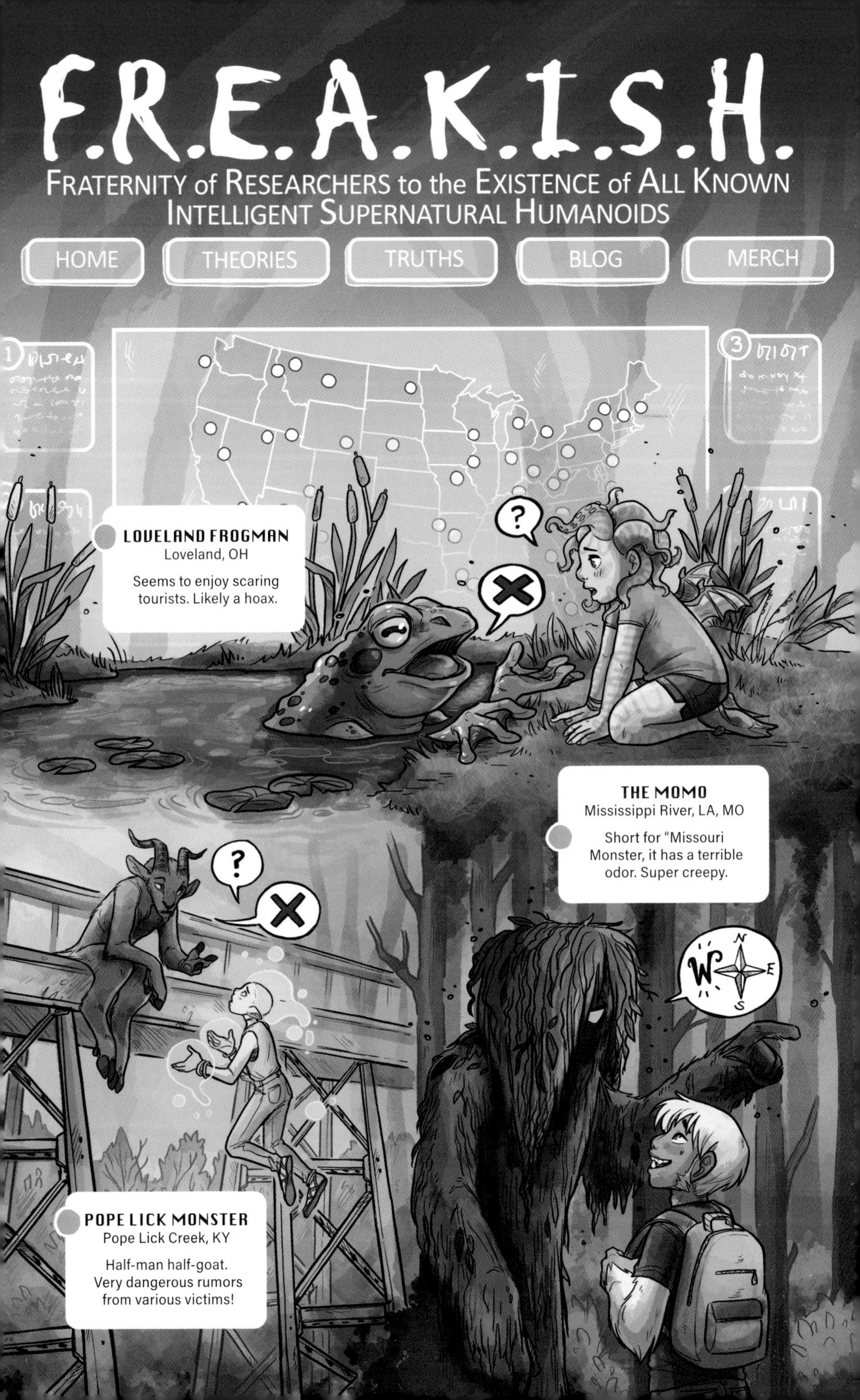

F.R.E.A.K.I.S.H.
FRATERNITY of RESEARCHERS to the EXISTENCE of ALL KNOWN INTELLIGENT SUPERNATURAL HUMANOIDS
HOME
THEORIES
TRUTHS
BLOG
MERCH
LOVELAND FROGMAN
Loveland, OH
Seems to enjoy scaring tourists. Likely a hoax.
?
THE MOMO
Mississippi River, LA, MO
Short for "Missouri Monster, it has a terrible odor. Super creepy.
?
W N E S
POPE LICK MONSTER
Pope Lick Creek, KY
Half-man half-goat. Very dangerous rumors from various victims!

FRESNO NIGHTCRAWLERS
Fresno, CA

Only seen through pixelated film, these Ghost Pants are thought to be alien life-forms.

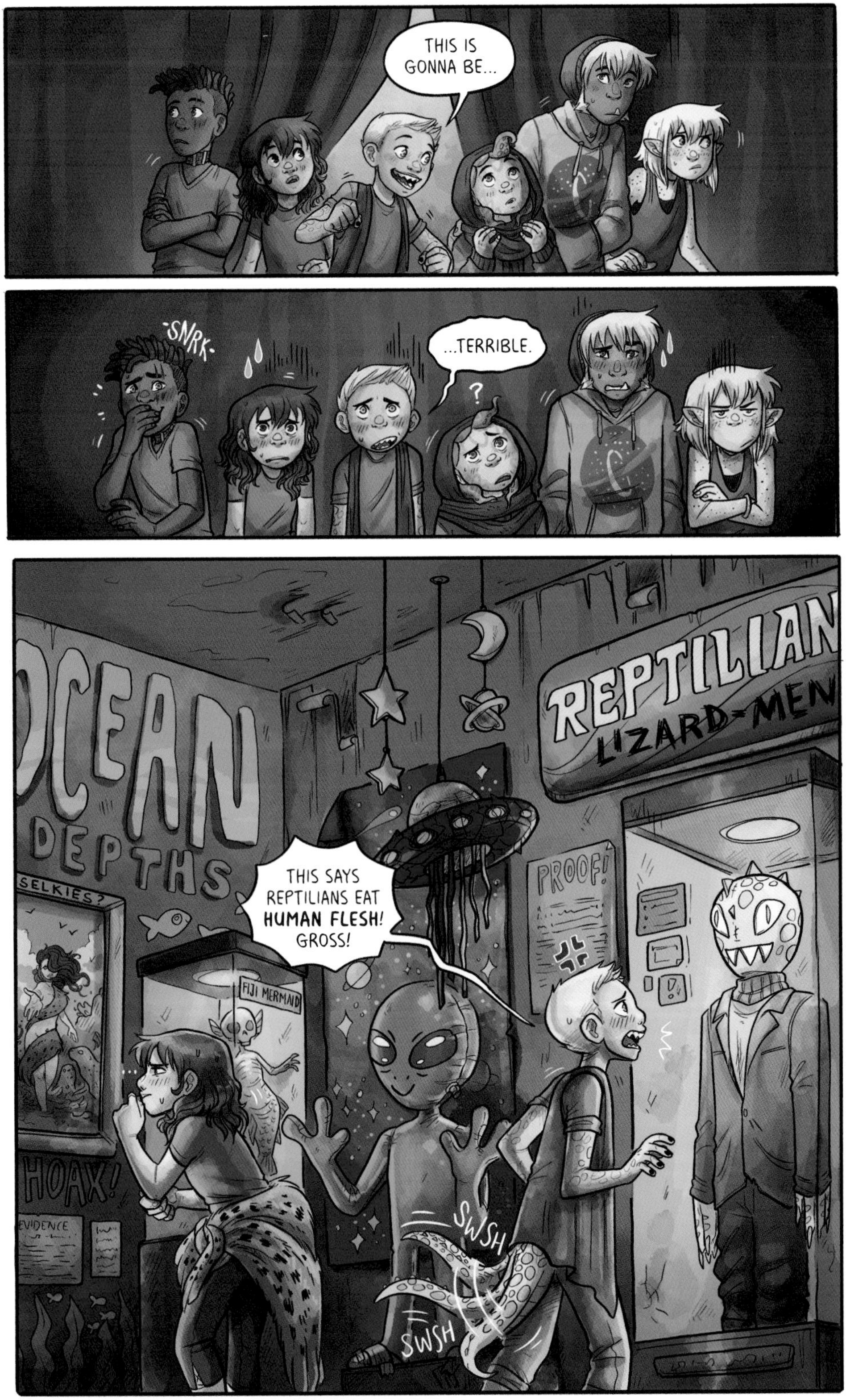
THIS IS GONNA BE...
-SNRK-
...TERRIBLE.
?
OCEAN
DEPTHS
SELKIES?
FIJI MERMAID
HOAX!
EVIDENCE
PROOF!
REPTILIAN
LIZARD-MEN
THIS SAYS REPTILIANS EAT **HUMAN FLESH**! GROSS!
SWSH
SWSH

186

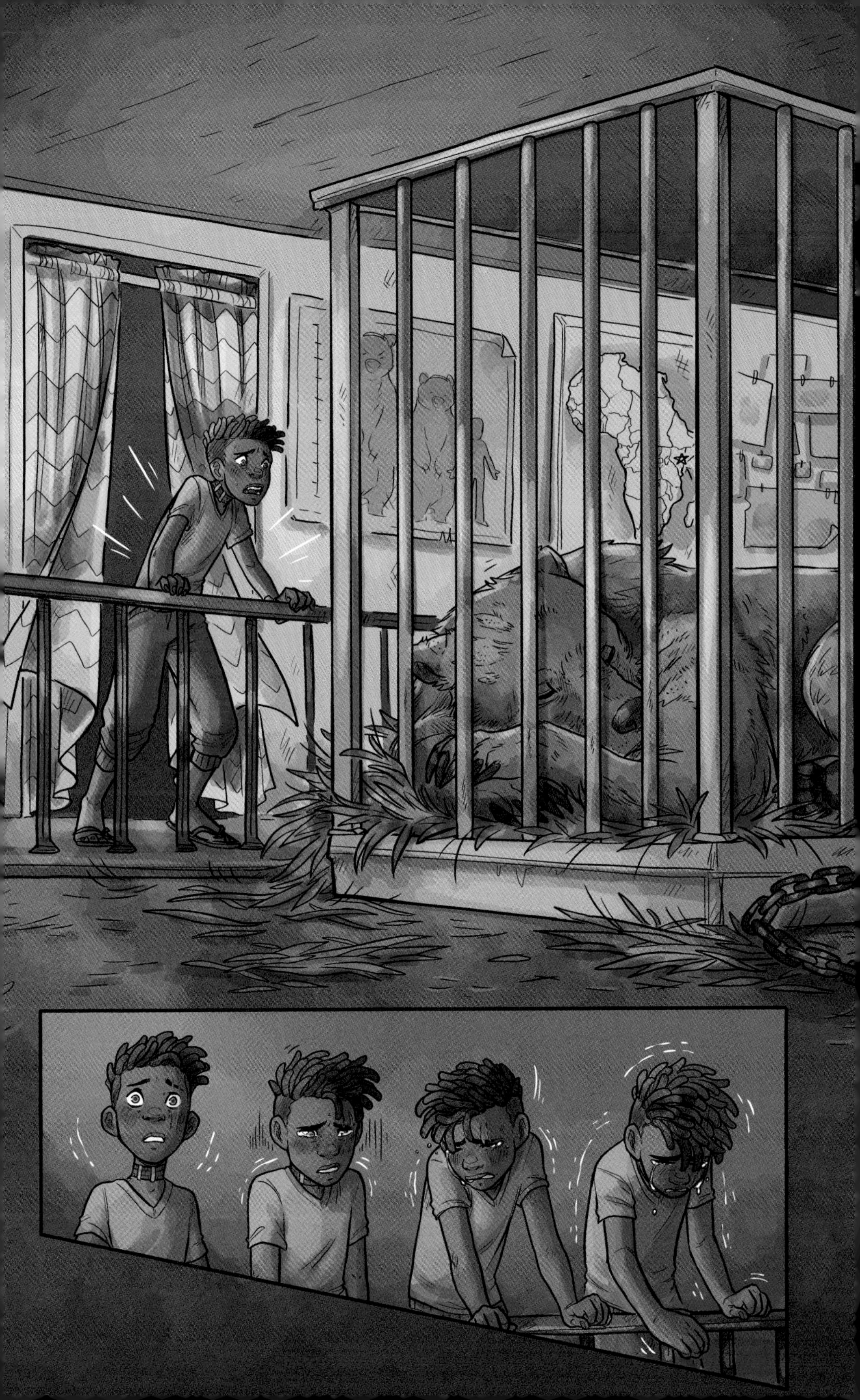

JAALI?

IS THAT REALLY A **NANDI BEAR**?

NO, I'M A NANDI BEAR. THAT'S JUST... A BEAR.

A **SICK** AND **OLD** BEAR WHO SHOULDN'T BE **IN A CAGE**!

CLANG

snff snff

whuff

I'M SORRY.

GIFT SHOP

EXIT

THAT WAS... A BAD SHOW.

YEAH.

ARE YOU OKAY?

SNIFF

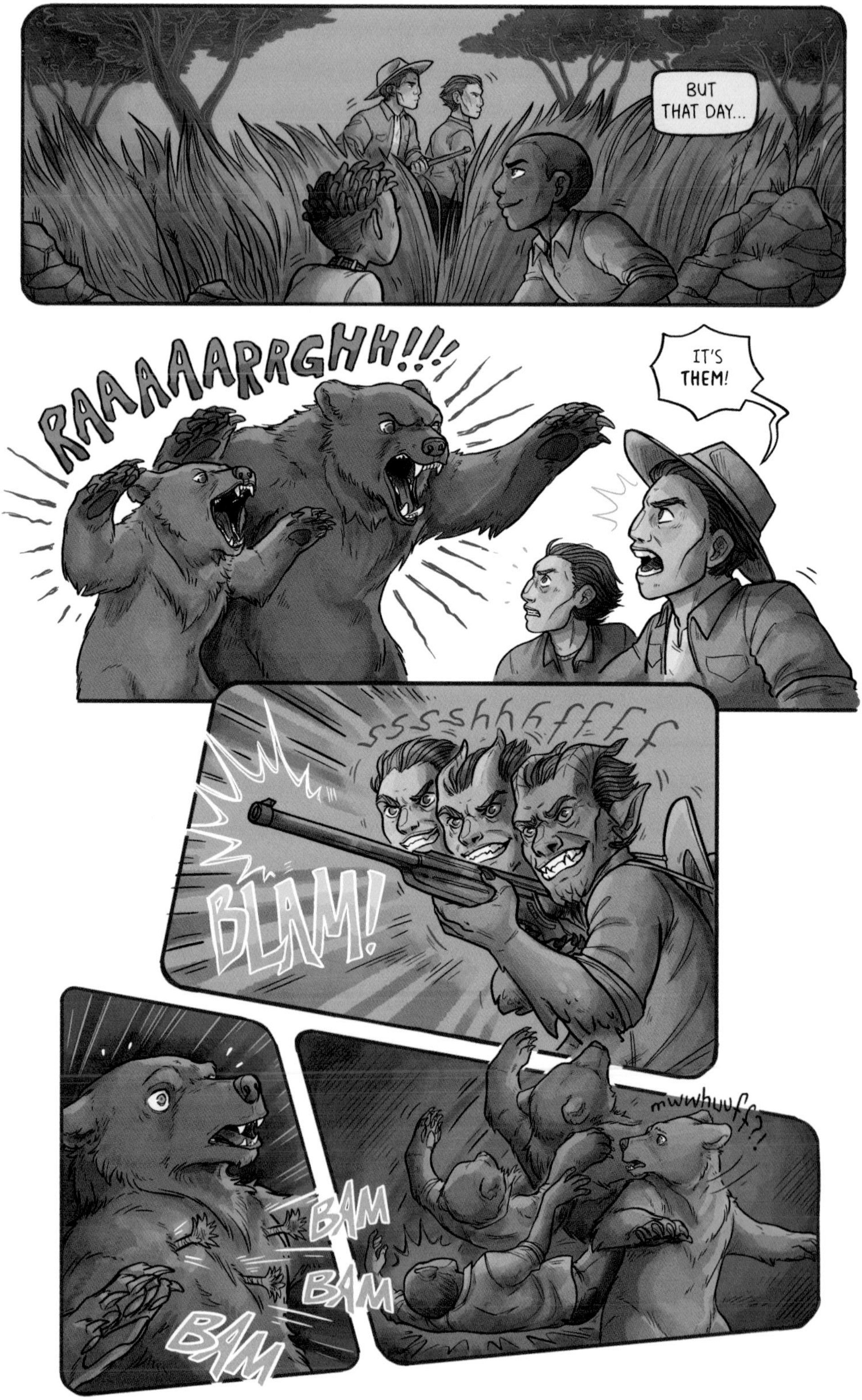
BUT THAT DAY...
RAAAAARRGHH!!!
IT'S THEM!
ssshhhffff
BLAM!
mwwhuuff?!
BAM
BAM
BAM

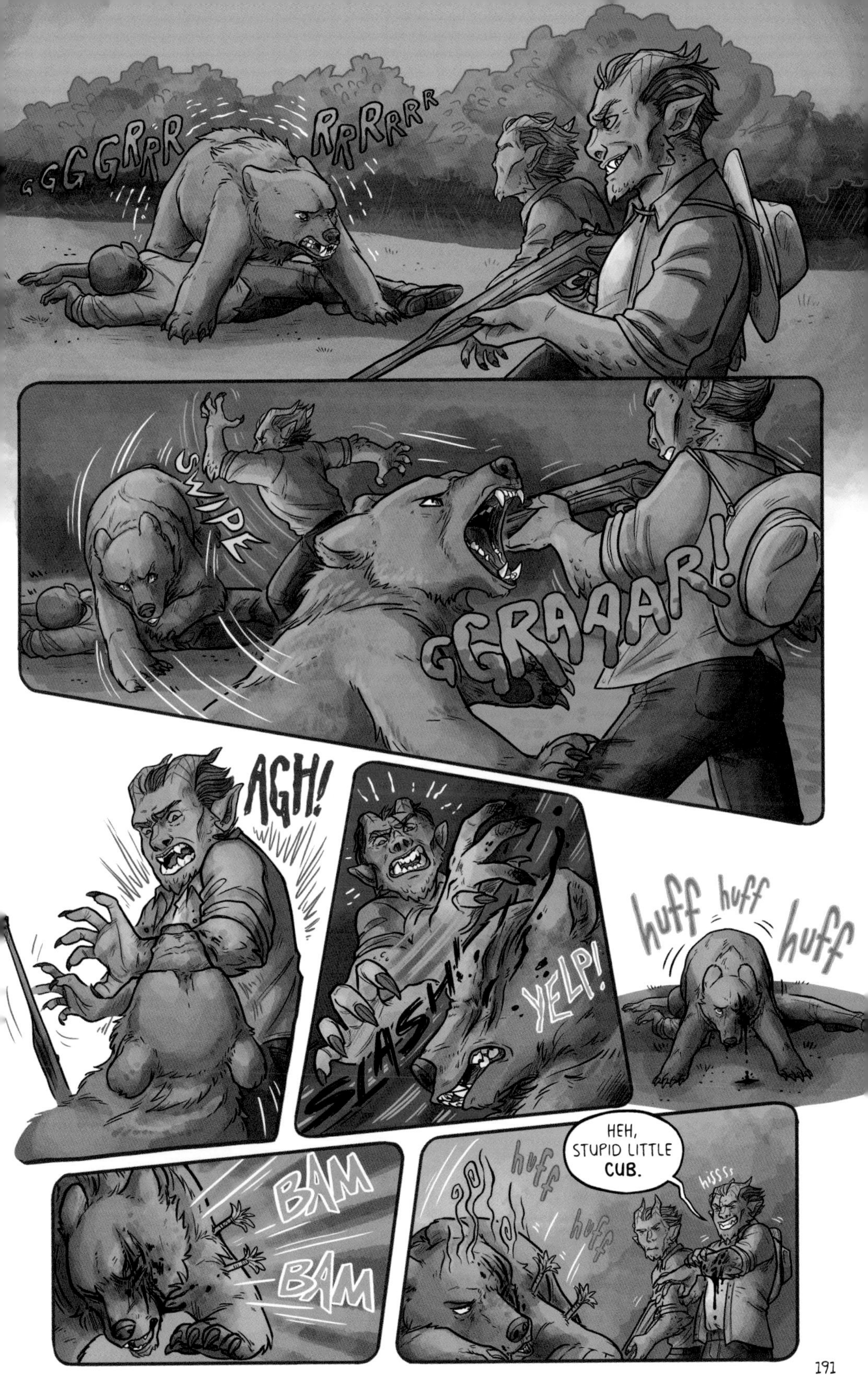
GGGGRRRR
RRRRRRR
SWIPE
GGRAAAR!
AGH!
SLASH!
YELP!
huff huff huff
BAM
BAM
huff
huff
HEH, STUPID LITTLE CUB.
hissss

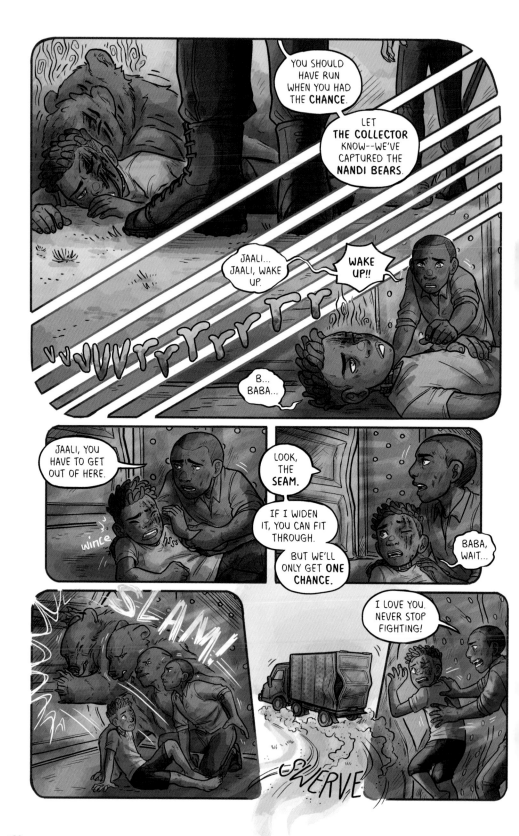

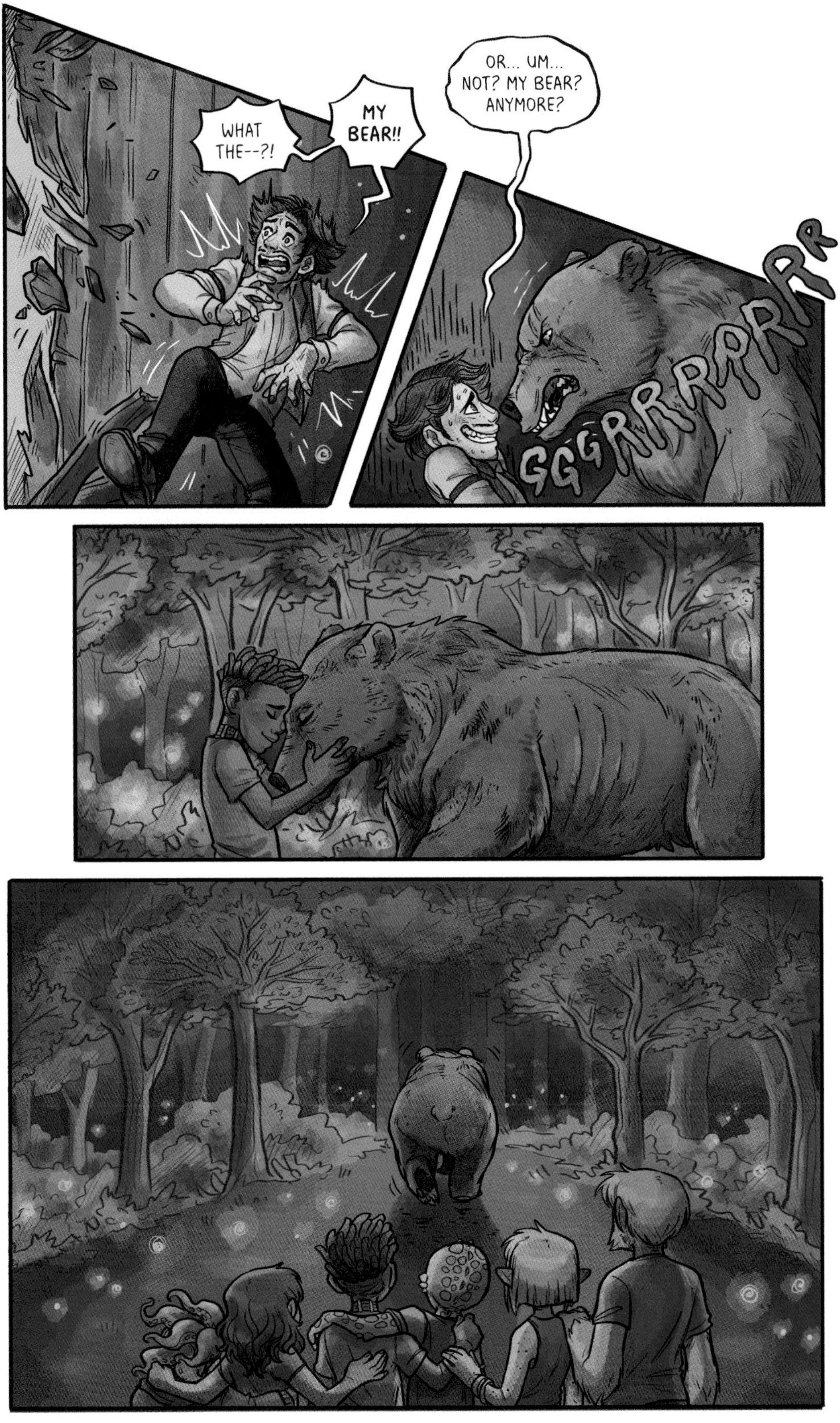
WHAT THE--?!
MY BEAR!!
OR... UM... NOT? MY BEAR? ANYMORE?
GGGRRRRRRRR

CHAPTER EIGHT

BRIEF RESPITE

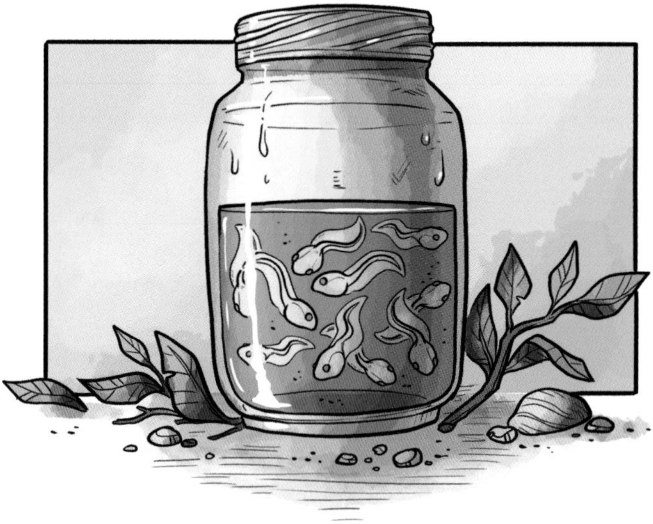

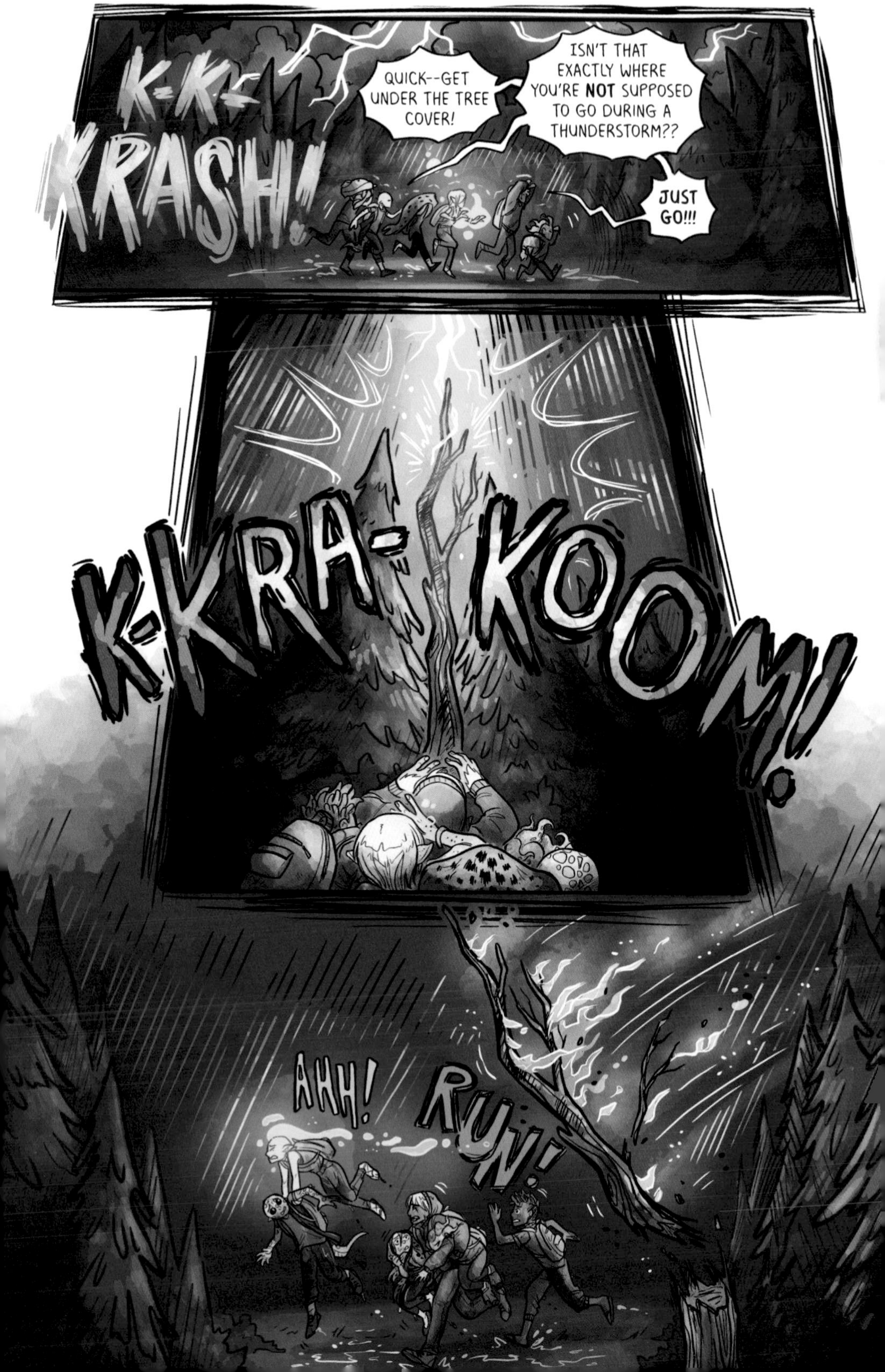
K-K-KRASH!
QUICK--GET UNDER THE TREE COVER!
ISN'T THAT EXACTLY WHERE YOU'RE **NOT** SUPPOSED TO GO DURING A THUNDERSTORM??
JUST GO!!!
K-KRA-KOOM!
AHH!
RUN!

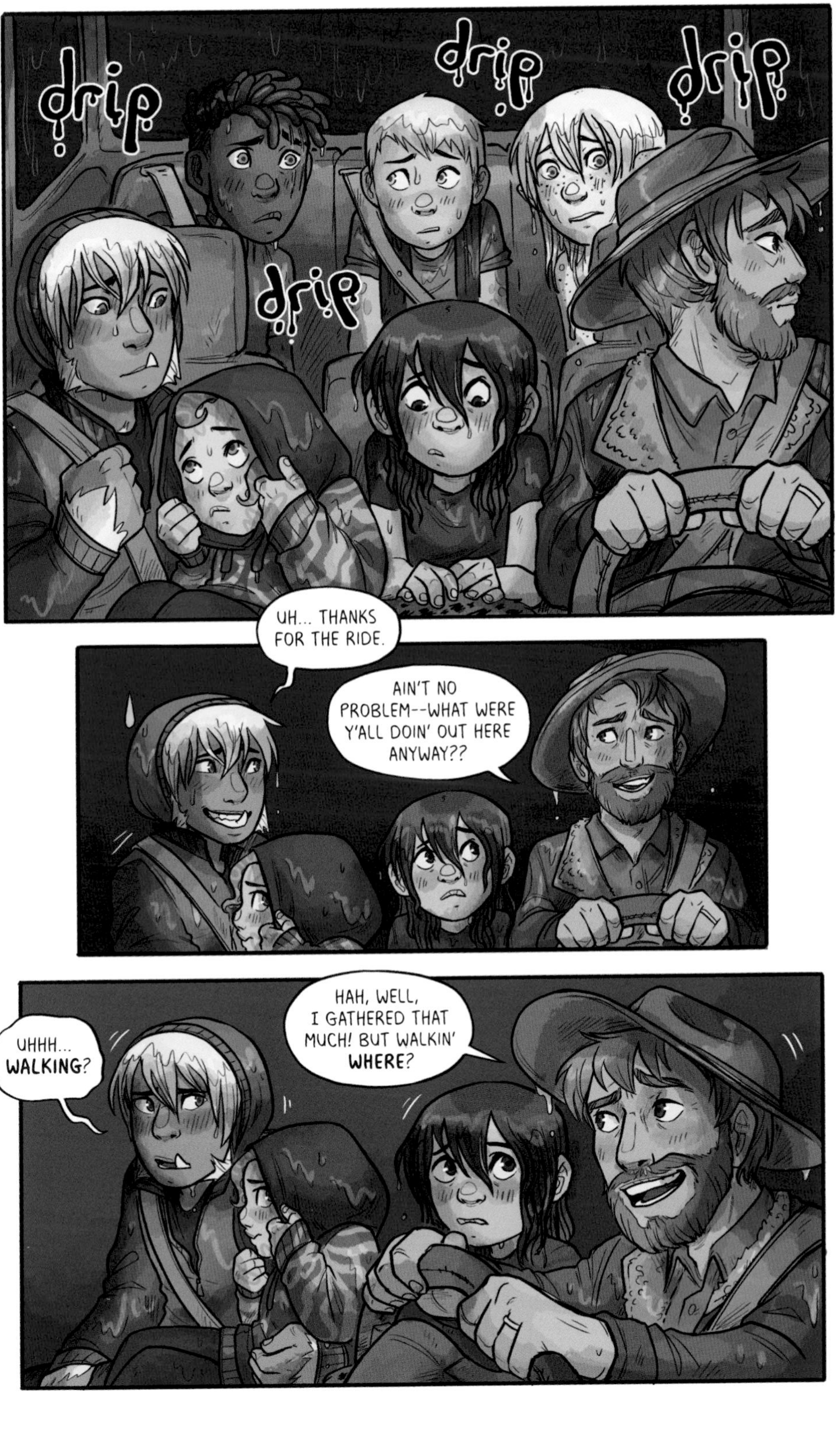

drip
drip
drip
drip
UH... THANKS FOR THE RIDE.
AIN'T NO PROBLEM--WHAT WERE Y'ALL DOIN' OUT HERE ANYWAY??
UHHH... **WALKING**?
HAH, WELL, I GATHERED THAT MUCH! BUT WALKIN' **WHERE**?

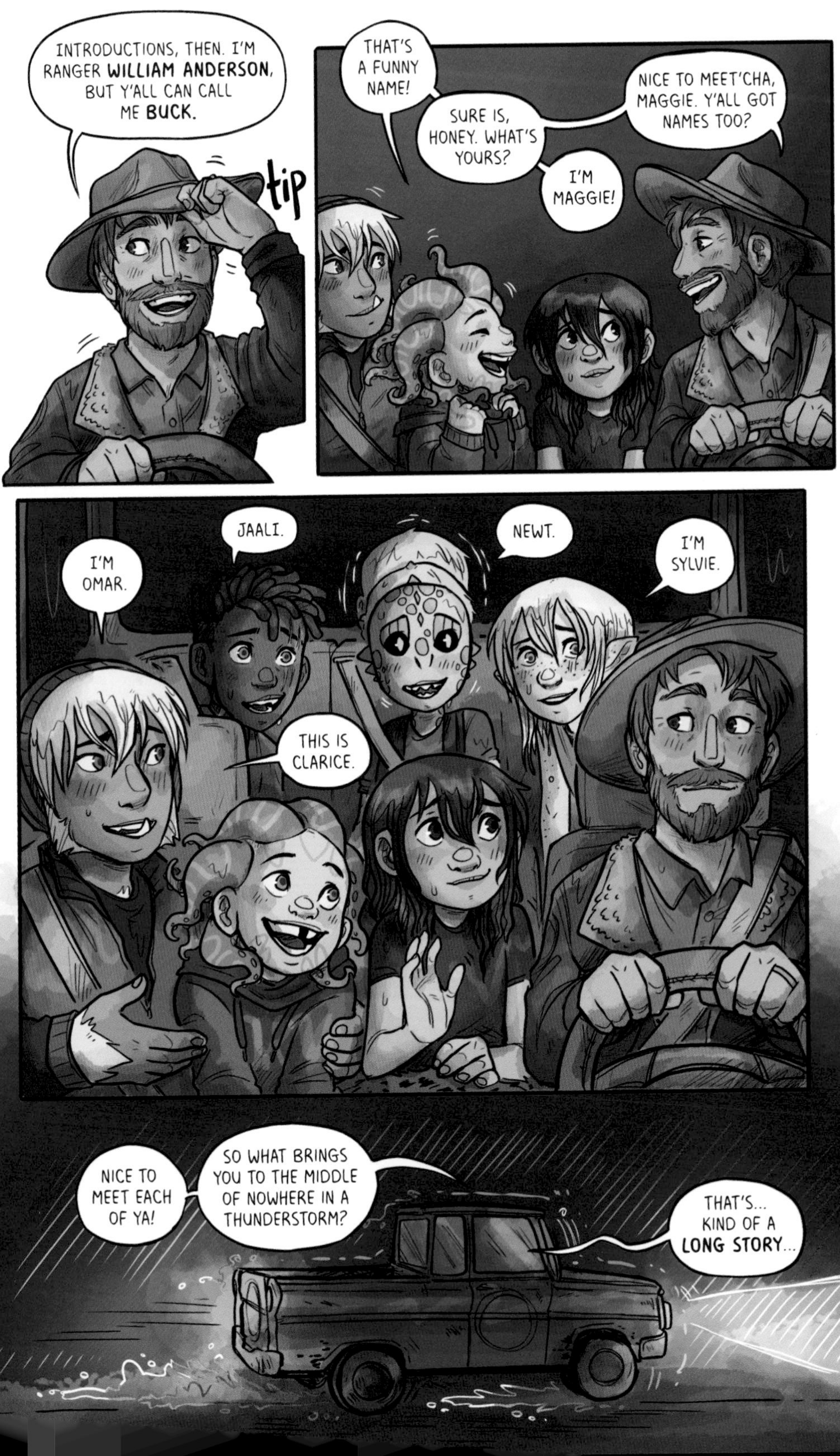
INTRODUCTIONS, THEN. I'M RANGER **WILLIAM ANDERSON**, BUT Y'ALL CAN CALL ME **BUCK.**
tip
THAT'S A FUNNY NAME!
SURE IS, HONEY. WHAT'S YOURS?
I'M MAGGIE!
NICE TO MEET'CHA, MAGGIE. Y'ALL GOT NAMES TOO?
I'M OMAR.
JAALI.
NEWT.
I'M SYLVIE.
THIS IS CLARICE.
NICE TO MEET EACH OF YA!
SO WHAT BRINGS YOU TO THE MIDDLE OF NOWHERE IN A THUNDERSTORM?
THAT'S... KIND OF A **LONG STORY**...

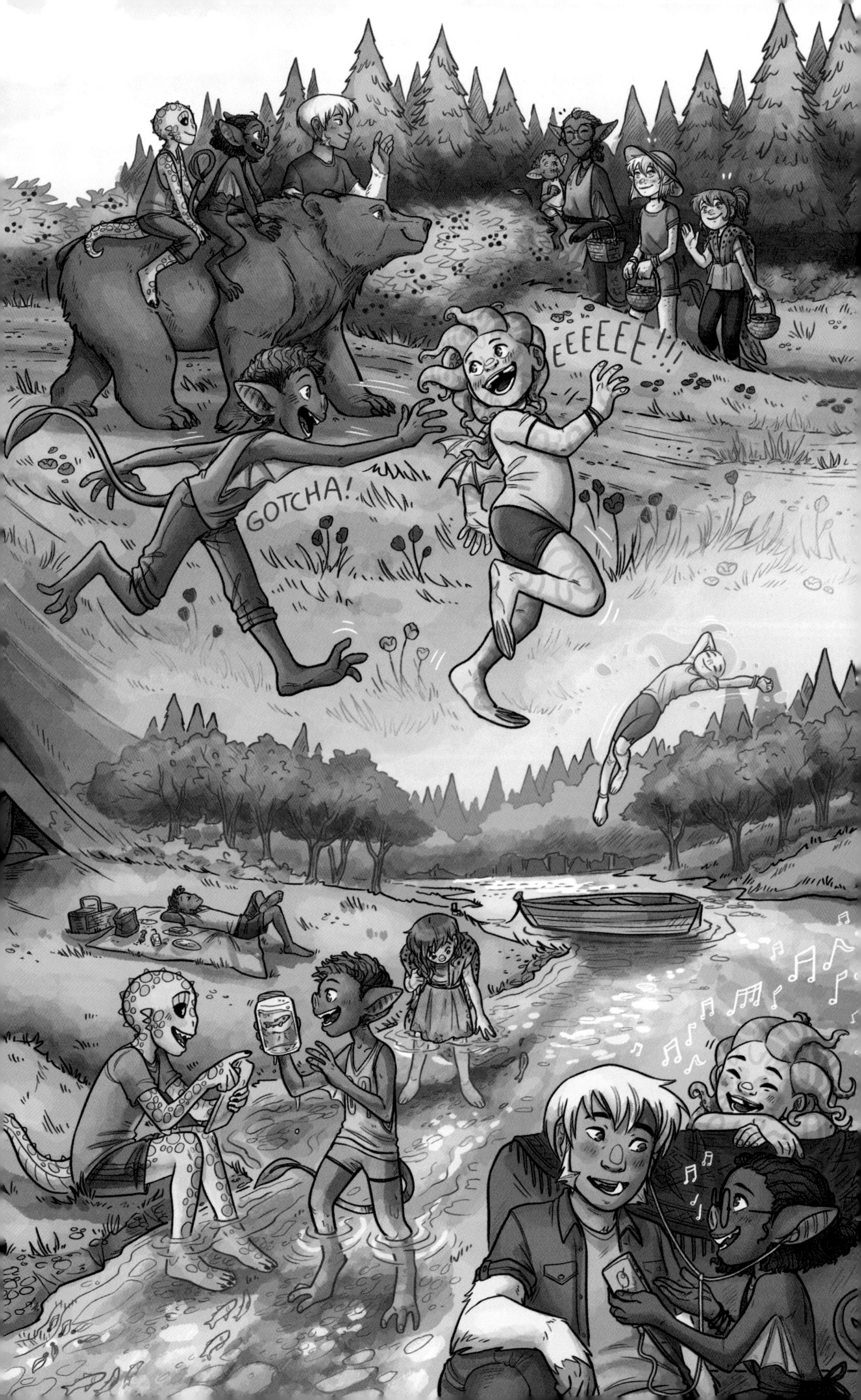
EEEEEE!!!
GOTCHA!

211

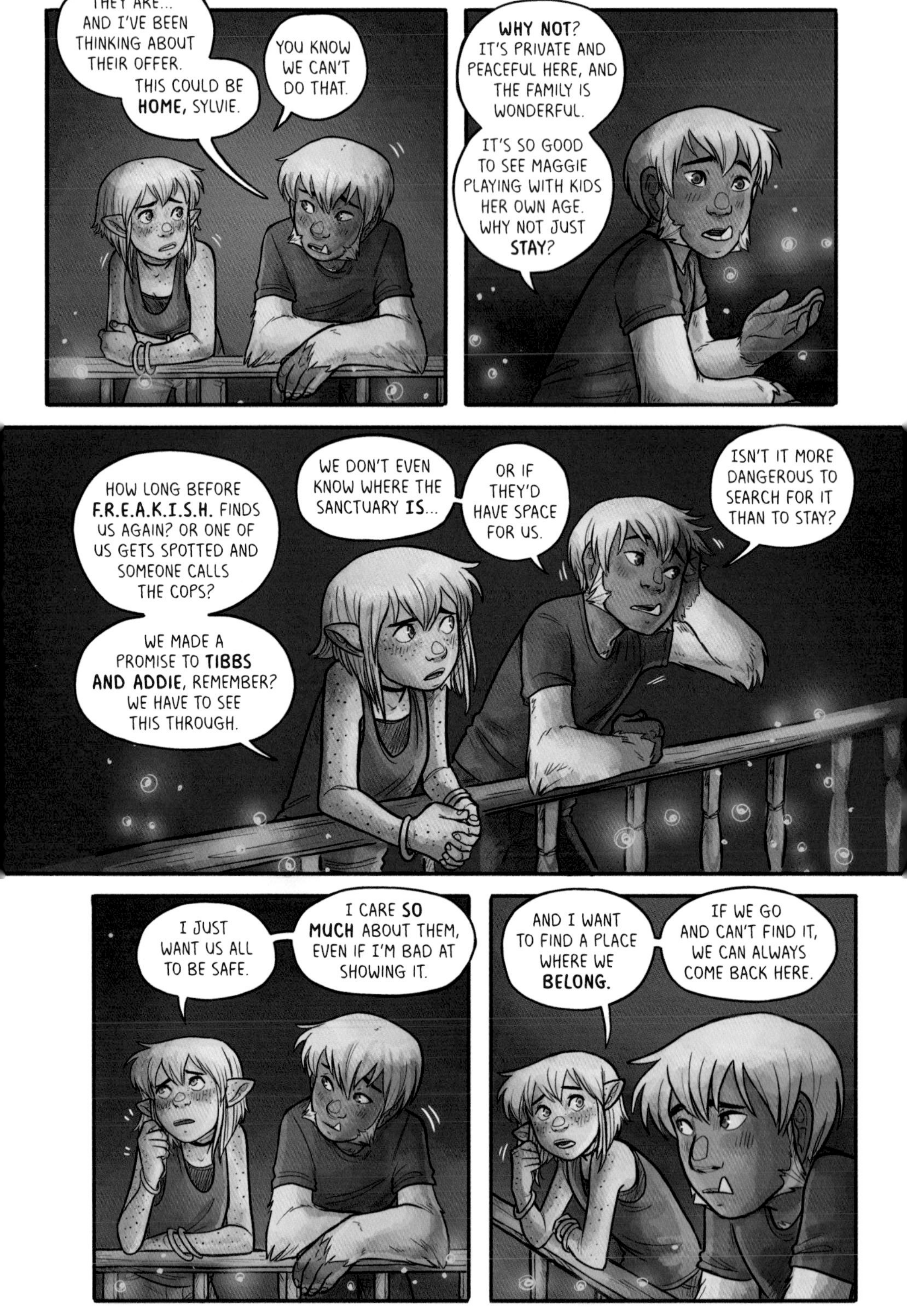
THEY ARE... AND I'VE BEEN THINKING ABOUT THEIR OFFER.
THIS COULD BE **HOME**, SYLVIE.
YOU KNOW WE CAN'T DO THAT.
WHY NOT? IT'S PRIVATE AND PEACEFUL HERE, AND THE FAMILY IS WONDERFUL.
IT'S SO GOOD TO SEE MAGGIE PLAYING WITH KIDS HER OWN AGE. WHY NOT JUST **STAY**?
HOW LONG BEFORE **F.R.E.A.K.I.S.H.** FINDS US AGAIN? OR ONE OF US GETS SPOTTED AND SOMEONE CALLS THE COPS?
WE MADE A PROMISE TO **TIBBS AND ADDIE**, REMEMBER? WE HAVE TO SEE THIS THROUGH.
WE DON'T EVEN KNOW WHERE THE SANCTUARY **IS**...
OR IF THEY'D HAVE SPACE FOR US.
ISN'T IT MORE DANGEROUS TO SEARCH FOR IT THAN TO STAY?
I JUST WANT US ALL TO BE SAFE.
I CARE **SO MUCH** ABOUT THEM, EVEN IF I'M BAD AT SHOWING IT.
AND I WANT TO FIND A PLACE WHERE WE **BELONG.**
IF WE GO AND CAN'T FIND IT, WE CAN ALWAYS COME BACK HERE.

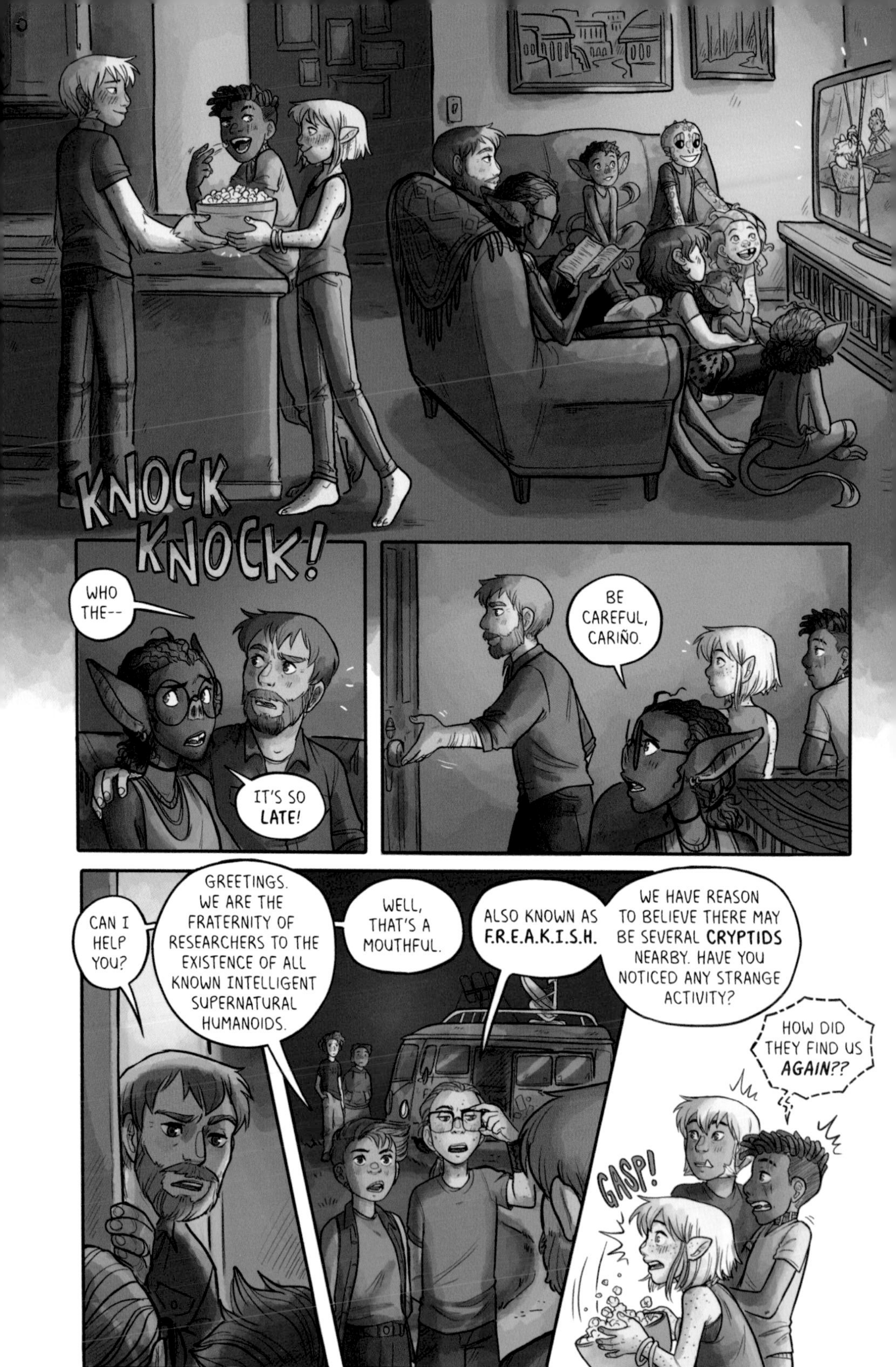
KNOCK KNOCK!
WHO THE--
IT'S SO LATE!
BE CAREFUL, CARIÑO.
CAN I HELP YOU?
GREETINGS. WE ARE THE FRATERNITY OF RESEARCHERS TO THE EXISTENCE OF ALL KNOWN INTELLIGENT SUPERNATURAL HUMANOIDS.
WELL, THAT'S A MOUTHFUL.
ALSO KNOWN AS F.R.E.A.K.I.S.H.
WE HAVE REASON TO BELIEVE THERE MAY BE SEVERAL CRYPTIDS NEARBY. HAVE YOU NOTICED ANY STRANGE ACTIVITY?
HOW DID THEY FIND US AGAIN??
GASP!

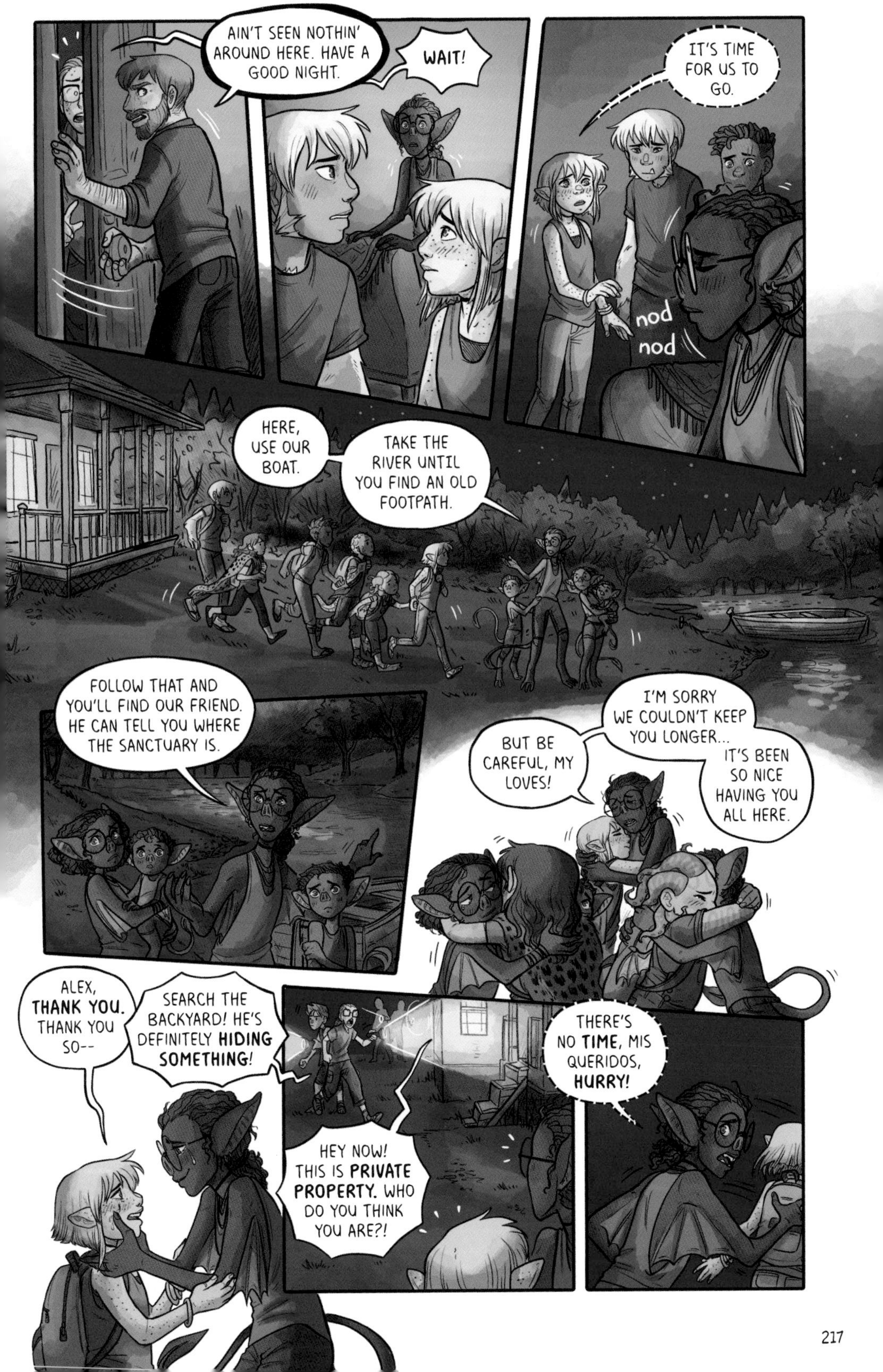
AIN'T SEEN NOTHIN' AROUND HERE. HAVE A GOOD NIGHT.
WAIT!
IT'S TIME FOR US TO GO.
nod nod
HERE, USE OUR BOAT.
TAKE THE RIVER UNTIL YOU FIND AN OLD FOOTPATH.
FOLLOW THAT AND YOU'LL FIND OUR FRIEND. HE CAN TELL YOU WHERE THE SANCTUARY IS.
I'M SORRY WE COULDN'T KEEP YOU LONGER...
IT'S BEEN SO NICE HAVING YOU ALL HERE.
BUT BE CAREFUL, MY LOVES!
ALEX, THANK YOU. THANK YOU SO--
SEARCH THE BACKYARD! HE'S DEFINITELY HIDING SOMETHING!
HEY NOW! THIS IS PRIVATE PROPERTY. WHO DO YOU THINK YOU ARE?!
THERE'S NO TIME, MIS QUERIDOS, HURRY!

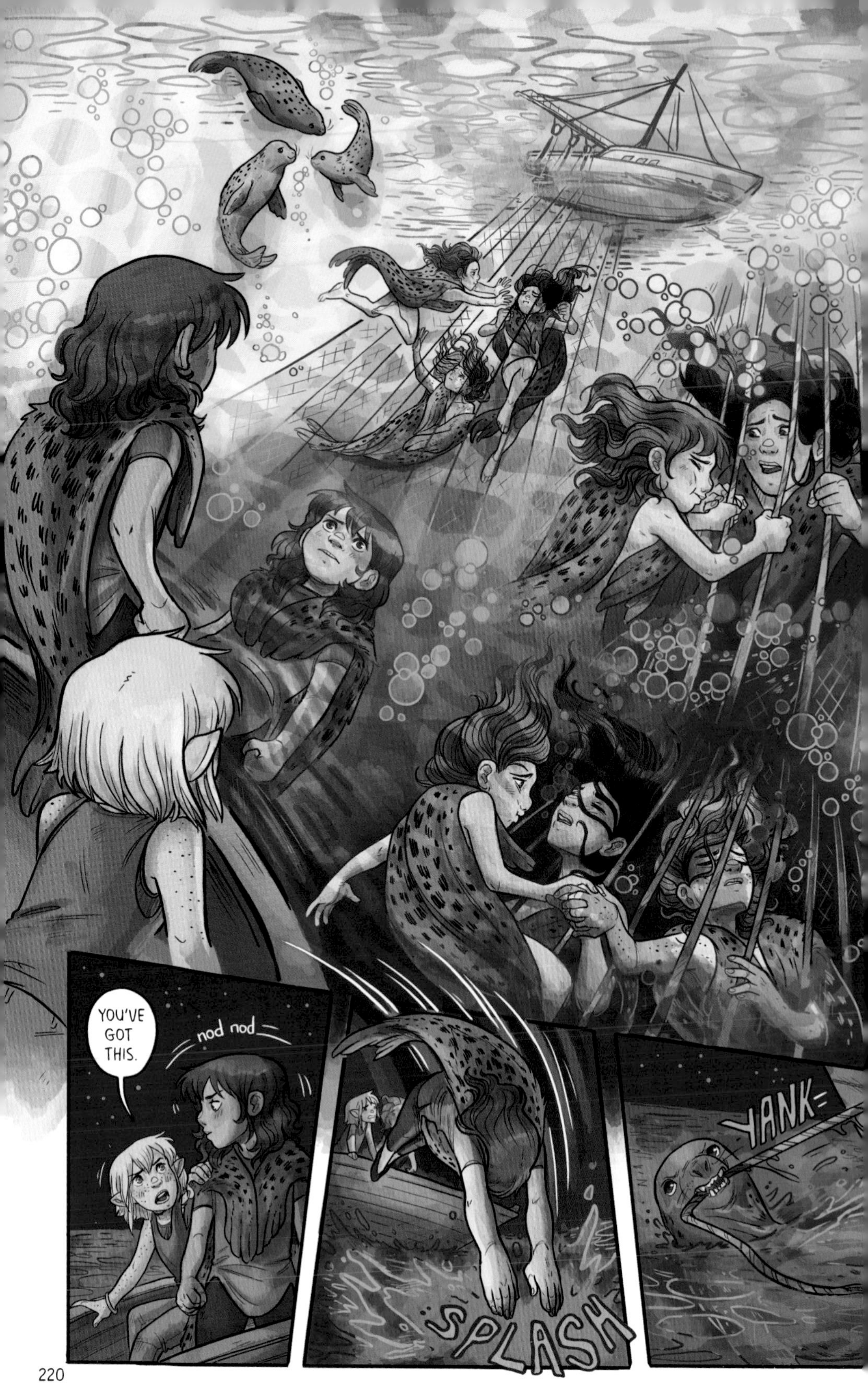

YOU'VE GOT THIS.
nod nod
SPLASH
YANK

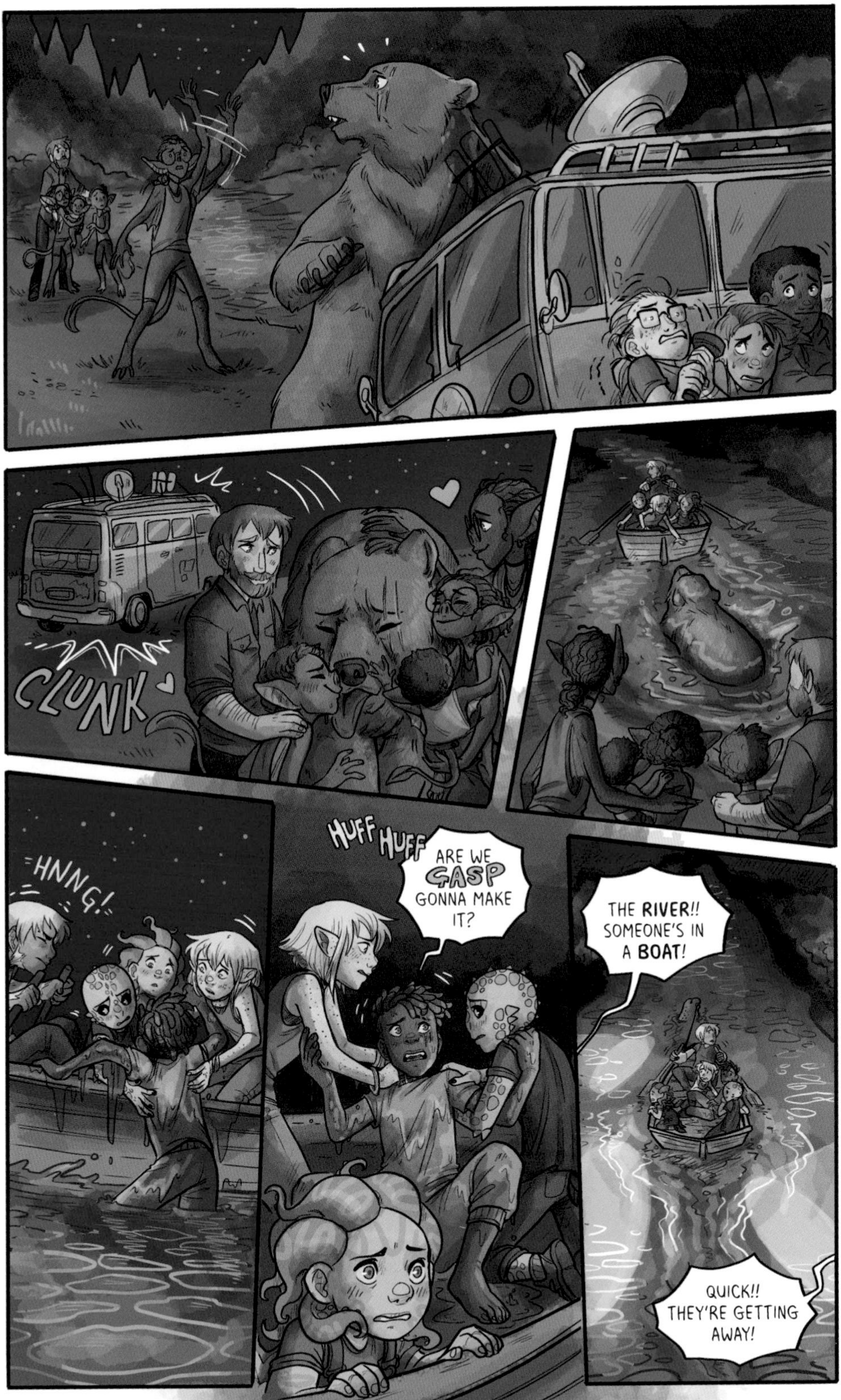
CLUNK
HNNG!
HUFF HUFF
ARE WE GASP GONNA MAKE IT?
THE RIVER!! SOMEONE'S IN A BOAT!
QUICK!! THEY'RE GETTING AWAY!

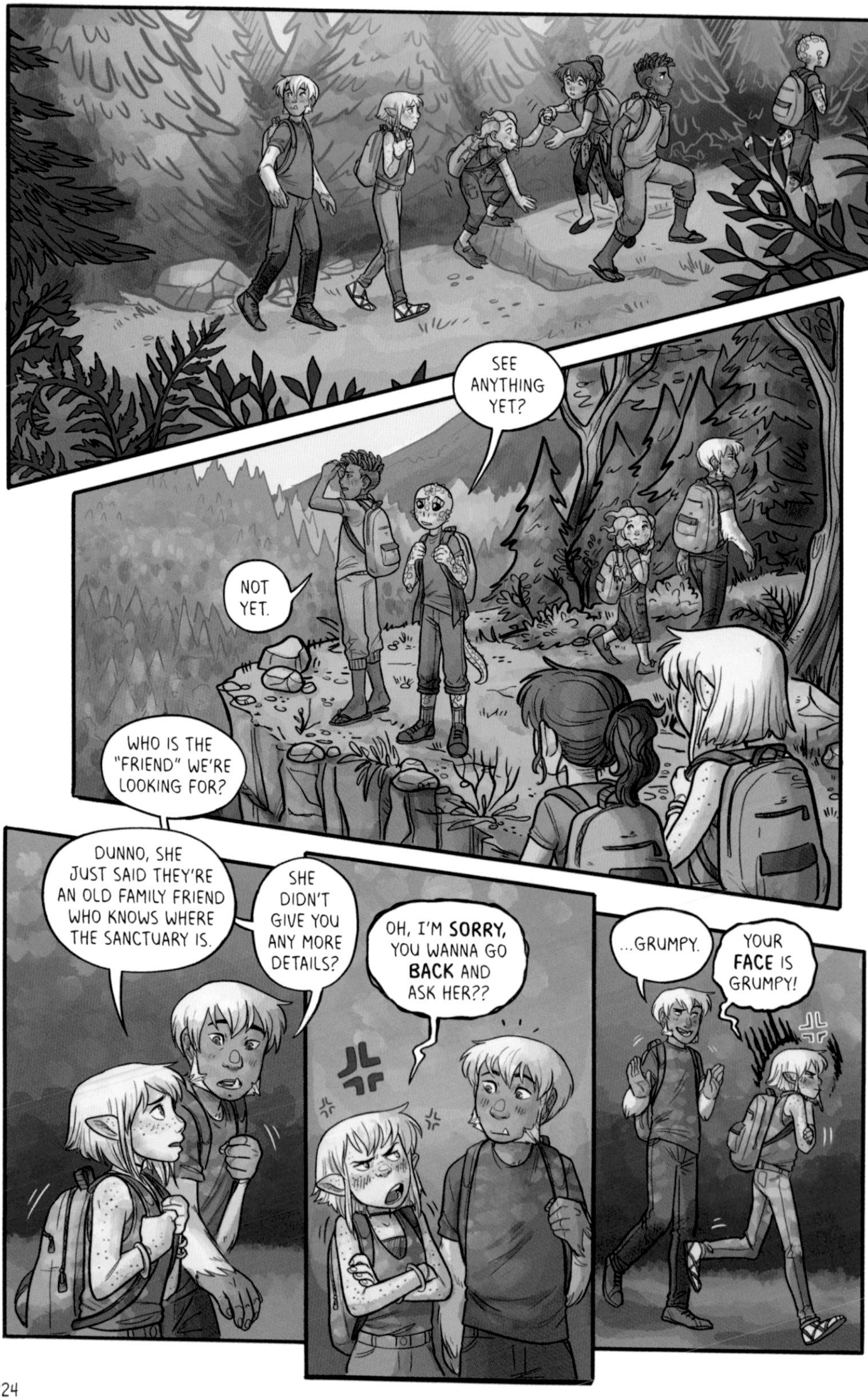
SEE ANYTHING YET?
NOT YET.
WHO IS THE "FRIEND" WE'RE LOOKING FOR?
DUNNO, SHE JUST SAID THEY'RE AN OLD FAMILY FRIEND WHO KNOWS WHERE THE SANCTUARY IS.
SHE DIDN'T GIVE YOU ANY MORE DETAILS?
OH, I'M **SORRY,** YOU WANNA GO **BACK** AND ASK HER??
...GRUMPY.
YOUR **FACE** IS GRUMPY!

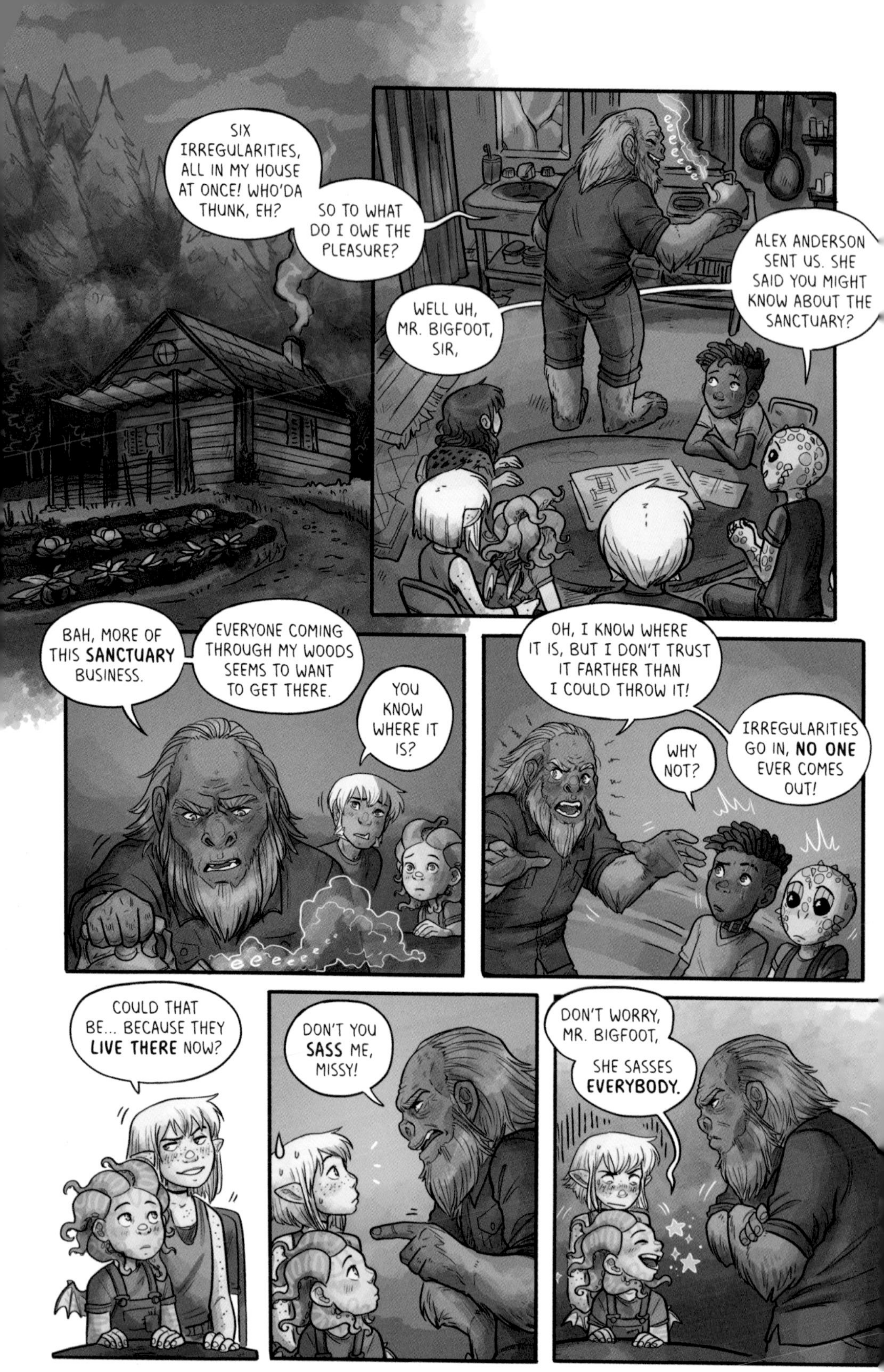
SIX IRREGULARITIES, ALL IN MY HOUSE AT ONCE! WHO'DA THUNK, EH?
SO TO WHAT DO I OWE THE PLEASURE?
WELL UH, MR. BIGFOOT, SIR,
ALEX ANDERSON SENT US. SHE SAID YOU MIGHT KNOW ABOUT THE SANCTUARY?
BAH, MORE OF THIS SANCTUARY BUSINESS.
EVERYONE COMING THROUGH MY WOODS SEEMS TO WANT TO GET THERE.
YOU KNOW WHERE IT IS?
OH, I KNOW WHERE IT IS, BUT I DON'T TRUST IT FARTHER THAN I COULD THROW IT!
WHY NOT?
IRREGULARITIES GO IN, NO ONE EVER COMES OUT!
COULD THAT BE... BECAUSE THEY LIVE THERE NOW?
DON'T YOU SASS ME, MISSY!
DON'T WORRY, MR. BIGFOOT,
SHE SASSES EVERYBODY.

CHAPTER NINE

UNRAVELING

GUH! I'M SICK OF WEARING ALL THIS **STUFF**!

IT'S **HOT** AND IT SQUISHES MY **WINGS**!

fumble

WE'VE TALKED ABOUT THIS--NORMAL PEOPLE WOULD **FREAK OUT** IF THEY SAW YOU.

I HAVE TO DO MY HUMAN FACE AND HIDE MY TAIL. WE ALL HAVE TO LOOK HUMAN.

BUT THAT ONE GUY THOUGHT I WAS WEARING A **COSTUME**!

BING-BONG

I KNOW BUT HE DIDN'T GET A VERY GOOD LOOK AT YOU. WE JUST DON'T WANT TO GET IN TROUBLE OR SENT BACK TO THE PLAYROOM.

SWIP

SWIP

ONCE WE'RE IN THE SANCTUARY I'M SURE YOU'LL NEVER HAVE TO WEAR IT AGAIN.

...FINE.

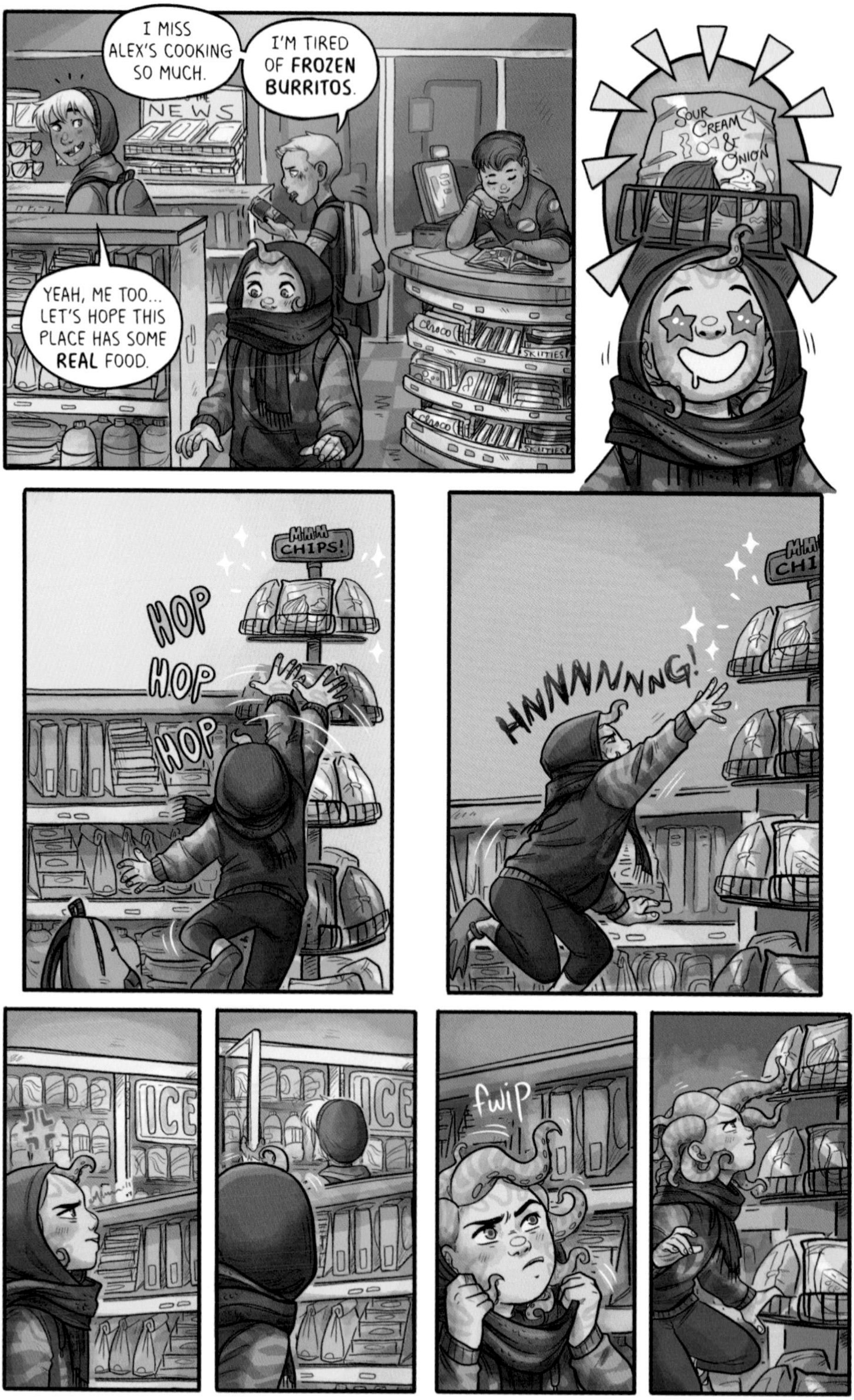

I MISS ALEX'S COOKING SO MUCH.
I'M TIRED OF **FROZEN BURRITOS**.
YEAH, ME TOO... LET'S HOPE THIS PLACE HAS SOME **REAL** FOOD.
NEWS
SOUR CREAM & ONION
CHIPS!
HOP
HOP
HOP
HNNNNNNG!
ICE
ICE
fwip

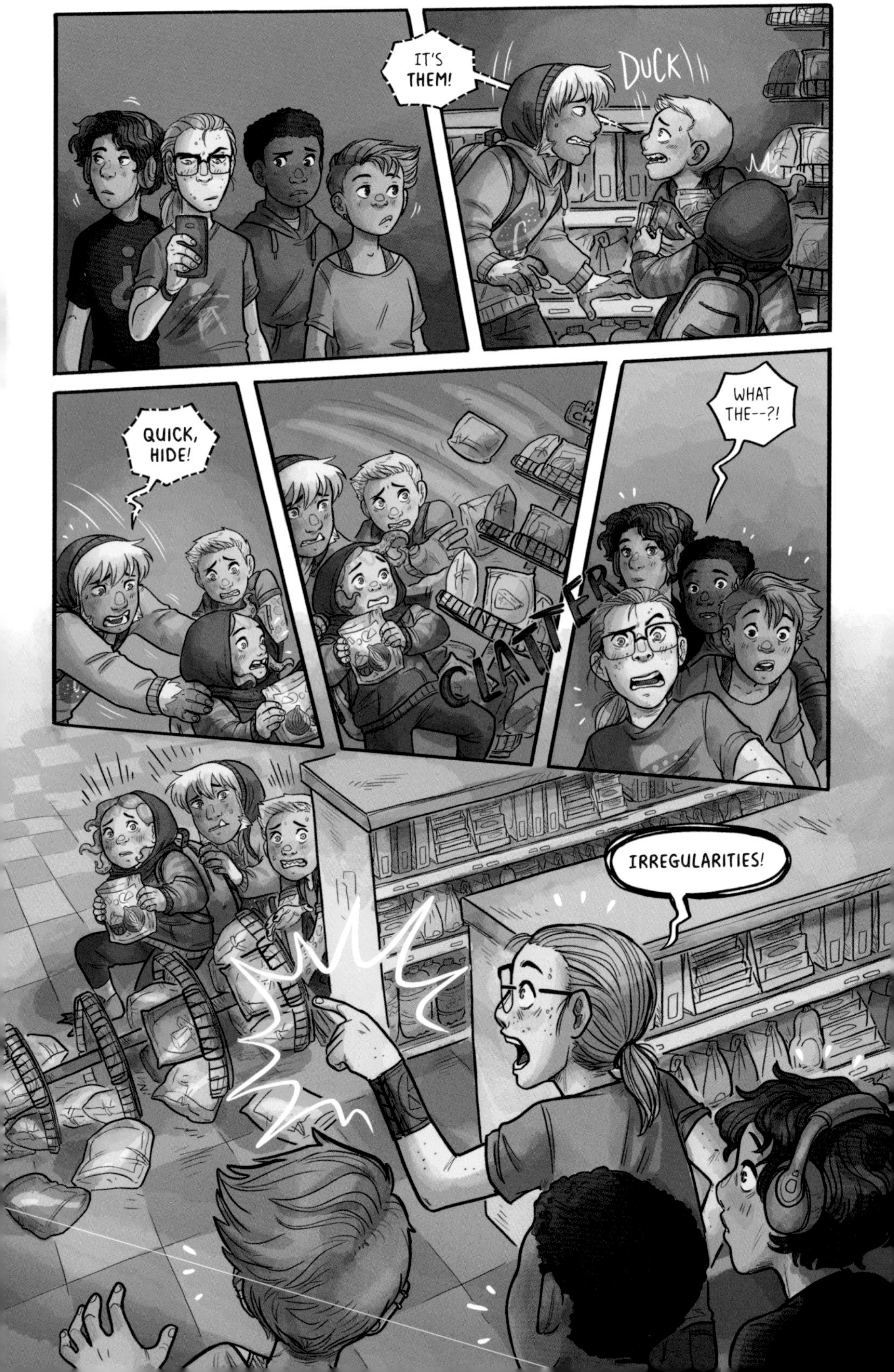
IT'S THEM!
DUCK
QUICK, HIDE!
CLATTER
WHAT THE--?!
IRREGULARITIES!

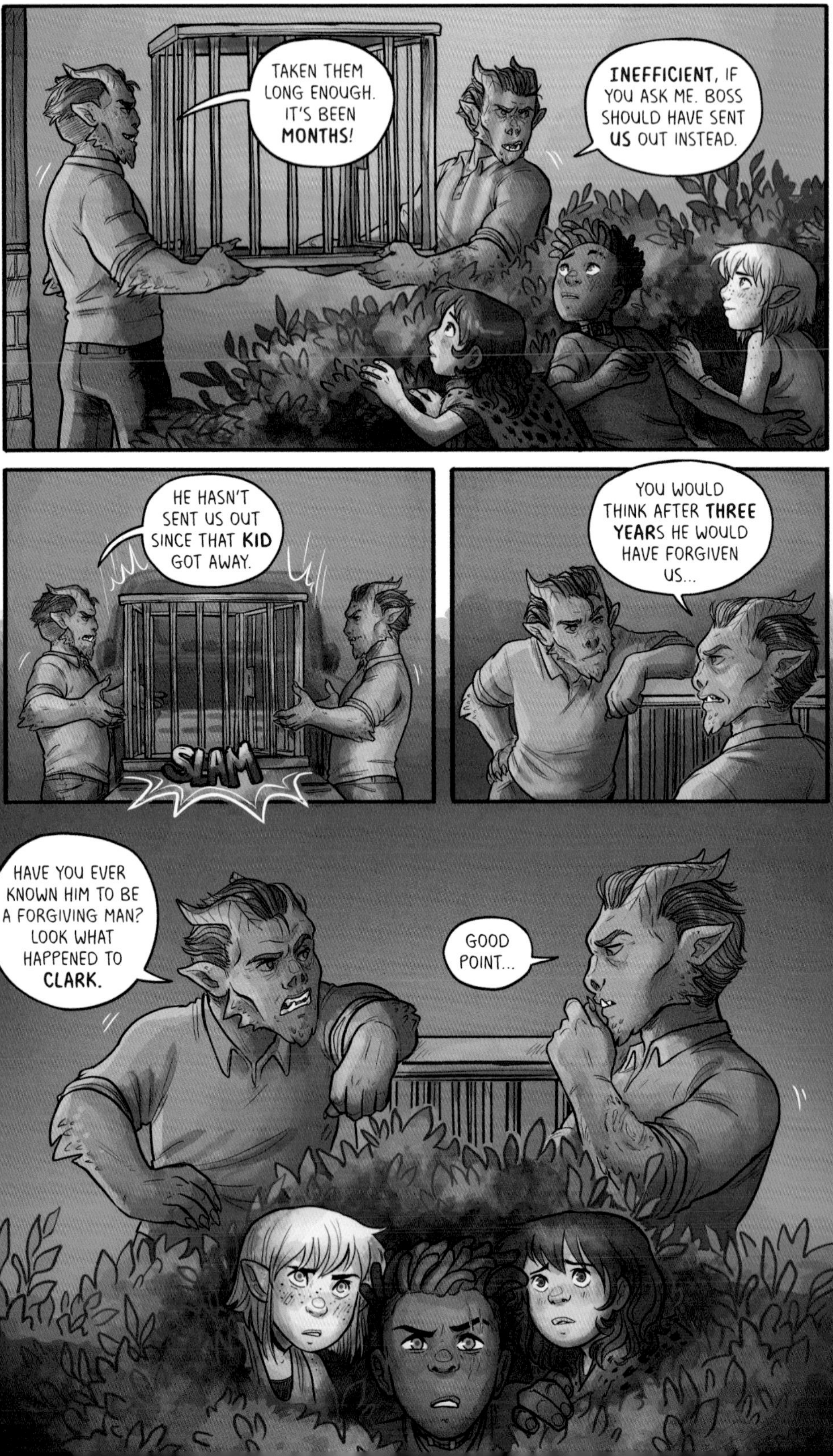
TAKEN THEM LONG ENOUGH. IT'S BEEN **MONTHS**!
INEFFICIENT, IF YOU ASK ME. BOSS SHOULD HAVE SENT **US** OUT INSTEAD.
HE HASN'T SENT US OUT SINCE THAT **KID** GOT AWAY.
SLAM
YOU WOULD THINK AFTER **THREE YEAR**S HE WOULD HAVE FORGIVEN US...
HAVE YOU EVER KNOWN HIM TO BE A FORGIVING MAN? LOOK WHAT HAPPENED TO **CLARK.**
GOOD POINT...

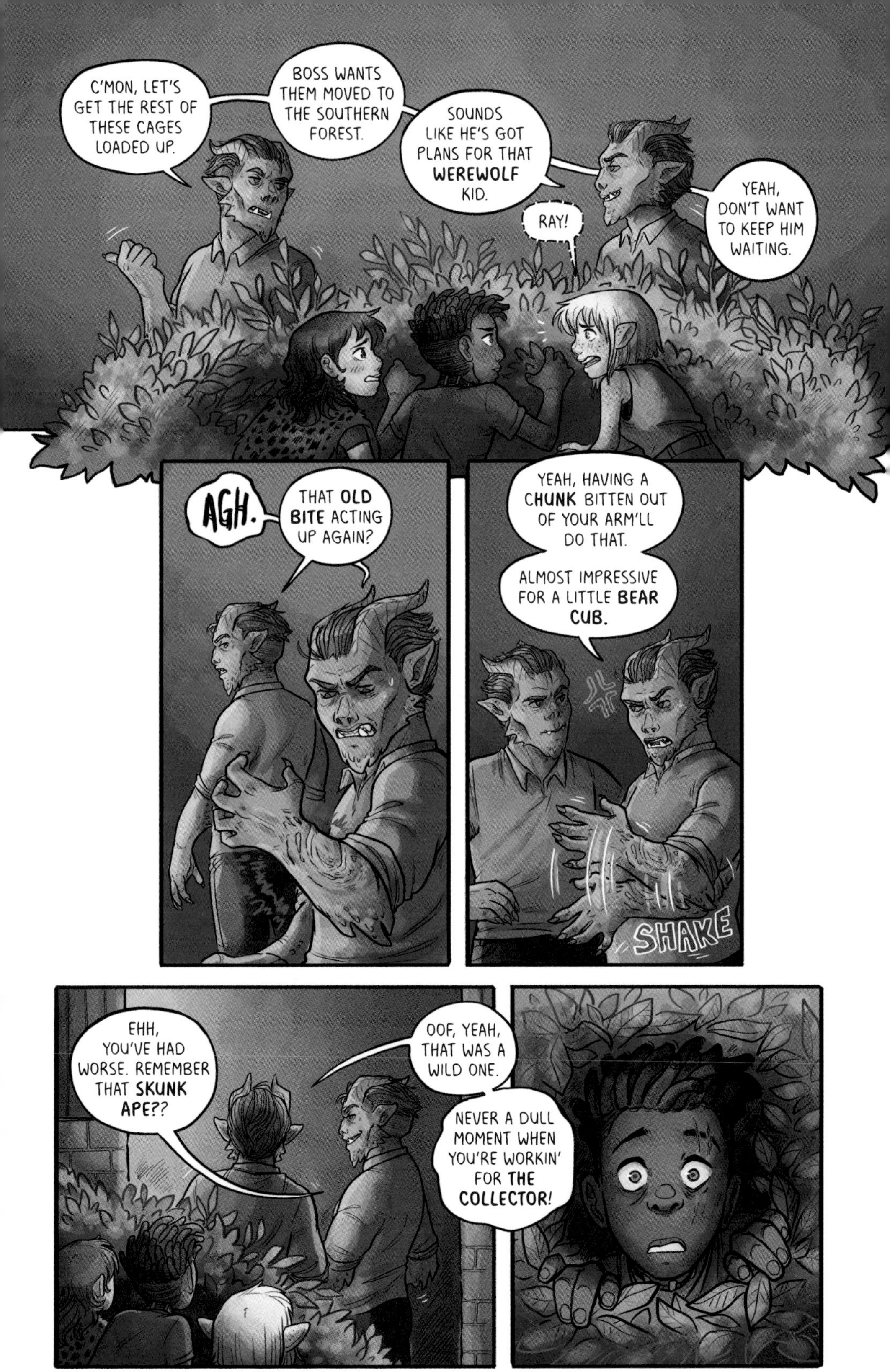
C'MON, LET'S GET THE REST OF THESE CAGES LOADED UP.
BOSS WANTS THEM MOVED TO THE SOUTHERN FOREST.
SOUNDS LIKE HE'S GOT PLANS FOR THAT WEREWOLF KID.
RAY!
YEAH, DON'T WANT TO KEEP HIM WAITING.
AGH.
THAT OLD BITE ACTING UP AGAIN?
YEAH, HAVING A CHUNK BITTEN OUT OF YOUR ARM'LL DO THAT.
ALMOST IMPRESSIVE FOR A LITTLE BEAR CUB.
SHAKE
EHH, YOU'VE HAD WORSE. REMEMBER THAT SKUNK APE??
OOF, YEAH, THAT WAS A WILD ONE.
NEVER A DULL MOMENT WHEN YOU'RE WORKIN' FOR THE COLLECTOR!

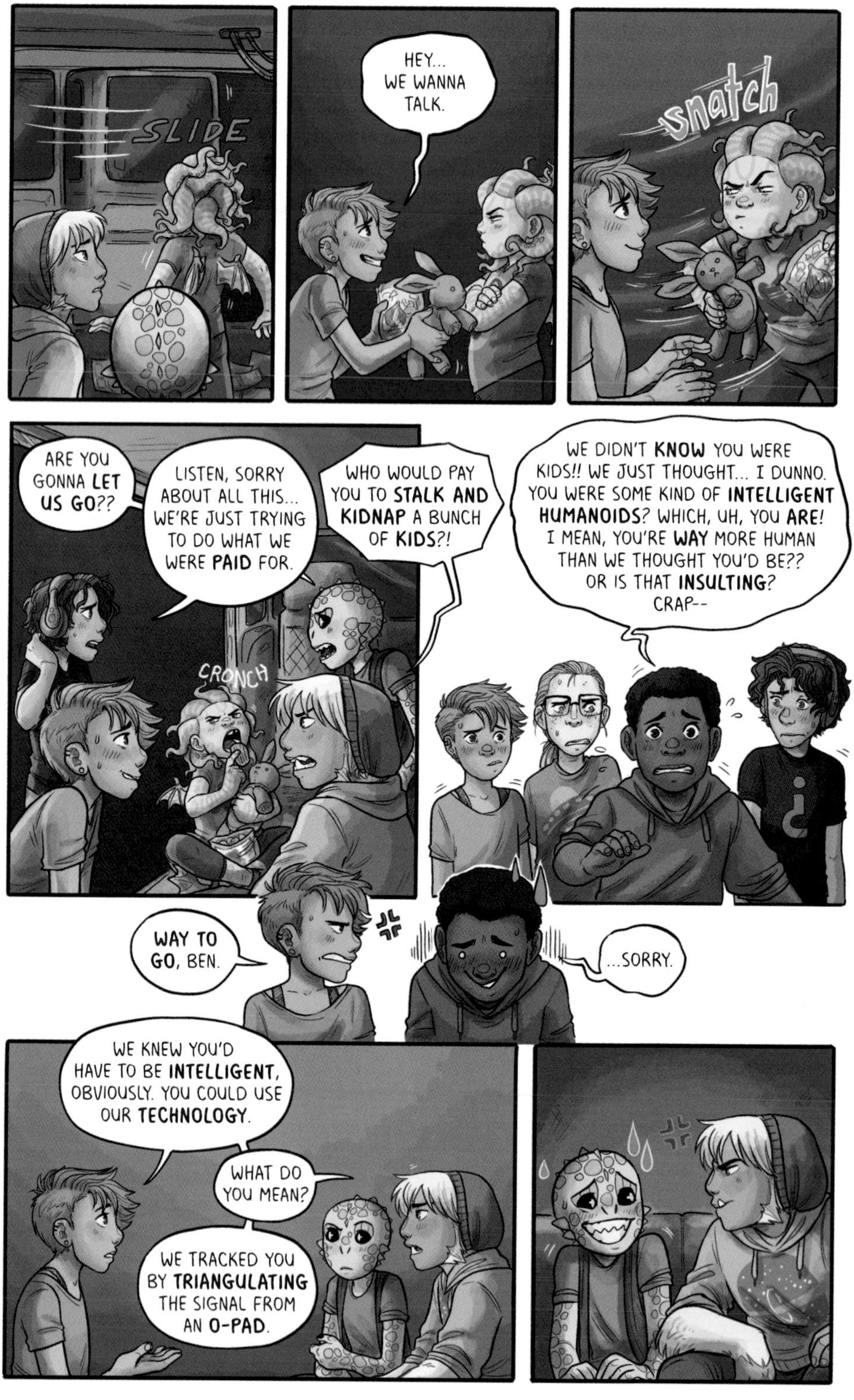
SLIDE
HEY... WE WANNA TALK.
snatch
ARE YOU GONNA LET US GO??
LISTEN, SORRY ABOUT ALL THIS... WE'RE JUST TRYING TO DO WHAT WE WERE PAID FOR.
WHO WOULD PAY YOU TO STALK AND KIDNAP A BUNCH OF KIDS?!
CRONCH
WE DIDN'T KNOW YOU WERE KIDS!! WE JUST THOUGHT... I DUNNO. YOU WERE SOME KIND OF INTELLIGENT HUMANOIDS? WHICH, UH, YOU ARE! I MEAN, YOU'RE WAY MORE HUMAN THAN WE THOUGHT YOU'D BE?? OR IS THAT INSULTING? CRAP--
WAY TO GO, BEN.
...SORRY.
WE KNEW YOU'D HAVE TO BE INTELLIGENT, OBVIOUSLY. YOU COULD USE OUR TECHNOLOGY.
WHAT DO YOU MEAN?
WE TRACKED YOU BY TRIANGULATING THE SIGNAL FROM AN O-PAD.

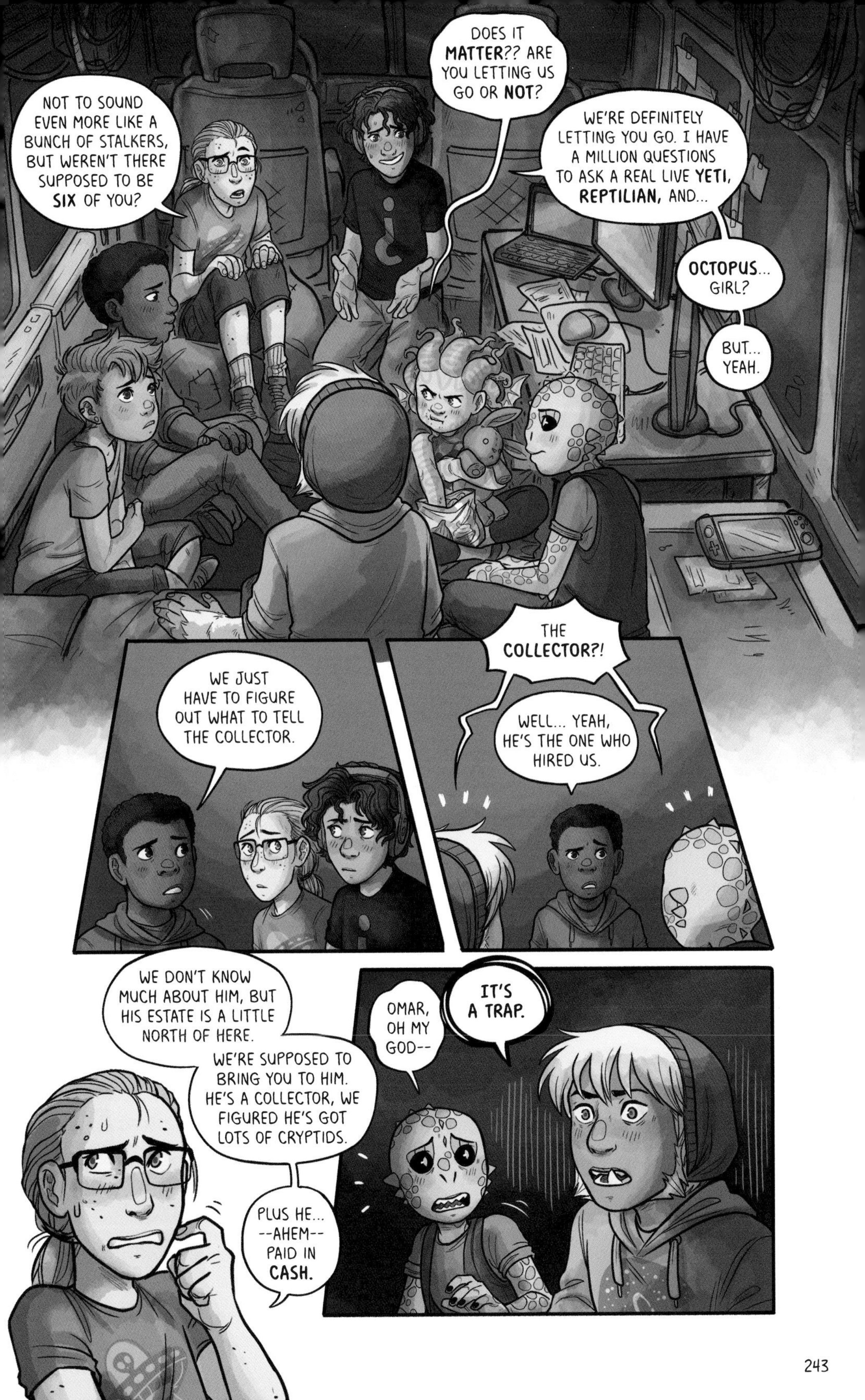
NOT TO SOUND EVEN MORE LIKE A BUNCH OF STALKERS, BUT WEREN'T THERE SUPPOSED TO BE SIX OF YOU?
DOES IT MATTER?? ARE YOU LETTING US GO OR NOT?
WE'RE DEFINITELY LETTING YOU GO. I HAVE A MILLION QUESTIONS TO ASK A REAL LIVE YETI, REPTILIAN, AND...
OCTOPUS... GIRL?
BUT... YEAH.
WE JUST HAVE TO FIGURE OUT WHAT TO TELL THE COLLECTOR.
THE COLLECTOR?!
WELL... YEAH, HE'S THE ONE WHO HIRED US.
WE DON'T KNOW MUCH ABOUT HIM, BUT HIS ESTATE IS A LITTLE NORTH OF HERE.
WE'RE SUPPOSED TO BRING YOU TO HIM. HE'S A COLLECTOR, WE FIGURED HE'S GOT LOTS OF CRYPTIDS.
PLUS HE... --AHEM-- PAID IN CASH.
OMAR, OH MY GOD--
IT'S A TRAP.

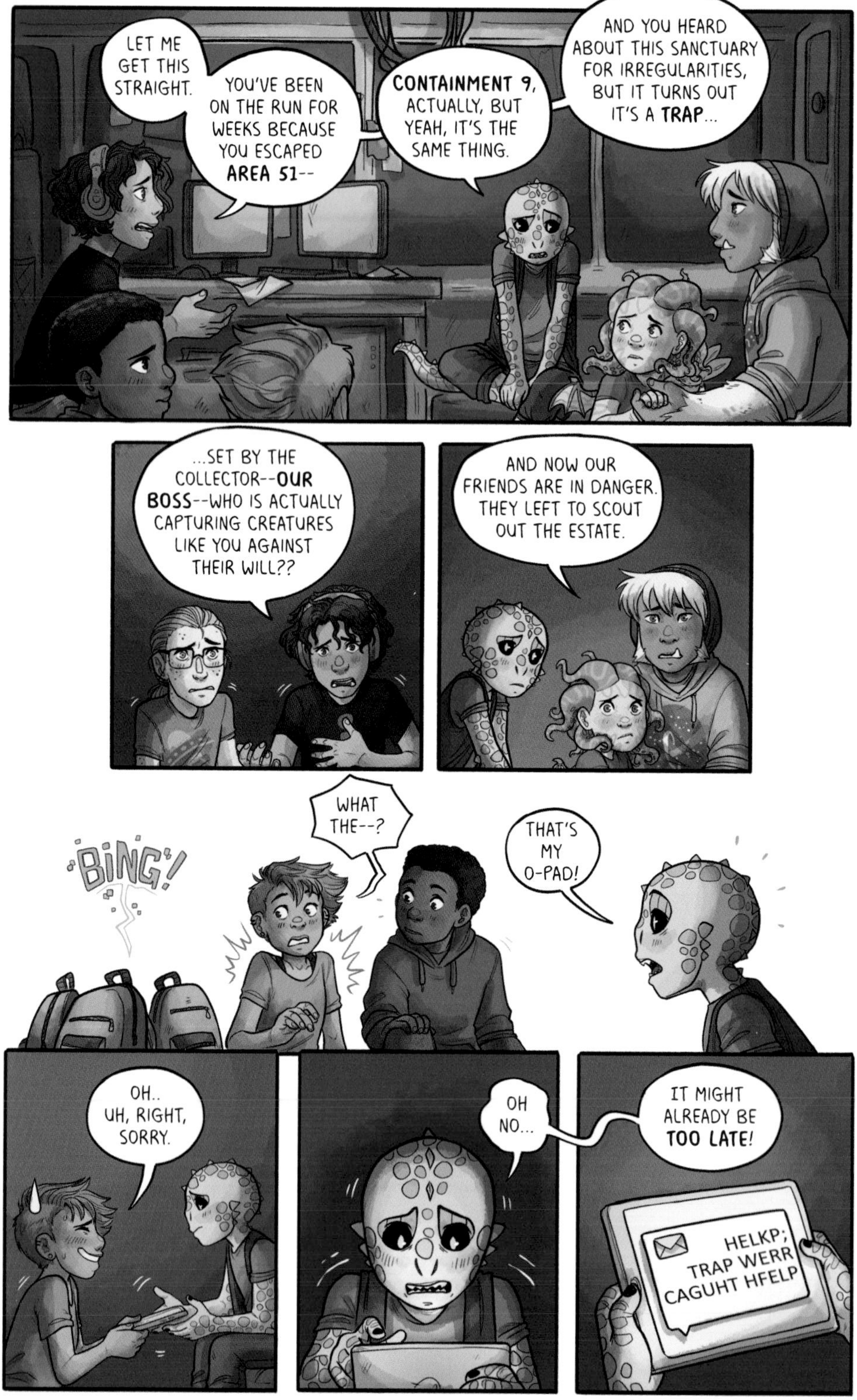
LET ME GET THIS STRAIGHT.
YOU'VE BEEN ON THE RUN FOR WEEKS BECAUSE YOU ESCAPED AREA 51--
CONTAINMENT 9, ACTUALLY, BUT YEAH, IT'S THE SAME THING.
AND YOU HEARD ABOUT THIS SANCTUARY FOR IRREGULARITIES, BUT IT TURNS OUT IT'S A TRAP...
...SET BY THE COLLECTOR--OUR BOSS--WHO IS ACTUALLY CAPTURING CREATURES LIKE YOU AGAINST THEIR WILL??
AND NOW OUR FRIENDS ARE IN DANGER. THEY LEFT TO SCOUT OUT THE ESTATE.
BING!
WHAT THE--?
THAT'S MY O-PAD!
OH.. UH, RIGHT, SORRY.
OH NO...
IT MIGHT ALREADY BE TOO LATE!
HELKP; TRAP WERR CAGUHT HFELP

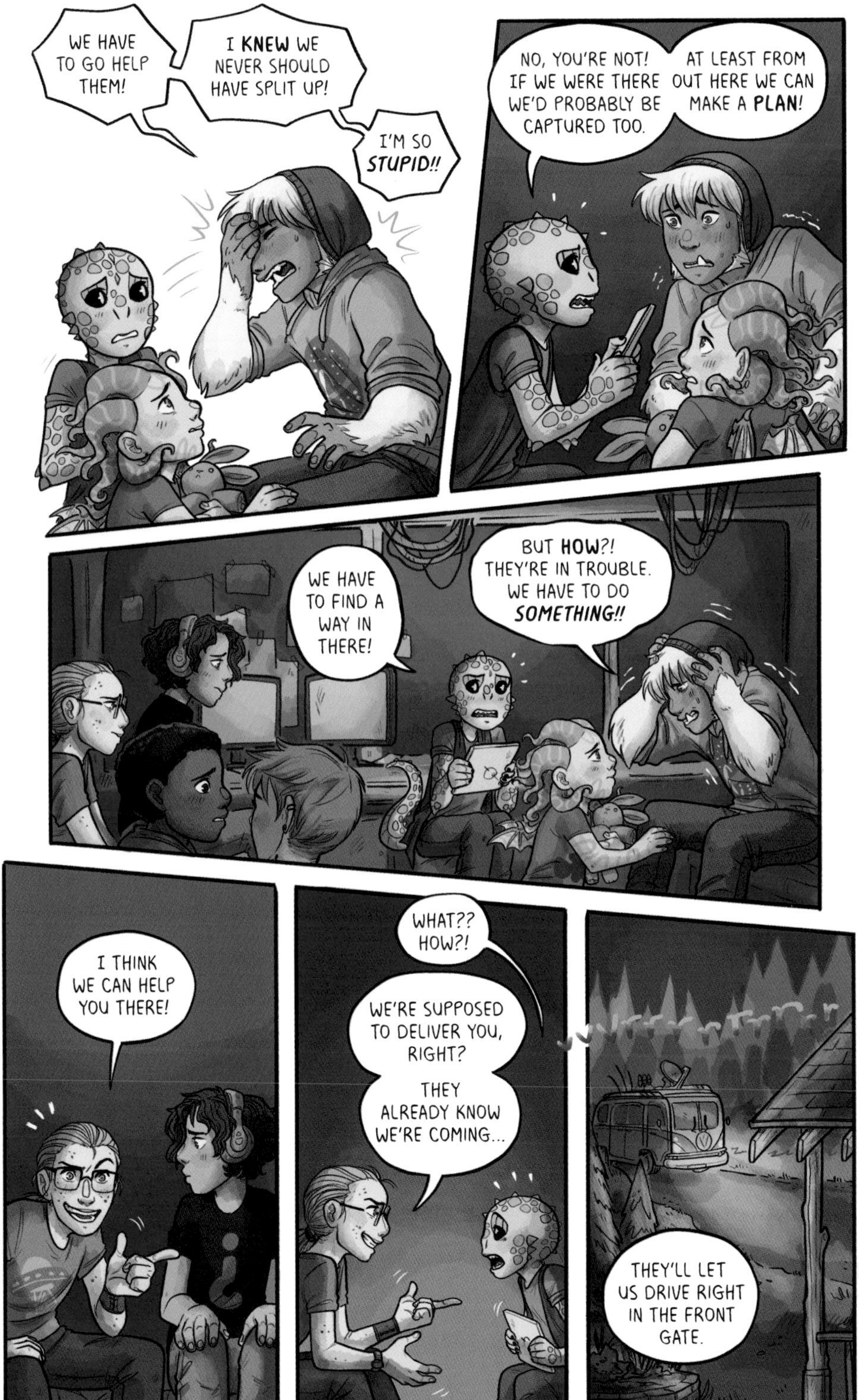
WE HAVE TO GO HELP THEM!
I **KNEW** WE NEVER SHOULD HAVE SPLIT UP!
I'M SO ***STUPID!!***
NO, YOU'RE NOT! IF WE WERE THERE WE'D PROBABLY BE CAPTURED TOO.
AT LEAST FROM OUT HERE WE CAN MAKE A **PLAN**!
WE HAVE TO FIND A WAY IN THERE!
BUT **HOW**?! THEY'RE IN TROUBLE. WE HAVE TO DO ***SOMETHING!!***
I THINK WE CAN HELP YOU THERE!
WHAT?? HOW?!
WE'RE SUPPOSED TO DELIVER YOU, RIGHT?
THEY ALREADY KNOW WE'RE COMING...
THEY'LL LET US DRIVE RIGHT IN THE FRONT GATE.

CHAPTER TEN

HOME

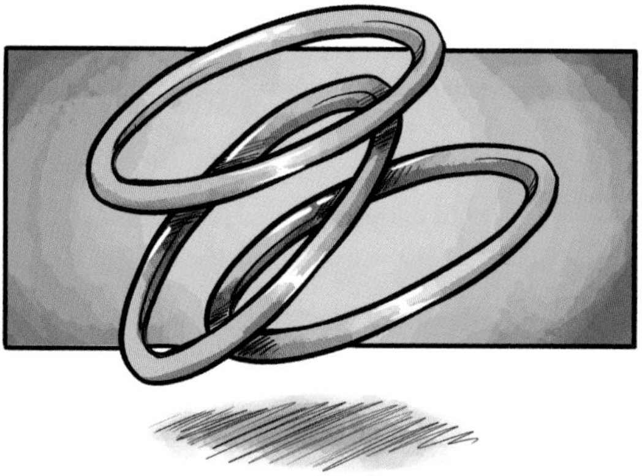

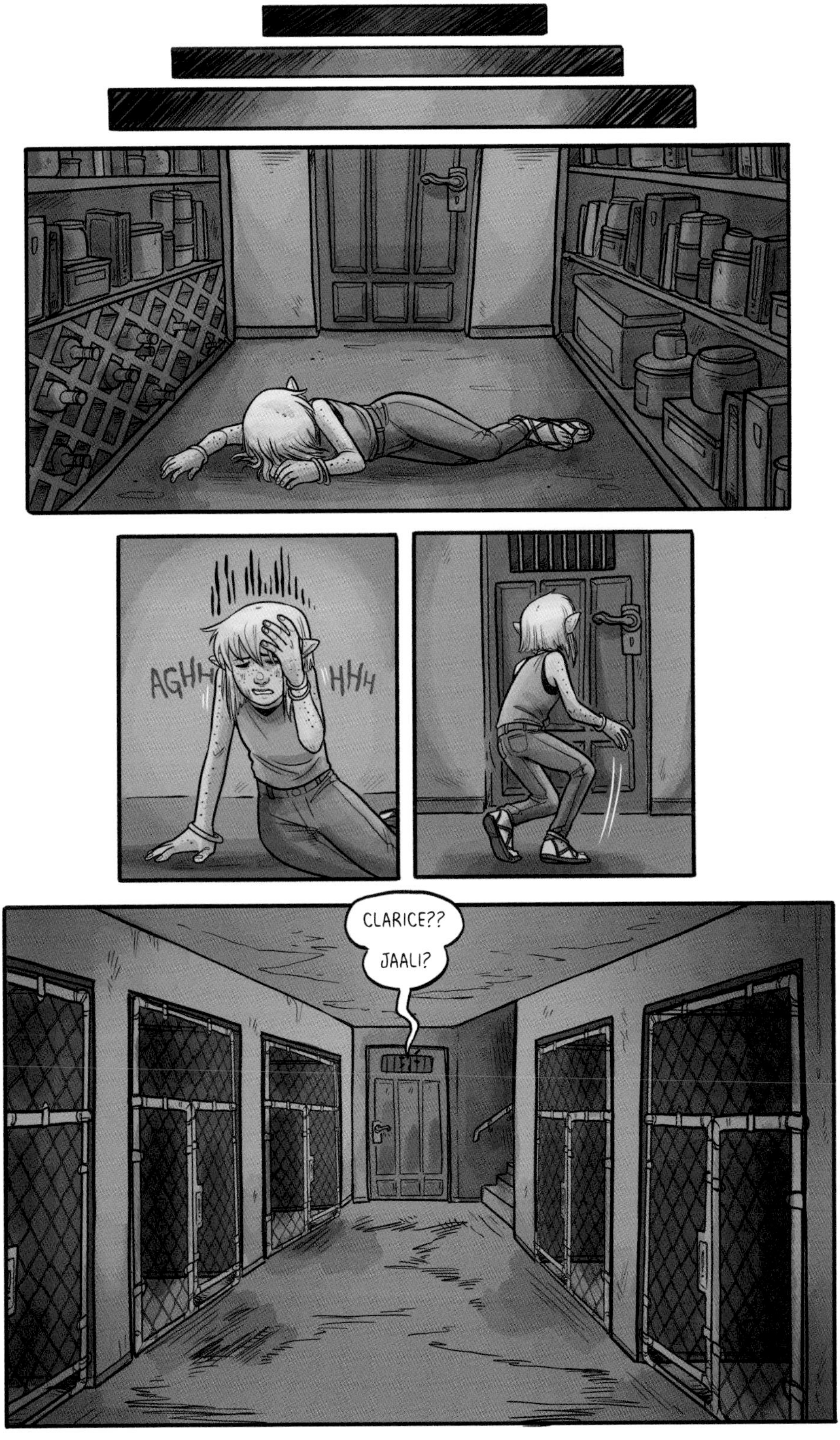
AGHHHHH
CLARICE??
JAALI?

ARE YOU **SURE** THIS WILL WORK?

OH YEAH, IT'S THE OLD "CAPTURED BY THE GUARDS" PLOY! IT WORKS ALL THE TIME **IN D&D!**

OWWWWWW

PUNCH

IT'S THE BEST PLAN WE HAVE. JUST BE READY THE SECOND THE DOOR OPENS.

OKAY!

nod

BEEP BEEP!

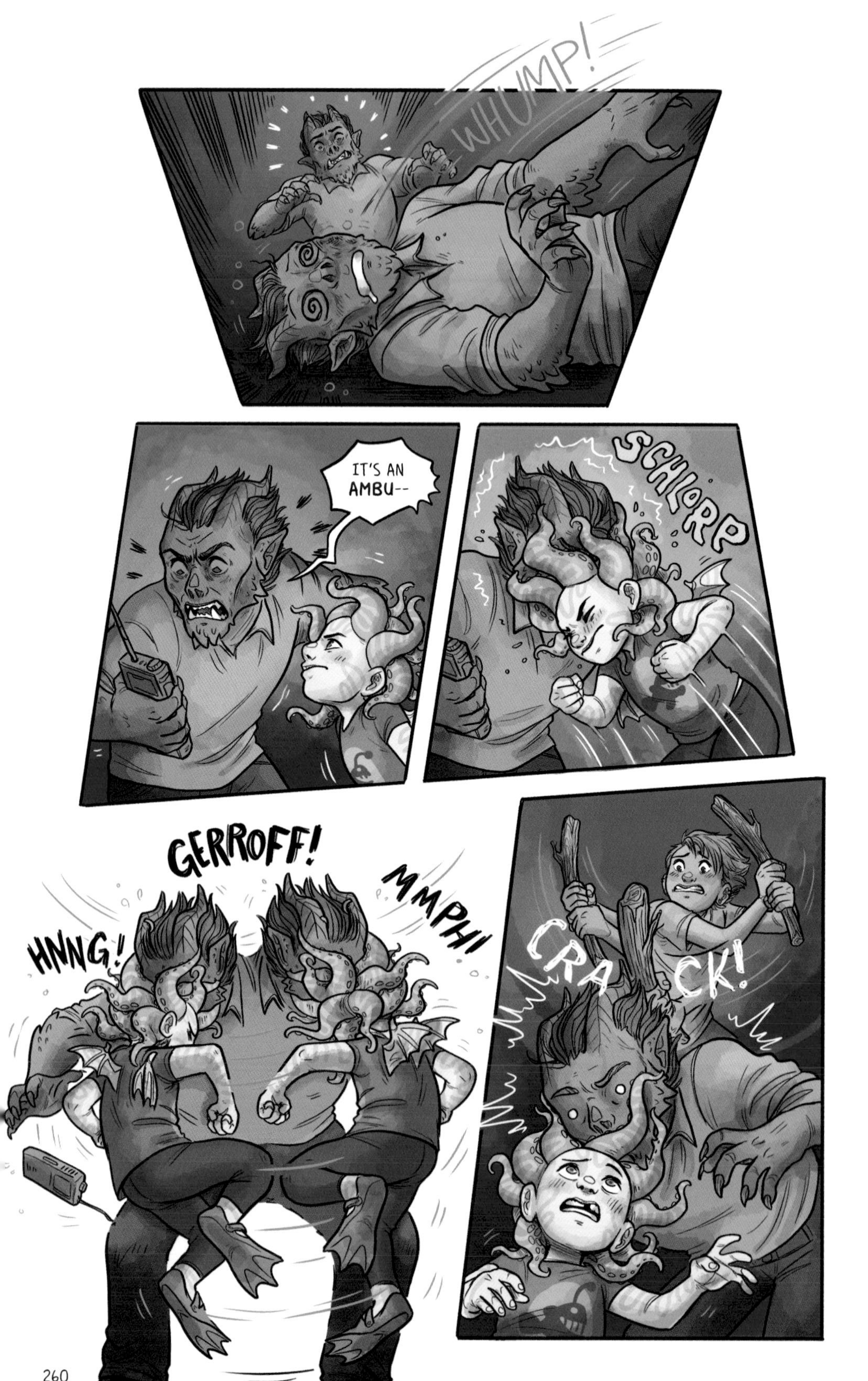
WHUMP!
IT'S AN AMBU--
SCHLORP
GERROFF!
HNNG!
MMPH!
CRACK!

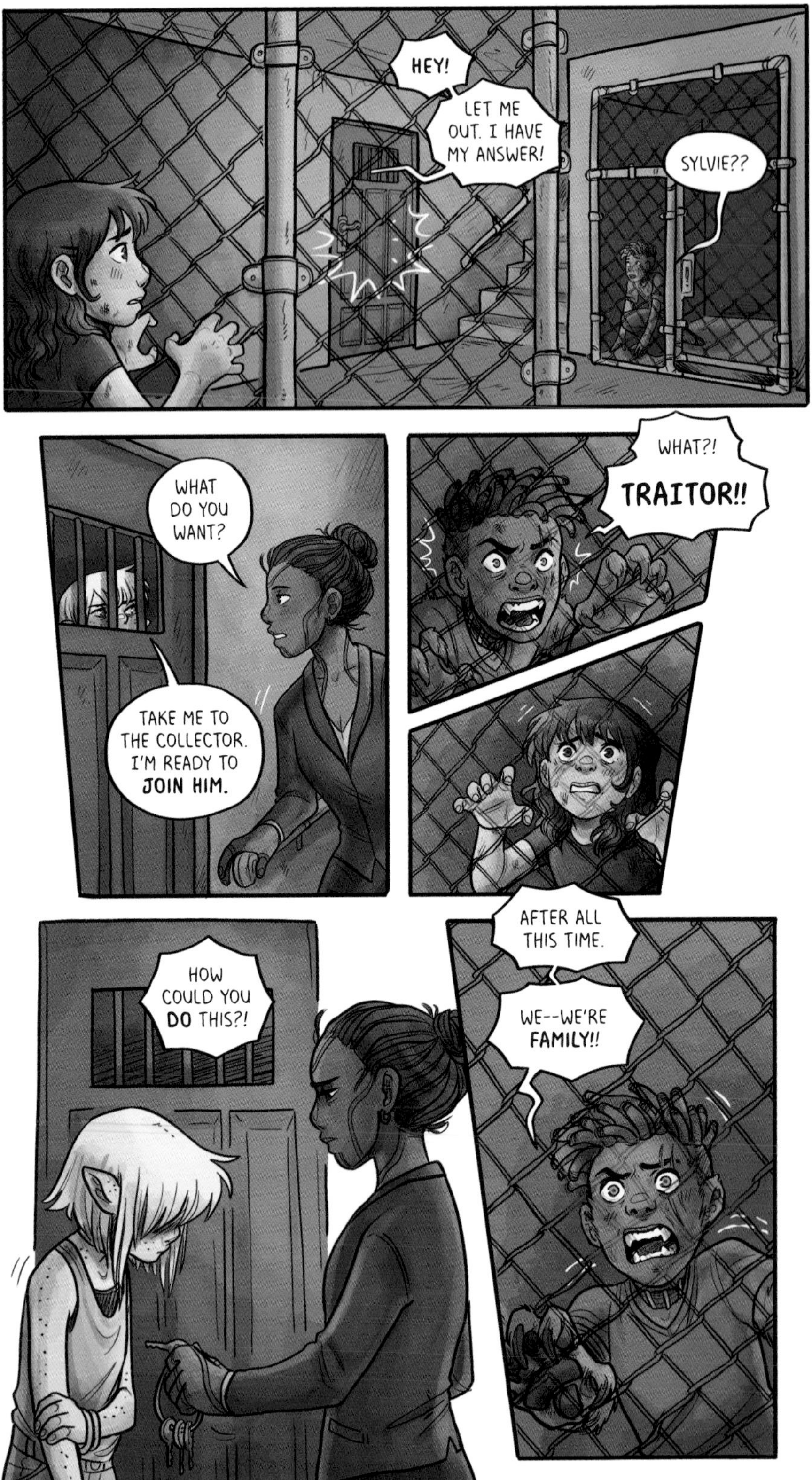
HEY!
LET ME OUT. I HAVE MY ANSWER!
SYLVIE??
WHAT DO YOU WANT?
TAKE ME TO THE COLLECTOR. I'M READY TO JOIN HIM.
WHAT?!
TRAITOR!!
HOW COULD YOU DO THIS?!
AFTER ALL THIS TIME.
WE--WE'RE FAMILY!!

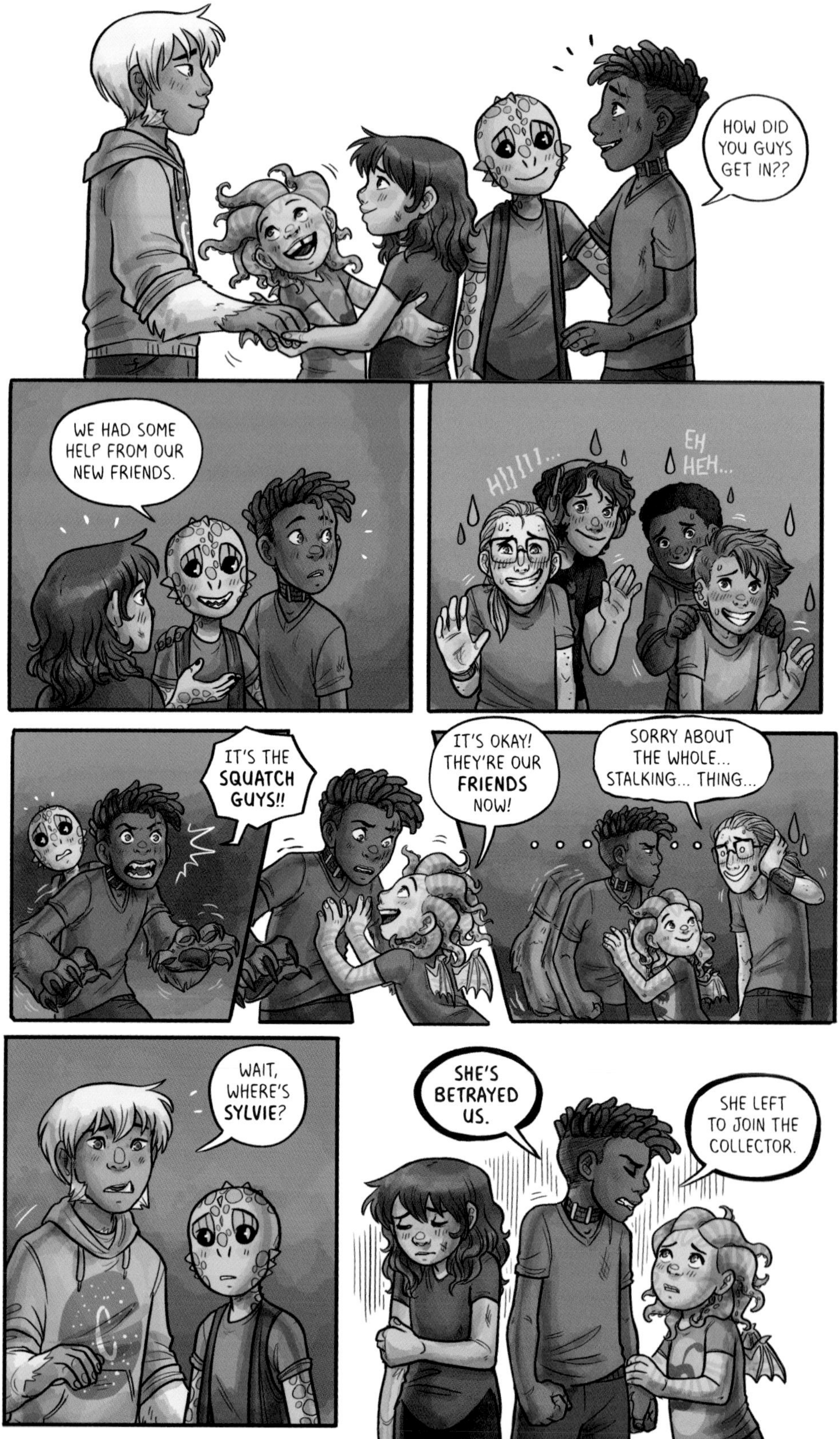
HOW DID YOU GUYS GET IN??
WE HAD SOME HELP FROM OUR NEW FRIENDS.
HIIIII...
EH HEH...
IT'S THE **SQUATCH GUYS!!**
IT'S OKAY! THEY'RE OUR **FRIENDS** NOW!
SORRY ABOUT THE WHOLE... STALKING... THING...
WAIT, WHERE'S **SYLVIE**?
SHE'S BETRAYED US.
SHE LEFT TO JOIN THE COLLECTOR.

270

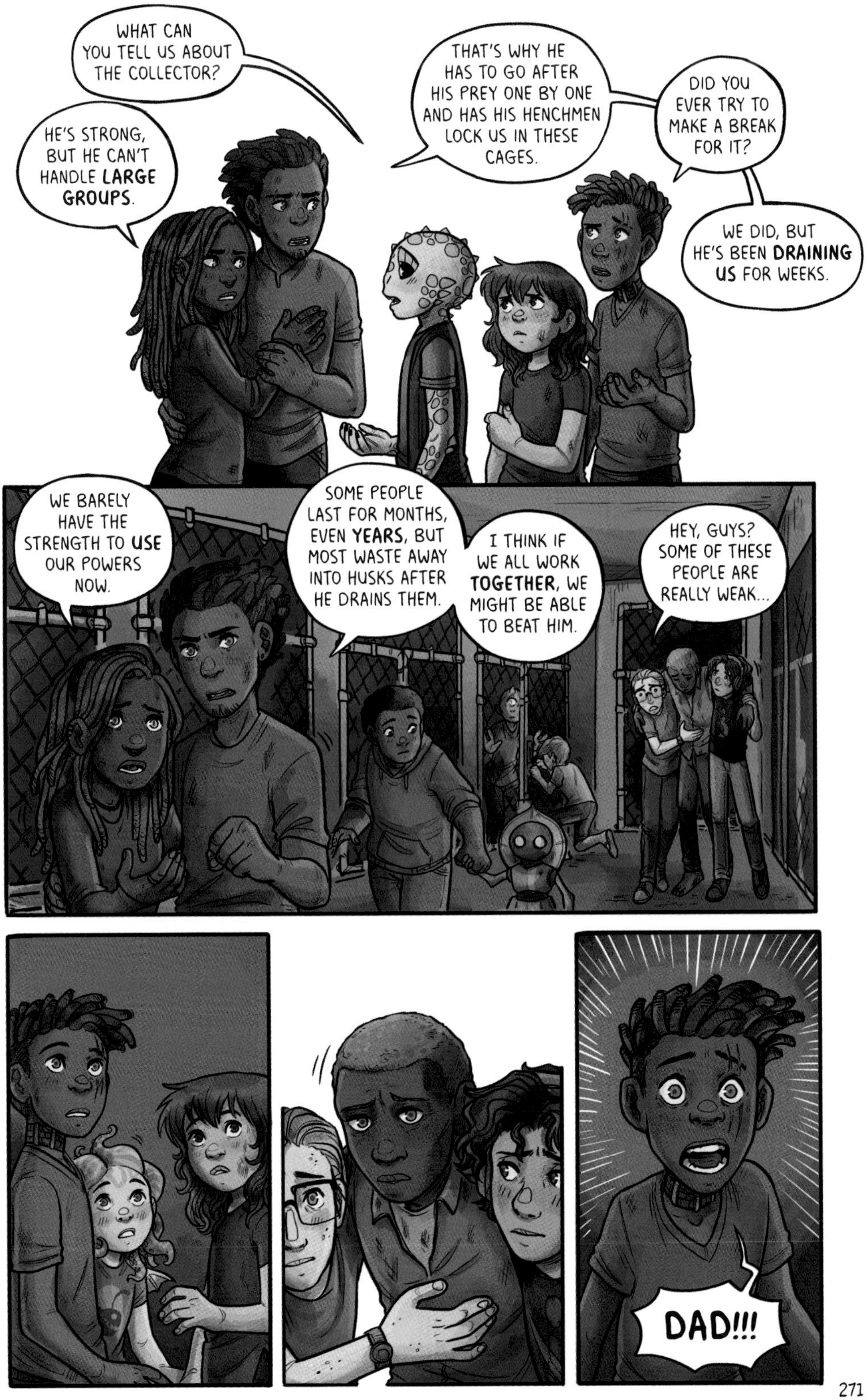
WHAT CAN YOU TELL US ABOUT THE COLLECTOR?
HE'S STRONG, BUT HE CAN'T HANDLE **LARGE GROUPS**.
THAT'S WHY HE HAS TO GO AFTER HIS PREY ONE BY ONE AND HAS HIS HENCHMEN LOCK US IN THESE CAGES.
DID YOU EVER TRY TO MAKE A BREAK FOR IT?
WE DID, BUT HE'S BEEN **DRAINING US** FOR WEEKS.
WE BARELY HAVE THE STRENGTH TO **USE** OUR POWERS NOW.
SOME PEOPLE LAST FOR MONTHS, EVEN **YEARS**, BUT MOST WASTE AWAY INTO HUSKS AFTER HE DRAINS THEM.
I THINK IF WE ALL WORK **TOGETHER**, WE MIGHT BE ABLE TO BEAT HIM.
HEY, GUYS? SOME OF THESE PEOPLE ARE REALLY WEAK...
DAD!!!

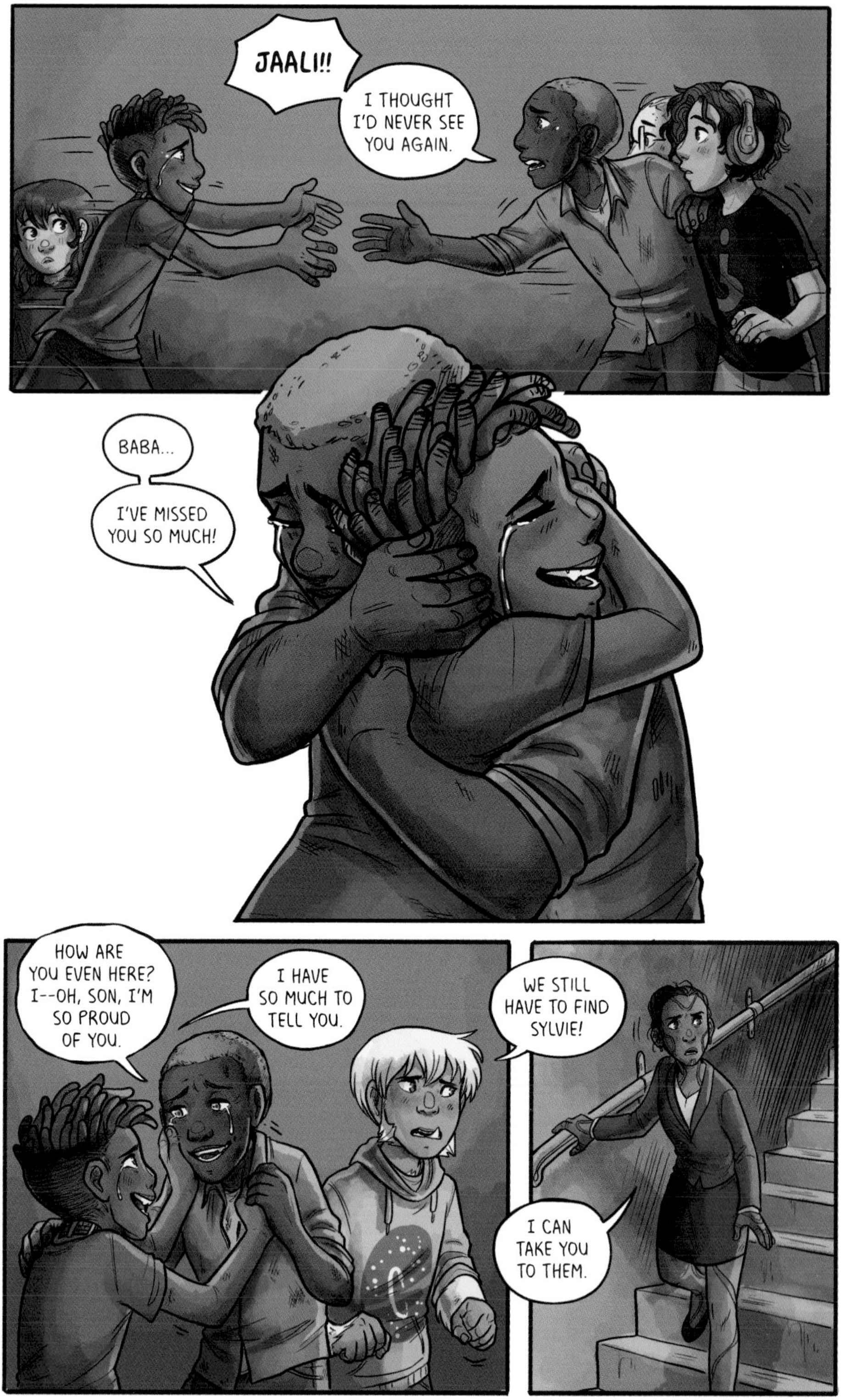
JAALI!!
I THOUGHT I'D NEVER SEE YOU AGAIN.
BABA...
I'VE MISSED YOU SO MUCH!
HOW ARE YOU EVEN HERE? I--OH, SON, I'M SO PROUD OF YOU.
I HAVE SO MUCH TO TELL YOU.
WE STILL HAVE TO FIND SYLVIE!
I CAN TAKE YOU TO THEM.

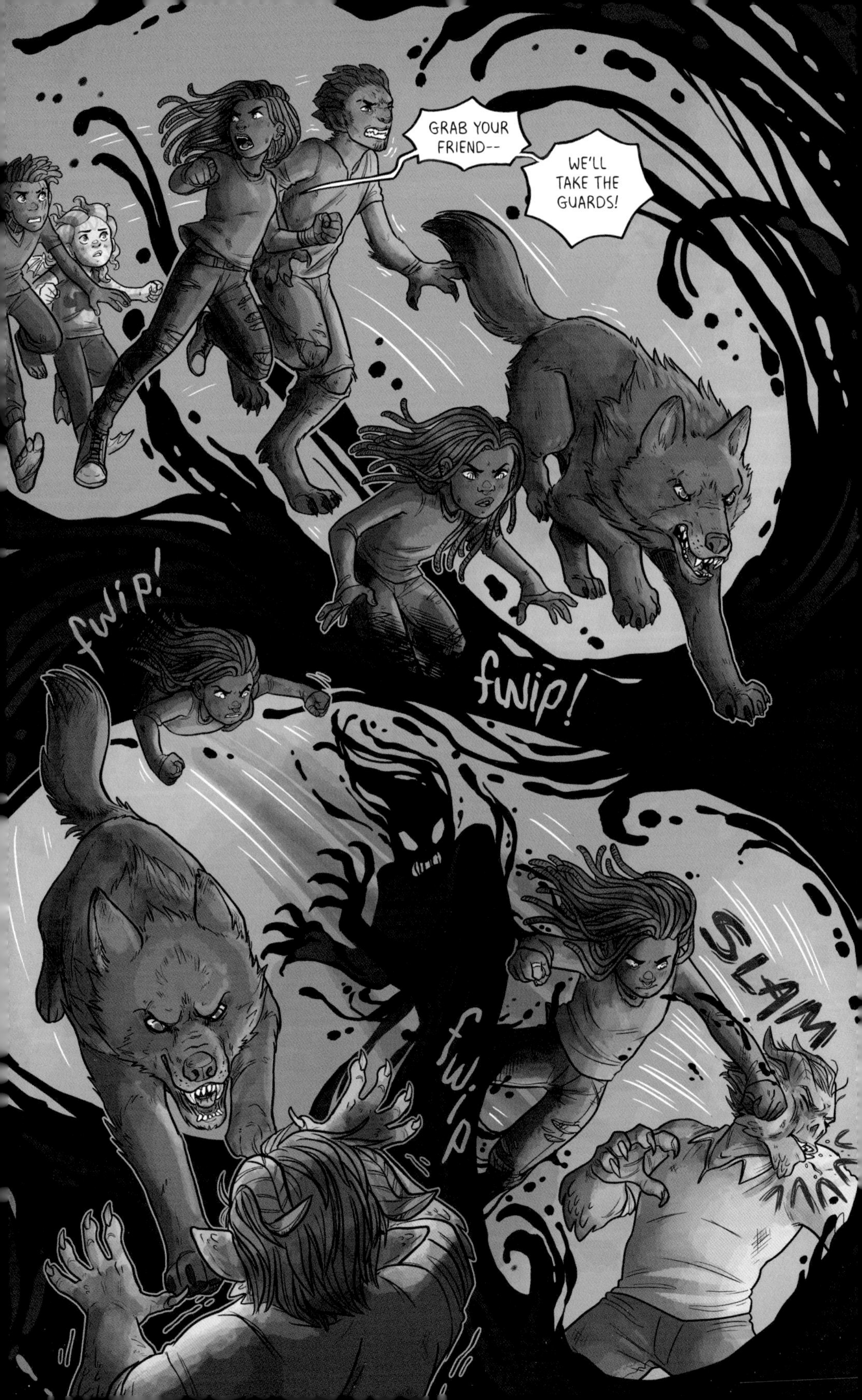
GRAB YOUR FRIEND--
WE'LL TAKE THE GUARDS!
fwip!
fwip!
fwip!
SLAM

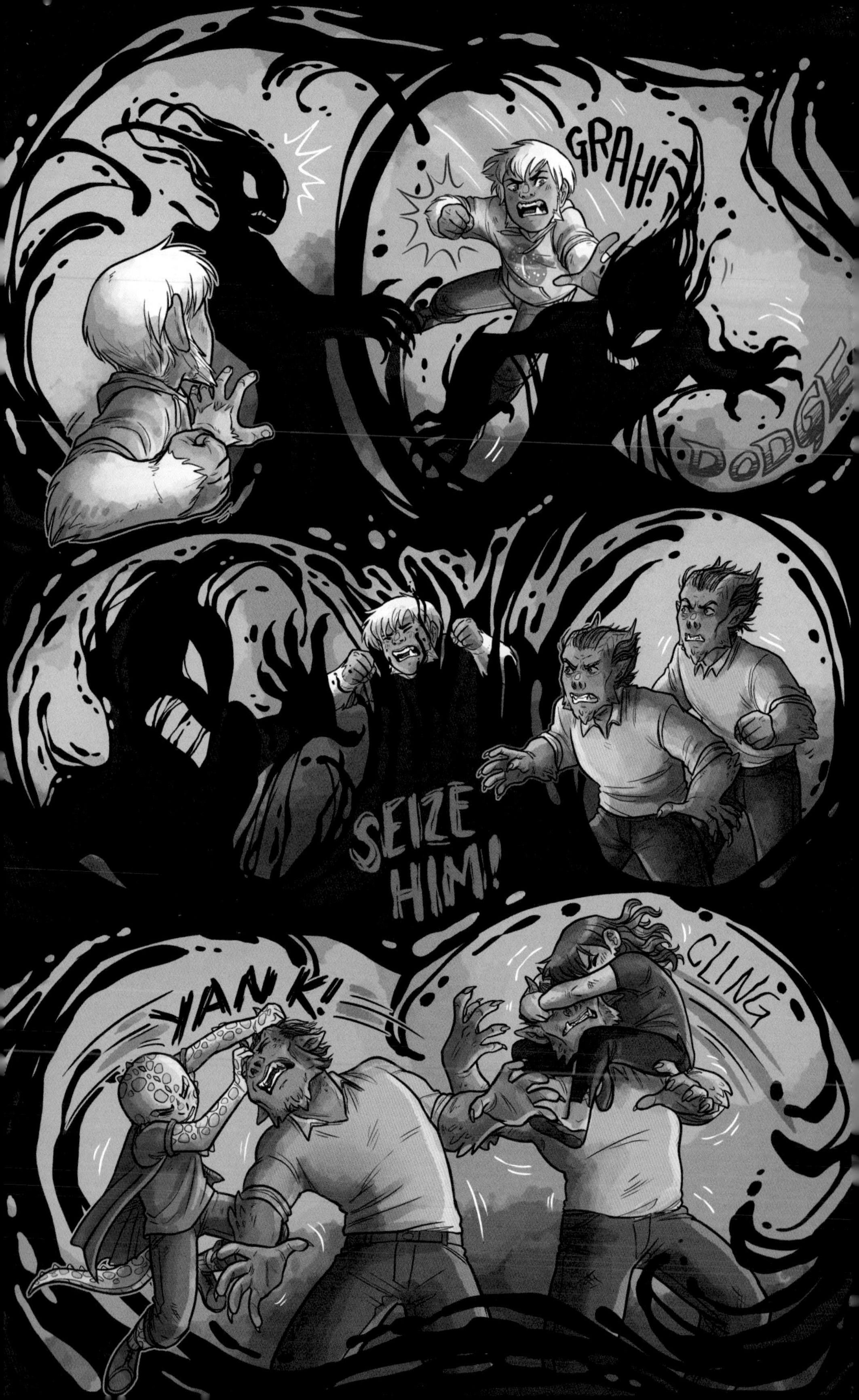
GRAH!
DODGE
SEIZE HIM!
YANK!
CLING

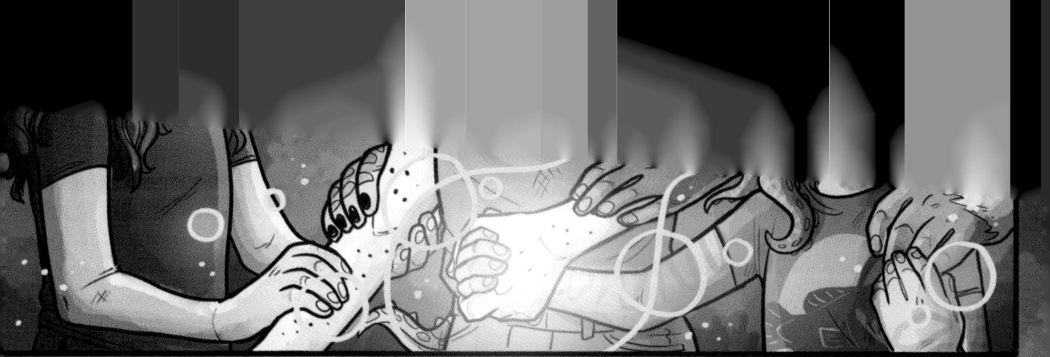

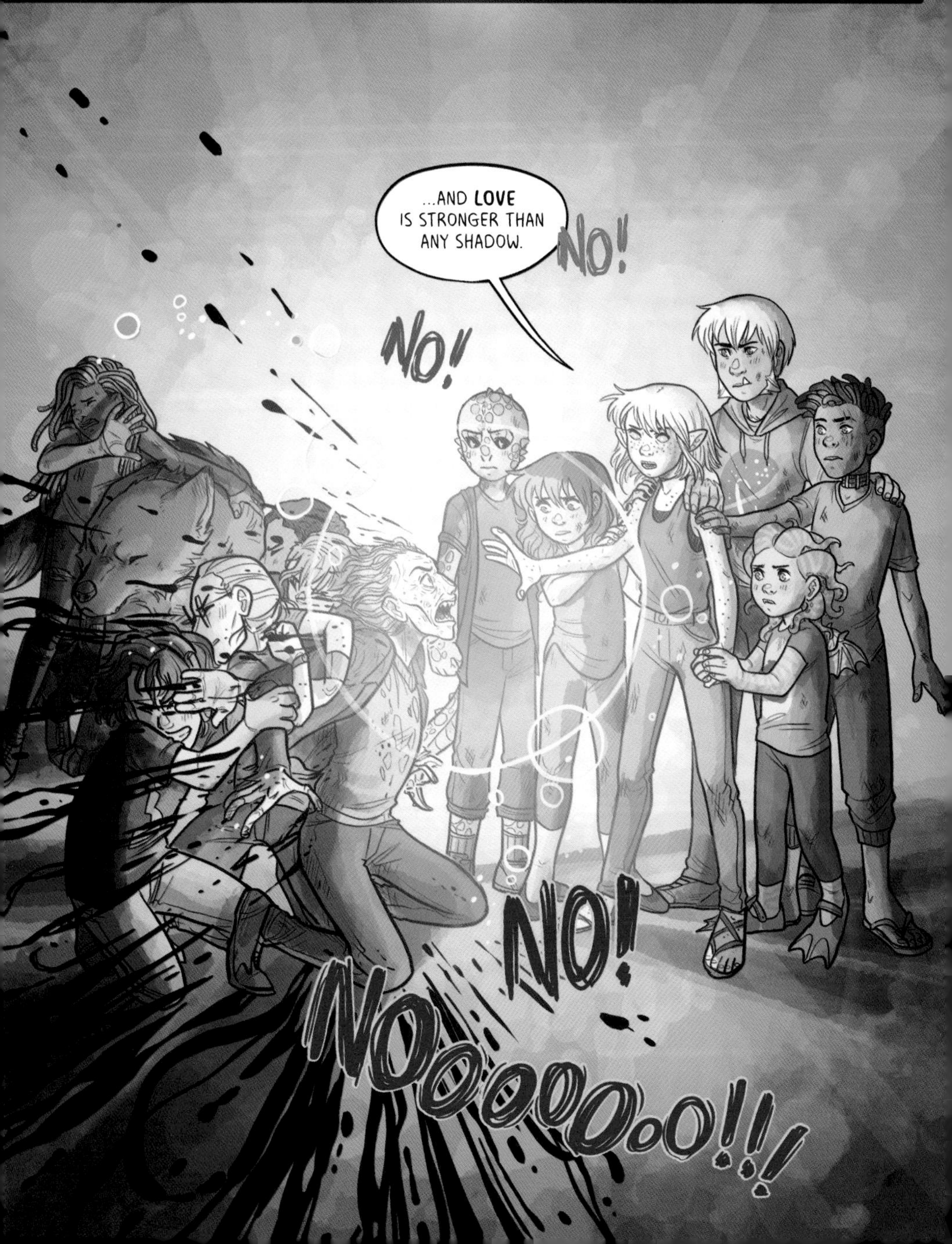
...AND LOVE IS STRONGER THAN ANY SHADOW.
NO!
NO!
NO!
NOOOOOOOO!!!

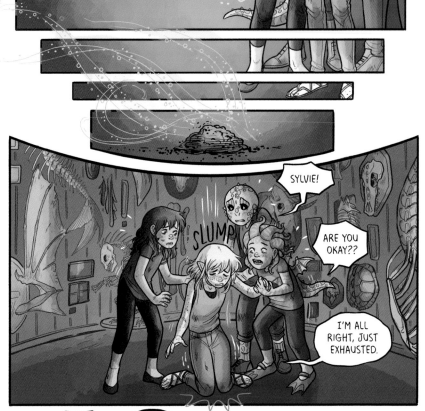

SLUMP

SYLVIE!

ARE YOU OKAY??

I'M ALL RIGHT, JUST EXHAUSTED.

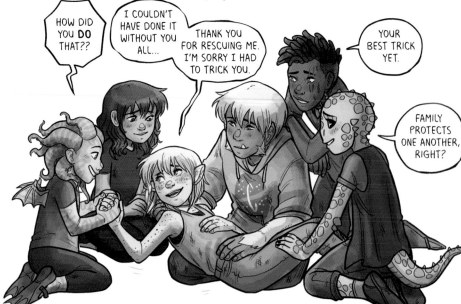

HOW DID YOU **DO** THAT??

I COULDN'T HAVE DONE IT WITHOUT YOU ALL...

THANK YOU FOR RESCUING ME. I'M SORRY I HAD TO TRICK YOU.

YOUR BEST TRICK YET.

FAMILY PROTECTS ONE ANOTHER, RIGHT?

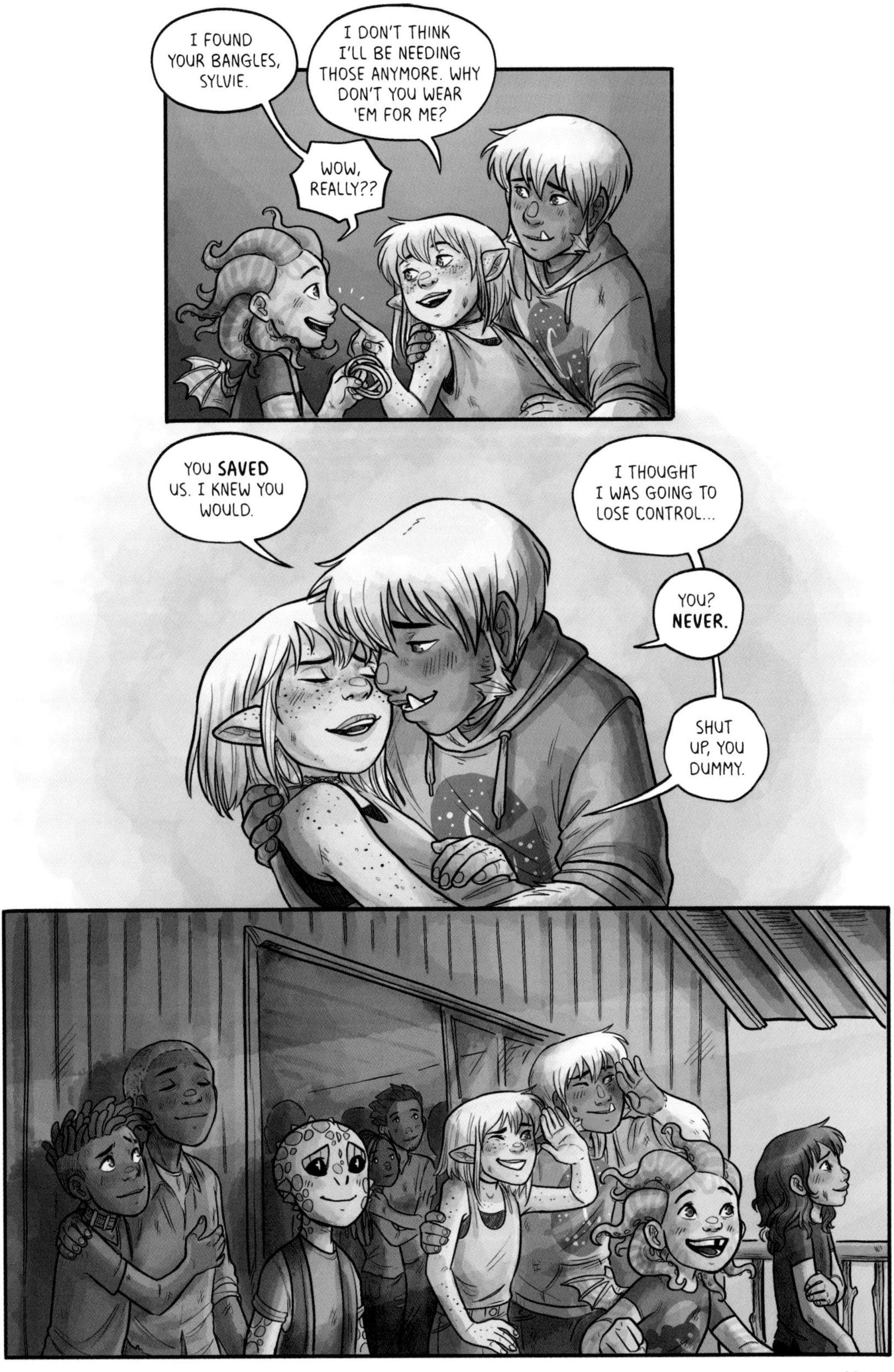
I FOUND YOUR BANGLES, SYLVIE.
I DON'T THINK I'LL BE NEEDING THOSE ANYMORE. WHY DON'T YOU WEAR 'EM FOR ME?
WOW, REALLY??
YOU **SAVED** US. I KNEW YOU WOULD.
I THOUGHT I WAS GOING TO LOSE CONTROL...
YOU? **NEVER.**
SHUT UP, YOU DUMMY.

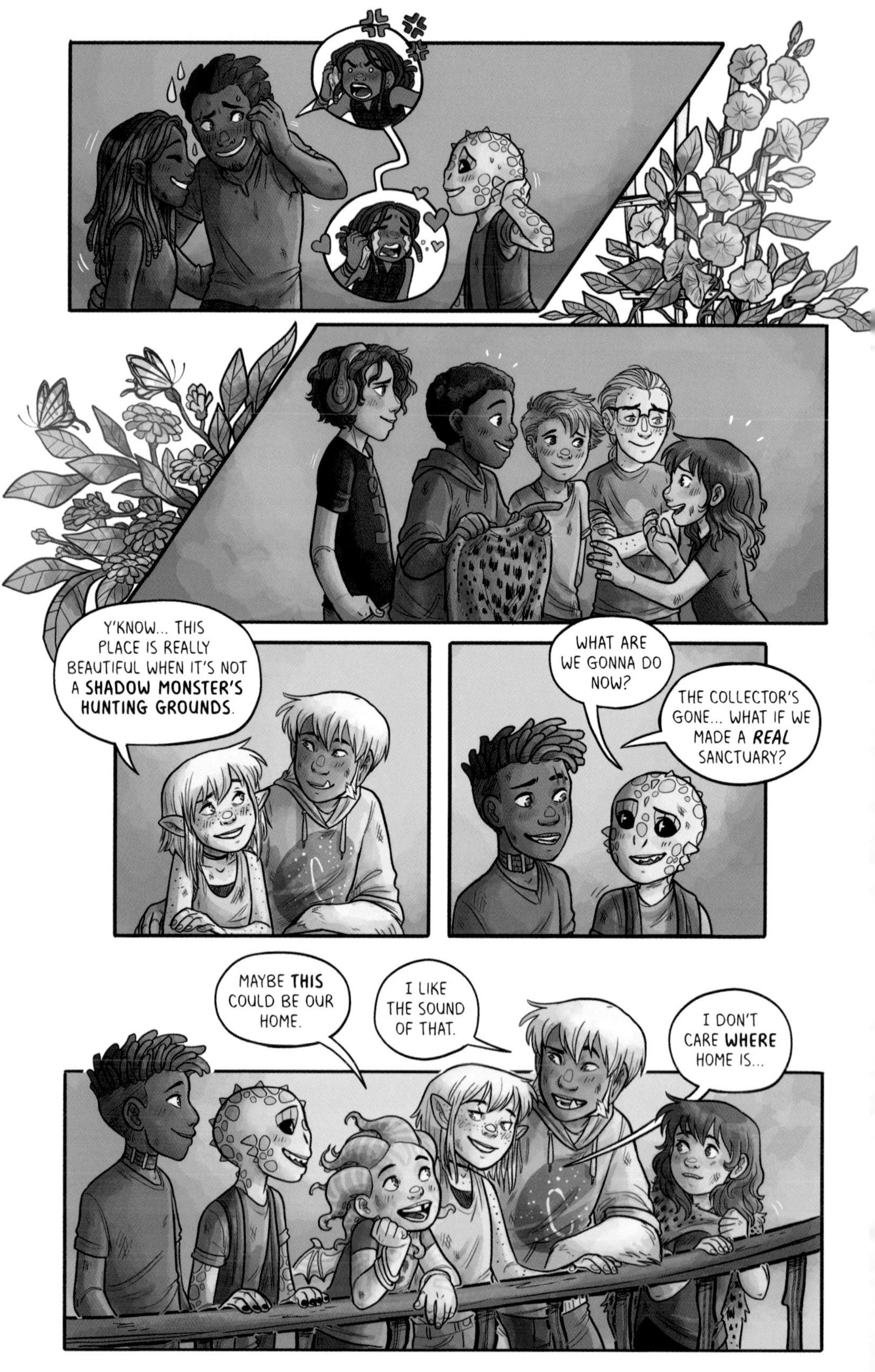
Y'KNOW... THIS PLACE IS REALLY BEAUTIFUL WHEN IT'S NOT A **SHADOW MONSTER'S HUNTING GROUNDS**.
WHAT ARE WE GONNA DO NOW?
THE COLLECTOR'S GONE... WHAT IF WE MADE A ***REAL*** SANCTUARY?
MAYBE **THIS** COULD BE OUR HOME.
I LIKE THE SOUND OF THAT.
I DON'T CARE **WHERE** HOME IS...

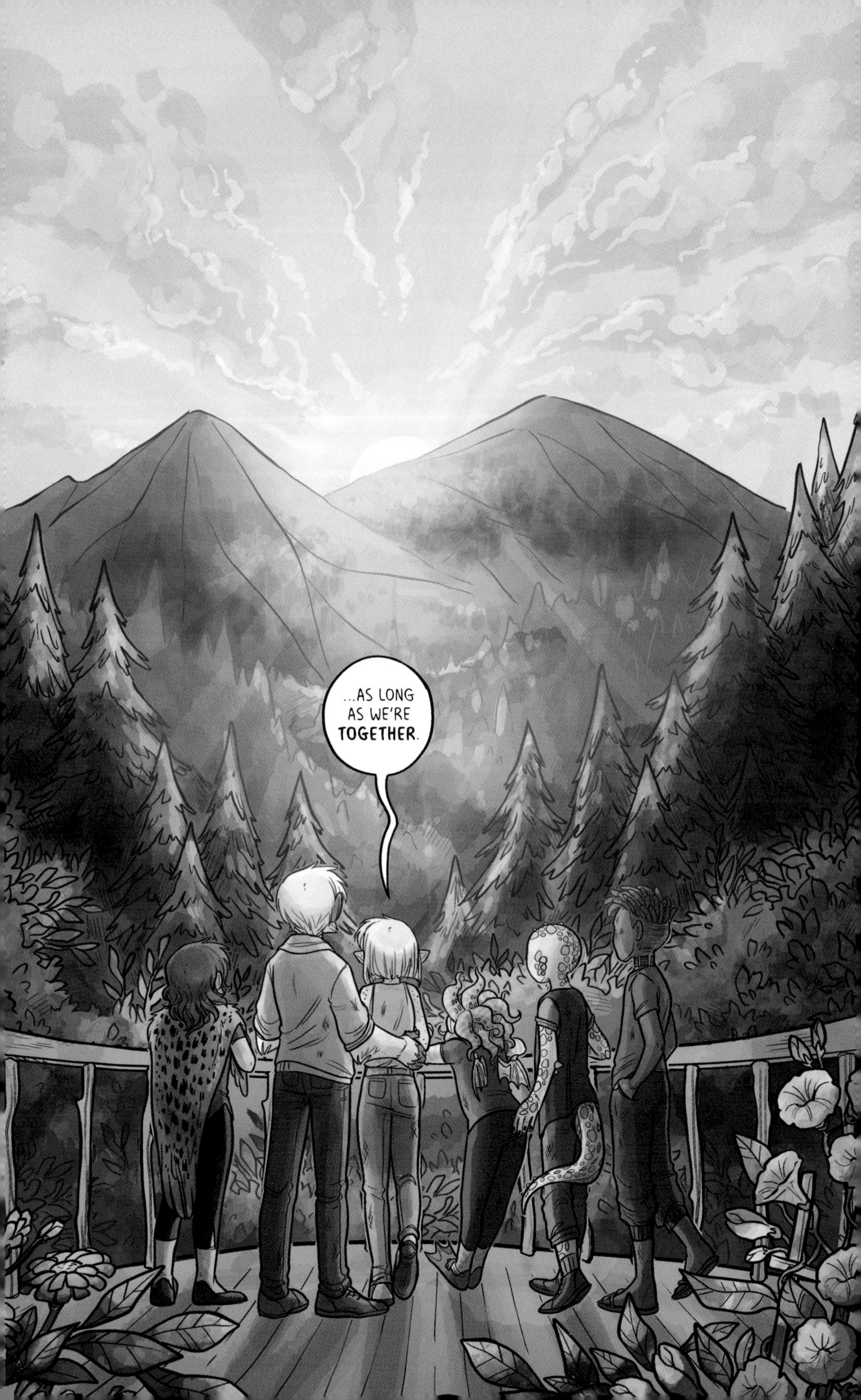
...AS LONG AS WE'RE TOGETHER.

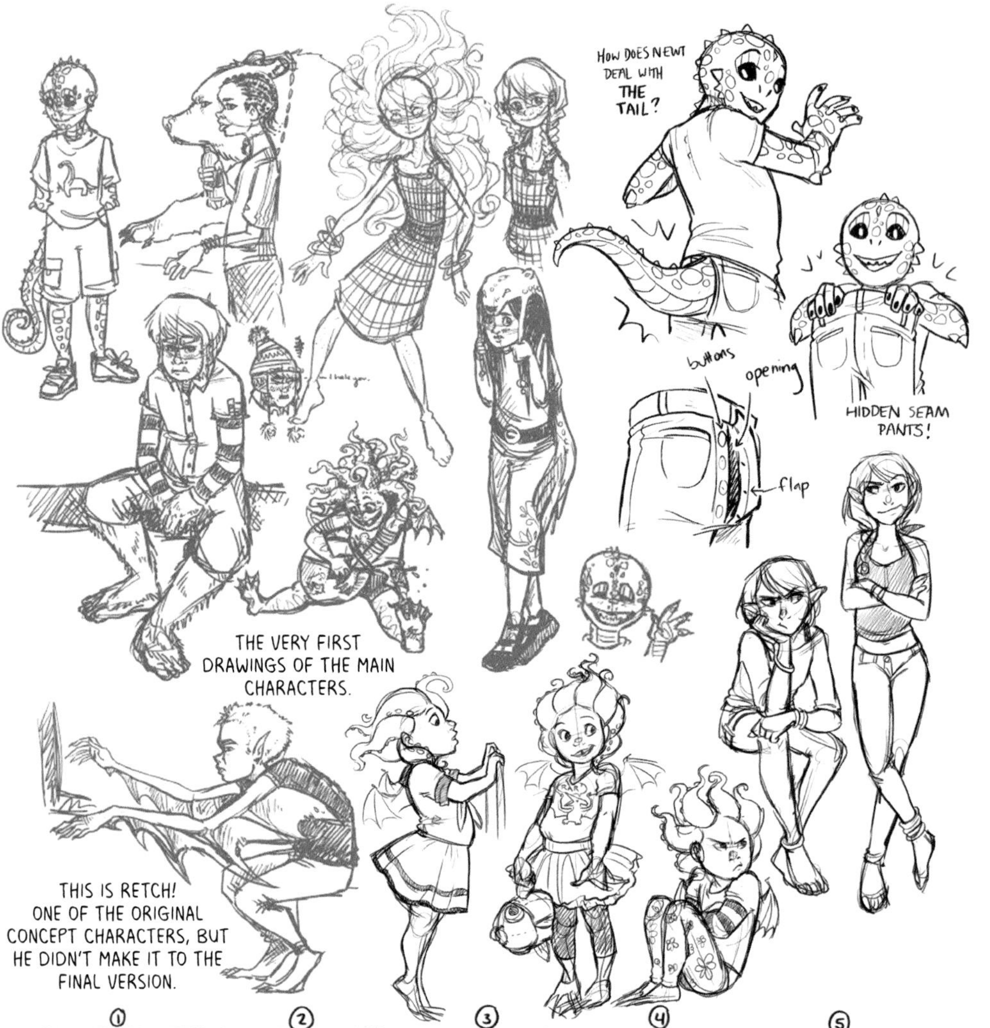
HOW DOES NEWT DEAL WITH THE TAIL?
buttons
opening
flap
HIDDEN SEAM PANTS!

THE VERY FIRST DRAWINGS OF THE MAIN CHARACTERS.

THIS IS RETCH! ONE OF THE ORIGINAL CONCEPT CHARACTERS, BUT HE DIDN'T MAKE IT TO THE FINAL VERSION.

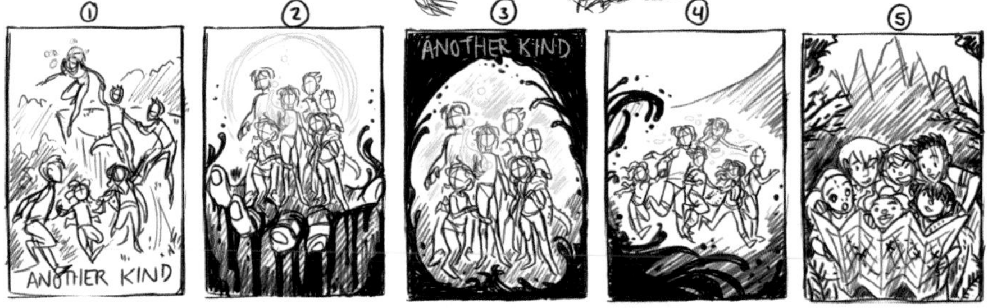
1
ANOTHER KIND
2
3
ANOTHER KIND
4
5

COVER SKETCHES

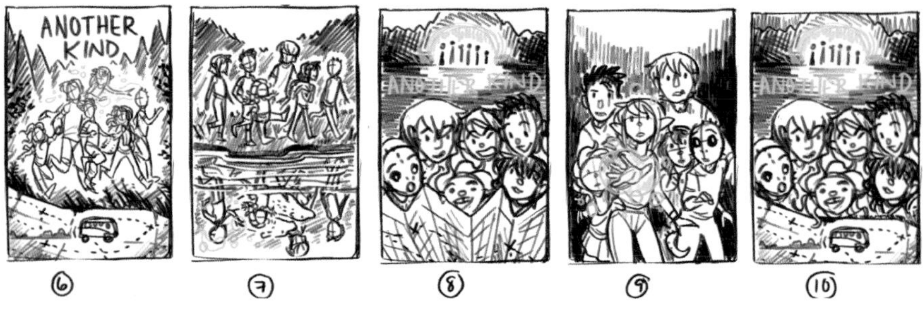
ANOTHER KIND
6
7
8
9
10

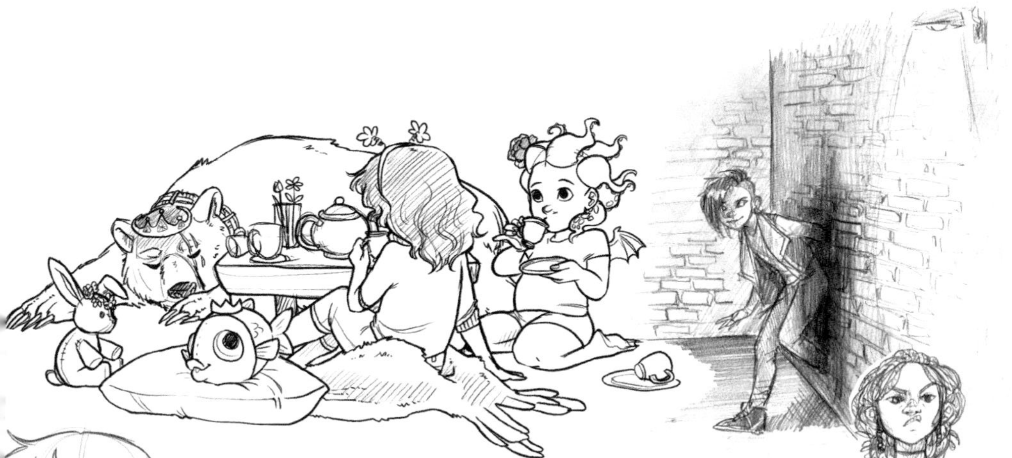

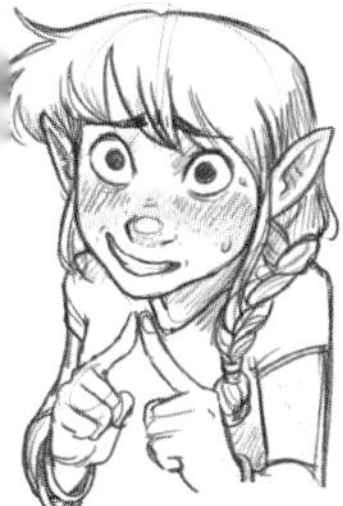

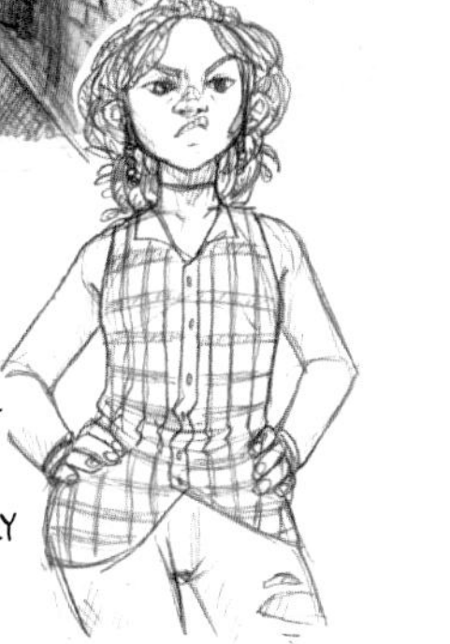

ACKNOWLEDGMENTS

THANK YOU TO OUR FRIENDS AND FAMILY FOR THEIR UNENDING SUPPORT AND ENTHUSIASM THROUGHOUT THE CREATION OF THIS BOOK. YOU KEPT US GOING AND INSPIRED SO MANY OF THE FAMILIES IN THIS STORY. WE LOVE YOU!

THANK YOU A MILLION TIMES OVER TO SAVANNA AND GIGI—OUR UNBELIEVABLY AMAZING FLATTERS WHO MADE THIS BOOK POSSIBLE THROUGH THEIR PATIENCE, PERSERVERENCE, AND DEDICATION TO THE MEME. BDB FOREVER.

THANK YOU TO CLAIRE, THE AGENT OF OUR DREAMS, WHO GEEKED WITH US THE WHOLE TIME AND IS MAGGIE'S #1 FAN IN THE ENTIRE UNIVERSE. THANK YOU FOR HELPING US MAKE THIS HAPPEN.

THANK YOU TO ROSE, ANDREW, AND JOE AT HARPER FOR BEING THE BEST TEAM WE COULD ASK FOR! Y'ALL ARE CHAMPIONS AND WE CAN'T WAIT FOR THE NEXT.

THANK YOU TO OUR HOME OFFICE FURRY COWORKERS FOR ALWAYS LAYING ON US WHEN WE WERE TRYING TO GET WORK DONE. MANY SCRITCHES AND PETS FOR YOU.

SHOUT-OUTS TO THE DIPPERS—OUR FIRST AND BIGGEST FANS. THANK YOU JOAN HILTY, ALEX FINE, THE ELDRITCH CREW, THE GIRL* GANG, THE PEPPER PAUPERS, LOREN COLEMAN, AND THE CRYPTOZOOLOGY MUSEUM. THANK YOU TO *BUZZFEED UNSOLVED*, *THE ADVENTURE ZONE*, *CRITICAL ROLE*, AND WAY TOO MANY PODCASTS FOR HELPING KEEP OUR MINDS OCCUPIED THROUGH THE TOUGH TIMES.

TO ALL THE CRYPTOZOOLOGISTS WHO HAVE COME BEFORE US. WITHOUT YOUR DEDICATION TO THE STUDY OF WEIRD PHENOMENA, WE MIGHT NEVER HAVE LEARNED TO LOVE THEM JUST LIKE YOU DO.

AND FINALLY—
THANK YOU FOR READING!

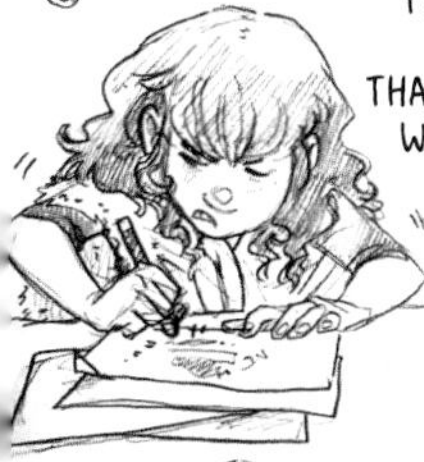

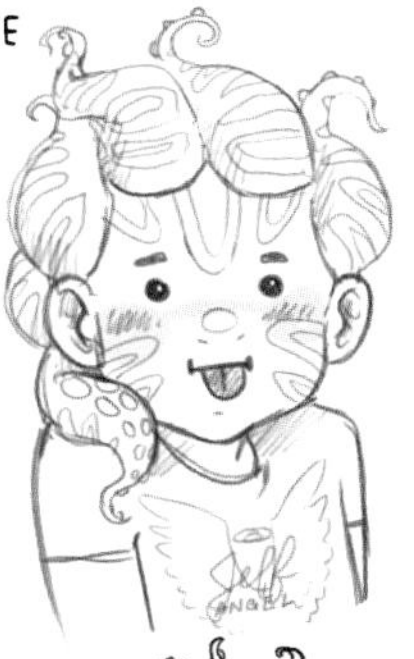

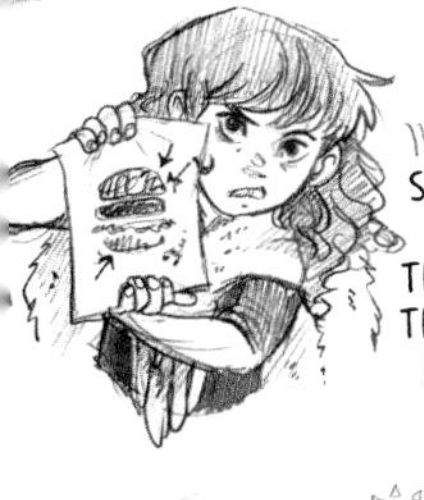

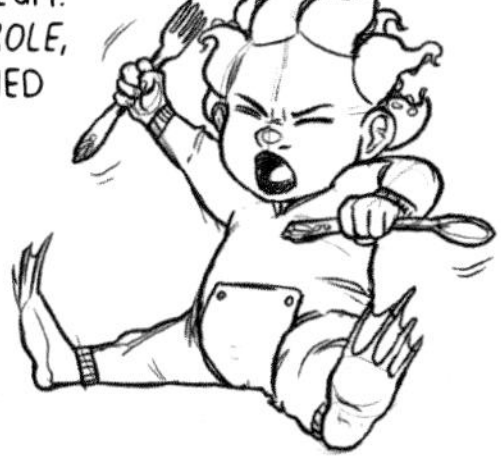

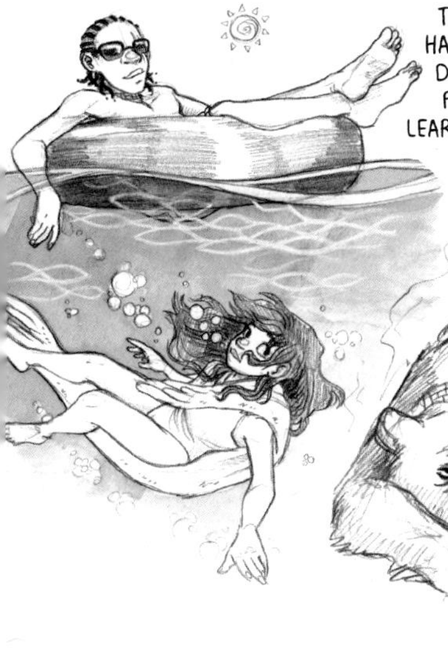

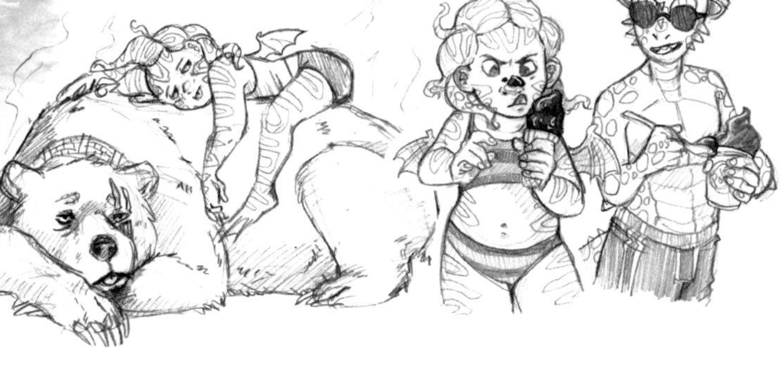

FOR DOYLE
AND FOR OUR FAMILIES,
OF ONE KIND OR
ANOTHER

HARPERALLEY IS AN IMPRINT OF HARPERCOLLINS PUBLISHERS.

ANOTHER KIND

LIBRARY OF CONGRESS CONTROL NUMBER: 2021939648
ISBN 978-0-06-304353-4 (PBK.) — ISBN 978-0-06-304354-1

TYPOGRAPHY BY JOE MERKEL

23 24 25   GPS   10 9 8 7 6 5

FIRST EDITION